From the Cold

Mia K Rose

ROSE QUILL

Published by **Rose Quill** 2025.

Gold Coast, Qld, Australia.

Book Cover by JV Arts.

Map by Coven Press.

Edited by Olivia Bedford, Dan Hanks, Angela Traficante.

ISBN: 978-1-7642515-0-1

Ebook ISBN: 978-1-7642515-1-8

First published in Australia 2025

For the ones who carried each other through storms, when the world was too heavy alone.

FROM THE COLD

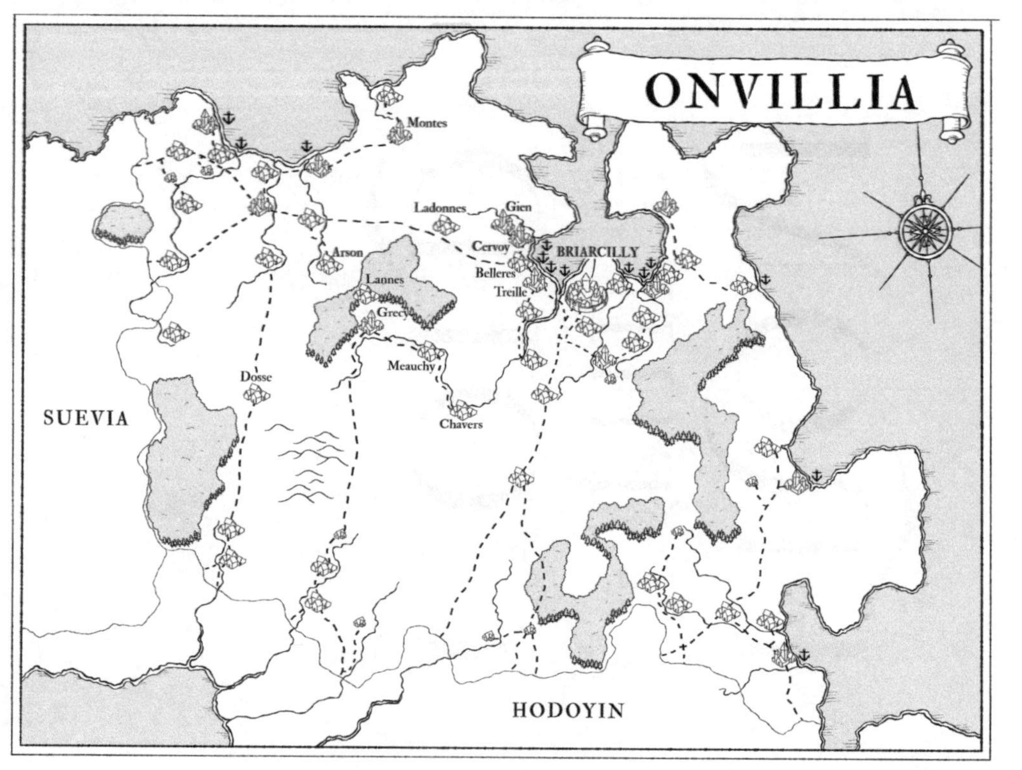

ONVILLIA
Montes
Ladonnes
Gien
Arson
Cervoy
BRIARCILLY
Lannes
Belleres
Treille
Grecy
Meauchy
Dosse
Chavers
SUEVIA
HODOYIN

A Stranger Arrives

Day 1

Each knife came free from the ashen tree trunk with a satisfying pull, with only Claris's ice-white fingertips visible in the woollen gloves. Her skill at knife-throwing was still a secret to most, considered unladylike, but it had never bothered those who loved her. Her mentor only cared about her strength in the impalement arts; her late mother had simply seen her as a bright light; her father's attention was focused on the wild streak running through her dutiful exterior.

To everyone else, she was Claris, or simply Demoiselle, poised to marry and bear the next Comte de Grecy.

At twenty, Claris should have been accustomed to the title and burdens that came with it. Her body was lithe, absent of curves the rich coveted, and her long flaxen hair constantly tied back in a multitude of plaits and braids. Neither aspect of her appearance supported the title, nor was she yet betrothed. It was her face, with the high cheekbones and deep-set brown eyes, that gave others pause. They gave weight to her stare and gravitas to her words.

She pulled the wolverine-fur-lined cloak closer around her shoulders after sheathing the knives. Argine, her merlin, sat hooded, feathers ruffling now and then in the wind, his small talons curling tight around the leather. She liked having him tethered to the nearby block perch while she practiced, the sound of him soothing.

Angry dark clouds hovered above, heavy with the promise of more snow. Claris shivered and readied herself again, hoping she would remain undisturbed in the eastern walled garden. Deep down she knew such thought was folly. Something always demanded attention, especially with the below-average intake of both food and taxes over the past year.

She narrowed her gaze, focusing on her target once more. With a swift, practiced motion, she hurled a knife, watching as it struck true, quivering as it embedded itself in the wood.

The faint rustle of leaves and the soft crunch of snow underfoot alerted her to a presence. She spun around, fingers reflexively readying another knife. Standing at the edge of the garden path was a garde, tall and sturdy as trained warriors of the county often were. A honed body of broad shoulders and musculature accompanied his golden brown skin. His face was not one she instantly recognised as one of their own and his surcoat absent of any heraldry. Her fingers tightened over the knife.

"Impressive," he said, forgoing propriety. He was of no Onvillian descent. The shaved left side of his head, with the right side resplendent with raven-dark hair, braided back and away from his face, gave it away.

She glanced at the breeches she wore, and the knives sheathed over her body. She'd never had a garde find her practicing. Despite the whispers in the household about her peculiar hobbies, someone witnessing it was a different issue altogether. Falconry they accepted, but not the impalement arts.

Claris masked her roiling emotions with a composed nod, sliding the knife back into her sheath. "Thank you," she replied.

"You practice often?" he continued, stepping closer, his height a head above her own.

"Often enough to stay sharp."

Her fingers, marked by tell-tale scars, twitched slightly as she met his gaze. He hadn't even blinked at her attire.

"Torsten." He gave a slight bow, his movements fluid and respectful. The faint, earthy, musky scent of him reached her as a light breeze stirred the air.

"Claris," she returned, keeping her tone even. She wanted to retreat, but his presence held her there. She felt seen, something she yearned to hold on to. Not seen as a means for titles and land, but simply as another person.

With a final shared glance, Torsten nodded, stepping back. "I'll leave you to your practice."

Claris watched as he resumed his path.

Jehan, the estate's seneschal, now came into view, dashing any hopes of continuing practice. Bushy eyebrows framed his large, wide-open green eyes. Claris wondered if he'd witnessed her encounter with Torsten. She shivered at the thought of his name, his stare.

"Demoiselle," he began, "Monsieur Henri Guignard, Vicomte de Chavers, has arrived."

Claris had hoped the foul weather would've delayed his arrival, but he'd arrived on schedule. Henri was a vicomte under her father's county and had entered negotiations with her father for her marriage to his eldest son, Alain. Thankfully, an agreement had yet to be made. Alain was pleasant enough to be sure, but the few moments of conversation they'd shared left much to desire. He hardly paid any attention to her, and he responded tersely to her questions. Claris sensed no warmth from Alain and she sighed at the thought. How she longed to go out on an adventure, to at least travel to other countries like young men her age got to do.

"See him to the parlour. I will be there shortly." Her current attire wouldn't be suitable to greet the vicomte. Not only would it be viewed as a sign of disrespect, but also place doubt that the comte was raising a well-respected daughter. Claris didn't want to risk her father's position.

Jehan gave a small bow and headed back into the manor. Claris couldn't do much without his support, for in her father's weakened state, Jehan took charge of all administration for the estate. She should've been learning from him, for assisting with the affairs of a household would be one of many duties a wife would assume, but she much preferred knife-throwing.

She'd planned to unhood Argine after her practice and let him stretch his wings. Claris brushed his wing in farewell.

Tucked near the door to the inside was a shed, primarily for gardening equipment, but Claris always had over-gowns tucked there. She slid a navy dyed gown over her breeches and went inside.

A purr at her legs drew her attention, as Pepin, her pet lynx, rubbed against her legs. His fur was soft to touch, a pale silvery-grey, with faint dark spots, though barely visible with his thick winter coat. She knelt to scratch behind his tuft ears. "We have the vicomte here today." He mewed in response and she smiled. Then with her shoulders back and head high, and with Pepin at her heel, she went towards the parlour.

The room was spacious yet inviting, its high ceiling adorned with intricate mouldings and large, mullioned windows allowing ample sunlight to flood the space during the day. Heavy, burgundy velvet drapes framed the windows, while the walls wore a sophisticated palette of muted greens and golds. In the centre of the parlour, a grand fireplace dominated one wall, its mantel adorned with delicate vases. Plush armchairs and settees, upholstered in rich brocades and soft leathers, were thoughtfully arranged around low, ornately carved mahogany tables. Claris spied the mahogany tea cart nearby, with an array of delicate porcelain teacups and saucers, each hand-painted with floral motifs. She hoped someone had removed the one that was chipped last week.

Vicomte Henri had sat himself close to the warm fire and remained seated upon her entrance. Pepin laid himself down upon one of the rugs, nearby Claris but not too close to the fire. One paw stretched lazily forward, claws briefly unsheathing.

"Demoiselle Claris, pleased to see you well," he said, with a small incline of his head.

"How was the trip, Monsieur?" Claris asked, taking a seat opposite.

"As well as one may expect with such weather. But, I am here to see about the comte. His absence at court is raising questions." The victome paused mid-sip. He'd spotted Pepin.

Claris folded her hands together in her lap, attempting to hold herself steady and serene. She and her father shouldn't still be at the Grecy estate. As soon as warm days ended, they should've headed back to the capital, but illness prevented the travel. Court attendance during the cooler months was expected of her father and every day away from court made her father lose favour. Claris knew Vicomte Henri wished for elevation, and what better than to take the place of an ailing comte.

"Of course." She swallowed. She needed something to dissuade any further actions by the vicomte. "He is resting today, for we leave to Briarcilly on the morrow."

The vicomte raised an eyebrow, but Claris schooled her features. She'd tamed her ire.

"That is good news. We can travel together."

Inwardly she cursed. Of course. She should've thought of that possibility. But it was too late to rescind her words. "My father would be most pleased to travel with you."

Jehan walked into the parlour, leaning down to whisper in her ear. "A solitary man approaches."

"Keep him in the courtyard."

"Is something the matter?" Henri asked.

Claris forced a smile. "No. A mere trifle requires my attention. Jehan will escort you to our guest chambers."

Jehan gave a small bow. "This way, Monsieur." Claris waited for the vicomte to stand and follow Jehan out of the parlour, then made her way to the stair turret, Pepin close behind her heels. Up high in the turret, Claris had a good outlook over the courtyard and the approaching path. There was only one way into the estate and its surrounding grounds.

It wasn't that he was solitary that stirred her interest. Nor the fact he carried no outward weaponry. It was that he was on foot, trudging through the snowfall, with not even a mule behind, while his hooded cloak shrouded most of his features. He couldn't be one of the locals of Grecy, none would wear lynx fur. Nor did he carry any supplies that indicated a physician. So, he wasn't there to help her father's health. To travel with nothing but what was on your back only boded ill. Claris didn't want trouble. Especially with the vicomte in residence. He needed no more ill claims against her father.

She waited a few moments more, watching for any signs there might be more on their way. Meanwhile, the garde on hand halted the lone traveller within the courtyard. She sighed and hoped this would have a quick resolution. With Pepin again at her heels, she left the turret and crossed over the salted snowy path to meet the traveller and garde alike.

Close up, she could see what lay beneath the hood, and the visitor's features gave her pause. He bore the same distinguishing large flat nose, prominent square bony jawline, and deep melting eyes as her late mentor. He was of Djeyun descent. His skin a light brown and ash brown curls cropped closely to his scalp. Those of Djeya lived at the very southern end of their continent, where the winters didn't bite as cold, but the summers harsher. He'd travelled far if he still called that country home.

Claris shifted her attention to one of the garde. "Well?"

"Say's there's some nasty business with a lich."

"Demi-lich," the traveller corrected. His tone deep and rich, yet soft. A subtle undercurrent of danger lacing the word.

Stories were told of liches, mages who'd found immortality by turning themselves undead by removing their very souls.

A dark stain on mages, and why many distrusted them. But Claris had never heard of a demi-lich before. Liches had powerful magic, able to spread corruption and decay, blighting the surrounding land. Some even told they instilled fear and dread, even paralysing those they encountered.

"We have heard of no such disturbance in this county," Claris said. Pepin pressed closer to her leg. "I will not waste the comte's time on the word of one man."

The stranger glanced at the lynx. "It doesn't leave witnesses," the traveller said. "Demi-liches are much worse than your average lich. What men I had, have died. The law—"

"I know the law," Claris snapped. The garde closest to her flinched, and Pepin mewed displeasure. She didn't need this. Her father was too ill to help with any fresh problem, and she'd already leaned so heavily on Jehan. The condestable would recite the law and do nothing more. But it'd bring dishonour if she turned this man away. Worse, it'd destabilise her father's position. The law dictated that any malevolent being upon a count's county was their burden, and his men shall cut it out before it infects another's land. "Where did you come from?"

"Dosse."

The township of Dosse lay to their south-west and was famous for its lead and silver mines. An important source for the creation of coinage. But it also fell under a marquis's responsibility.

"And did the Marquis de Argentum not lend aid?" Like her father, the marquis would have had an obligation, especially as Dosse lay in a march, a region at the boundaries of the kingdom.

"I did not seek his aid," the stranger said. "Grecy is the aid I seek. Men I need."

She couldn't readily see any deception in his eyes, but his lips twitched in the corners, as if amused by her presence.

"You must understand, it would be a good trap to strip away the garrison for a hostile takeover." It may have appeared paranoid to many, but Claris would not trust someone so easily and endanger her father. Especially now that the vicomte was in residence. Someone more skilled in subterfuge might be able to see a connection.

The traveller reached into his cloak, the garde and Pepin tensed, and pulled out a strip of bark. But it wasn't ordinary bark. The colour had faded from the surface, and a light frosting covered it. Claris took it and turned it this way and that, and even let Pepin take an experimental sniff. But she found no sign of chemicals or magical runes indicative of magecraft. She let out a barely audible sigh. Only a particular group of people would have such an item.

"You are a ley tracer," Claris said. They weren't common, but some made a living hunting down the malevolent, seeking them out for whatever purpose. "We have no current bounty." Perhaps his arrival coinciding with the vicomte was happenchance.

The traveller shook his head. "I don't do it for the coin."

"Very well," she said. "Come inside and I will see what I can do." She held up a hand, indicating that the garde needed not follow. Pepin continued to stay at her side.

At the doorway, Claris stamped her leather boots to shake free the snow. She waited for the traveller to follow suit and led him into the parlour. Pepin hung back, not being fond of fire. By the fireplace, the traveller held out his now degloved hand. "I'm Brahim."

Claris pulled her hands free from her own gloves and took his offered hand. "Claris." His fingers bore similar tell-tale scars from throwing knives like hers (though Pepin, and Argine, had also contributed with a few). She also couldn't shake the knowledge that Brahim shared more than a common appearance with her late mentor.

"Are you one of the comte's wives?" he asked.

"No, he is my father." Claris couldn't help the uncomfortable squirm of being appraised by the stranger. He likely took in the downturned edges of her mouth and port-wine stain near her left ear and took pity on her. Claris didn't think her life warranted any such thing. She was also glad that her father only had taken one wife. If he hadn't, she'd likely had never got the chance to study knife-throwing, nor had the freedom with Pepin. There'd be too many other eyes scrutinising her behaviour.

"And this is your lynx?" he asked.

She couldn't help but smile towards her pet. "Yes. I raised Pepin. He is as loyal as they come."

He stepped away from the fire and knelt. "Do you mind?"

"That will be up to Pepin." She focused back on her cat. "Keep watch, boy." She went out into the vestibule, where the seneschal already waited.

"Anything you need, Demoiselle?" Jehan asked.

"Is the vicomte settled?"

Jehan nodded. "I can keep him occupied if needed."

"That would be wise. I will see if Father is well enough to receive this new guest," she said. "Pepin is in there."

Through the hall and up the stairs, her father's valet stood stoically outside, giving her a polite nod. Claris entered the northern solar, which was her father's room.

His colour appeared healthier than the day before, but a sheen of sweat coated his brow, and he curled slightly in on himself. His receding hairline made the sweat more obvious, and his black hair had more flecks of grey than before. She missed seeing his smile. It was a good smile.

"Father, we have a visitor," Claris said. "He brings news of a demi-lich in our domain."

Her father blinked a few times, coming awake with comprehension, and shuffled to prop himself up on the bedhead. "A demi-lich?"

"That is his claim." Claris hoped Brahim to be wrong, for if the demi-lich poisoned the crops nearby, they'd be in even further strife.

"Best bring him up here then," her father said. Claris opened her mouth to protest, but he waved a hand. "Go. Let's not keep him waiting."

She hesitated. "Vicomte Henri is also here. Should we really let a stranger see your weakness?"

"If the vicomte is here," he said, "then all the more reason I see this stranger. Show I am not too weak to attend to affairs in my county."

Claris reasoned he spoke sense, and she would not question her father's decisions. He still had his mind.

She paused when back on the parlour's threshold. The seneschal still hovered nearby, and Pepin curled himself up away from fire and stranger alike.

"My father will see you now," she said and beckoned Brahim to follow. Although Pepin's tufted ears twitched, he made no move to follow as well. Once the man was beside her, she decided the truth would be the best. "He has the bloody flux," she warned, "but he will pull through this."

Brahim stayed silent at her side as he followed her up the stairs and to the solar. She didn't miss that his gaze didn't even stray to the paintings that lined the hall; paintings that would fetch a high price for a thief.

He waited at the entrance while Claris went in.

"Father," she said, "this is Brahim." She nodded at Brahim, and he took a step towards the bed.

"Comte Arnoul," Brahim said and bowed. "I trace malice in our land, and this demi-lich is in yours. One cannot take such a creature alone." Brahim glanced at Claris. "And, if you permit, I would have Ziri accompany me."

Claris stiffened slightly at the mention of her mentor. The comte also glanced towards her. "I'm sorry to say, but Ziri passed on last winter."

Claris took the opening. "How did you know Ziri was in our employ?"

Brahim angled himself to address Claris without showing disrespect to her father. "We're kin, and kin like to keep in contact when we can. I'm sad to hear of his passing."

Claris was a little sceptical. Ziri had never spoken to her of any kin and surely kin would know when one had passed? "I will take you to his mourning stone once this is done."

"But why request Ziri?" her father asked. A brief glimmer of pain lanced through his face. She'd get the pincerna to attend him.

Brahim glanced again at Claris, and she shifted her weight to her other foot, not liking the attention he gave. "This isn't pleasant business."

The comte waved a hand at his daughter. "She is well hardy."

Claris stood a little straighter at her father's recognition. She knew he wasn't referring to going through the loss of her mother, but her wilder streak with taming Pepin, and the numerous cuts upon her hands.

"A demi-lich has a single weak point, so tiny only a fine blade has the chance of piercing," Brahim said. "And no one wants to stand toe to toe with a demi-lich."

"But you yourself have such a skill," Claris said, confident she'd recognised his scars correctly.

Brahim gave a small nod. Again, his lips twitched slightly. "I've taken many a chance, which is something I shouldn't repeat. A second knife thrower is what I truly need." His eyes strayed to Claris. Had he recognised her knife scars on her fingers? "But without such, I'd welcome some of your men."

The comte grunted. "You want the assistance of my garde?"

Claris held her tongue, despite wanting to volunteer herself to be that second knife thrower. She had blinked and missed the opening, and would be remiss to voice her opinion now.

"Handful, not a large company," Brahim said. "And soon. Each day, the ley trail weakens."

"Claris," her father said, "please find Levlan and send him here. We have much to discuss."

Claris nodded her assent. Levlan was the estate's mareschal, and voice of the garde. "Brahim, if you will." She gestured to the door, and as her father did not indicate otherwise, Brahim exited the room.

Hubert, the ever-silent valet was nearby. "Please fetch the pincerna for Father," Claris whispered on passing.

Claris led Brahim back to the parlour. Pepin lifted his head and tracked her movement. "Please, wait here, and I will take you to Ziri's stone once I am done."

She waited until Brahim had taken one of the chairs before departing. Back outside, out near the southern pond, she located Levlan from behind. His broad shoulders and stubbornness to never cover his bald head for warmth a giveaway.

"Levlan," she said. He turned and inclined his head from respect. "My father wishes your presence. It is to discuss garde who shall accompany that traveller."

His eyes flicked up to the house, before focusing back on Claris. "Demoiselle." He stepped around and trudged up to the house.

Claris only lingered outside in winter if need necessitated it, or she was practicing, but the thought of inside and the stranger, one who knew Ziri, didn't appeal as much as she'd first thought. Especially as she'd foolishly promised to take him to Ziri's stone.

She traced her fingers over the hidden scars on her opposite hand. Scars from hard work and mistakes. Blood she'd shed under Ziri's tutelage, an escape found after her mother's death. Brahim's presence was bringing up all the thoughts Claris wanted to keep buried. The fear crawling under her skin that she may also lose her father. How many losses can one endure before they break completely?

Yet this stranger had also seen loss. His eyes gave it away. No one can ever really hide the sheen of loss that covers one's eyes.

She didn't think it was the loss of his men, either.

Knowing she'd dallied enough, Claris made her way back indoors. Pepin was no longer in the parlour, but Brahim remained seated where she had left him. His eyes were closed, as if deep in thought.

Claris gently cleared her throat so as not to startle him. "If you would like, I have time now."

Brahim's eyes opened in a controlled way, similar to the way he came to his feet. "Much appreciated."

She led him out to the western walled garden, past the bee boles, and towards the three downy birches that framed the estate's mourning plaza. Frost caught on the branches gave them cascades of white, and nestled in amongst the cobbled mosaic paths and gardens were the limestone mourning stones. Claris would often come out there and stand before her mother's stone, simply to talk and work through all the fears that plagued her.

No one in the kingdom was buried; instead, they were turned to ash, and the hollow interior of the stone filled with the remains. Ziri never spoke to Claris about doing it any other way. His stone was the only one not of Claris's long family lineage to be mourned at the estate.

She stopped in front of his stone, dropped to one knee, and knelt her head against the cold front of it for a moment before standing. Brahim did no such thing.

"Would you like time alone?" Claris asked.

He shook his head. "How did he pass?"

No one died, simply passed. An ancient Onvillian belief was that one passes as their soul continues, and to die is for the soul to die too. It comforted her, that notion.

"The influenza. He... We tried everything. But his body eventually gave in." It seemed so strange to her at the time, for someone so strong-willed and healthy to succumb to such a simple illness.

"Winters have been harsher," Brahim said. "There's no surprise a demi-lich has risen in such a climate."

"But they can exist beyond the climates of winter, no?"

He nodded. "Of course, but death's grasp is always keener in the cold."

She shivered involuntarily. After a moment, Brahim motioned he was ready to move on. Pepin slunk over to them, pressing himself up against Claris. He licked his lips with content.

"Did you find a rabbit?"

Pepin purred in response. She reached down and gave his side an affectionate rub.

Claris then led Brahim back towards the house, although Pepin remained outside. The nightkeeper had restoked the fire and laid out a hot pot of tea and cakes in their absence, likely under the seneschal's directive. Most nightkeepers avoided being seen or heard. They were fiercely loyal beings if you met their conditions; creatures eager for human dreams. Many argued for their purging, to classify them in the same class as a lich, but most found their dreams were worth an extra pair of hands, especially when it saved coin. Claris had been letting theirs feed on her exclusively. Even before her mother passed, nightmarish fever plagued Claris's night dreams, providing terrifying shadowy creatures that she couldn't even name. They only worsened upon losing her mother. Thankfully nightkeepers didn't differentiate between good and bad dreams, and without their aid she was certain she'd never sleep well these days.

Claris took the pot and carefully poured out two cups. Brahim accepted the offered drink and took a tentative sip. A grimace quickly passed through his face and Claris contained her smile.

"Bark tea can be a little bitter," she said. "Cake will help weather it. I'm afraid our honey ran out a couple weeks past." Another reason to pack up and leave for Briarcilly. If they continued to dip into the winter stores, the people of Grecy would have even less to last them through the winter.

Brahim politely declined and took another sip. Claris took a large gulp, cherishing the liquid burning down her throat. She looked out the open window, watching the sun set behind the walls of the garden. It would spill oranges, reds, and purples across the deepening sky. The heavy clouds were a distant threat.

A door clicked shut and heavy footfalls came towards them. Claris didn't make to move. Jehan was of lighter foot, so she knew it was Levlan who stood at the threshold. He tilted his head slightly. "Comte would see you, Demoiselle."

Claris set her cup down, her hands trembling.

Would her father send her with Brahim?

A Choice Made

DAY 1

Inside his room, he remained propped up.

Claris moved to his side. "At least lie back down."

He grunted once, but let his daughter help him slide back down. "Levlan and I have agreed that six garde will go with this man," her father said. "Surely that will be enough to appease the law."

Claris pursed her lips. She wanted more than to be married off. Though ramifications would be a long list, she had to take the gift of opportunity. "Did you count me in that number?"

The comte tried to rise, but Claris gently pushed his shoulder back down. Finally, she had the chance to prove that all those lessons were not wasted, that she was meant for more. None in the garde had the same skills. Besides, she was as good as Ziri had been with a knife. Brahim couldn't say no to that.

"You know I am the best option to end this demi-lich," she said.

"That man said he could manage."

Claris shook her head. "You should not stand for *could* now. This is our land. Our people. You would risk them on a could?"

"Imagine the talk if I allow my daughter, a woman, to go on the road with men. Your reputation, my reputation. It could spell our ruin." He grimaced in another attempt to rise from the bed.

"The ruin of a demi-lich would be worse," Claris said. "Imagine how the others in court would whisper about our failure to defend our people. You must let me go. In accomplishing this task, I can be seen capable of ruling. I could be Comtesse without need for marriage."

He sighed deeply. "But you help so much."

"You know most of that is Jehan," she replied, though she wished his words to be true. "I already told the vicomte you would travel with him tomorrow to Briarcilly. You must be the one to tell the king. Word of a demi-lich will not be received well."

He reached out and took her hand. "You never cease to amaze me. Levlan will also help, I suppose."

"Then it is settled," Claris said. "In the morning you shall depart for the capital, while I accompany this Brahim and six of our garde."

"You best get our new guest settled for the night then," her father said. "And inform Jehan. I'll want at least one garde to stay here for the vicar."

Claris pulled the blanket up around his shoulders and kissed his forehead. "Water and rest."

Back out in the hall, she took two deep breaths. She knew if her father wasn't so ill, she wouldn't have got her way. She could do this. No, not could. Must. She knew this was a real possibility to prove her worth in battle, like many other male nobles, and in doing so elevate herself above just a vessel of marriage.

Brahim stood on her return. She noted he had taken a cake after all.

"You will share in supper, rest with us, and then we will depart in the morning," Claris advised him.

"Thank you."

She gave a terse nod and went once more outside. Levlan and a few of the garde stood around a fire. They went quiet on her approach, likely in the middle of organising who would accompany Brahim on the journey. She didn't spy the one who'd interrupted her practice earlier.

"Levlan, a word," she said.

He separated away from the others. Further in the shadows, Pepin prowled over, padding near Claris, but eyes trained on Levlan. He gave the cat a wary glance.

"Tomorrow, you will arrange an escort for my father back to the capital. Ensure one garde stays here," Claris said. "The vicomte will accompany Father."

"And you, Demoiselle?"

"I am to travel with Brahim." She watched the garde and swallowed. Surely, she could push a little more? "Ensure those that join in the journey are aware they will be answering to me." She didn't want the reaction of shock to her presence in the morning from the garde, and she needed to know they would see her as their leader, like they would her father if he had accompanied them instead.

"Of course." His expression indicated he had more to say on the subject but wouldn't voice such thoughts. "The vicomte has two of his own garde with him, so your father will still have ample protection on his journey."

"Thank you, Levlan," she said, turning back towards the house. She wasn't entirely used to her requests being granted so easily.

Claris also sought the fauconnier. She'd have to ensure Argine would continue to be cared for in her absence. She wouldn't take the merlin, but the lynx would have to come with her. He'd bonded to her, and wouldn't tolerate another.

"What do you say, Pepin?" Claris asked her pet. "Ready for an adventure?" He mewed his pleasure and loped in front of her, eager to be inside once more.

The scent of boiled cabbage filled the house as it flowed from the kitchen. Claris went to retrieve Brahim from the parlour, but found him absent. Surely, he'd have more respect than to wander another's home unaccompanied? Claris pursed her lips momentarily in thought, then composed herself and moved towards the dining area. Perhaps he'd been ushered there by Jehan... even though that would be abnormal, to seat a guest before the host.

Her father had already seated himself in one of the chairs; sweat dotted his brow. She was too shocked to move or say anything. Claris spied the vicomte and Brahim also seated. Claris moved to her father's side. "You should be resting."

He gave a pointed look at their guests. "I'll not let some passing ill give me bad grace."

"Your wellbeing is far more important than any perceived slight," Claris said. Pepin had curled up under the table.

Her father scoffed, and Claris hoped her embarrassed flush went unnoticed. "Take your seat." At least Brahim had the decency to keep his head down and pretend to not hear the exchange, while the vicomte looked on with rapt attention.

Once seated, her father rang the little dinner bell. The dinner cart pushed out from the kitchen, the nightkeeper invisible to the eye. After the bowls and bread were laid out, the comte cleared his throat.

"Tonight, we dine to a quick and successful quest to clear the land of this new malevolence."

Claris raised her glass of cold tea, realising the vicomte now also knew the plans, and about the demi-lich.

"For the delay in ashes," she said.

Her father, the vicomte, and Brahim reciprocated the sentiment.

After a few beats, allowing all a few mouthfuls of food, the comte spoke again, this time to Brahim. "I'm sure you're aware I've granted your request for men. Six of my garde will accompany you."

"You're most generous," Brahim said, displaying no outwards sign that the number of men was enough or not.

The vicomte cleared his throat. "In fact, it will be five of the comte's, and one of my own. I urged the comte that I provide at least one to show my support. All of the county stands to lose much if this demi-lich is not dealt with."

Claris went to tell Brahim how she'd be joining him as well, but her father's subtle shake of his head snapped her mouth shut. It wasn't as if Brahim had a choice if he wanted the men. Or so Claris hoped. It'd be like her father to change his mind. The vicomte would know the truth well enough when she did not join them on the trip to Briarcilly.

"I do look forward to our trip together, Arnoul," the vicomte said. "Will give us time to finalise those marriage terms."

Claris's hand stilled. Surely her father would have to pause such negotiations. She dared not look towards him. Instead, she offered the vicomte a small smile. "Then I will be sure to travel separately to give you the necessary space."

The vicomte narrowed his eyes for but a moment before breaking into a wide grin. "A most gracious offer."

Her father raised his glass in a silent toast.

They continued to eat in quiet, a silence that gnawed at Claris. The emptiness demanded to be filled.

"Brahim," Claris started, "what brought you to our kingdom?"

"A restless spirit lives within me," he said. "Left my homeland for it." He took a sip. "Wasn't until I reached this land did the spirit quieten. It was here I started to ley trace."

"Is that common among your people?" Claris asked. Ziri never spoke much of his origins.

"Spirits can live in any soul, regardless of origin. Much like the malevolence rise, they give little care of their surrounds. It rises from forces outside perceived control."

Claris wasn't sure if she truly followed what Brahim said, but she nodded in slow understanding. It at least gave her something to put away to think further on. She was sure their new clergy would not like such talks of spirits inside a body. The clergy of Aurelanity preached the virtues of duty, sacrifice, leadership, and unity under the grace of the creator, Luminar. Even the old Onvillian traditions, now known as the old gods, were considered shadows subservient to

Luminar. The people would view such spirits in a body as a form of malevolence, something that the light should purge.

The comte hunched forward, making a poor effort at disguising the sickly coughs shuddering through him. Claris pushed her chair back, startling Pepin up, to tend to her father.

"Excuse us," she said to Brahim and the vicomte as she helped her father up from his chair. His entire body shook. Pepin pressed his body against her father's other side. He shouldn't have left his bed, but Claris kept her admonishments quiet as she led him away, not wanting their guests to hear such domestic matters.

In the comte's room, Claris helped him back into his bed and she waited until he'd taken a good few mouthfuls of water before she let him rest his head down.

"Pepin," she said, "please bring the pincerna here."

The lynx looked between her and the comte before letting out a single mew and padding from the room.

"I likely will not see you again," said Claris. "Not until that lich is dead. And when I do, you will be healthy again." She leaned down and pressed a kiss above his brow. It wasn't normal for her to think of the future, knowing how fickle it was, but she needed a small thread of hope.

He reached out to touch her hand. "You be safe for me. I'll not mourn you too."

"Promise you will not worry?"

He gave a slight nod. "I won't. It wouldn't be good for the health." A small smile tugged at his mouth.

"Good." She tucked up his blankets and departed from the room, resisting the desire to give him another lingering look. They both must remain positive.

Brahim had returned to the parlour in her absence. Rather than sitting, he stood in front of their meagre collection of books. Most of them were reference volumes, maps, and transcribed histories from other lands. Thankfully the vicomte was nowhere to be seen; he must have retired to his own chambers, or to speak to his own garde.

"Do you get much opportunity to read?" Claris asked Brahim.

He turned around. "Afraid not."

She refrained from more questions. "We have a guest bed you can use for the night." Brahim nodded and Claris took the cue to lead him to the small solar that filled the space between her father's and her own larger solar.

"The men will be ready at dawn," she said, holding at the doorway for a moment, debating if she should tell him about her joining the journey.

"Your hospitality is most generous," was all he said in return. Not once did he look up to acknowledge her lingering presence. So she murmured her good night and headed to her own room.

Pepin had already made himself comfortable on the bed. She walked over and stroked his back, eliciting contented purrs. But Claris was in no rush to fall asleep, though she knew her dreams would be eaten. It was the unsettling thrill of anticipation sitting in her gut that kept her wide awake. She busied her hands by sharpening and oiling all her throwing knives under the watchful gaze of Pepin.

The selfish part of her wanted this journey to prove to herself that she could be like a Suevik blade-maiden, fierce in battle and beholden to no man. The dutiful side knew it was their only option. She must be there to ensure the demi-lich was taken care of and she must help her father keep his position as comte, not for her own future, but for the legacy of his forebears. It would devastate him to lose such a position from ailing health. Taking care of the demi-lich could perhaps even change the need for her to wed Alain. She smiled at the thought. A way to distance her father and herself from the vicomte.

Only when the candle guttered did she fall asleep.

A Struggle to Lead

Day 2

Before dawn, Claris stood before her mother's mourning stone. Pepin sat at her side; his tail swished over the mosaics. Talking at the stone brought Claris a sense of peace. Her mother always had an ear to lend when Claris had lost her way.

She'd dressed unladylike for the trip, with a surcoat over breeches with ankle cuffs. It'd make riding a horse far easier than any gown could. If it wasn't for the length of her hair, she likely could've passed for a young man.

"I know you would not have approved of me following a similar path to the Suevik blade-maidens," Claris said. "I know I have said it was a hobby, a way to take my mind off everything else, but now I think it is a true path I can follow. A way to take a modicum of control back. A way to forge a different future, a future you'd be proud of, a future where I can be the comte's legacy, to carry on his name without a loveless match." She paused, distracted by snow sliding from branches at the orchards that peeked over the wall. "Father has approved this, and I hope you too can see the need in my going. I promise it is not foolhardy, and I will take what caution I can." She kissed her fingers and rested them against the stone's top.

Pepin stood and touched his nose to the stone. Claris gently stroked his head.

She made one last stop to farewell Argine. She'd enjoyed the last four years of falconry, especially when it was all three of them.

Returning inside, no other sounds murmured through the house. She wanted to be ready before Brahim, so he couldn't leave without her. He might not like her presence, but that'd be non-negotiable. She'd have to prove to him she was an excellent student and Ziri taught her well.

After tucking the last of her knives into a thigh strap (the arm strap was already full) she slung her travel bag over her shoulder and left her solar. Pepin diligently stuck by her side.

Pausing outside her father's door, she debated if she should check in or not. A part of her wanted to see him one last time, just in case. She wasn't a fool. Going up against any malevolent wouldn't be easy, and she hoped the outcome was favourable, but she knew saying goodbye again to her father would crack her resolve. She shook her head. Nothing was certain, and she knew it wasn't worth worrying about the future.

The sky was still clear, a good way to begin, especially for the comte's trip. Travelling in winter wasn't common with the roads harder in the snow.

Garde stood nearby eight horses, all long haired and very muscular, bred to carry a rider for the best part of a day and still able to gallop for an attack. At least one was a stallion, and another a gelding; the remainder were a good stock of mares, all bay, dun, or black coloured. A mule stood nearby, loaded with supplies.

She approached the garde, keeping her hands at her sides so not to twist them in anxiety. Coming across as weak wasn't on her desired list. But as the gap closed between them, her steps stuttered. Amongst the six men was the one who'd found her in the garden, Torsten. He had to be the vicomte's garde.

They noticed her approach and fell silent, halting all action. Torsten's gaze found hers. His blue eyes, such a rare colour in Onvillia, halting all reasonable thoughts in her mind.

Claris swallowed. "The vicomte volunteered you?" she asked, her voice coming out quieter than intended. She didn't dare repeat herself. They were taller, larger than her, and it didn't seem natural for her to stand before such a group alone. In fact, she never had. Ladies had to be escorted if unwed, usually by another lady. Claris had none. She was the sole woman left at the Grecy manor.

She hoped her father would have a good reason for her absence on his return to Briarcilly. If it became common knowledge she travelled with a group of men, unchaperoned, it would ruin any prospective marriage proposals and weaken her father's claim on the county.

Torsten stepped away from the others. "A show of his support." The shadow of stubble on his strong jaw and the puckered scar at his throat added to his rugged appeal.

Her eyes flicked to the garde of her house. "A word, then." She moved away from the others, not wanting the attention. Pepin strayed near the horses. Thankfully all the horses were accustomed to the lynx's presence.

"Is this where you give me a warning?" His lips twitched in the corners. They had a soft curve to them. In fact, his entire face was pleasing to look upon.

"No." Again, her mind faltered, unsure why he'd think such a thing. "You are Suevik?" She swallowed, her eyes not quite meeting his.

"Yes. Is that the problem?"

She sucked in her lower lip, enjoying the rough texture of his voice. "Neither your heritage nor your fealty to the vicomte is of my concern."

He smiled. "Then..." He took a step closer, but Claris refused to step back.

Pepin slunk forward, keen to inspect Torsten.

"Is he friendly?" he asked.

Claris smiled down at Pepin. "Unless I do not want him to be." She looked back up, finding her eyes didn't want to land anywhere but on Torsten. His eyes lazily studied her, slowly drifting down to eye Pepin again, as the lynx prowled closer to his legs.

With his eyes no longer on her own, she snapped from her trance. With a subtle shake of her head, she stepped backwards, right into someone else. Claris bit her lower lip to keep from drawing attention by gasping.

"You're joining?" The voice belonged to Brahim, and Claris side-stepped, so she had both him and Torsten within her line of sight.

From the corner of her eye, she noticed the other garde went back to the business of securing supplies, and the general act of feigning activity. Pepin went back over to them, curling between horse and human legs alike.

"I can throw as well as Ziri," she said to Brahim, though the weight of his stare brought her own eyes down. "I will not risk the lives of the people in this county on one alone."

His eyes took in all the knives strapped to her body. "Show me." He pulled out one of his own knives and held it out to her.

Claris bristled at the request but took the knife. She'd not be cowed. She knew her worth, but not acquiescing would be a worse way to begin. Pepin came over, pressing his body up against her legs. Knife in hand, Claris walked to an appropriate spot at a standard distance from a tree outside the courtyard. Brahim, Torsten, and Pepin weren't the only ones to follow, all the garde couldn't pass the chance up to see Claris perform. Of course, those in the manor all heard the whispers of her training, but few had witnessed it. The extra eyes didn't dissuade her. Besides, the more the better. They'd soon understand she was dangerous in her own right.

This knife was weighted differently, blade heavy (different to her own handle heavy knives) but she figured that was another part of the test. She spent a few moments with phantom throws, getting a feel for the weight. Angled at the tree, she took a step forward and released the knife. It landed a little lower than she anticipated, but it still struck true.

"You have an ability," Brahim said, "but that's no true mark." Claris frowned, and Pepin mewed displeasure. "The demi-lich has one weak spot. You miss, we all die." His eyes narrowed and Claris's throat thickened, finding herself unable to speak.

Brahim let out an exaggerated sigh. "I'll not reject the help, though I doubt it necessary."

Torsten cleared his throat, still hovering quite close by.

Claris glanced towards the garde, all still lingering nearby. She knew she was better than that one throw. She faced the tree once more and in quick succession she'd thrown two of her own knives. They landed side by side.

Brahim huffed. "Very well."

She stomped through the snow to retrieve the knives, though she knew she should hide her embarrassed anger from the men. When she held out his blade to him, he shook his head. "Keep that. Practice. You can't rely on having your own blades."

What he said made sense, but Claris still didn't swallow it easily.

"Do we have a direction?" she asked, keen to deflect attention from herself.

"North," Brahim said and headed back towards the horses.

"Right, Lannes," she said to herself. Pepin nudged her side, and she gave him a reassuring pat. Back in the courtyard Levlan stood near the horses, keeping a close eye on the stock he'd raised. He held the reins out on a black mare. "I've readied horses for the comte's travel as well."

"Many thanks," Claris said. "But what of that stallion?"

Levlan shook his head. "I tried to dissuade the garde lordling, but his father insisted. But a warhorse for this? It's madness, Demoiselle. Warhorses are for battle, not travel." Levlan patted the mare's flank. "She's good riding stock."

"Some you cannot talk sense," Claris replied with a slight smile. "Will he keep up?"

He nodded. "Of course. But come a fight, that horse may bite and kick the others in his aggression. So keep a wide berth if it comes to that." Levlan unhooked a hatchet tucked into his belt. "Take this. Your blades may be good afar, but in close, you should have something."

Claris took the small axe, though she'd never held such a thing before. "I may do more harm than good with this."

"I'm sure you'll surprise yourself." He then handed over another leather strap to belt around her waist to hold the hatchet.

"Thank you." She looked back at the estate. "Please ensure that Father gets plenty of rest on the travel and be sure he is careful. His health should not be pushed by want of speed by the vicomte."

"Of course, Demoiselle. I shall look forward to your return."

He then pointed out the wrapped bedroll tied horizontally across the cantle of the saddle, and informed her supplies, like spare clothes, were in the saddlebags.

Levlan bent to give her a hand, but Claris shook her head. "I will not expect one of the garde to offer such a service, thus I will manage alone."

Levlan nodded and took a step back, allowing Claris to mount the horse on her own. Pepin looked up at her but made no attempt to join her up on the horse's back.

The men had all fallen into formation and were mounted, with Torsten taking up rear guard. He looked back and faltered at her stationary presence. Claris waved him on. She'd catch up. She knew the moment she left, it would be months before seeing her father again.

Months of not having her dreams vanish, too. She clenched her hands tighter over the reins at that thought, hoping her dreams wouldn't disturb the others or draw unnecessary attention. Having not dreamt for so many years left her wondering if they'd even still be there.

She shook her head, pushing her doubts down, then patted the horse's neck and gave a gentle pull on the reins. As expected, it didn't take long to catch up with the group, with Pepin also keeping pace.

Brahim was in the front alone, astride a dun mare. The surrounding snow churned into a slurry and movement was slow, as expected, especially as the horses grew accustomed to the gait in the snow.

Knowing they headed for Lannes unsettled her. To the west was a forest, under Forest Law, and she hoped the demi-lich had not made its path through there. Entry into such a forest had to be granted by the king. A request they likely had no time for. Encouraging her horse to increase the pace, she moved around the men and came up on Brahim's side.

His jawline hardened and he tilted his head away. "Do you think us equal?" he asked with a sneer.

Claris didn't take the barb, even if she seethed at his arrogant, dismissive tone. Clearly he did not want her with them. "Do we head to Lannes because that is where the demi-lich went? It is heavy with trees."

Brahim glanced down at Pepin, who took to pawing at the snow. "It would have gone around woodland, but this is a direct route."

"But we will not lose its path?" Claris asked, still a little ruffled.

"A necessary detour," he said. "I wanted Ziri." He looked her up and down. "Not a girl with rose blossoms in her cheeks."

Claris flushed. She was no longer a girl. "One knife throw should not be how you judge my worth."

"One throw is all you'll have."

He urged his own horse to pull away from Claris now and her eyes narrowed at his back, but she didn't press to keep up. She kept her head held high, knowing the garde had watched the exchange.

When it came time to set up camp, Claris found herself only in charge of her own bedroll and horse. One of the garde took command of her tent, clearly thinking it their responsibility. She stepped out of their way while they did so, warring with herself about whether she should've taken over or if that would've caused offence. She really should have asked Levlan for more advice. But she watched as they hammered in the last stake. The tent, a wedge of stained canvas patched with waxed leather, dropped slightly on the windward side, but it would hold. She ducked inside once finished. It smelled of wet wool and ash and she laid out the bedroll, taking the fur back out to sling over the tent for added insulation.

The rest of the garde set up the camp and stoked a few small fires with haste. Clearing the snow seemed almost fruitless, but enough was cleared that tents could be set, and it would suffice for the night. At least none assumed that Claris would voice a complaint. Hushed murmurs passed between the men while they carried out their tasks. She waited patiently as they did so, wanting to hold off sleep as long as possible, not eager to know what dreams filled her.

Torsten took a step towards her, then paused, then continued. In the low light, Claris decided that he must be close to her own age. Pepin had curled up inside the tent already.

"Would you like that word now, Demoiselle?" he said.

Claris glanced between him and Brahim. She wanted to correct Torsten into calling her Claris instead, but she was eager to approach Brahim and clear the air with him. "I have forgotten already." She offered Torsten a smile. "Excuse me."

His hand reached out as if to stop her, but his fingers stopped short of contact. "You'll sleep alone?"

Claris swallowed. It wasn't deemed common, or usually acceptable, for one to sleep alone. But she had done so since her mother's death, since she insisted her father dismiss her handmaid. She hated being followed and fussed over, especially when she wanted to roam with Pepin, or throw knives. By removing the handmaid, she removed a source of gossip. She had Pepin, and that was enough. "I have my cat. I will not be alone. Now, excuse me." Claris knew that the garde would share space, with their primary concern on keeping warm to avoid freezing to death. She had ensured she had an extra woollen blanket, and Pepin gave good warmth with all his fur.

Torsten shifted sideways to let her pass. She didn't want to be rude and hoped her smile would be enough. He worked for the vicomte, after all, and she was certain he'd tell his monsieur all about her upon their return.

She fought hard not to blush as she came quite close to his body. Bolder ladies would've taken the opportunity to brush against him and her mind skipped back to his question on her sleeping arrangement. Had he been offering to share the same space? Her skin flushed at the very thought. She shook her head and took a deep breath, banishing such absurd notions. He was a garde. She resisted looking back at him.

"Claris," Brahim said, sensing her approach.

"Is there anything else you can tell me?" she asked.

"About the demi-lich?" Brahim shifted to face her but made no effort to stand. It was a small slight, and by remaining seated, it meant he saw no threat. Her fingers curled up into her palms.

"You are positive it is no standard lich?"

"Yes. I can handle a lich on my own." His hand strayed to a pocket, likely where the lich bark sat. "But only seeing it will truly persuade you."

"What makes a demi-lich deadlier?" Claris asked.

"They transcended, becoming something different, but even less mortal, less tied to this plane."

Much of the malevolence in the country, and their neighbouring ones, had been eradicated, but many still lingered, some still able to be pulled from other planes. It was why many cautioned against those versed in magecraft. The widespread belief was that magic, and misuse of it, created the malevolence. Now mages were rare, and those who practiced openly faced hostility and strict governing laws, especially in Onvillia. The king had made a Charter of Magic that covered all such punishments, none of them pleasant, for those accused of abusing their magic.

Claris had studied the Obscurum War, where humanity went against hordes of malevolents, costing over 100,000 lives. Thirty years of hard conflict, a hard-won victory. Her father had been only two years of age at the conflict's end. It was in that learning where she first encountered mention of the Suevik blade-maidens, women warriors who fought side by side with Suevik males to fight back the malevolence. Even to this day, women were openly permitted to train in weaponry and join the Suevik armies.

"But why a blade, not an arrow?" she asked. She'd heard it before that a knife thrown was far weaker than an arrow shot.

"Arrows are no good against such beings. Too fast, too simple. The old magics recognise only what is bound to hand and will. A blade thrown from the self can wound the unliving." Brahim looked towards the garde, then back to her.

"We will not stop until it is dead," Claris said. She found it hard to look at Brahim, his features far too reminiscent of Ziri. The memories threatening at the corners of her mind were an unwanted side-effect.

"Even if it crosses into another's county?"

A small furrow creased her brow. "If that happens, then we have failed."

"You'd give up?" His head tilted slightly.

His literal take on her words didn't slide easily over her. "It would be hard to do when ashes."

"Death either to it or yourself?"

"If that is to be the price." A shiver passed over her. A thought she wouldn't have voiced, not realising how true and right it sounded now that it had been said. A promise into the future she never gave much pause for.

"An attribute all need when facing malevolence," Brahim said and shifted his attention away. Claris paused, waiting to see if he'd focus back, but he appeared lost in whatever thought had snared him.

She glanced over at the garde gathered around the fire. Torsten must've sensed her gaze and stared back at her. She averted her regard quickly, before colour bloomed over her cheeks, and she steeled herself, knowing she had to build a camaraderie with them if she hoped they'd listen to her. She'd yet to know their names. Making her way over, she didn't sit immediately. They all quieted as she stood over them.

"If you would please," she said, and swallowed. Garde shouldn't make her nervous. "I would like to know your names."

A garde with wide shoulders and thin hips spoke first. "Sigibert." His eyes, deep-set and steely grey, reflected a no-nonsense attitude. The crow's feet at the corners of his eyes and the faint lines etched across his forehead hinted at years of service.

The garde next to Torsten with a round face, large eyes, and long nose went next. "Flore, my lady." Claris sucked in her bottom lip. They had a deep and strong tenor, and she always appreciated a nice voice. Though she doubted they regarded her in favourable light. She'd had many a fellow lady comment how her body wouldn't please most men. Not that their comments bothered her. She liked her slender strength. One thing she learnt from her research on blade-maidens was that they used speed to their advantage, not their strength.

"Roul." The next man along inclined his head, Claris noting his wide green eyes and long blond hair. Even seated, she could tell he would stand taller than the rest. He was also the one who brought the warhorse.

The garde next to Roul wore fitted braces on his wrists and ankles, a bow resting against his legs. His jaw set firm, and without a smile, he introduced himself, "Dalfin." Claris noted to ask about the braces later.

"Odo," said the last, his jawline clean-shaven, with long, well-groomed chestnut hair. The garde who had set up her tent. "And if it is not too forward, we heard what you said."

Her eyes widened.

"You share our duty," Sigibert said. "Death is a price we all prepare for."

Flore held out a parcel of food for her.

"Thank you." Claris held the food and became uncertain if she should eat beside them or not. None of them made to move to make her feel invited. Perhaps they thought it inappropriate for her to be within their presence. Heat clawed up her neck.

Flore cleared their throat, drawing Claris's attention back to them. "Did your cat need food as well?"

She hoped the firelight didn't give away her embarrassment. "No... no, Pepin is fine. Thank you for the food, and your names."

She moved away from them and back towards her tent. Pepin was still curled up where she'd left him. He raised his head to sniff at her food as she sat beside him. He turned his head away in disinterest.

"Not raw enough for you." Her smile cut short as her earlier revelation still nagged at the corners of her mind. Of course she didn't doubt it. She was here to see the demise of the demi-lich, no matter the cost. But even the garde echoing her sentiment, even knowing that 'death with no regrets' was a common garde motto, still unsettled her. Had she doomed those she only just met?

Part of her, maybe the youth of her years, never gave much pause to her own mortality. She was young and healthy. Thoughts of such shouldn't cross her mind. But the deaths of her mother and Ziri went against that belief. The way Brahim spoke of the task ahead, if they kept their distance and aimed true, suggested the demi-lich would die. She shook her head, for it couldn't be that simple. If it was, Brahim wouldn't have needed to seek help.

Pepin nudged her hand. She hadn't even begun to eat. "You are right, boy." She spooned the food into her mouth with her fingers, barely registering the taste.

Footsteps crunched behind her. Heavy. Intentional.

"Fire's warmer if you get closer," said Brahim. He didn't look at her. Just stood there.

"I'm warm enough," she said.

"Never spent a winter beyond walls, have you?"

"No."

This time, he looked at her. "It isn't too late to go back."

The statement struck cleaner than her best knife. She said, "This is important."

Brahim's mouth twisted. He nodded. Then he walked off. Leaving her to wonder why he kept trying to deter her presence.

A loud commotion startled her from the reverie. Pepin was up on all fours. Claris stood, poking her head out of the tent.

Roul towered over another, his back blocking her view of who. Another garde let out a shout, and another tumbled to the ground. Roul had pushed him down. Claris took a step forward. Before she intervened, Torsten stood before Roul.

Claris couldn't be seen to avoid conflict, especially between those under her charge. She closed the gap and watched as Sigibert helped Odo from the ground. Torsten, arms crossed, watched as Roul went to a tent.

"Is everything okay?" she asked, eyes flicking over the garde.

They all nodded, dispersing away from the fire, and to tents. Torsten stayed behind. She sighed and sat down. He stood before her, and Claris didn't know if she should stand, or he should crouch to her level. She licked her lips and gazed up at him. His eyes were intent on her, causing a shiver to run through her. No one had stared at her like that before.

"What was that about?" she finally said, lowering her eyes to escape his gaze.

He lowered himself to a kneel. "He has an air of self-importance. One not shared by us. He's simply trying to assert himself."

"And?" Claris shifted slightly, noticing how much closer his face was now to her own.

"And, I thought you may like company." He smiled widely; her heart stuttered. It was very forward of him, but there was also no one here holding anyone to the high standards of proprietary. Her attire screamed as much. Yet she did notice a few other garde look their way. She had no idea what they might report back to her father upon their return.

She held in a sigh, torn between building bonds with those who travelled with her, and any perceived notions many had towards noble ladies in Onvillia.

"Sit." She patted the space near her. "Were you born in Suevia?"

Torsten shifted and sat near, but not too close. "Yes, but we moved to Onvillia when I was younger. I did stay with my mother's sister for a few years. What I miss most is seeing the sun set over the western shoreline."

Claris brought back up her studies in geography. "You visited Ravden?"

He nodded. "Yes, she lives there. You would like her, I think, she's a blade-maiden."

She hummed deep in the back of her throat, knowing she indeed would have loved to know more of his aunt. "And you have pledged too."

"Nothing is more honourable than serving in combat," Torsten said, leaning back onto his hands splayed out behind his back. "It simply made sense to do as my father chose." He turned his head to face her. "Have you ever travelled beyond Onvillia's borders?"

Claris looked away. "No. Maybe one day."

She felt eyes on her and noticed Sigibert frowning towards them. Perhaps there was a line of being too familiar. "I should rest. Goodnight."

He waited a few moments, but when she continued her silence, he stood and retreated. The absence of his warmth sorely missed.

Though she only spoke at her mother's stone that morning, Claris wished she could again. Speak to ease the nagging at her mind.

She fell asleep knowing she'd have an uphill battle proving herself to Brahim, as Pepin pressed himself up against her, sharing his warmth and easing her passing to sleep with his rumbling breaths.

A Necessary Stop

Day 3

As dawn broke, spilling orange hues over the white ground, the whole camp was packing up. Claris stuffed away her belongings early and went to work practicing her throw. Pepin went off to find his morning feed.

Her nightmare had kept her restless. She couldn't force the imagery from her mind. A twisted, nightmarish figure had loomed before her, gargantuan in size. Its skin was a patchwork of scales and festering sores, and its stench clawed at her senses. The creature's guttural growl reverberated through her bones, whispering an ancient tongue. She rubbed at her head, willing the memories away.

Focusing on her practice as best she could, she alternated between her own knives and the sole one of Brahim's. But each time Brahim's blade wouldn't fly as true as her own.

She felt a presence behind her and debated if she should acknowledge the bystander or not.

"Are you sure Ziri taught you?" Brahim's voice had a short bite.

"There is nothing wrong with my throw," Claris said, turning to face him. His eyes caught hers, but she saw no cruelty there.

"Enemies don't stand still," he said. "No enemy is the same size, or height."

Claris's fingers tightened reflexively over the knife in her hand.

"He never gave you a moving target, did he?"

There was no gain in lying, but voicing it wasn't easy. Instead, she went the easy path and shook her head; meeting his gaze wasn't an option.

He grunted. "I've had your life in training. You're barely a woman, and you want my trust that you'll help. That if I fail, you can succeed."

"And I can. Know my resolve is as strong as yours. This is my home, and that is worth defending. Worth anything." Claris raised her head, the simmering anger warming her, giving her more strength to stand.

Brahim stepped closer. The warmth from his body an uncomfortable proximity to her own, though it didn't radiate the same uncomfortable pleasantness that Torsten's closeness had. "Do you really believe that, love?"

"How—"

"Words mean nothing." Brahim stepped away, took a few paces, and spun back around, releasing a knife. Claris felt the air as the knife kissed the space beside her jaw and thunked into the tree behind. She was too stunned to react, and he'd already walked away by the time she'd composed herself. Only then did she notice one of her own knives was missing; Brahim must've lifted it when he stood so close.

Over at the tree, she collected all the knives. Her missing one wasn't there, but another of Brahim's was. She added it to her own arsenal and had no intention of giving it back.

Pepin approached from her left, a rabbit clamped between his jaws. He dropped it down at her feet and sat back on his haunches.

"Is this for me?"

Pepin pushed it closer with his head.

"Thank you, boy." She knelt to give him a scratch and picked up the dead rabbit. As she stood, Pepin stood too.

Torsten approached as Claris joined the rest of the camp. She brushed down her clothes, conscious her hair had escaped the braids and plaits.

"We're ready to move out," he said. His gaze flitted between the dead rabbit in Claris's hand and the lynx at her side. Between the time they left the Grecy estate and the morning, Torsten had become the voice for the rest of the garde. Her mind twinged a little at such a fact, seeing as Torsten was not one of her father's men, but perhaps that was why he ended up in such a position.

She noted Brahim had his belongings strapped to the back of his horse, ready to continue. She almost expected him to head on without them.

"Claris?" Torsten said.

Her eyes snapped to his. It was the first time he'd said her name. The word bundled up in coarse, but husky, delivery. She swallowed, angled her head so the stain near her ear was less visible. His eyes widened, realising what he'd said. "Sorry, Demoiselle."

"Claris is fine," she choked out, "thank you." She cleared her throat, heat warming her neck and cheeks. "Signal the others. Time is precious."

Torsten gave no indication of her awkward disposition, inclined his head, and then returned to the others. Claris tried to tame her flyaway hair strands, took a deep breath, and secured the rabbit in one saddlebag after packing it in snow; her horse having already been saddled for her.

Brahim set the pace upon seeing the garde mount. Pepin looked up at Claris once before loping off after the other horses.

All were glad that no new snow fell overnight, as the existing blanket of it was enough to slow even the most earnest of gaits. Only the crunch of white under hooves accompanied Claris as they rode, while the sky above was an uninterrupted blue. The garde rode in loose formation. Not tight enough for discipline, not loose enough for comfort.

She couldn't bring herself to ride near or by Brahim, his disdain getting under her skin. She pulled her cloak tighter over her shoulders and focused on Pepin, who had found his way atop the mule and appeared quite snug.

A smile played on her lips.

The further the party rode, the more the murmur of conversation increased. Flore appeared intent on provoking a smile from Sigibert's face, but Claris hadn't even spied a single lip twitch from him.

Claris nudged her mare forward, boots brushing the stirrups. Her thighs already ached. No one had warned her. She'd ridden before, but not for such extended periods.

She wouldn't go to Brahim, or Torsten. Flore seemed occupied. Odo, young. She'd barely heard Dalfin speak. So she picked Roul. With his long blond hair, and warhorse.

Her horse drew up beside his. She ignored the warning look he gave her. Ignored the fact that both horse and him towered over her.

"You have been in my family's service for a while," she said.

Roul didn't glance at her. But he gave a slow nod.

"Have you ever fought malevolence before?"

This time, he did glance at her. "You didn't come here to talk about the weather?"

"No."

He was silent again.

"I need men who are not afraid," she said. "I need men I know I can trust."

Roul gave a dry laugh. "And you think I am yours?"

"No," she said. "I think you will not want dishonour."

He looked at her for a long second. Long enough that she wondered if she'd made a mistake. He had a scar under his left eye, pale and spiderweb thin.

"My honour will never be questioned." He spurred his horse ahead.

She watched him ride forward, but didn't call after him. Or try to follow.

As the sun reached its apex, Brahim held up his hand to signal a halt. Claris frowned. It should be her responsibility, or at least one of the garde. As consolation, they made no move other than to halt, choosing to stay astride their mounts. Roul's stallion snorted, and Pepin leapt down to come beside Claris's horse. She encouraged her mare onwards towards Brahim. Her own cursory look at their surrounds gave her no indication to why he would call everyone to a halt. Nothing but the sprawling expanse of white. They'd be approaching the farmlands of Lannes soon enough.

"Why call a stop?" Claris asked, now at his side. She couldn't see her knife anywhere visible on his person.

Brahim didn't acknowledge her straight away. Claris tried to keep as still as possible and tempered her annoyance.

"The demi-lich passed this way not long ago," he finally said.

Claris's eyebrows pinched together. "How can you tell?"

Brahim gestured to the space around them. "The snow carves a different path." Claris squinted but couldn't discern any differences, so she shook her head. He pointed. "Walk over there."

Claris dismounted and took a few steps, then a few more with Pepin close at her heels. She took note that the crunching underfoot changed to a creak, the snow wetter than the hard surrounds. Pepin crouched down, acting like he stalked prey. She took more experimental steps in the region, noting each time the snow consistency altered. How Brahim could tell on horseback was another trick she knew not. She returned to her horse. "Are you sure that is from the demi-lich?"

"No prints or carriage indentation, thus giving one reason," Brahim said. "A demi-lich glides. The magic reverberating around them melts the cold, but their speed prevents the snow turning into full slush."

"But the liches embody cold?" Claris glanced down at the snow. Could he simply tell by sight?

"Magic does not," was his response. His lips twitched and she itched to smack his mouth. No noble-born man would dare speak as such to a demoiselle like her.

Claris sucked in her breath. "How far ahead?" She caught movement from the corner of her eye. Torsten approached. The garde must be restless.

"Not far, we won't lose it," Brahim said. "But here comes the Suevik." He winked at Claris as she turned to address Torsten.

"Get the garde moving again," she said, tamping down her flustered state.

Torsten's eyes went between her and Brahim. "Of course."

'Not far' to Claris turned out to be very different to what Brahim had suggested. They rode for a good few hours more, and still there was no signs of catching up to the demi-lich. When farms appeared, with no damage visible, Claris was both relieved and doubt filled. Surely the demi-lich wouldn't leave these in its path untouched? Brahim continued leaning down and pausing at erratic intervals, inspecting what little greenery and shrubs poked up from the snow. And sometimes even dismounting to take a closer look.

A pair of serfs came out from the fields towards the party. Claris signalled the halt and dismounted to meet them on equal ground. Pepin came over to her side.

"How is the crop?" she asked. She spied no signs of decay or blight that a demi-lich was known for.

The older of the two men tilted his head in acknowledgement. "Well. Keeping the frost at bay is a challenge." He spoke to her as though she too was lowborn. It was an odd sensation, but she didn't dare correct him.

"Is all quiet?"

They didn't seem to mind that Claris spoke to them, and not one of the men.

The men looked at each other. "All's quiet here," the older man replied. Nothing about their demeanour or the appearance around indicated they'd be lying. They only seemed wary about Pepin's proximity.

"Fare well then," Claris said, and waved the men to continue. Nearby, Brahim had taken a keen interest in some ropy vines around a portion of the farm's fence. Claris paused to run her hands over the vine, but it appeared to be like any other plant she'd seen before—completely unremarkable.

With the farms in sight, the nearby forest border village of Lannes wouldn't be far. They'd arrive before the sun set completely. Maybe then Claris would get more insight to why they hadn't encountered the demi-lich if they were following close behind on its ley trail. She comforted Pepin with a scratch. "We will rest soon, boy." It had been hard enough for the lynx to adjust from his natural nocturnal tendencies to suit when Claris woke and slept, and being uprooted from all he knew couldn't be easy.

Back on her horse, she hung back from the rest, keen to observe Brahim and the things that drew his attention, trying to ascertain any patterns or clues. She also strayed further afield at times, testing to see if she could tell if the snow was different depending on the horse's gait.

The village came into sight as the sun had almost disappeared behind the horizon. All around them towered the black and white spruce of the forest. To one side, an orchard sat resplendent before the trees, while a path opened ahead. One that was salted and scraped at least once a day, by the looks of it.

The whole party slowed and dismounted from their horses. A well sat in the village centre, with a church framing one side. Further along, past a butcher, was a pub; sounds currently flowed down from the establishment. The salted path surprised Claris, for she didn't imagine Lannes to be a popular travelling stop, even for merchants, in the winter.

Of course, when the king visited for a hunt, that was a very different tale. The church was small, with stone walls and narrow windows of blue and green glass.

She turned to address Torsten and the others. "I will speak to the bourgmestre for lodging." She waited a moment, giving any a chance to interject, but all remained silent. The bourgmestre's house sat opposite the church, and was easily the second largest structure. Most of the farms would've been the bourgmestre's.

Claris reached into her saddlebags to pull a kirtle out and over her clothing, at least making her a little more respectable in the bourgmestre's eyes. Having visited Lannes many times, especially when her father had to accompany the king on one of his hunts, she was familiar to the bourgmestre, though never lodged with him before.

Brahim followed her up to the door. "If they cannot accommodate us?"

The door opened inwards a couple of moments after Claris knocked.

Two women stood there, both with dark hair and light eyes. One had a faded scar on her right cheek.

"Greetings," Claris started, "I am Demoiselle Claris, daughter—"

"Of Comte de Grecy," the scarred one finished. "Welcome to Lannes. I'm Yvain, and this is my sister-wife, Aalis. Our husband is currently away on business. Please, come inside."

Claris and Brahim followed the wives inside to a modest parlour with a well-stocked fireplace. How had they known who she was? She was sure she had never been introduced to them before. Mind you, she hadn't been to Lannes in three years, perhaps the bourgmestre was only recently married.

"How many travel with you? Though I am surprised you are not at the palace. Unless you are here at behest of the king?" Yvain asked.

"Eight, including my six garde," Claris said. "My reasons here must be kept quiet. Please."

"And the lynx?" Aalis asked, watching as Pepin padded in through the door.

Claris gave him a reproachful look. "He is well tamed and will cause no trouble."

"We have two spare rooms," Aalis said with a glance at her sister-wife.

"Does the pub have lodgings?" Claris wanted at least one night inside for all the men, for she wasn't certain when they'd next have the opportunity. Brahim shuffled closer to her. Surely the king and his retinue had lodgings near, but she'd never dare go there.

Aalis shook her head.

"Would you be opposed to some using this parlour, or the loft in your stables?"

The couple exchanged a silent communication before Yvain answered, "That would be agreeable. Five could bed here."

"And two could share the other room?" Claris had noted that Brahim also slept alone in his own tent the prior night, but that wasn't a possibility tonight.

"Of course," Aalis said, "and you will have your own." She glared at Brahim. Claris imagined she didn't approve of his proximity to her. "Let me show you there now. Yvain will see to your garde."

"I have a dead rabbit in my saddlebags..." Claris trailed off.

Yvain nodded. "I can use that for a meal for your men?"

Claris cleared her throat. "Please, garde, not men. And that would be welcome." Claris let herself be led away from Yvain and Brahim by Aalis, with Pepin dutifully following her. The rooms were up the stairs, and the room was enough for a bed and small dresser; it was also dry and clean. A brazier of wood and low fire helped keep warmth within the room. Pepin made himself comfortable up on the bed.

Aalis wore a frown but voiced no complaint. "The washroom is at the end. Is there anything else you'll need?"

"When did the bourgmestre leave?"

"He left only yesterday," she replied. "Did you travel this way for him?"

"No. We're simply passing through."

Aalis hesitated, as if on the verge of voicing a thought, but then thought better of it. Claris had an inkling she was either going to mention Claris's unwedded and unchaperoned state, or the company she kept. As Aalis went to leave, she startled when the door opened. Brahim was framed in its entry.

"Come with me," he said, gaze directed at Claris.

"We will stay for supper," she replied with a nod at their hostess.

Brahim shook his head. "No. We're going to the pub." He flashed a grin at Aalis, who looked sharply away. "And remove that kirtle."

Claris didn't like the order, didn't like the way it undermined her. A flush heated her neck. He shouldn't speak to her that way in front of the wives.

"Excuse us a moment," Claris said to Aalis. She inclined her head and left Claris alone with Brahim.

"You must know that those who live here will likely recognise me," Claris said. "I am no stranger to this village. I am here to put an end to this demi-lich, not to ruin my father's image, my image. Court is not kind."

Brahim raised his eyebrows, clearly such matters were not his concern. "If you wear no kirtle, cover that mark up on your face, surely you'd look different enough to pass cursory scrutiny."

"Wait for me outside." Claris sighed and closed the door after ushering him out. She made quick work of untying all her braids, finger-combing her hair and letting it fall around her face and down her back. It wasn't perfect, but it would have to do.

Back outside her room, she affixed her cloak and found Aalis. "My garde will still be grateful for supper," she said, then eyed Pepin at her heels. "Stay here, boy." Her cat lifted his head and took interest in grooming himself.

Aalis appeared a little flustered but nodded her consent. Torsten approached as Claris exited the manor.

"The horses have been stabled," he reported, his eyes flitting to the cloak she still wore, and her long hair falling freely around her shoulders.

Claris nodded, fighting the urge to push the hair away from her face. "Brahim and I will be at the pub. Stay here, rest, eat with the others." Claris couldn't envisage much trouble to be found in Lannes. Torsten gave a slight nod and said no more.

Outside, she went up to Brahim. "Why the pub?"

He didn't glance her way.

"At least tell me why there is no sign of the demi-lich if we were on its path?" She paused in front of the butcher's shop.

"Are you so sure?"

Her gaze narrowed. "No lich, demi or otherwise, would leave such a place unharmed."

"That's good," he finally said. "Once this demi-lich has glutted, then it'll be too late." He walked onwards and Claris hurried to keep pace.

"Glutted?" Claris had never come across the word before in relation to liches.

He leaned closer to whisper. "Once they take enough souls, nothing can stop them."

She noted a few locals standing nearby, and she wondered about the bourgmestre's absence. His position wouldn't afford him absences, especially in winter.

The pub was what Claris would've considered busy for the small village. The air inside heavy with wood smoke and sweat. Claris couldn't help but notice that many stared towards them, their eyes moving between Brahim's darker skin and Claris's masculine clothing. None of the patrons looked nervous, or at them with distaste, simply out of curiosity. Strangers wouldn't be common in such weather.

The interior was dimly lit, with the scent of stale cider permeating up from the floor. Rows of painted portraits lined the walls, but none looked like the same artist was responsible.

A bit of tension leaked out of her. She shouldn't be on edge. Nothing had warranted suspicion.

"Passing through?" the barkeep asked, a gentleman of aging years.

"Is it normally this busy?" Claris replied.

The barkeep shook his head. "Not this early. But with the bishop out of town, there's no service to attend."

"The bishop left?" Suspicion nipped at the edges; both the bourgmestre and bishop gone at the same time wasn't normal.

He nodded. "What will you have?"

"Cider, thank you," replied Claris, knowing it'd be impolite to not try their local drink.

"The strongest drink you have," said Brahim.

The barkeep poured two drinks and set them down. Claris slid a few coins across in payment. She then glanced over at Brahim's drink, and assumed he'd been provided with a wine, a deep garnet red.

He took his glass and swivelled on the stool, gazing out over the other patrons. Claris kept her frown in check. If they were only here to gather information, Claris would do that without complaint. A rumble from her guts, though, reminded her she should eat too. She sipped her cider for a few moments before signalling the barkeep again.

"What is being served from the kitchen?" she asked.

"I can do cabbage stew," he said.

"That would be most welcome. For both of us, please." Even though Brahim hadn't indicated his wish for food, he still needed to eat. And Claris noticed that other patrons had ordered the stew as well.

After a few moments of waiting, a prickle at the back of her neck urged her to turn around as Brahim had, but she didn't want to be rude to the barkeep upon his return. Yet she knew someone was staring at her and she wanted to know why.

The barkeep set two bowls down, and Claris thanked him and slid over more coins. He glanced over at Brahim beside her, then leaned down.

"He's with you, with your consent?" he asked.

A smile tugged at her lips, his concern touching. "Yes," she said. "He is my travelling companion."

"We don't get many of his kind here, that's all," he said. "With a village like us, different can spell trouble." He nodded towards a few locals in the back, and the way they stared towards Brahim.

Her face shuttered. How dare he? Claris had encountered such distasteful behaviour when Ziri was her mentor, their closed mindedness abhorrent. And something she would not stand for. "I assure you, we are not here for trouble. And he would be the least likely to instigate it."

"Take care then," the barkeep said and went off to another patron.

Brahim turned around and took a mouthful of the stew. He turned his head towards Claris. "Trust is hard."

"I am sorry." She wanted to reach out to offer comfort. "Many think caution can help save a life."

"It also kills life," Brahim said. Claris frowned, but he turned his focus back to the food. Of course, she knew caution was a double-edged blade, yet a more open discussion with Brahim wouldn't go amiss. She turned to her own food with no other option.

Not long after she'd finished eating, not unpleased with the taste, Brahim slipped away from the stool. A stab of worry mixed with annoyance pricked at her. He shouldn't leave like that. Not without a word. It didn't take long for her to spot where he'd gone, though, for she soon saw two villagers throwing knives at a board. Neither of them was very good, but that might've been from inebriation.

Brahim went up to them and held his hand out, clearly wanting to be given some knives. One villager nodded and handed over three knives. At least not all shared the same sentiment as the barkeep. Claris slid from her stool to get a closer view. Brahim didn't wait to familiarise himself with the blades and threw all three in quick succession. Each one landed neatly around the centre circle. Claris didn't want to be impressed, but she couldn't help it. One villager retrieved the knives and handed them back, eager for Brahim to repeat the feat. The other villager signed to the other, who nodded.

Claris's fingers twitched, eager to also have a go. She was certain the armoury of knives strapped to her arm and thigh hadn't gone unnoticed by the villagers. She doubted they recognised her; they wouldn't think her a lady. Perhaps that is why Brahim insisted she remove her dress, as she blended better without it in such an establishment.

"Five silver if you get a circle of five," said the villager who'd nodded. That was a large sum for a villager to offer, especially in the middle of winter. Other villagers, listening in, had now gravitated over.

Brahim nodded and took the five knives without comment. Claris simply focused on his movement, zoning out all other distractions in her peripheral. If there was something he thought lacking in her own skill, she'd be keen to know what.

His stance was stable, feet shoulder-width apart, and he leaned slightly forward. His first throw a fluid motion, combining both arm movement and a wrist flick, so quick and decisive. With no pause, Brahim established a rhythmic cadence, throwing each knife in succession. Claris blinked, trying to memorise the movements, but before she could, all five knives formed a circle in the middle of the board. The gathered villagers cheered, and the coins were handed over. The deaf villager signed towards Brahim. His friend was about to speak, but Brahim was already signing back. After a cursory nod to the others, he walked over to the counter. Claris followed close behind and itched to know what was said.

"Here," Brahim said to the barkeep, passing over his winnings, and didn't say anything more, or let the barkeep respond, as he then headed towards the exit.

Claris offered the barkeep an apologetic look and followed Brahim back out into the night. He'd already made ground and she hurried to catch up.

"What was all that about?" Claris asked, reaching out to touch his arm.

His step faltered and he spun around. "Someone follows."

She halted, one of her hands straying to her thigh strap, nudging one knife up with a finger.

Brahim looked over her shoulder. "Left. Aim to startle," he whispered, barely letting his lips move.

The momentary thought that he was merely testing her crossed her mind, but then she pulled the knife up into her hand, spun on her heel, and threw the knife in the direction he'd indicated. She aimed low and quick, a statement that they knew whoever it was had followed them.

"Stay your blade," a masculine, but abraded, voice called out, the tone familiar to her ears.

"Torsten?" she asked but edged out another blade in case. Brahim seemed to be holding in a laugh at her side.

Torsten had his arms held down low, palms facing outward, his chin and gaze dipping low. "Sorry." He rubbed at the back of his neck. "You weren't even meant to notice me." He stopped and pulled the blade free from the building beside him.

"I hope he follows instructions better than he stalks prey, or he'll get us killed," Brahim muttered, shaking his head and walking back towards the manor.

Claris held back a sigh. Torsten continued his approach and held out her knife.

"I'm glad you didn't aim to maim," he said, "or worse."

She reached out to take the blade back, but his fingers lingered at the other end. "Do you not trust Brahim?"

"I'd bring shame upon myself if I'd let something happen to you."

The back of her neck prickled. Her eyes strayed to his and down to the scar on his throat. She swallowed. It wasn't polite to stare.

"Do you make it a habit of ignoring orders?" Claris tucked the knife away as he released it. She needed to remove her feelings from the equation. He was a garde and meant to do as ordered. A tiny tickle at her mind made her second-guess if what she'd said to Torsten was really an order or not.

A subtle lift of one shoulder and shadow of smile made her look away. She couldn't be anything but the leader she wanted to prove to herself she could be. Claris gestured they should walk on, and he joined her at her side.

"I am grateful for your concern. Yet, when the time comes, you must have equal concern for all, or your own life will be forfeit. Concern, too, for my orders." Side by side she enjoyed the warmth he gave off. His physique was also pleasing, even with the fur cloak. That she couldn't deny.

"To the Suevik, death in battle is a passage to eternity," he said.

Claris imagined he had many ways to skirt around a conversation when required. "I am sure that is comfort to many." They reached the manor's entrance and Claris went in first. "Be sure the others are ready at dawn to continue." She looked back at Torsten, who stayed at the foot of the stairs. "And do consider this an order to follow."

He grinned in response, and Claris fought to return the smile.

"I will see the horses are ready," Torsten said.

Claris's eyes widened, remembering about the horses and Brahim's want to journey through the forest. She knew Levlan would've chosen horses suited to such a journey, but taking them through a winter forest was another matter entirely. All manner of dangers would be hidden in the snow that could lame one of the horses.

"We will have to go slow in the forest with the horses," she finally said.

"The garde will take care of their rides," Torsten said. "The journey through is not long."

Claris forced the myriad of bad possibilities from her mind. "Fine." They'd have to ask for the king's forgiveness later for going through his forest without consent.

Torsten hesitated, but when Claris said no more, he gave an incline of his head and then turned to go to the stables. Footsteps stopped Claris from moving. Yvain came around a corner, surprise crossing her face.

"Demoiselle." Yvain's tone was curt, her lips pressed into a thin line.

"Going out for air," Claris said, and turned to go back outside.

Yvain cleared her throat. "You may find your lynx out there. He seemed quite insistent to get out."

"Thank you... If he damaged anything, I will pay to cover the cost of repairs."

Yvain forced a smile. "I think only to Aalis. She isn't a cat person."

Claris returned the smile and slipped back outside, and around the opposite side to the manor. She needed to practice. The air was crisp and clear, enough to let through the bright moonlight and starshine.

With the forest so close, Claris was spoilt for choice of target. Though some trees clumped far too close together to give her a good throwing distance. The weight of the hatchet at her side made her hand stray there. Testing it with a few experimental swings crossed her mind, but she knew her focus had to be on the throwing knives. She needed the pace she'd seen from Brahim. Needed to eliminate her momentary hesitations. Needed her instincts to rule more than knowledge.

She went through the motions first of her standard technique, letting the knife spin through the air and land into the target tree. But the key to speed meant no full spin of the blade. Spin on a blade may not be enough to slip into the sole point of a demi-lich. Claris rubbed at her temples, too many thoughts crowding her mind.

Brahim had made it sound simpler than what was truth. She shouldn't have been naïve, but the longer they took to find the demi-lich, surely the worse it'd be.

"Falling sick won't help any." Brahim's voice startled her and the knife in her hand slipped through her palm, slicing open flesh. Blood dropped onto the white snow, the deep red vibrant even in the dim light.

"Such cold I am accustomed to. But I need to practice," Claris replied, holding her palm to her chest. The stinging pain showing through in the grimace on her face. A mewl flowed through the darkness. Pepin smelt her blood. He'd be upon them soon.

Brahim held out his hands. "Show me." Claris swallowed and let him take her injured hand. He prodded at the flesh near the cut, and she clenched her teeth to avoid flinching. "Only shallow. Should be fine." He bent down, scooped up some snow, and compacted it over her wound.

A low, rumbling growl stilled Brahim and Claris both.

"Don't move," she whispered to Brahim, then, "It is okay, boy. He is helping me," she said in bright intonation. "Here." She crouched and waited for Pepin to pad closer, his eyes not straying from Brahim. Pepin smelt her wounded hand, chirped, and licked the snow. "I will be fine. Thank you for caring." She used her good hand to give him a pat.

Once satisfied that Pepin wouldn't attack Brahim, she stood. "Thanks," she said, relishing the icy numbness that spread up her hand.

Brahim reached down and collected her fallen knife. "You may need new gloves."

Claris smiled. "That seems likely." They were good woollen gloves, a bit worn from the years, but perhaps she needed leather ones; a pair that would be a little sturdier against a blade. Maybe then she'd have fewer scars. She'd always intended on asking for some, but there never seemed a right time to indulge in that request. Not when their funds had to be allocated to more important matters, especially to ensuring their continued good standing at court.

Pepin walked ahead of Claris, glancing back to ensure she was there. Back inside her room she peeled off the ruined glove, damp from snow and blood, and dunked her hand into the water heated over the brazier. The water swirled a brownish red. Pepin rubbed against her legs.

A quiet knock sounded at the door, and then Aalis slipped in, her gaze falling to Pepin at first. She wore her night robe, and shut the door back with a click. "You've hurt your hand?"

Claris felt the fool and lifted her hand up from the water.

"I do hope you were not roused from sleep," she said.

Aalis shook her head. "He was right to have me tend you." She took Claris's hand and made the same assessment as Brahim, that it was a shallow cut. "I'll bind it and with rest it'll heal over." A comfortable warmth came to Claris's face, but also conflicted in how Brahim had gone out of his way for her. She hadn't got the impression he cared overly much for her presence, but this gesture spoke differently.

"Will reins bite into it?" Claris asked, now worried how she'd travel. She'd dealt with hand injuries before.

Aalis's lips puckered with thought. "If you are capable, one hand will suffice."

Claris flushed; she should've thought of that herself. "Of course."

Aalis gently patted her shoulder. "Sometimes being away from what you know can be hard, and thoughts will flit away often."

"You speak from experience?" Claris looked into Aalis's eyes, searching for truths she wasn't sure she had questions for.

Aalis shrugged. "Becoming a wife may have been hard, but my sister Yvain has been by my side for all of it. Our family are from Arson, so moving here to Lannes was also hard. From river to forest is different. Different sounds."

She finished tying off the bandage and closed Claris's fingers into her palm. "Good. You'll want to continue movement."

Pepin mewed once towards Aalis, rubbed against Claris, and jumped onto the bed.

"Your sister, Yvain, does not seem to like me," Claris said.

"We're both worried for you. You travel alone with men, something no woman of your station should do." Aalis sighed. "Unlike Yvain, I understand the desire to do something more. Society is different for women in other countries, so I see no harm in exploring a different path for oneself. But I do ask of you to exercise caution."

Claris nodded. "That I will do."

Aalis smiled and patted her knee. "I shall leave you to get your rest."

"Were the garde behaved?" Claris asked.

"Quieter than I expected," Aalis replied. "Sleep well, Demoiselle." With a little bob, she then let herself back out of the room.

Claris gave her hand another experimental clench and was satisfied at the minimal pain.

A Surprise Find

Day 4

Sunlight slanted into the room from the eastern window. The sun shouldn't have been that high.

Claris jolted up. It was far too late in the morning. They were meant to leave with the rise of the sun.

Had the sister-wives convinced the men to leave her behind, or was it Brahim's doing? She shook her head. That wouldn't make sense. But she wouldn't put it past Aalis and Yvain to ensure they left her here, where it was safer for her, or at least safer in their eyes.

Slipping her cloak back on, and crudely wrapping cloth over her wound, she went downstairs with Pepin only to find Torsten milling in the hall. She swallowed, steadying the sudden uptick to her pulse. But at least the others had not left.

"Where are the others?" she asked. Pepin padded over to the front door, and Claris quickly let him out.

His eyes went to her injured hand. "You should take a seat." His deep tone soothed some of the edge to her nerves.

She tucked her hand behind her back. "We should be leaving."

He opened his mouth to speak, then paused. "The garde are indisposed." He shook his head. "We can't leave today."

Claris didn't want a delay. They'd already lost most of the morning. It would push the demi-lich further away from them.

"Let me see them then," she said.

His lips quirked into a small smile. "If you're sure."

"I'm used to taking care of the sick," Claris replied. "Are they in the parlour?"

Claris started towards the parlour when Yvain came out of the room, shutting the door behind her. "It appears the supper did not sit well with them."

"The rabbit?" A sinking feeling flooded Claris.

Yvain averted her gaze. "The rabbit was fresh. I'm... I'm not sure of the cause."

Aalis hurried in. "Please, do not punish her. Their stomachs may not have liked the spices we use." Claris's eyes widened, horrified they'd think her likely of such an action. "You can stay another night without issue."

"I guess we have no choice," Claris said, though she knew the sister-wives wouldn't be behind making her men sick on purpose.

Yvain looked up. "At least it will give you a chance to heal that hand."

Claris clenched her hand. "Would you be so kind for a spot of food?" She turned to Torsten. "Where is Brahim then?"

He shrugged. "Said something about tracing ley lines."

Claris shook her head and went into the dining room, taking a seat opposite Torsten. "Then it appears you are stuck with me for company."

"There's worse than you," he replied, a touch of smile in the corner of his mouth.

A flush heated her neck. She'd never had much interest from men and couldn't decide if Torsten took a liking towards her or not. Her seamstress had made many a comment on how men liked woman of ample bosom, and nothing she could do would help Claris in that department. Breastbands couldn't enhance her. Many noble ladies wore dresses that exposed their necks, shoulders, and upper part of their breasts, all designed to draw attention to their beauty. Her seamstress had only commented positively on her long slim neck, ensuring Claris's gowns at least exposed her neck and shoulders. Her current clothing choices had no such qualities.

Yvain shortly returned with a plate of fruit and cheese.

Claris thanked her and turned her attention back to Torsten. "And what did you do this morning?"

Torsten finished chewing, swallowed, and said, "Took the horses for a stretch."

They continued to eat in silence, and Claris did her best not to look at him too often. Neither the fruit nor cheese was overly fresh, but the taste was still welcome.

"Shame we will have to waste the day," she finally said. Her hand was tender, and the skin around the cut still angry and pink. At least the extra day gave her a little longer to heal.

"How does a demoiselle normally fill her day?"

Torsten's question took Claris off guard, and she almost swallowed a piece of cheese whole.

"Back at the capital, among others my age, we'd do needlework together," she said, with a little scoff. "We may also take classes in music or dancing. Sometimes, we even get to paint."

"You'd prefer your time at the estate?" He pushed the remaining fruit towards her.

She glanced down at the food. "It's complicated."

"I like the time I get to work with the blade and armour smiths," Torsten said. Claris was grateful that he hadn't pushed her to talk. "The heat in the forges is quite welcome."

"I've never been in a forge." Her father had always got one of their servants to procure her throwing knives, or Ziri had gone himself. Not once was she invited along.

"Then shame this village has none."

Claris picked further at the fruit, but found her appetite gone. She hated to dwell on things that seemed impossible to change in her life, though her being here now spoke otherwise.

"Do you think it strange both bourgmestre and bishop are gone at the same time?" she asked. Brahim had made no comment last night; it appeared his sole concern was the demi-lich.

"They are?"

Though the barkeep had told her, it didn't appear to be widely spread knowledge.

"Perhaps we should seek a church service. Or, at the very least, a blessing for our journey," Claris said. It was a reckless notion, but one that gave her a shiver of thrill. She still wasn't sure on Luminar and the teachings of Aurelius, still finding comfort in those who now had to be referred to as the old gods, particularly in Wodan and Baldr.

Torsten narrowed his eyes and Claris instantly doubted herself. Surely it wasn't both her idea and company that displeased him.

"You're serious, aren't you?" he finally replied.

"We do have time to pass," she pointed out. "And neither do I have any needlework nor estate to pretend to know how to manage." With those words she stood from the table. "I guess all that remains is if you will join me."

Torsten stood. "Consider me your escort."

Not quite the words Claris wanted to hear.

She averted her gaze, having hoped he saw her like an equal, how a Suevik man might treat a Suevik woman, even if she wasn't Suevik. She wasn't sure where Aalis or Yvain would be, so she headed for the front door, and wondered how far Pepin had roamed.

Outside, a light falling of snow came down around them. Claris pulled the hood of her cloak up. Torsten stayed close at her side.

"How does one acquire a lynx as a pet?" he asked.

"By finding his dead mother and littermates." It was both a sad and fond memory for Claris. She had wandered out past the estate walls, down closer to the river, when she heard the scavenger birds squawk and circle. At first, she intended to leave the birds to their meal, but she had seen movement at the lynx mother's rear legs, where two of her litter were huddled dead against her. Claris shooed the airborne scavengers away and pushed at the dead body. There, hidden partially from view, was a surviving kitten. She didn't hesitate to bundle it up into her arms and carry him home. They'd been inseparable since.

"Taming the wild is a feat," Torsten said.

She found herself nodding in reply, but also wondering if Pepin truly was wild anymore, or simply a larger version of a domesticated cat. Was Pepin a reflection of herself? Many tried to tame her, to force her into the proper woman role, but she wanted to stay a little wild, just like she hoped Pepin kept a wild spirit.

Torsten paused before the arched church doors. Rubies were inlaid into gold handles.

"Extravagant for a village," Claris remarked and pushed open the doors, which had no resistance. Clearly the bishop did not mind who sought out the church.

Torsten hesitated at the threshold before following her in.

No candles burned, and a thin layer of dust already coated the wooden pews. The altar lay bare.

"This place has seen no one in some time," Claris said, and headed to a side door, which surely led to the bishop's own quarters. Torsten stood still in front of the altar. Claris beckoned him over, snapping him from his thoughts.

A tentative mew from the church's entrance had Claris quickly withdraw her hand. Pepin had pushed open the church doors and stood partially inside, likely following her scent.

Her heartbeats steadied again. "Inside, Pepin." It wasn't like she had broken into the church. Pepin sniffed the air as he prowled inside and towards her. Claris ran her fingers through his fur once he was at her side. "Do you smell anything?"

Pepin looked up at her and stayed silent.

Torsten stepped in behind her and pushed open the bishop's door. "After you, Demoiselle."

There appeared to be no natural light, and Pepin went in first. Claris followed him in, doing her best to stem the swarming doubt. Torsten waited a beat before coming in after. Pepin had gone straight to another door, which was faint while Claris's eyes adjusted to the gloom. They appeared to stand in an austere hallway, and Pepin stood at the only other door.

"Is it right to feel guilty?" Claris asked, her hand resting on the door, hesitant to push it open. It was, after all, the bishop's private quarters, but if something was amiss, it was her duty to figure it out. She was also responsible for the county.

She couldn't decipher Torsten's silent response. With a Suevik background he might not put much stock into the sanctity of the church. As far as she knew, the teachings of Aurelius hadn't spread into Suevik lands yet.

Beyond the door lay the bishop's living quarters. The room was sparse with a neatly appointed cot, brazier, wooden chest, and a wooden desk with a high-backed chair. There wasn't even any parchment on the desk, or ink and quill. It was as if the bishop had never lived there. Pepin showed disinterest in the entire space.

"What were you hoping to find?" Torsten asked and walked over to the single narrow window.

"Anything indicative of travel," Claris said, trying to mask her disappointment.

"There appears to be a lockbox outside."

Pepin paused grooming himself at Torsten's words.

Claris crowded next to the man, hyperaware of his body heat. The window gave a clear view of a dead garden, and a tiny gazebo. Tucked under the seat in the gazebo was a lockbox.

"I guess we will see," she said. "But it will likely need a key."

She went back over to the desk and opened the drawer, frowning at how easy it was. The only item sitting in the middle of the drawer was a key. Her hand hesitated above it.

"Are you sure?" Torsten asked.

Before the doubt won, Claris picked it up. Then she led Torsten and Pepin out the back door and into the garden, as Pepin put himself between her and the garde, though pressed closer to her legs. Pausing at the edge of the garden, she eyed the lockbox.

She didn't know why she hesitated. She had the key.

Torsten stepped past her and went to the lockbox. Pepin went over and pawed at the box.

"A little small for you, I think," Claris told her cat, a smile ghosting on her lips, as she finally came to the box as well.

The key fit the lock perfectly. The only items within were a gold piece of parchment and a pouch that smelt of cypress and lavender. With the parchment in hand, guilt warred with Claris. The combined absence likely had nothing to do with the demi-lich and shouldn't be her concern. But both were subjects of her father, and if they knew his current weakness... Claris opened the parchment without another thought. Torsten peered over her shoulder.

Forgive us. If you have sought this out, then we have failed and have not returned in three moons as promised. The younger Suevik princess was our goal. We'd heard her interest in the church. An alliance with the Suevik crown might help stem the tide of liches they send into our lands.

Claris rocked back on her heels. "Surely this is not right." Her stomach clenched, as her thoughts scrambled to understand. Though not directed to anyone, surely it was for the sister-wives. The bourgmestre had no one else. They weren't at Lannes because they sought an alliance, one behind the king's back. This was happening right under her father's nose; under hers. She'd heard nothing of liches until Brahim turned up with news of the one they now hunted. Did the sister-wives know this lockbox was here, waiting for them to open after three moons?

Torsten growled lowly as he too read the parchment. "They imply our mages willingly turn to liches for the crown's bidding."

Her eyebrows pinched together. Claris didn't know if she felt hurt or rage. Treason against her father, against the crown, was one thing. But the implication that someone guided malevolence into her country, controlled it, had her chest tightening at the very thought. Suevia shared a border with Onvillia to the west, their lands less than half of her own country's. Before the Obscurum War, the War of Three took place. Lasting only a mere three years, it was fought over borders between Onvillia, Suevia, and Hodoyin. What came after was a tentative peace, and no change to borders, but better trade agreements. Perhaps the Queen of Suevia now wanted to change that.

Claris folded up the parchment and tucked it into her clothes.

"Do you think that possible?" Claris asked.

"All men are capable of treason."

Claris reached out to pet Pepin, eager for something familiar. "No. That a lich could be forced on a path. That they are but a puppet." She knew treason was no small matter. She'd pen a letter to the capital, along with the found parchment.

Pepin stiffened under her touch and hunkered down; even his tail stilled. Claris also held her movement. Though it seemed like whoever it was wanted to mask their approach, the small sound of crunching snow gave them away.

Torsten shut the lockbox, swooped down, and pulled Claris up to his own body. She stifled her surprised gasp and tried to ignore how their bodies pressed against one another, the hardness of his against hers. Thoughts warred within her, torn between the worry of someone knowing exactly what the bourgmestre was up to, and what they might do if they thought she knew. Her pulse quickened at the other thought, that they'd see her in the arms of a garde and gossip, ruining her and her father.

"Apologies in advance, Demoiselle." Torsten's whisper sent a chill down her neck.

She thought he meant for the compromising position he'd put her in, but then his lips were near her own. Not quite touching her skin, but enough to alight her with heat. Her mouth dried.

His lips moved against her cheek. "Giggle for me." Her eyes widened, and time seemed to slow.

Overcoming the initial shock, her first instinct was to protest, but she let out as silly of a giggle she could manage. Ones she heard many times before from other court ladies. Her cheeks reddened. How foolish she felt, even though it was like all her insides vibrated.

His hand reached up to her cheek, his thumb ghosting along the line of her jaw. He bent a little closer, the faintest touches from his lips caressed her own.

"Oh." A startled gasp pulled Torsten away from Claris.

She steadied herself on her feet. Pepin, unconcerned, laid down in the snow. Aalis stood with a woven basket tucked under one arm.

"Apologies, Demoiselle," she said, and looked down. "I didn't know you would be this way."

Claris watched her for a moment, but Aalis didn't seem interested in the lockbox. "That is quite alright," Claris said and brushed snow from her cloak. "Your discretion would be appreciated."

Aalis glanced up and looked at Torsten once before averting her gaze once more. "But of course. My silence is yours."

Claris went over and touched her hand to Aalis's arm. "Thank you." She clicked her tongue, making Pepin stand and come over to her side. "We will let you on your way."

Torsten followed Claris as she walked back towards the village centre, and she hoped her face was no longer red. She needed to shake the lingering thrill of heat that lit her whole body up.

Once certain they were out of earshot, Claris spoke. "Did she continue on?"

He nodded. "And again, I'm sorry for my actions. But it would distract any from looking too closely elsewhere."

"A secret tryst?" Claris cleared her throat, the last word choking her up.

"One reason that could be believed," he replied. "It'd be no stretch to think it. You are, after all, pretty and alone with many men."

She latched onto that one word, pretty, and knew her face heated. Hearing it from someone without obligation to say so had her fighting her own inner voice saying otherwise.

She swallowed, willing her face to remain impassive. "But a comte's daughter?"

He smiled. "Even better. You are away from home and free from such oversight."

Claris couldn't help but return his smile. "I am sure Aalis will tell Yvain." She hoped it wouldn't spread further, for then there'd be a chance of it reaching her father. Not only would it crush his heart, but destabilise his position, for he'd no longer have a marriageable daughter to strengthen his holdings over his county. Perhaps she needed to blend in with the garde, truly embrace a Suevik blade-maiden persona. Distance herself from nobility.

They made their way back over to the manor and paused outside.

"What will you do now?" Torsten asked.

After what had happened, Claris knew she had to put distance between them. She couldn't let rumours spread. Some damage may be done, but moving on from Lannes, she'd do her best to mitigate it. "Rest my hand. I need it healed."

Though her mind danced back to when he'd called her pretty.

A light knock stirred Claris from her thoughts. She'd gone out earlier to organise a messenger for her letter.

"Come in," she called.

Brahim opened the door. "It is time to go."

A glance out her window reinforced it was early night, and she hadn't dozed off. "We would be fools to travel through the forest at night."

He chuckled without humour. "We go to the pub."

The light snowfall made Claris pull the fur-collared coat closer around her body as she followed Brahim across town, leaving Pepin to stay behind. Like the night before, the pub was doing good business and almost immediately inside the place, Brahim's step hesitated momentarily. Claris peered in the general direction he gazed to see a sole gentleman at a table in the corner, shrouded in the shadows cast by the oil lamps.

Brahim continued to the service counter and Claris followed, though she glanced back at the man as they took seats on the stools. The figure hadn't pulled the hood back off his head, and he was hunched forward, as if trying to minimise how much of his body was exposed.

Claris leaned towards Brahim. "Who is that man?"

Brahim gave a subtle shake of his head but did not answer.

She turned back around to order some drinks and food. This time she was acutely aware that Torsten had followed them and stationed himself outside. Her pulse fluttered at the very thought of him, how he'd pressed up close to her, how he'd called her pretty.

Once she had a drink in hand, she kept an eye on the man in the corner, noting how everyone gave him a wide berth, and how he barely seemed to move. He mustn't have even been nursing a drink.

A jab in the side of her ribs snapped her gaze away. "What was that for?"

"Don't attract attention," Brahim said.

She glared at him before turning her focus on the food set before her. She didn't miss how the barkeep's regard went to her injured hand and the thin line stark against her palm. She'd left it ungloved and unbandaged at Aalis's directive to let it breathe.

Clearly, Brahim was interested in the man in the corner. It increased her growing suspicion that he might be responsible for the bad food keeping the garde abed.

"Did you make the others sick?" she asked suddenly.

His lips twitched. "What would give you that idea?"

"Because clearly that man over there is of interest to you," she said. "Perhaps he's why we came here last night. And since he was not present, you made sure we'd be here another night."

"But we left before they ate," he said, "before I even knew who would be at the pub."

Her eyes narrowed. The smirk on his face told her she was right, but she was still not sure how he'd made them sick.

When only a few patrons remained, Brahim pulled out a pouch, scooping out a fine dust that had a blue hue. He spun on the stool and blew the dust into the air. Claris scrambled up from her seat, wary of the dust. It travelled and flitted through the almost still air, carried by an invisible force.

Patrons scrambled up from chairs, eager to flee the blue cloud.

The man in the corner finally looked up, his eyes catching Claris's. As the dust settled over him, runes set into his skin lit blue, glowing from beneath his clothes. He pushed back his hood, revealing a bald head with more runes scattered across it. Brahim stood and approached the man. Claris stuck close to his side.

The straggling patrons, seeing the runes on the man, also up and fled, leaving the barkeep cursing vehemently for the loss of his patrons.

Torsten charged into the pub, sword drawn. Claris held her hand up at him. He looked around, saw there was no immediate danger, and went back outside.

As the man stood from his corner, he reached down and pulled out a huge mage-hammer from underneath the table. It too had runes lined up the shaft and over the hammer head, all glowing an eerie blue. Claris's eyes widened. The man was clearly a mage, and not too pleased about his unveiling.

"Zut," Claris muttered, not pleased to have provoked a mage's ire.

Brahim closed the distance, and the mage stood a head taller than him. The mage's brown skin and blue eyes likely meant he was from Suevik, a land more common to foster mage powers. The sheer size of the hammer's head could easily crush a man's skull with a single swing. The mage wasn't small of frame either, with broad shoulders and a bulk that could only be from muscle mass.

"Mage," Brahim said.

Claris recalled the buried letter and wondered if mages could command a lich, being they used to be a mage themselves.

The mage made a humming noise in the back of his throat.

"We're hunting a demi-lich," Brahim continued, as if he wasn't close to imminent skull crushing. "Your skills would be valued."

The mage gazed at Claris. "The woman?" But the question wasn't directed at her, and she'd not be cowed by his rude manners.

"A good throw," Brahim replied. She blinked, surprised he'd give the praise after being so critical towards her. She tried not to smile.

"I'm Halvar," the mage said. The glow of his runic symbols died away.

Claris cleared her throat and held out her hand. She didn't want to be ignored, or sidelined. She was meant to be leading this group. "Claris. Your help will be appreciated."

Halvar ignored the gesture and tightened his grip over the hammer. Claris let her hand fall back to her side.

Brahim held out the pouch of dust to Halvar. "I'm Brahim. You'll join us?"

"No one should suffer a lich to live," Halvar said and took the pouch, tucking it away somewhere in his large fur coat.

Claris became intrigued by not only what the dust was worth, but what it meant for a mage. Her father and tutors alike sheltered much of magecraft and mage life from Claris's learnings. Apparently, it wasn't appropriate for a demoiselle's upbringing. She knew enough to not be completely ignorant, but now face to face with a mage, she wished she knew more.

Halvar flipped his hood back up over his head, shadows casting back over his face. "Depart in the morning?"

"Through the forest," Brahim said. Halvar made no sign of acknowledgement, and then left the pub. Claris and Brahim were the last ones left.

Brahim rested a few coins on the counter before he led Claris out of the pub. Claris's eyes strayed to where she knew Torsten waited in darkness for their reappearance.

"Why do we need a mage, when you said a demi-lich can only be killed in one way?" Claris asked.

"If we trap it first, the kill will be easier," Brahim replied, as if that fact was obvious.

"And you trust him?"

Brahim shrugged. "One can trust a mage to wish death on malevolence."

At the manor she let Brahim go in first but did not follow, nor did he turn back to see if she did. She turned and waited a few beats until Torsten showed his face.

"If I am to pass as a blade-maiden," Claris said, "what are your suggestions?"

Torsten peeled off his gloves. "When I first saw you, in leathers and braided hair, I thought I had walked in on a blade-maiden."

Claris took a sharp intake of breath. "Really?"

"All that was missing was a sword."

"Levlan gave me a hatchet," she said, "though it is more decoration than a weapon right now."

"It's good to have, the willingness to learn."

Claris peered up at Torsten. "Is that an offer?"

He smiled, and her attention drew to the single dimple in his left cheek. "We'll see." He pushed open the door and let her go in first. The warmth was welcome, flooding back through her limbs. Torsten walked over to the fireplace and removed his cloak, warming his hands by the fire.

"We will leave at dawn," Claris said, "and we have a mage joining us."

"I did see that," he said, glancing back over his shoulder. "They say Suevik is the birthplace of mages."

Claris warred with herself if she should stay longer, but he'd turned back to face the fire. "Sleep well, Torsten."

"And you... Claris."

A small smile played on her lips as she went upstairs and to her room but stilled at the threshold. Pepin had curled up on the chair, as a tied bundle lay in the middle of the bed. The cat appeared unperturbed by its presence. One hand hovered near her knives as she peered around the room and headed towards the bed. Nothing else was disturbed. Pepin opened one eye up and watched her. She felt a little foolish; she trusted Pepin.

There was no note on or near the bundle. She slipped the tie loose and stood back as the cloth peeled away from its contents; nothing airborne escaped. What lay inside was a pair of leather gloves, the wrists lined with rabbit fur, and a leather vest with fur trim and a thick hide lining.

Claris looked over to Pepin. "Was this Torsten?"

He perked his head up and mewed once.

The sudden urge to thank him drove Claris from the room. She found no signs of him in the parlour, and figured he must've gone out to the stables to check on the horses, as he had done the night prior.

Approaching the stables, she heard muffled sounds and a voice; it was Torsten. Claris figured he must be talking to the horses. She smiled at the thought and quietly peeked into the stables, not wanting to startle the horses or him.

She stifled her gasp at what she found.

A Cold Loss

DAY 5

Torsten's upper body was naked, and clan tattoos inked in dark blue marked his shoulder blades and spine. His muscles bunched and moved as his arms embraced another person.

Claris's eyes stung, and her body heated with embarrassment. It was an intimate moment she had stumbled into. Their shared whispers and kisses undeniable. As Claris went to leave, Torsten's lover's head looked up. Odo gasped as his eyes found her. Heat flooded her face.

"Sorry," she mumbled and spun away, hurrying back to her room before she'd have to truly face them. Once there, she slid down the door into a puddle on the floor. Pepin chortled with concern and left the chair to bundle on top of her lap, his head pushing at her hand. She obliged and gave him a pat, even as she held back her tears.

She'd been so stupid. Every part of her seemed impossibly hot. Of course Torsten had no true feelings for her, he was the vicomte's man. She pressed her fist to her chest, willing the tightening to cease. He wanted to get close. He wanted to break down her barriers. All for the vicomte. All for the quest for more power.

It was all too much and the tears fell. Pepin nestled in closer, pushing his head into her. Her fingers absently stroked over his fur.

Taking a deep breath, she angrily wiped the tears away. She should have seen this coming. She knew the vicomte had designs for the county and he'd purposely sent one of his men with the group. If her reputation was ruined, and proof carried back to the vicomte, he'd easily be able to replace her father, and step around the need for her to marry his son.

"I need to be smarter," she said to Pepin, who chirped in response.

She'd have to keep her distance from Torsten.

Her dreams didn't give her an easy rest, and she yearned to have a nightkeeper at her side. Pepin had to lay on her, to settle her thrashing each time she tried to break free from the nightmares. Screams of anguish still rung through her head.

Giving up on sleep, she was dressed and ready before any others stirred, and even had time to check on the horses twice. Anything to keep her mind occupied. As she went outside a third time, with Pepin close behind, Halvar loomed outside. Even leaning against the wall, he cut an imposing figure, especially with the large hammer by his side.

She took a deep breath. "What brings you to Lannes?" Claris asked, coming to stand near him. Pepin slunk behind her legs.

Halvar looked down at her, eyes drifting to the lynx. He sniffed. "A rotation of mages."

The garde were busy strapping down their belongings to their horses, and Brahim was crouched to read the ley.

Claris let the words process through her mind, brain whirring with possibilities. "You travel to all places?"

Pepin peered out at the mage but made no effort to get closer.

"To those that require it." His hand rested on the hammer's handle. "Lynx yours?"

"He is. And he's normally not this shy."

"Many sense magic and wary for it." Halvar pushed away from the wall. "Seems we depart."

Halvar had no horse but seemed unworried by that fact as the others led the horses to the forest's edge. Clouds bruised the sky and refused to let much of dawn's light down onto the earth. The forest would only give some cover from the threat of snowfall. The air had chilled considerably from the day before, the threat of frost compounding.

As everyone paused at the tree line, Claris took the chance to assert herself. "Inside the forest we must be careful, or we risk laming a horse. It will take most of the light to cross through, and we do not rest until nightfall." Pepin took the moment to get up on top of the pack mule.

"The loups-garous are said to roam these woods," Roul said, peering into the trees, hand resting close atop his blade.

Claris resisted rolling her eyes; such creatures, which were human but could transform to a wolf at will, had been eradicated from the area. The king had wanted them completely gone. These were his hunting grounds after all.

Halvar stood beside Roul, the mage's height taller than even Roul's. Claris didn't think Roul was used to being smaller than anyone else.

"You have nothing to fear," Halvar said to Roul.

Roul scoffed. "I am not afraid."

Brahim shook his head. "We head for Arson. There is a high chance of encountering the demi-lich. Their path will take them there."

"Keep alert and watch your step," Claris said. "The snow can hide many traps." Her eyes found Torsten's, and she hastily looked away. With a constricted throat she looked down, also keen to avoid eye contact with Odo.

It wasn't uncommon for men to find comfort and pleasure with the others they served with, especially if they were on long travels. That didn't bother her one bit. It was how conflicted and twisted inside she was towards Torsten. His flirtations with her, and the crushing hurt realising it was a ruse. A way to ruin her. The familiar weight of her knives gave her a comfort, a reminder she could be strong without need for attachments.

Brahim entered the forest first, and Claris followed straight after, her horse whickering softly at her. The dense press of trees would likely add time to their travel, and Claris's hope they'd reach Arson in two days would be lost.

Hoarfrost streaked up the trunks of trees, with feather frost tracing along plants. Claris became aware of her breath condensing in the cold. The snow crunched under boots and hooves alike, with the boughs and branches creaking and groaning from the wintery wind. Claris kept quiet; she didn't want to the puncture the air with any other noise.

A presence came up beside her, and she gazed over at Halvar as he strode beside the horse, his hammer strapped tightly over his back. Underneath the hood Claris could only see peeks of the runic symbols over his skin. Her mind flashed to Torsten's naked tattooed back, and she forced it away. That wasn't a smart line of thought.

Claris spied Pepin, who'd hopped down from the mule to instead slink behind Halvar. She chuckled under her breath.

Pulling at the fur vest tight over her chest, she was conscious of the scrutiny the mage gave her. She wasn't attracted to the older man, but such regard couldn't help but make her self-conscious of her appearance. The darkened flesh under her eyes had likely only worsened over the past few days.

"Have you ever seen a demi-lich before?" Claris asked, her voice sounding louder than she thought it was.

"Once," Halvar said.

Claris waited a few beats, but Halvar didn't elaborate further. She held in her sigh. "And did you see it die?"

"It took out eight good men before it succumbed," he said.

There were nine of them in the party, and a lightness filled Claris's insides, as if everything in her fled. No sinking dread, or nerves, but a simple absence of disconnected understanding. She knew planning for the future was foolish, but all that loomed before her was her inevitable death at this venture. Her father knew it was a risk when she volunteered and he, reluctantly, agreed. Her death would make his county holding unstable, with no heir, but a grieving father always had a little sway with the king, who'd lost one of his own children when they were a young child.

"Your expertise will be valuable," she replied, hoping he would have some wisdom to impart that would help save at least a few lives.

He rubbed at his shaved chin. "If that is the Will."

His emphasis on the word didn't slip by Claris. She took note how he treated it as a noun, as something specific. Again, she self-admonished. She should know more of Suevik beliefs. Claris had always been focused on the blade-maidens more than anything else. Her vague memory told her that the Will was a core belief, a higher power, like a god's guiding hand. Before last night she would've thought to ask Torsten.

A biting wind wailed through the trees and Halvar fell back, angling himself between horses and trees for cover. Pepin bounded up close and Claris patted the horse's head in a reassuring stroke before allowing Pepin up for shelter. It wasn't long until snow joined the wind, flakes whipping through the branches, wind sheering frost free. Claris hunched over, hoping to save her face from the brunt of the cold. Pepin pushed himself closer to her chest.

Brahim glanced back, as if assuring himself the others remained close and hadn't been disorientated or lost. Claris had been making the same checks ever since the wind picked up speed. His eyes caught hers as she gazed forward. His gaze seemed to stray first to her new gloves, then to what he could see of the vest. He nodded, as if in approval of her wearing them. Perhaps she was wrong to think them from Torsten.

Time ticked by as the group trod through the new snowfall and wended their way through the trees. Claris was sure pushing through until they left the forest would be the best option, but in the cold, keeping strength up was equally important. She hated having to go against her own word. She threw up her hand but couldn't even hear her own voice over the howl of wind.

"You wish for us to stop?"

Halvar's sudden appearance caused Claris to jump, and she took a few deep breaths to calm her racing heart. Pepin yowled in displeasure and jumped from the horse. Doubt nipped at Claris with Halvar's question. Was it wrong to call a stop?

"Yes?" Halvar prompted.

That he asked again gave Claris a spur of encouragement. "We should, for food."

He pushed up his right sleeve and touched one rune etched near his wrist. It pulsed a low blue colour once. "Halt." Claris's eyes widened in shock. Halvar's voice boomed out around them, surely even waking those deep in slumber for the winter. A few of the horses neighed with displeasure.

As best as everyone could, they clustered in around Claris. Pepin leaned up against her legs. She mentally counted the garde and horses, paused, and did it again. The mule was missing. She said a silent thanks that Pepin had no longer been upon it.

"Where are our supplies?" she asked, doing her best to keep her voice controlled and even. She could not let the emotions threatening within spill over. Brahim stood beside her, his presence giving her added courage. His horse's warm breath welcome against the back of her head.

No one spoke up, and Brahim gave her a small nod. "Who was in charge of that mule?" she said. She would be listened to. That mule had their tents, their cooking pot.

Torsten cleared his throat, staring straight into her eyes. "I assigned Odo that duty."

Claris was struck still. She didn't want to face away from Torsten, for visions of his naked torso and him kissing another danced at the surface. That the one he kissed was responsible for the animal in question only made it worse. Brahim went to move, but Claris held out her hand. If she wanted their respect, she had to do it herself.

She stepped towards Odo, pleased to note he was of equal height. "Is that true?"

"My horse spooked," Odo said, his voice breaking a little. "And in that moment, as I calmed her, the mule spooked. I lost hold of the rope." Even the wind couldn't mask his stammering excuses.

"Yet you did not think to halt us?" Claris looked at the others. Pepin prowled in front of Odo, forcing him to take a step back. "How did no one else see this?" Her eyes lingered on Torsten. He was at the rear and should've noted if the mule had taken flight.

Again, none offered an explanation, and Claris's initial fear of losing their supplies was supplanted by a growing anger. In the dense press of the forest, it should've been impossible to lose a horse, let alone a mule.

Brahim spoke up. "The mule is from our reach now. We should press on."

Pepin mewed at Odo and stalked away.

"Once we break for camp, Odo will hunt for our supper," Claris said. Odo looked at her but did not raise any objections. She did, however, note the clenching of his free hand.

She waved the group on. Brahim clapped her on the shoulder. "Well done, love." He winked and walked onwards. She lingered to fall into pace beside Torsten, but she couldn't bring herself to look at him at such proximity.

"Was it the visibility?" she asked.

"A curtain of white," he replied, "but that shouldn't be an excuse. You should have me help Odo."

Heat raced up her neck. "Do you ask because you believe your guilt, or for another reason?"

"Do you wish me to explain what you saw?"

She glanced sideways at Torsten. "Is there a need?"

His lips twitched, causing her own to pull into a traitorous return smile. "I'm not ashamed. Nor is it something I hide."

Her face flushed. Claris repeated the refrain that he was the vicomte's man in her mind to steady her heart. "Do not think that is why I ordered Odo to do what I did, to punish him for what he shared with you."

"I'm happy to share my warmth with others." His voice was lower than normal, his head inclined down towards her.

She hummed for a moment, certain he wouldn't hear over the wind. Pepin returned to her side and rubbed against her with a contented purr. She insisted to herself she'd not be swayed by his words.

"If he approves of course," Torsten added and held out a green pear in front of her. She took a quick few bites, not caring much for flavour, but the need for food. "Never hurts to have food handy," he said, taking a bite of another pear he pulled from a saddlebag.

She peered over at his horse. "How many have you stashed there?" Pepin came by to check out the fruit but turned away quickly.

"That is between me and my horse."

She didn't bother trying to hide her smile and took another bite from her pear. Claris gave a small wave to Torsten and pulled her horse along as she pushed forward, the lynx close behind. She needed the distance before her feelings got twisted too much; before Torsten clouded her mind entirely. With the pear almost all devoured, Claris held her hand out with the remains to her black mare. She gave it an experimental sniff before taking it from her hand. The horse seemed to agree that it was quite alright.

The wind eventually eased, as did the snowfall, but the light dimmed quicker than Claris anticipated. Before her remained the wall of woods, and with low visibility it was hard to discern if they were near to exiting the forest. She admonished herself. She shouldn't have called that halt. It cost them time with no gain.

By the time the group broke through the tree line, the sun had disappeared below the horizon, leaving the sky muted and darkness creeping in fast. Pepin paced around the camp set-up once before bounding back into the forest. Claris went up to Odo, hoping she wasn't about to make another bad call.

"Do not stray too far in the dark," she said. "We still need you."

"I will try my luck in the woods," he replied, slinging a bow and quiver over one shoulder. She wondered if he was as skilled with that as Dalfin was.

Claris found she couldn't look him in the eyes. "If you are not back soon, I will send after you." Odo gave a curt nod and headed towards the trees. Halvar headed into the trees as well, but in a different direction.

Claris peered over at Roul, who was already seated by the fire, while Sigibert tended to Roul's and his own horse. Her eyebrows furrowed. Dalfin sat off to one side, using a whetstone to sharpen his arrowheads.

"We will resupply at Arson," Brahim said as he came up from behind her. "The pears Torsten had will get the horses by."

Claris held out her gloved hands. "Do I have you to thank for these?"

He didn't turn to face her. "I asked the sister-wives to procure new ones for you. I do need your hands."

"I thought my help would likely not be required?" Claris shifted her attention away from the garde.

"We shall practice." Amusement danced in his eyes, and he pointed at the nearby trees.

Claris didn't think much of the light conditions but followed Brahim over towards them. Where he stopped, so did she.

"Throw as many as you can before I tell you to stop." He nodded towards one of the further trees.

She took her stance, rolled back her shoulders and shifted her cloak aside for easy access to her knives.

"I said throw." His voice wasn't harsh, or loud, but it cut low, and Claris knew her time had started and still not a single knife had been released.

She threw her first knife, adjusted slightly and took another to throw. Both struck the tree true.

"Left," Brahim said.

She glanced at him, wanting confirmation, and he pointed at the tree left of where her first two knives struck. Again, she took precious moments before taking the third shot. After two more throws, Brahim directed her back to the centre tree.

"Right."

Claris felt she had got into a good rhythm, her knives in her thigh straps depleted and she reached for the ones on her upper arms.

"Stop." Brahim's forehead creased in a frown, and Claris sensed the waves of disapproval crashing down from him. He came around and stepped before her. "We need to change where you keep the knives."

Claris looked down at herself and then at Brahim. He sported a single thigh strap and then a belt of them.

"Ziri suggested the position of my knives," she said.

Brahim raised his eyebrows. "If it was a hobby. But in battles, in a fight, you need them more accessible."

She touched the strap on her upper arm. She thought Ziri found her skills good, but clearly he too had relegated her interest to a hobby and nothing more.

Brahim reached up and undid both her arm straps. He leaned down and went to see if it'd fit above her knee. Claris initial reaction was to pull away, but she forced herself to stay still. The back of her neck prickled with the sense of being watched. She didn't need the garde thinking inappropriate thoughts from this.

"We have no materials to make something," Claris said, needing to puncture the silence. Whatever Brahim was trying to achieve, it wasn't working. Her existing sheaths wouldn't fit anywhere else.

"Then we must acquire some at our next stop," he replied, handing the straps back to Claris. "You'll also need a wrist sheath."

"So, you have more faith now?"

He gave a wry smile.

Voices raised from behind them, and Claris turned to see what the commotion was. Odo had emerged from the forest but was empty handed. He looked uninjured and the thought he'd simply given up left a bad taste in her mouth.

"The boy returns," Roul announced. "Likely expects us to eat poisonous berries he's picked."

Claris went to go over, but Brahim put a hand on her shoulder. "Give them a moment." If Roul viewed Odo as boy, who likely was similar to her own age, Claris didn't like thinking Roul would view her in the same light.

Torsten had already gone over to Odo, with Sigibert close behind.

Pepin's rumbling purrs drew her attention. He'd also returned from the forest, but he wasn't empty handed like Odo. The lynx laid a dead rabbit at her feet.

She knelt. "Thank you, boy." She leaned her cheek against his face and stroked her hand through his fur. "Always know where to find the rabbits."

Claris took the creature and walked over to the gathered garde. They all went quiet as she approached. Odo raised his head, either to show defiance or no shame, she wasn't sure. She held out the rabbit. "We can eat this."

A few of the garde exchanged looks, before Sigibert spoke up. "We're not fond of rabbit. Not after last time."

"It is a fresh kill. You can either share it, or it will be a meal for one."

Flore finally stood and took the rabbit from her. "I'll prepare it." They hesitated, as if waiting for her to stay something, but Claris stayed silent.

"You've a fine ally in that lynx," Sigibert said.

She looked over at the others, her gaze lingering a little longer on Torsten, before she nodded her acknowledgement. Flore had gone to one side to skin the rabbit; the sound of it tearing turning her stomach slightly. "Excuse me."

Brahim stood a few paces away and she went to his side. Pepin padded over to the horses.

"The mage still has not returned," Claris said. "Should we be worried?"

"He's safer alone," Brahim said. "And I think he's found us a larger meal."

Claris followed his gaze. Halvar walked out of the forest with an elk strung across his shoulders. The weight not even seeming to bow his back or slow his stride. If the king knew they'd hunted within his forest, they'd all be fined, or worse, corporal punishment.

"We will have to try and preserve that meat," Claris said and headed back over to the campfire that Halvar had reached. Flore had placed the rabbit over the fire.

Halvar pointed to it. "Exchange."

Torsten stood, removed the rabbit and presented it to Halvar. With a nod, Halvar took the half-cooked rabbit and left the elk on the snow. Claris was certain his runes flashed blue as he walked past.

All the garde looked from the elk to Claris.

"Cut only what we need tonight," she said. "Preserve the rest." She hoped the mage might help with that, for snow-packed elk might not last for long.

"We'll be conservative," Torsten said, unsheathing a knife strapped behind his back.

Roul's face pulled into displeasure and Claris knew she couldn't afford to lose the garde so early. She shook her head. "No, we can be generous. It will last us to Arson."

Dalfin, still sporting the ankle and wrist braces, stood and offered her the wineskin. Claris politely refused. Sharing the same wineskin as the garde would be a step too far. They needed to continue seeing her as their demoiselle, as a person they owed allegiance too, not a comrade. She may not yet command their respect, but she would command their duty.

Once more she moved away from the garde, though she liked the proximity to the fire. Halvar stood next to Brahim and had clearly shared the rabbit between them. She didn't wish to interrupt them either. She walked closer to the trees and rested a gloved hand against one of the trunks. It wasn't her mother's stone, but it was solitary.

"I feel a fish in an ocean too large," Claris said, "and I am not sure I know the right direction. Mother, you know with you gone, the future is not a path to dwell on, but maybe that is what I must. No matter how dangerous such thoughts could be. How much further pain it will cause. I need the shore I am not sure I can reach."

Approaching footsteps pulled Claris away from the tree. She turned to see Torsten almost upon her.

"You should stay closer to the fire," he said. "And closer in case of any attack." He took another step closer to her.

His body emanated warmth, likely the lingering effect of the campfire.

She peered around him at the other garde. "What do they think of your presence over here?"

His eyes stayed locked on her. "That I'm doing my duty."

"Yet no one else seems to offer." Claris swallowed. The gap between them had grown smaller again.

"That's because I won't let them."

She tried never to stare, but her eyes drifted to the scar on his throat. Catching herself, she averted her gaze.

"Does it make you uncomfortable?" He touched his neck.

She flushed. "My discomfort is not due to any injury you have."

He closed the gap, leaning his head down to hers. "Or is it my naked flesh you can't remove from your mind?"

Her cheeks burned red. Her throat dried. She needed to put a stop to this. Remind herself that Torsten was working for the vicomte, not her father, not her.

"What did happen to your throat?" She took a step back.

His face shuttered. "A story for another time." Torsten glanced back towards the camp. "The food will not be long now. Let us return."

Claris swallowed. She needed to get her emotions under control before facing everyone else. She also needed to bury the resurfaced image of Torsten's back. It wasn't appropriate.

She staggered her gait, so she wasn't at Torsten's side when they reached the campfire.

Sigibert and Flore were busy with pulling the meat away from the fire and portioning it out. Sigibert stood and held the first serving to Claris. They'd used strips of bark to serve the food on.

"Thank you," she said. "It smells good."

"I always carry salt with me," Sigibert said.

Claris spotted Pepin off inside her makeshift tent of furs draped over branches, keeping himself clear of the fire. She nodded to the garde and went over, letting him press up against her as she sat.

Pepin lifted his head and rested it back down on her lap.

"You best not have annoyed the horses," she said to him.

The lynx purred, but Claris didn't have a free hand to stroke him. She ate her food before it turned completely cold and tossed the bark aside into the snow. Pepin glanced up at it before returning to her lap.

Claris gave his fur a stroke as she watched the garde and Brahim talk, while Halvar stood off to one side. The fire had lessened and would be kept at a low burn while everyone slept and one kept watch. Claris knew if she were a man, she could sit among them, drink the wine, and still have their respect as their leader. She sighed.

She gently shifted Pepin aside. "Time to sleep, boy." He stretched out and repositioned himself to lie beside Claris once she'd thrown her blanket on.

Unfortunately, sleep eluded her. The chill, even with the blanket, sat deep within her bones. The one spot that warmth emanated was from Pepin's body pressed up against the curve of her back. She shifted, careful not to disturb the lynx, and peeped outside her shelter, curious who was on watch. Blue eyes immediately locked onto hers. Torsten stood and made his way over.

"Is there something wrong?" he asked, looking out at their surroundings, but in the night gloom she doubted he'd see far.

She rubbed at her nose with the back of her hand. "Simply cold. Makes it hard to sleep."

A smile tugged at his lips. "As I have said, I am happy to share my warmth."

"I am a demoiselle." She cleared her throat, averting her gaze.

"And I am unworthy?"

Her eyes shot back to him, quickly shaking her head. "I said no such thing. But you work for the vicomte." There, she said it. Aired her suspicion aloud, that Torsten was there only to gain the vicomte more standing towards claiming the county as his.

He leaned down, his face dangerously close to hers. "I won't tell."

A choked sound escaped her lips as warmth flushed through her body. Her body may be betraying her, wanting to give in to temptation, but she steeled herself. "Goodnight, Torsten."

He smiled widely. "Sleep well... Claris."

Her insides twisted. Before she changed her mind, she ducked back within the shelter, closing herself away from his gaze. From his lips.

A Cave Detour

Day 6

Claris woke with her hair full of snow. A quick assessment of the shelter showed a neat cut up the side of the fur. She knelt and took a closer look, her finger running along the cut. Only a blade could've achieved such a thing. She frowned, looking around. Pepin had clearly abandoned the shelter before she woke, and there, resting out of her sheaths, was a single throwing knife. She took a deep breath. She must've done it during her nightmares. There was no time to patch it as everyone packed up to continue their journey. Once they stopped again, she'd see to it.

Flore was the one to come over and pack away the shelter. They nodded at her, their eyes straying to her hair. "Rough night?"

A pat of her head and she knew she needed to redo her braids and tame the hair all back down. But doing so blindly would likely end in a similar result. Claris slipped the hood of her cloak up over her head.

"Nothing I cannot manage," she replied.

Brahim stood over near his horse. The weather was already miserable, with little sunlight squeezing through the dense dark clouds. Snow drifted down in a steady pattern.

The remains of last night's elk were strung on the back of Torsten's horse. Pepin was over there, smelling the dead animal in interest.

Claris moved to her own horse, strapping down her bedroll and blanket. Flore brought the ruined fur over.

"Thank you," she said as they went to move away after their task was done.

"Of course, Demoiselle," they replied, their inflection stressed.

Her eyes narrowed after them, uncertain if they were being polite or rude. Claris sighed. She likely was overthinking it.

Halvar loomed up beside her. "Do you need help to sleep?"

She blinked a few times. "Is my appearance that bad?"

His gaze fell over her and he shook his head. "You tore a hole in your shelter. Perhaps sleeping with blades is unwise."

"You saw this?"

"I took a watch." He shifted his weight. "I can help."

"At what cost?" Claris wasn't too naïve to expect help for free from a mage. Magecraft always cost something.

Once more Halvar's gaze roamed over her. His eyes settled on the silver brooch of a bee clasped on her cloak. "That will suffice."

Her hand went to the brooch protectively. It was a decorative piece, but it was a piece of home.

"One who does not look to the future should not dwell in the past either," Halvar said, as if sensing her thoughts.

After some deliberation, Claris unclasped the brooch and placed it into Halvar's waiting palm. "It will work?"

His hand closed over the brooch and Claris lost sight of it. "You'll slumber peacefully."

A return to restful slumber was a welcome thought, but that brooch also belonged to her mother. Her throat constricted at such a thought. She hoisted herself up onto the mare as Halvar moved towards the others. Brahim had already mounted and led the group onwards. With the weather as it was, Claris doubted they would reach Arson before night fell. At least they still had elk. Out in the white expanse Claris didn't think they could find much food. The winter landscape broke the unwary.

They hadn't travelled far when the snow intensified and cold bit into her cheeks. Flakes clung stubbornly to her lashes, no matter how many times she flicked them away. Everyone moved as close together as the horses allowed. Brahim manoeuvred his horse to come up to Claris.

"We won't get far like this," he said.

All that stood before them was a swirling wall of white. The air bit with a fierce cold.

"Do we stop?" she asked.

"There are the caverns," he said.

Claris almost pulled her reins in shock. "Caverns?"

"The demi-lich has been traversing them."

She shook her head. "We need Arson for resupply. And wouldn't an encounter down there with the demi-lich be unwise?"

"Halvar and I looked over the maps," he replied. "There is a way out of them near Arson. Halvar says they will not be blocked. The demi-lich won't be in there now."

The idea sat uneasy with Claris. They would abandon the horses. And if something went wrong, they'd be trapped underground.

Halvar came up beside them. "The horses will return home safe."

She swallowed. She'd never heard of mages reading thoughts, but Halvar behaved as if he read hers. It was a vital decision. Heat plucked at her eyes. The horses' gait had slowed considerably. Though certain the garde could each carry the burden of weight from their own supplies, Claris knew she'd struggle. And if they didn't catch the demi-lich at Arson, they'd have to keep travelling.

"We must decide now." Brahim slipped down from his horse.

"You have used these caverns?" she asked Halvar.

"Yes."

Claris hated that he didn't specify how recent his use had been. She held up her hand and called for a dismount. Torsten and the others came over to them.

"Are we erecting shelter?" Torsten asked.

Claris glanced at Brahim before answering. "We take what we can carry, and we will use the cavern passageways."

Roul scoffed. "They are for thieves and scoundrels."

"We follow the demi-lich, and the demi-lich went under," she said. "The mage has ensured every horse will return to Lannes safe."

"And if they don't?" Roul crossed his arms. The snowfall had intensified and soon all visibility would be lost.

"Then the comte will reimburse the loss," Claris said. "There is little time to waste."

A flurry of activity burst around the horses as all took what they could and strapped it to their backs. Claris managed her bedroll and fur, but knew many of the supplies in the saddlebags would be lost.

"Leave it," Brahim said, as he walked past her.

Claris clucked her tongue at Pepin, who came out from the horse's legs. "Time to go, boy. The horses will not be following." Everyone clustered together and Claris deferred to Brahim.

"Halvar and I will lead us through," he said. "The caverns are not wide and have many dead ends. You will all be responsible for one another."

"We have but two torches," Flore said, holding them aloft.

"I will light some way," Halvar said, his deep rumbling voice putting a stop to any lingering murmurs.

Claris ensured Pepin was still close by her side as they followed behind the others.

Torsten fell in beside her. "You shouldn't take the rear."

"Pepin does not like fire," she replied. "And I will not leave his side while we are down there." The lynx mewed in response and rubbed against her leg.

"Then I must insist." Torsten reached around her waist, Claris flinching at the contact, and the weight of rope he hung from her. "I've had the others do the same. Should we put rope over Pepin?"

Pepin hissed in response, and Claris smiled. "He is smart. He will be fine. But you should have asked me. You're lucky I also did not hiss at you."

"I'm merely glad I found no blade buried in me," he said.

Claris glanced down. "I am not sure I am quick enough for that."

"Perhaps there'll be target practice down in these caverns." He flashed her a smile.

The wind picked up, carrying Torsten's last words away. Snow battered into them. Claris hunched down into her cloak, eager to shield her face. Torsten walked ahead of her and the rope went taut for a moment. Claris picked her feet up and Pepin stuck as close as he could.

A dark rocky maw appeared ahead, and Claris hurried in behind all the others. Everyone took a moment to shake and stamp away the snow before Brahim led them on. A soft blue glow emanated from the front, and orange light flickered from the torches. The cavern walls were abrasive if brushed against, the rocky surface unforgiving.

"You cannot go off and hunt in here," she whispered to Pepin. "We will get you food, but you must stay beside me." He rubbed against her leg again and softly mewed.

Everyone remained close to one another, and the ropes almost seemed pointless to Claris. She shifted her shoulders and back a bit, the extra weight unfamiliar, but she was grateful it seemed manageable at least. Only the sounds of rock crunching underfoot and the sizzle of flame permeated the air. Claris would've expected at least small creatures to find refuge within the caverns, but so far there were none. She kept one hand close to her blades in her thigh strap. The lack of life down here surely wasn't a good sign. The demi-lich could still be around.

Soon enough, it wasn't feasible to have two abreast, so they walked in single file. There'd be the occasional pause each time the cavern branched in another direction before one was chosen and everyone continued. Claris peered down the unchosen paths, but all there was to see was un-interrupted gloom, while the air was almost stagnant with a damp chill clinging to all sides.

Pepin's restlessness was hard to ignore as he weaved in front and behind Claris as she walked. It was a sense of confinement to the lynx, one he was not used to. But she couldn't let him roam.

Then, suddenly, his yowl echoed through the passageway. Her skin prickled and she halted. The rope pulled once before going slack. Pepin was behind her, hunkered down and peering in the direction they had come from.

Murmurs broke out as everyone came to a stop. Claris expected Brahim to come check, but the blue glow strengthened as Halvar approached. He looked between Pepin and the darkness beyond.

"Did you see anything?" Halvar asked and Claris shook her head.

He crouched beside Pepin, who still hadn't moved, and it put Claris on edge.

"What do your eyes see?" Halvar said to Pepin and rested his hand on the lynx's head. Claris tensed. Runes flared underneath the mage's hood. She readied a blade near her fingers.

Pepin relaxed, mewed once, and went to Claris's side. Halvar stood.

"There is nothing to worry on."

She frowned. "Pepin would not react in such a manner over nothing."

Contrary to his words, Halvar unslung his hammer. "We move on."

Claris reached down to pet Pepin. "You did good, boy." A single tug on her rope pulled her gaze up.

"Anything?" Torsten asked.

"The mage says no," she said. Claris glanced back to be sure, but nothing was visible. She lowered her voice. "Weapon ready, to be safe." Torsten nodded and slid out his short sword. If the mage thought it prudent to have his hammer ready, Claris would remain alert for an attack.

She had hoped that if others frequented the caverns, there'd be markings or sconces for torchlight. But every passage seemed quiet and uninhabited. Perhaps it was the effect of a demi-lich passing through. Though Pepin appeared undisturbed, she noticed he would turn his head to look backwards more frequently than she considered normal. Torsten still had his sword at the ready. But with everyone carrying more weight, could they react quick enough to defend successfully? Claris needed out of her own mind lest such dark thoughts consumed her.

She tugged on the rope. Torsten looked back and she ushered him closer.

"Did you see something?" he asked. Pepin looked up at him and then moved to the other side of Claris.

She shook her head. "Yet something is down here with us."

"Could it be the demi-lich?"

Doubt squirmed within. If it was, that meant it had taken a route that positioned it behind them. A shudder went through Claris. That train of thought didn't help her.

"Surely it is before us," she said.

Torsten took in their surroundings. "Then perhaps the creatures it drove to hiding are resurfacing."

Claris watched Pepin for a moment. "I think it is more than that."

Torsten lessened the space between them. "Do you want me to take the rear guard?"

She knew he'd follow her direction, but that made it difficult. If something indeed stalked them, Torsten would be first attacked. She knew it was his job, but it didn't lessen the burden or the knowledge that if he was harmed, it'd be from her choice.

"Claris?"

The sound of her name brought her attention back to Torsten. She shook her head. "Pepin will be our best alert."

Worry creased Torsten's forehead. "But my job is to be your armour." She swallowed, believing his words were sincere.

"Then do no stray far."

Just then, the orange glow from one torch ahead flickered and guttered out. The blue glow and remaining torchlight still permitted enough visibility to see by.

A heated exchange carried towards them. Whoever held the torch couldn't get it lit once more.

"Hand it here." Roul's voice boomed down the passageway, bouncing from the rocks. Pepin's ears flattened.

"It is done." Sigibert's reply had equal volume. He did not refer to the torch's reignition, though, but the fact it would no longer sustain a flame.

"There is no harm in letting him try," Flore said. Everyone had gravitated towards the commotion, and Flore found Claris's eyes, as if imploring her to resolve the matter.

Unfortunately, she knew nothing of torches, seeing as she normally used oil lamps at home.

Halvar pushed his way into the centre of the clustered group and took the torch from Sigibert's hands. Claris expected him to light it once more, but instead he tossed it to one side.

"He was right. The torch is done."

Claris looked down at the discarded torch, tempted to salvage it. Pepin went taut at her side. Her hand strayed back to her knives.

Roul grumbled and they moved onwards.

"Quiet," Claris called. Everyone returned to stillness. Pepin's claws extended, and Claris untied the rope, letting it fall to the ground.

Skittering noises against the rocks echoed towards them.

Brahim came up beside her and she pointed in the direction they had come. This time the skittering was accompanied by a chittering that set Claris's nerves on end. No ordinary creatures could make such a noise. She'd never seen a hint of anything but controlled composure from Brahim, but she swore his face paled a little.

He made quick, sharp gestures with his hands to indicate all should hurry onwards. Being silent made no difference now.

"What?" she whispered.

His eyes darted back. "Corpse crawlers."

Claris had no urge to encounter whatever creature had been given such a name. Torsten reached out and pulled her forward, kick-starting her legs into motion. Pepin kept a quick pace in front of her. Halvar's blue light intensified to aid the quick traversal.

The cacophony of noise from the combined chitters and skitters pumped Claris's heart faster. Her only thought was to keep moving, to not stop. Her belongings smacked into her back with every stride, Pepin and Torsten before her. Brahim right on her heels. The surrounding temperature plummeted, but she saw no signs of an exit. She wasn't sure she could throw a knife as her heart raced.

Chitters came from all directions now. Yet she didn't slow the pace.

Halvar called, "Right." A few of the garde had outpaced the mage's gait. Roul's own pace flagged, and he'd fallen behind.

"Ambush," Dalfin shouted.

The group gathered, all weapons drawn. Three of the creatures were before them. They had eight jointed legs like a spider, a body the size of a goat, and two large round eyes close to a pointed snout and hidden mouth. The chittering died down and Claris's skin chilled. A glance behind showed two more boxing them in, even with the widened passage.

Halvar intensified the output of his light, but the creatures stood their ground. In such close confines Claris was concerned her knives would only be a hindrance. She glanced down at the hatchet, but she had little faith in that either. Even after a few deep breaths, her pulse hadn't settled. Her throwing hand shook.

"Do they have a weakness?" she asked, loud enough for all to hear, but her question directed at Brahim, who had turned to face the ones behind them.

"The legs," he said. "The body is thicker than it looks."

Of course, the smaller targets are what Claris had to focus on. She pulled free one of her knives.

"Don't let them bite you," Brahim continued, "for their venom will kill you."

Without warning he flung a knife out, catching one of the legs of the closest creature. A thick grey ichor leaked from the wound.

Shrill, high chitters burst around them, and the creatures surged forward.

An arrow from Dalfin hit another of a crawler's legs.

Between her unsteady hand and the quick movements from their foe, her first knife missed the mark. She struggled to free a second knife. Her vision narrowed. She took a deep breath, swallowed, and lifted her hand to throw again. The shaking stopped. She released. It landed low on a leg, but it was a front leg, and the creature stumbled a moment.

Torsten stepped in front, sword ready.

The crawlers closed in, rearing up on their back four legs. They thrust out and lashed with the others.

Claris ducked reflexively. Pepin swiped at a leg. A shrill cry went up from one. Torsten had cut through a rear leg. More grey ichor slicked over the rocks.

Brahim gave up his knives in favour of a thick-bladed short sword. Claris fumbled for her hatchet. Flore pushed past her, coming to Torsten's aid. Together they finished one of the creatures.

"Claris!" Brahim's voice was sharp but strained. His sword held before him, two legs weighing down his blade.

Pepin dashed forward, leaping at one of the rear legs. Claris couldn't watch him get hurt. She stepped forward and swung at the leg, her hatchet connecting but sticking in the limb. The crawler's head swivelled towards her. One of the front legs swiped at her.

A sword passed before her face, cleanly slicing through the leg, and Claris pulled her hatchet free to swing again. This time the creature collapsed. With the two rear now dead, the four of them faced forward and Pepin came to her side. But the others had no need for their help. All the corpse crawlers were dead and Halvar's light flared bright again.

"Casualties?" Brahim asked, walking up to the mage.

He shook his head. "A few injuries. All minor."

Claris still held the hatchet, but she couldn't loosen her grip. She wanted to sit or lean against something. Her skin tingled. She took a shaky breath.

Torsten came before her, resting his hand over the handle.

"It's okay now," he whispered. Claris blinked. "Let me take it, Claris."

She swallowed and looked down at the weapon. Ichor clung to the blade still. Pepin purred at her side. Her fingers loosened and Torsten took hold of the hatchet. He wiped it clean and tucked it back into her belt.

"Thank you," she whispered, still caught in a daze. She looked towards Brahim. "Those things are called corpse crawlers?"

"They rise from the earth when they sense death," he said. "The demi-lich must've woken them. They feast on necrotic flesh." He faced the others. "We move quickly and hope no more find us."

No one argued, and Halvar took up the lead once more. The second torch they had lost in the battle, so only Halvar's blue light guided them in the dark now. Pepin stayed close at Claris's side and Torsten wasn't far from her either. Brahim had moved to take rear guard.

The further they walked, the more Claris settled, enough to note the few empty slots in her sheaths. She should have retrieved the blades. And when it came to the demi-lich, she knew she couldn't freeze as she had with those crawlers. She couldn't be a weak link, a reason someone else died because they had to aid her.

Claris kept her head down as the thoughts rattled through her mind, not keen to know who looked at her, who judged her for her weakness. She had enough ire for herself alone.

Pepin mewed, startling Claris, but he'd already dashed forward. Then her feet trod on snow and she understood. They'd finally reached an exit; they were finally back outside.

From what she could see, the sun had already set. Pepin had likely gone hunting for some food.

No one gave any orders, but the implicit agreement that rest was the only course of action had the garde immediately in motion to make camp. Claris was grateful to relieve the weight from her back. Flore came over to start another small fire and construct a lean-to.

"Try not put a hole in this fur," they said and set it up.

"Is that not yours?" Claris asked, her voice still hushed.

"Us garde will crowd for warmth."

She was thankful Flore paid her no attention as her cheeks warmed.

Flore stood back from the erected shelter. "But do try not to ruin this one." Their little smile made Claris feel a little better at the displacement. Perhaps they had started to accept her.

"Thank you," she replied.

The central campfire ignited and more of the elk was placed over the flame. Pepin pushed himself into the shelter as Claris finished laying out the bedroll and blanket. He licked his lips. Claris sat back and let him settle on her lap.

"You were brave today, boy," she said. "Braver than me."

He purred and nudged her hand. She ran her fingers through his fur, stroking his back.

"I am glad you are with me."

His contented mew brought a smile to her face.

"You decent?" Brahim's voice called.

"Sorry, boy," Claris said to Pepin as she shifted him from her lap and got up.

Brahim stood outside. She steeled herself.

"Was that your first fight?" Neither his tone nor features signalled displeasure. Claris felt as if she was about to fall. She temporarily forgot how to form words, so she merely nodded.

He pulled three knives from his cloak. Her knives. "You should always recover them if you can."

Claris licked her dry lips. "Thank you. I did mean to... but..."

"It's easy to forget the simple things when one is overcome," he said. "You did well. The more battles, the easier it gets."

She took the knives. "We should practice more then."

He gave a half smile. "I'd prefer not to see another corpse crawler again."

Claris didn't want to let her guard down but couldn't help returning a small laugh. "I think we all agree on that."

"The others have found a hot spring," he said. "I told them you should go first."

Claris stood silent for a moment, but Brahim said nothing further. His eyes seemed sincere, and his mouth bore no smirk. "That is kind. Thank you."

"I'll show you the way," Brahim said, "but I think your cat will be guard enough for you."

Her eyes widened and she glanced over at the garde. None paid them any mind. She didn't have the energy to defend herself. All she thought was how hot water would be welcome. She glanced back at her shelter. "Let me grab fresh clothes."

She clucked at Pepin. "Want a swim?"

He watched her for a moment before uncurling himself and following her.

They followed the rocky outlines of the caverns they'd left until they reached a copse and the pools of water beyond. The banks of the pools were still covered in ice and snow, but steam wafted up lazily off the water. She turned to thank Brahim, but he'd already made himself scarce. Pepin went to the water's edge, dipping his paw in. Claris placed the bundle of clean clothes and blanket near the edge. The air warred between warm and cool.

With a glance around, ensuring she was indeed alone, she stripped off her bloodied clothes and slipped into the water. As Pepin paddled a circle around her, she unravelled all the braids and plaits in her hair, detangling with her fingers. She then let the water lap over her head, eager to wash all the grime away. The heat helped soothe some aches from the battle and the prior days atop a horse.

Her first battle wasn't what she expected. The stories painted such different pictures, though a part of her knew they weren't reality. The fight was chaotic, and any moment of hesitation could see someone hurt. Her mouth dried at the thought. Without Torsten, she might've fared worse. Pepin nudged his head into her shoulder. He always knew when she was lost in her head. She offered him a smile and scratched behind his ears.

A prickle at the back of her neck warned her of being watched.

The lynx seemed unperturbed by anything in their surroundings. She looked around and then spotted him. Torsten stood amongst the trees, keeping a respectable distance.

"I know you are there," she called out.

Torsten stepped from the shadows. "I'd be remiss in my duties if I didn't stand guard."

"Indeed." She spied her clothes off to the side. "You should turn around to allow me some decency."

He lifted his eyebrows but did as she asked. Claris also turned her back to his and hurried to dry and slipped on the kirtle. Pepin padded off to the tree line.

"How do you feel?" Torsten said when she'd finished dressing and turned to face him.

She looked at him, really looked. He had no visible wounds from the fight. A weight lifted from her chest. "Clean."

He closed the gap between them. "No one thinks you behaved like a coward, or poorly."

"Torsten..." But Claris didn't know what to say. Or if she could say anything at all. That voice urging her to remember he worked for the vicomte was drowned out by her erratic pulse.

"You were right there with us," he said, his voice unwavering. "Every blade counts, and you added yours."

He moved closer; their bodies pressed up against one another. His warmth radiated over her. He took a few strands of her long hair in his fingers, letting it fall back down.

Claris looked up at him.

He put one hand gently at her back and leaned towards her. Her pulse picked up. His lips pressed against hers, warm and soft. Hesitant at first.

She reached a hand to his face, her body arching in welcome.

Warmth consumed her. Her arms wound around his neck. All she could taste was the moment, letting all the worries on her shoulders fall away. She could easily lose herself in that moment.

But she couldn't. That nagging voice resurfaced. Claris pulled back and swallowed.

She couldn't let this happen. She could be playing right into his hands, right into what the vicomte might want. Her ruin. Her father's ruin.

She couldn't let this happen, even if that had been her first taste of a kiss. The type of kiss she'd felt before over her cheeks and back of hand, but never on the lips. A kiss she wanted more of. Her hands fell away from his body.

"We should head back," she said, stepping away to put more distance between them.

His eyes roamed over her face, lingering on her lips, before he nodded. "Of course." He let her lead the way.

Back at the camp Claris pretended to not notice anyone else, and that Torsten near her was a mere coincidence. The food was cooked, and she took her offered portion from Sigibert; his upper right arm had been bound with cloth.

"Will it be okay?" she asked.

He looked at his arm. "But a scratch, Demoiselle."

"I am glad."

Everyone was subdued, and Claris turned into her shelter. Pepin joined her soon after. It didn't escape her notice that Brahim had integrated himself amongst the garde, or that Torsten watched her every movement. She wondered if the other garde had noticed the interactions she'd had with Torsten, and what they might think. She rubbed at her temples, all the worries slamming back into her at full force.

A Doomed Encounter

Day 7

As promised by Halvar, Claris had a sleep undisturbed by bad dreams. Pepin was still curled at her side when she woke. Even after everything last night, she couldn't deny she felt refreshed. Perhaps Halvar was a good sort, and she'd do better at putting trust in him?

Claris kept her face impassive as she found Brahim outside her shelter again.

"A word?" he asked.

She nodded and gestured they should walk for a moment of privacy. Pepin stuck his head out but made no move to follow. Her stomach flipped, waiting for what Brahim would say.

"There is a high chance we might encounter the demi-lich soon. We'll also reach Arson." He looked towards the garde. "Will you be ready, if we do?"

Claris looked at her knives and then the hatchet. She swallowed. "I will be." She had to believe those words.

Behind her, the camp was vanishing. The last coals kicked into the snow.

"I'll let you finish getting ready," he said.

Back at the shelter, Claris longed for a mirror while she braided her hair. She was sure it was messy. She even felt a sore niggling at her chin, which must be unsightly. Such frivolous thoughts; she needed to push them away. Blade-maidens surely didn't care about their appearances. Claris needed to remain focused on the important things: the demi-lich, the potential treasonous actions of those in their county, and the vicomte's motives.

Without horses, everyone grouped near Brahim and Halvar for direction. Claris pulled back her shoulders and headed over.

She cleared her throat. "Once we reach Arson, Dalfin and Sigibert will acquire us new supplies."

"What of horses?" Roul interjected.

Claris shook her head. "I will not take the burden, not if we are forced again onto a route horses cannot traverse." She peered at each of the garde, taking stock of the minor injuries. Odo sported a scratch up his forearm, while Dalfin had multiple tears in his pants. "We will have a good night's rest before we continue on after Arson." She gestured to Brahim. "Lead on, please."

Wanting space to think, to work through all on her mind, she only wanted Pepin for company as they headed towards Arson—yet Torsten came to her side. They moved in a loose formation and Flore had taken up the rear guard in Torsten's absence. Neither of them spoke straight away, and Claris kept her attention on the space ahead.

Torsten reached out to her hand, but she pulled it from his grasp.

"Is your hand fully healed?" he asked.

"It is fine." Her hands clenched. "But what happened yesterday will not happen again." She jerked her head towards Odo. "Keep him company. I'll not give you gossip for your vicomte."

His lips twitched, and for a split second she wished she could see his dimple as he smiled. "The vicomte is not here."

She clucked her tongue at Pepin and stomped forward, leaving Torsten behind. He was bound to be playing her. But she also needed to hide the flushing colour in her cheeks. She walked by the other garde before reaching the front where Brahim and Halvar were. The mage waved her over to him. She still felt small in his presence. Pepin skirted around Halvar to go over to Brahim's side. Though Claris didn't think her cat had warmed to him.

"He seems to not like you again," she said to the mage.

Halvar grunted. "I'm unnatural and he knows it."

"Our nightkeeper never troubled him so?"

"Those around him, that were there as he aged, would never not be accepted by him." Halvar reached back to tap his mage-hammer. "Just as this will always accept me."

"Because of the Will?" To Claris, the weapon looked ordinary, except for when the etched runes glowed blue of course.

"No," he said, the look in his eyes faraway, "a part of me is inside it."

With the momentary pause, Claris's step faltered. Surely he couldn't mean he'd placed a part of his soul within the weapon?

The snow underfoot creaked as everyone walked. Leaving Halvar to his thoughts, she hurried over to Brahim. "We are back on course?"

He had the bark clutched in one hand. "It is close."

"Is this close like the last time?" She had no desire to be misled into false thought again.

"No. I can taste it." Part of the bark crumbled away, lost now amongst the snow.

She looked down at her lynx, but he seemed unworried by their surroundings.

Brahim faced her. "It may be at Arson."

Her heart skipped a beat. If the demi-lich was there, it was too late for everyone. She looked at the garde, especially Roul, who carried the demeanour of a leisurely stroll.

"Pick up the pace," she called, snapping some from their inattentiveness. She turned back to Brahim. "We need to reach it. Stop it before Arson." After readjusting the supplies on her back, Claris picked up her stride and soon all matched her speed. Pepin loped beside her too.

She liked to think herself capable, but her fitness level was no match for the garde. It didn't take long for her pace to waver, as the snow kept dragging her feet down longer with every stride. Claris gritted her teeth regardless. She would not give in so easily.

Birds circled high in the distance. Fear crashed into her. That was too many for them to be hunting prey. They were scavengers. If they'd arrived for the feast, then they were too late. There'd be no one to save. Her stride slowed, and the garde pressed on past her. Even Torsten and Flore went by. Pepin bounded up to her, nudging into her side.

"This journey seems hopeless, boy," she said. Arson was part of her county, her father's county. It was their responsibility to keep the people safe.

Pepin mewed and nudged her again.

Claris stopped and knelt. "What is it?"

He pushed his head to her left side. She swallowed and icy spiders skittered down her spine. Though Pepin was worried, not alert, Claris didn't like the idea something was close by. She turned to her left. A few large rocks and dead shrubs were the only things she saw. "Over there?"

He mewed. Claris stood and walked over towards the rocks. But the rocks weren't there by chance. Someone had arranged them carefully. She wasn't sure of the shape they were in, but they had the familiarity of the runes etched over Halvar's flesh and weapon. A Suevik mage rune.

"Halvar!" she called as loud as she could muster. The group came to a halt, but only Brahim and Halvar jogged over to her location.

"What have you found?" the mage asked.

Claris waved towards the rocks. "I hope you can tell me."

Halvar walked the perimeter of the rocks once. Brahim had crouched close by. The mage looked down at Pepin, who hissed in return. Claris frowned, but Halvar only chuckled.

"The magic once in this rune has now fled," Halvar said. "Only a trace remains."

"What purpose did it serve?" Claris asked. The garde would get restless without direction soon.

Brahim stood. "A beacon."

Halvar glanced at Brahim. "It acted as a guide for the lich to seek."

There was no warmth left in Claris. "Someone is guiding this demi-lich?" She did her best not to look at Halvar. The letter left by the bishop came to the front of her mind, how they believed the Suevik were leading liches into Onvillia.

Halvar touched one of the rocks and it crumbled at his contact. Pepin yowled and darted away.

"It is a rare occurrence," Brahim said. "But there may be a way to use this to trace the demi-lich's path."

"Should we not hurry to Arson?" asked Claris, glancing up at the birds circling in the sky.

Halvar straightened. "Gather some rocks. We will see."

"Arson will not be there, will it?" A hollowness filled Claris's voice. Bile burned in the back of her throat.

"If people make the place, then no." Brahim stood, the gathered rocks bundled into his cloak. "But it may still be there."

"We should keep moving," Halvar said, and walked towards the others.

"And the rocks?" Claris asked.

"After we reach Arson," Brahim said.

She leaned down to pat Pepin, even as her hands shook. "Good find..." The rest of her words dried up in her mouth. This was so much more than stopping a demi-lich. A deeper treachery ran underneath it. A shudder swept through her. Not only did she want to end the monstrosity, but she had to find the one responsible for its path of devastation. The person who saw the destruction of Arson.

Claris dismissed her negative thoughts. She had a purpose. The people of Arson would be avenged.

Brahim had got the men moving again by the time Claris bridged the gap between herself and them. Torsten stared at her, as if hoping she'd have an explanation, but she said nothing in return. Flore had moved up, leaving Torsten solely at the rear, with Claris trailing behind.

A part of her expected smoke or fire to signal Arson's downfall, but as the buildings came into view, it was quiet; the simple absence of anything. Pepin yowled and Claris's hairs stood on end. Something shifted ahead, deep into the town's centre. Brahim halted the group, drawing them to quiet. Hands went to weapons and Claris walked as softly as she could to Brahim's location.

"Is that..." She swallowed. The very air shimmered around its location.

"The demi-lich." Brahim had already unsheathed a knife. The men grouped closer.

She peered towards the creature. Though not close, even the vague features she discerned unsettled her. It hovered a little above the snow, the battered torn cloak hanging past the feet. Through the tears in cloth, bits of scarred flesh and bone, all with a grey glow, were clear.

Pepin pressed himself down low to the snow.

"We must go quiet. Circle around," Brahim said.

"Try to trap it?" Claris asked.

Halvar unhooked his mage-hammer. "I am not ready for that. I will help another way."

"Dalfin, Sigibert, you will go with Halvar to its north," Claris said, determined not to look at Brahim; she couldn't afford doubt to worm through her. "Roul with Brahim to the south. Flore and Odo can take west, while Torsten and myself east."

The garde all looked amongst themselves, and Claris braced herself to be told otherwise. She counted, and she got to four before someone spoke.

"We should attack now," Roul said, unsheathing his sword.

"Only attack on my order," Brahim said. "We will have one shot alone. I'll not have it wasted." Claris tried to assure herself that his eyes didn't linger longer on her than anyone else.

She would have felt better if an equal number were assigned, but she thought the spread of skills would be enough, provided she hadn't misjudged. Surely Brahim would've spoke if otherwise. He wouldn't risk this failing.

"Luck be with you," Claris said to them.

"Will guide us true," Halvar added.

Everyone shucked their supplies, not wanting the impediment. There was little worry for thieves. Claris had expected to see corpses littered throughout, but there were none. Not yet. The birds circled above though, so reason told her they would be present.

"You stay with me," she said to her lynx as everyone moved to their assignments. Torsten came to her side too.

"Am I here because you trust me the most or expect us to die first?" he asked, his sword and shield ready.

She nodded at his blade. "Because if it gets near us, I can do nothing."

He smiled despite their dire situation. "You trust me."

Her jaw clenched. She wanted to tell him it was the opposite. A man of the vicomte was best close by, where she could keep an eye on him. Wild thoughts made her even consider the vicomte responsible for the demi-lich.

She shook her head and slowly picked her way to their designated location. The closer they got, the more dread and disgust roiled inside her. She could now see why the birds were circling. It was because the corpses were in a pile. One the demi-lich presided over.

Claris dared not look too closely, not eager for the sight of children. The glimpse she caught was enough. Somewhere in that pile was likely Aalis and Yvain's family. She took a deep, pained breath. The sick feeling swirling in her stomach had to be pushed away. She had to focus. They had to end the demi-lich. It couldn't be allowed to do this again.

Torsten and Claris crouched low, using the buildings and snow mounds to cover their movements. Pepin barely made a noise beside them. He was used to stalking prey.

Torsten rested a hand on her shoulder, slight pressure pushing it down. Claris nodded and he removed his hand. She pulled free two knives; one to throw and another ready. Pepin sunk down into the snow; not even his tail moved. From their hunkered vantage, Claris had no sight on anyone else. Could the others see each other?

They seemed to be at the fringe of the demi-lich's magical influence, with the air a touch warmer in the space before them. Claris didn't want to know what the creature wanted with the bodies. Once the lich was dead, she would burn all the corpses to let them pass.

From here she could see that hung around the lich's neck was an amber-hued jewel. It pulsed like a steady heartbeat.

A thin slice of air shifted past her. She knew that feeling. Claris turned on her heel and found the thrown knife embedded in the wood behind them. She pulled the blade free, and Torsten peered over her shoulder. His proximity frayed at her nerves. She heard his breaths, could almost feel the beat of his heart. Etched into the side of the blade was a single command: 'Don't break jewel'.

It seemed like the perfect time to strike, and yet Brahim's words only puzzled her. The demi-lich was not moving and still was unaware of their presence. She took a deep breath and lined up her shot, then lowered her arm. She'd be ready when it was time.

A shout sounded at their south. The demi-lich seemed to shimmer and face the shout's direction in an instant. A wave of warmth crashed over them and dissipated as quickly. Brahim was in that spot. Was that the signal?

Torsten tapped her shoulder and pointed in Brahim's direction. Claris nodded. The demi-lich hadn't moved any further. Roul came into view, weapon raised and marching straight for the creature.

Time seemed to slow. Numbness tingled over her skin. Her head shook in denial.

"This is not the plan." Claris was certain Brahim would not permit such a reckless action.

The demi-lich glided towards Roul.

Claris would not watch one of her garde die so carelessly. She stood and threw her first knife. But the demi-lich moved at the last second and the knife sunk into its upper arm. It didn't even seem to notice the metal protrusion. Torsten pulled her back down. The other garde had the same thought as Claris though, all of them coming out at the demi-lich as if to box it in. Dalfin even let an arrow fly free, but it too seemed of no bother to the demi-lich.

"They're going to get themselves killed," Torsten said.

She pulled her cloak free from his hands. "That is why we cannot simply watch." The mage should've acted by now.

Torsten stood with Claris this time. She had another knife ready.

Roul was far too close to the demi-lich. Her voice caught in her throat.

The demi-lich stopped and reached out with his hand, his fingers only bone. Roul came to a standstill. One by one, the demi-lich curled its fingers into its palm. Roul stood before the creature, which towered over him. Claris blinked more than once. Snow dripped water from the buildings around them. Roul's arms were slack at his sides and he appeared to struggle against invisible bonds.

The demi-lich thrust his hand into Roul's chest, the crack of bone shuddering her senses.

Claris had her opening. Clenching her teeth, she forced the sound and visual from her mind. She threw her knife.

It should have struck.

But it fell uselessly to the ground just before the creature.

Roul's anguished cry pierced the air.

A blue glow caught Claris in the corner of her eye. Halvar had his mage-hammer raised. She still couldn't see Brahim. The other garde had halted their charge. As Halvar's hammer struck the earth, a force lifted Claris from her feet, and she slammed backwards into a building. Her head cracked against wood and white flared in her vision. Pepin yowled and she felt his paws on her chest. She closed her eyes.

A Death and Lies

Day 7

"Open them, Claris."

Torsten's voice was near, and her eyes snapped open to see blood trickle down from a cut on his forehead. Her head pounded and she wanted to purge everything inside her.

"Roul?"

Torsten held out an arm. "The mage appears to have scared the lich away."

"It got away?" She reached up and clasped his arm, letting him pull her up.

"For now," he said.

Her head spun and he helped steady her, as Pepin pressed against one of her sides.

"I must check on Roul. On the others." She moved away from his arms and towards where she'd last seen Roul. Her head still pulsed and she was sure it'd crack open. Torsten's voice was muffled, but she kept walking.

Water pooled where the demi-lich had stood, and Roul's crumpled form half lay in it. With unsteady steps she made her way over, collapsing down beside him.

His eyes fluttered open. Blood leaked from five puncture wounds in his chest.

"You will be fine, Roul," Claris said, though doubt fluttered in her chest, shifting around to put her arms under his shoulders. She pulled and dragged him from the water, falling backwards into the snow from the effort. His lips had turned blue. "I need heat," she called to anyone.

Torsten came over and Pepin sat, head tilted in curiosity over Roul.

"There is a building close by," Torsten said. "We should move him in there."

"I'll help," Brahim said, coming up from behind them. A bruise blossomed under his right eye.

Claris shifted out of the way and stood, retrieving Roul's fallen sword from the snow. Torsten and Brahim lifted his body, and Claris was relieved to see the other garde approach them. Halvar was still not visible. She hoped he had given chase to the demi-lich. Pepin had gone over to the water and Claris clucked her tongue. "Leave that." He cocked his head but came to her side as she hurried before Torsten and Brahim.

The building used to be someone's home. Plates sat on the wooden table, ready for a meal. Claris swept it all aside, cutlery clattering to the floor, so Roul's body could be laid down. Flore strode in and headed to the hearth.

"Is he still breathing?" Claris asked.

Brahim nodded. "He has but moments."

Roul groaned. His wounds still bled.

"He is still alive," she said. Claris slipped free a knife and sliced open his leather vest and woollen tunic underneath. The holes were neat, not at all what Claris expected bone fingers would make. They also were deep. Heat slowly filled the space with the fire lit in the hearth.

Claris looked at Torsten; his eyes showed no more understanding than her own.

She was no physician, but she refused to give up. While Roul breathed, she would do everything she could to save him, even if the others thought it futile.

"Flore. Find me the mage." Her eyes went back to Torsten. "Hot water. Clean cloths." She sighed towards Sigibert, who walked in with one arm limp at his side. "Sit before you pass out."

"Roul will not live," Brahim said.

Claris refused to believe that. "We will do what we can."

Sigibert sat. "Dalfin is also injured."

She scowled. "The mage could have killed us all."

"The demi-lich would've got there first," Brahim said quietly.

Her hands were slick with blood, but no matter the pressure she applied, Roul's wounds kept bleeding. It wasn't natural. Roul's breathing was irregular and shallow. She knew losing garde was inevitable, but she refused to let it happen without doing all she could.

Claris's head pounded, and nausea swam near the back of her throat. She blinked rapidly, forcing her vision to focus.

Torsten came back with a pot of water he sat over the fire and placed torn shreds of cloth nearby for her. Flore entered straight after with Halvar close behind, who looked unscathed. He went to the opposite side of Roul and pushed Claris's hands out of the way in favour for his own. She took one of the cloths to wipe her hands.

After a few moments of silence, and nothing visible happening, Claris spoke. "Can he be saved?"

Halvar removed his hands. "No. He is already gone."

Her eyes widened and she looked for signs of life in Roul but found none. He had passed. She swallowed and her eyes stung with the threat of tears.

"We need a pyre," she said. "Not just for Roul, but for the rest of Arson's souls."

"Their souls are already gone," Brahim said. "The demi-lich took them. It almost took Roul's."

Claris recoiled as if struck. "Halvar?"

The mage nodded. "It is what powers it so."

"That jewel?" Claris asked, eyes narrowing. She swayed a little on her feet. She should sit. "Then why not destroy it?"

Brahim looked to Halvar first before answering. "It would've sent it into a rage, and we weren't prepared for that."

She rubbed at her temples and took a deep breath. "Halvar, see if there is anything we can do for Sigibert's arm. Then I need to speak to you and Brahim."

She stared at Brahim for a moment. Her second knife should've struck the demi-lich. Claris left the house with Pepin at her heels.

Outside, she closed her eyes and took in deep breaths. Her head still ached and all she wanted to do was lie down. Pepin mewed once and dashed off. She let him, he was hungry.

Torsten jogged up to her. "Care to help me salvage?"

"Sigibert said Dalfin was injured?"

"A cut to his leg, but he's moving fine. A cut by Odo's sword in the chaos of whatever the mage did," Torsten said. "What about you?" Concern pinched his eyebrows.

Claris sighed. "I will be better after rest." She peered around the dead town. "We should be able to find what we need." She needed to keep herself busy, keep her mind off Roul.

"No horses though."

She didn't think there would be. They likely broke free and fled at the demi-lich's arrival. A small part hoped a few of the townsfolk escaped on them.

Her eyes snapped to Torsten's. "Did anyone escape up the river?" Arson sat at the river's end of a channel that went out to sea, where a prosperous port city sat proud.

"I don't believe anyone's checked," he said.

Claris orientated herself and headed towards where the river would be. It took them on the opposite path to where the others worked on preparing to burn the bodies. A few trees had been felled; their trunks lay forgotten in the snow. Past them, it didn't take long to reach the river's edge. A pier jutted out onto the water, where two rafts were secured. Claris walked onto the pier but saw nothing to indicate there had been a third vessel.

"If anyone did manage," she said, "it wasn't by water."

"Unless they swam." Torsten came up beside her. "We could always go upriver ourselves."

A fleeting desire to do that went through her, but she knew they couldn't. She'd failed those in Arson. There was only one way to stop it happening again. She turned back towards the land. "We must follow that lich."

Brahim found them on their return. "You wanted to talk?"

"Continue without me, Torsten," Claris said, following Brahim to a different home where Halvar stood before the hearth's fire.

"What happened?" Claris said, pointedly staring at Brahim, the bruise under his eye more prominent.

"We found another rune," he said and sat in one of the available chairs. "I told Roul that fighting the demi-lich was pointless. He punched me, called me a coward, and went to march to it."

Her eyes narrowed. "Another rune?"

Brahim looked to Halvar before he replied, "Like the other."

"How does a beacon make killing a demi-lich pointle..." She looked between the two of them and knew she'd be sick. The beacon wasn't to guide the lich. She staggered back and fell into a chair. "You lied." Her voice barely audible.

Halvar pulled his hood up. "You two should talk."

Claris wanted him to stop; he was complicit too. But no words formed. Brahim had led her into a futile encounter; her own garde into likely death.

Brahim knelt before her. "We expected."

Her eyes snapped to his, a flare of anger sparking through her. "We could have fired an arrow. No one had to get close. No one had to die."

He scowled. "If he wasn't a hot head, no one would have."

She let out a noise of disgust. "You best tell the truth."

"Someone has warded the demi-lich," Brahim said, and collapsed back to sit. Claris's insides churned. "A ward only a special blade can pass through. A blade we don't have."

"Can the mage remove the ward?"

"No," he said. "Wards like this are tied to life. We'd have to find the one responsible. The blade is quicker."

She breathed deeply; she needed to rein in all her roiling emotions before they flooded out.

"Claris." She looked back at him. Her name unfamiliar on his tongue. "We will have to go off path to get what we need."

Her gaze narrowed. "Did you tell the truth of the jewel?"

"It is a soul gem," Brahim said, a flash of pain crossing his face. Roul's loss must've have hit him hard. "Souls may power the demi-lich, but the ward guards it too."

Ziri flashed in her mind. "How do you know what we need, and where we would find it?"

Brahim stood. "That's my job."

"We will need to tell the others," she said and swallowed.

"Only if you trust them enough." He secured his cloak and left Claris alone. She wasn't sure if she could mislead the garde, not if she wanted their respect. But if they knew the truth... Claris shook her head. It would cause dissent, especially with Roul's death. She didn't want to be like Brahim, withholding information, even if was for the better good. The taste of it was like ash in her mouth. But she was no stranger to deception.

Once she composed herself, Claris went back outside. The pyre had been lit, and billows of smoke had scattered the birds away. Pepin had curled himself in front of a building a good distance away from the fire. All the garde stood before the burning bodies, heads bowed. Claris walked up and did the same. The smelled itched her nose and threatened to choke her throat, but she stayed. When Sigibert broke away, so did Claris. The nearby snow had melted down.

Both Pepin and Torsten approached her as she moved far from the fire. She knelt to give her lynx an affectionate rub.

"Without horses, we won't be able to carry too many supplies," Torsten said, "but I have collected what I think important. Please come look."

"I am sure you have done what is right," Claris said. She was drained and simply wanted to rest. She didn't even care for food.

"Please," Torsten replied, "I insist."

He appeared sincere enough, so Claris assented. He gave her a small smile, but she had no energy to reciprocate. Pepin followed behind them. Torsten led her to a small home near the town outskirts, close to the river. At the front of the home were all the men's bags and supplies in neat bundles, ready to be packed. But Torsten didn't stop there. He headed towards a side room, where heat drifted from. Pepin hung back and opted to stay near the front door. The room held a tub filled with water and a fire heating it from below. Torsten doused the fire.

"I thought you might like a bath," he said.

Tension ebbed away from her. She still hadn't quite figured how to place Torsten, but after everything, it was exactly what she needed.

Claris walked over and tested the water, eager to wash the blood from her hands.

"Thank you," she said. Torsten had even found soap. "But I do bathe alone."

A smile spread over his face. "As you wish." He took hold of the wooden screen and manoeuvred it to be before the door and he stepped back into the other room. "Call if you need me."

Not wanting the water to cool too quick, Claris shed her clothes and slipped into the bath. The soap smelt of lime, and she was convinced Torsten had scented the water with rosewater. Soap meant for another. They should be enjoying a rosewater bath. They should not now be a corpse, their soul stolen. She sucked in a shaky breath. She hoped she wasn't in Aalis and Yvain's family home.

As she washed the blood away, the water turned a pink hue. She was hyperaware of Torsten's closeness and heard him shuffling through the supplies. It was entirely inappropriate for a lady to bathe so close to a man's presence. Pepin slunk into the room and pressed his face against hers.

"No one will take me from you," she whispered to Pepin. He sat back and gave her a slow eye blink. She reached out and gave his head a scratch.

All those people dead. Roul dead. Her breath grew ragged. Her fingers trembled. Pepin purred softly, nudging his head under one of her hands. It shook from her spiralling. It wasn't the right time to cry, not here, in a bath, with Torsten so close.

The water was turning tepid when she realised there was no cloth to dry herself with.

"Torsten," she called.

"Yes, Demoiselle?" She swore she heard amusement in his tone.

"You appear to have neglected a key item. Pass a cloth over the screen, please." She paused and glanced at Pepin, his tail swished slowly. "Pepin would be more than happy to see you not comply."

A cloth was flung over the screen, as well a clean surcoat. Once dressed, Claris went back out. Torsten crouched down around the bags.

"That was nice," Claris said. "What do you hope for in return?"

His eyes shifted over her. "You should be afforded luxuries when opportunities arise." She crossed her arms, as her eyes narrowed. His actions, his words kept shaking the foundation she'd thought he stood upon. Perhaps she was wrong to think him a spy for the vicomte... but he did seem more wary of the demi-lich than the others.

Her next breath shook as she let it out. The stillness from the bath, the time to think, crashed over her. She swallowed heavily. A tremble took her hands.

"I..." Her throat thickened, and she couldn't form any more words.

Torsten closed the gap between them, pulling her smaller form into his chest, wrapping his arms around her body. "All will be okay. You're okay."

Claris didn't want to cry. She closed her eyes and took a few deep breaths. This was different to her mother's passing, and even Ziri's. This was violent, and avoidable. She knew setting out that losses were likely, but reality hurt. Pepin rubbed against the back of her legs. She had to ground herself again, not let herself be overwhelmed. She could do this.

Torsten didn't move, staying as still as possible.

Only when she was ready, Claris pushed herself back against his arms and he relaxed them to his sides. She dared not look up at him.

She walked to the front door. "I will be practicing outside if you have need of me." Pepin followed her out and she headed for the nearby trees. Without any to watch, she reverted to the practice she enjoyed most, throwing at a far distance.

Once she'd thrown the first few knives, the lynx bounded into the trees. Neither were concerned she'd strike him.

"There is the talent I need." Brahim's voice came from behind her.

She threw the knife she currently held and turned to face him. "Is there something you need?" She had no desire to converse with him idly. She'd not succumb to his praise so easily.

"We have a plan to acquire what we need," he said. "You may wish to partake."

"We?" She went towards the tree with her blades.

"Halvar gave me input." Brahim followed a few steps behind her. "But you know your land best."

Claris took her time in removing the knives, not wanting to face him. Not wanting him to see her uncertainty. Her knowledge was passing at best, and he only said what he had to try and appease her anger at him.

"Very well," she said. They sky above deepened, an orange glow highlighting the undersides of clouds. Pepin dashed around a tree. She wished she felt as free as the lynx in that moment.

Halvar stood in the doorway of the hut they were in previously. Claris scratched Pepin on the head and made her way over. She sat in one of the chairs around the hearth. She waited for one of them to speak first.

"Two items will be hard to acquire," Brahim said. "And then we'll need a smith to forge the weapon."

"Which will be a throwing knife," Claris said, not expecting it to be anything else.

"Aurichalcum is one item," Brahim continued, "and the other is volcanic glass."

"Did those rocks from the rune help?" she asked Halvar.

"Their dust will help," he said.

Claris pursed her lips. The mage divulged little and barely had a straight answer. She was beginning to think that was simply his way.

"And you know where to find such items?" she said, directing her gaze back at Brahim.

"We must travel across to Gien. There is a trader acquaintance that procures such glass."

Claris mentally recalled the map, knowing full well that Gien was not part of her father's county. It'd be more important than ever to shrug off her nobility in favour of a blade-maiden persona.

"But the aurichalcum we retrieve ourselves," Halvar added.

"Which will be on the way," Brahim was quick to add.

Claris looked between them. "That is the plan?" Brahim nodded. "And you propose a direct route?"

"With an ally at the demi-lich's side, delays are unwise," Brahim said.

"There will be the river town Ladonnes on that route," she said. "We will stop there for a night."

Halvar said nothing, and Brahim finally nodded.

"And we will have to tell the garde," Claris added. "We leave at first light."

She stood and went back outside.

The others had created a campfire to gather around, a good distance away from where the bodies still burned. What she really looked forward to was sleeping indoors for the night. She spotted Odo and Torsten to one side, heads close together. They were likely going to share space. She swallowed the heavy lump caught in her throat and turned away.

She didn't need Torsten anyway.

A Slow Procession

Day 8

Halvar shouldered Roul's old pack. Any one of them could've died, but it had been Roul. A fool, but defiant even in the face of death. She admonished herself. He might still be alive if she had only questioned Brahim and Halvar more strongly about those runes. Insisted on a more cautious approach to the demi-lich. Such mistakes were not ones she wanted to repeat.

The sun timidly peeked above the horizon, the day still early. None were sad to leave the ghosts of Arson behind. Flore and Torsten took the rear guard together. Claris pushed up front to beside Brahim.

He glanced at her. "How is your head?"

"Without issue," she replied. "We likely will not encounter the demi-lich again, will we?" Especially as their route would take them from its path.

"Does not mean there'll be nothing to trouble us," he said.

Claris stared out at the expanse of snow and trees, her mind preoccupied with worries of another snowstorm. She dreaded the idea of being forced into seeking shelter in caves again. Pepin, full of playful energy, darted around their legs and pounced at the snow.

Sigibert's arm was pulled tight to his chest in a sling, and Dalfin walked with favour on one leg. If there was trouble, Claris worried a few more might be lost.

She sensed Brahim shift beside her, her eyes meeting his before turning her gaze back to Dalfin. She still hadn't gotten to asking about his braces.

"At Ladonnes, you could leave them there," Brahim said.

"Garde would not accept that." It'd be a great shame to their families to forfeit a duty.

"They would if you ordered it."

Claris doubted it, but she cast a glance back at the garde. So far, they had shown no signs of wavering in their loyalty to her, but after Roul's death, she couldn't be certain how long that would last. After all, it had been her plan that led them here.

The sun reached its zenith when Odo jogged up to them. "We must rest. Dalfin cannot walk much further."

Claris held up her hand, signalling a stop. "It will not be long."

Odo nodded and went back to the others.

"If he keeps slowing our pace, you may be forced to," Brahim said and moved over to Halvar's side.

She sighed and went to check on Dalfin. The gash at the side of his left calf was red and angry, the flesh around tender to touch. Odo had cut the wound open again and washed clean water over it. The blood appeared dark. She wondered if he tended so carefully to Dalfin, because he blamed himself for the injury caused.

Claris crouched beside him. "Will he keep the leg?"

Odo whispered, "With how much we walk, it's uncertain. The rest helps, Demoiselle."

She nodded and stood. "As soon as Dalfin stands, we move." Claris went over to Torsten. "At the next town we may have to leave him there."

Torsten turned them away from the others. "He won't like it—"

"He cannot walk," she insisted.

"But we aren't without reason," he finished. "If you make Dalfin stay, then you should do the same for Sigibert. He cannot wield a weapon efficiently."

"That leaves us with three garde." She glanced back as Odo helped Dalfin back to his feet. "Time to move." Claris went back to the front. Pepin, now subdued, padded quietly at her side.

As the sun descended towards the horizon, Claris felt a sense of relief that the day had been uneventful so far. They had already made two stops along their journey, yet all they had seen were endless stretches of snow and trees.

She walked between Brahim and the garde, their footfalls creating a steady rhythm in the otherwise silent landscape. Their path cut through the rugged countryside, there was no rivers or paths here. Even the forest stood tall in the distance to their east.

Pepin went taut, his tail straight in the air.

Claris shot her hand up. "Halt!"

An arrow went over her shoulder and slammed into Sigibert's chest, who'd turned to look back at her.

"Down!" called Torsten.

Everyone hunkered down, and two more arrows speared the ground near them. Claris slid free a knife. The attackers likely believed they had the upper hand, but why were they there in the first place? If they were those that fled Arson, arrows wouldn't be a way to greet potential saviours. And yet if they were bandits, they must be desperate to be so far from the trade routes. She let out a shaky breath. Her father should've had the bandits under control in the county. The stability of his land was shakier than she ever knew.

A party of fifteen circled around them. Pepin pressed in close to Claris. Odo crawled over to Sigibert's prone form. She hoped it wasn't a fatal shot.

One of the marauders with a red beard spoke. "Give us your supplies, and you can live."

Claris ensured her cloak and hood hid most of her features.

"Or we can let you live." Halvar's rumbling reply jerked Claris's attention. He stood, and the runes on both his flesh and mage-hammer flared blue. Only a handful of marauders laughed.

She caught Torsten's gaze but couldn't discern the subtle gestures he made with his hands. Pepin growled. One of the marauders had come too close for the lynx's liking.

"There's a cat here," he called, and took a smart step back.

Claris clucked her tongue at Pepin and pulled him closer to her body.

"I would leave us be," Halvar intoned, his hammer ready at his side.

The few marauders near the leader murmured amongst themselves. A glance at Sigibert showed he still hadn't moved. Odo's hands were bloodied. Claris went hollow inside.

"Are we meant to be afraid of—" A knife stuck in the leader's throat. His hands grabbed at his neck; he fell forward onto his knees.

The others were momentarily stunned. Another two fell from Brahim's knives and chaos erupted. Halvar's hammer slammed into the ground. A few marauders were flung high and far. The garde stood with weapons ready. Pepin freed himself and pounced at the closet foe.

Claris had never taken a life, and she had no desire to do so. But she also knew she could not do nothing. She instead aimed to immobilise. Her first knife caught one in the shoulder, his grin feral when he spotted her. He didn't get far. Pepin was on him, jaws over his throat and claws sunk into his chest.

Blood pooled and splattered against the white landscape as Claris threw another knife, this time aiming for a knee, and then another at a hand. When only five marauders remained, they dropped their weapons and raised their hands in surrender. Pepin stood protectively before Claris, his fur matted with blood. The garde surrounded the defeated attackers.

Claris drew her shoulders back and walked over. A few other marauders lay in the snow, their moans telling her they still lived. She pushed past her garde and drew back her hood.

"You have two choices," she said. "Keep your lives and tend to your friends. Or die." Pepin prowled at her side, claws out.

"Little girl." The man's grin was feral.

"You won't survive out here," one said and spat blood onto the snow.

She stood before him, her gaze unyielding. "Live or die."

He looked between her, the lynx, and his fellow marauders. None of the others had the inclination to speak. He leaned forward. "Will you let me—"

Claris felt the knife go by her cheek and turned her face away as it struck his neck, blood bursting free.

"Live or die," Brahim said and came up to her side.

The remaining four nodded and wished to live.

Claris nodded towards Flore. "Take their weapons."

Turning away, her eyes alighted upon Sigibert's prone form. Her scalp prickled. Odo sat beside him.

She knelt and looked at Sigibert's unblinking eyes, his still chest. A heavy lump choked her throat. Her hands shook as she reached up to lay her palm upon his chest. To lose two garde in such a short span of time sat heavy and unbearable with her.

"If I was only quicker," she whispered. She'd barely got a chance to know Sigibert, or Roul. They were soldiers, figures in the party, but she knew so little. They deserved better from their leader.

"His death is not your fault," said Odo.

She closed her eyes momentarily. "We will see his body burned."

Odo peered at the marauders. "We should put distance between them and us, Demoiselle."

"I will not leave his body unburned," she replied. "He deserves better than that."

"We will carry his body and burn it at the next camp."

"Do what you must," she said. If she couldn't save her garde, she would do right by them in their passing.

Torsten walked over to her as Odo enlisted Flore to help with Sigibert's body.

"You have blood on your cheek," Torsten said.

She reached up and touched her face, her hand coming away with a few spots of blood.

"Let me." He reached up, braced one hand over her neck and used his cloak to wipe at her face. His lips turned into a small smile, and she focused on his sole dimple.

"Is it worse?" she asked, her voice soft and quiet.

"A little pink," he replied. His thumb reached over and slid over her cheek. "But the rose here enough to pull attention away from a little smudge."

She lifted her gaze to his and she felt herself warm under his sight. Clearing her throat, she stepped back, breaking the intimate moment. Torsten's hands fell back to his sides.

"We should get moving again," she said, her voice shaky.

"Of course... Claris."

She pulled her hood back up, hoping he wouldn't notice her blush.

Flore and Odo had used Sigibert's blanket and cloak to make a makeshift sled to pull his body along. Brahim watched over the marauders and only moved once everyone else was ready to depart. Rather than take the front, he fell to the back, likely to keep an eye on those they were leaving behind. Halvar took the lead in his stead. All evidence of glow from his magic gone.

The sun had begun its earnest descent to welcome the darkness, and Claris hoped they would put enough distance between themselves and the marauders by nightfall. She'd have to send messages to her father once they reached Ladonnes. He had to know. Action had to be taken to stop them.

Between Flore and Odo dragging Sigibert's body, and Dalfin's hobble, they covered little ground when darkness edged away the light. Claris went to Brahim as the others erected the camp. They'd salvaged two tents from Arson.

"Were we followed?" she asked.

"No, they were staying to tend to the wounded," he said. "And with snow on the way, our tracks will be covered."

A small campfire had been lit and Torsten and Flore worked to construct a pyre to burn Sigibert's body.

"We will not have enough garde once we return to the demi-lich," Claris said.

"As long as there is us, and the mage," Brahim said.

Pepin mewed for attention, and she leaned over to give him a head scratch. His fur still had traces of blood from those he killed. She stilled her shudder.

Torsten walked over. Pepin peered up at him, rubbed himself against Claris's leg, and then bounded away.

"I guess he trusts me," Torsten said.

"He simply knows you are no threat." Those words stilled her for a moment. Did that mean she could trust him? Claris shook her head, still unsure. She moved towards the campfire. "Is Sigibert's body ready?"

"Yes," he replied, "ready to burn."

Snow fell in light flakes. "Let us get it done."

The other garde already stood near the pyre, while Halvar and Brahim stood away to the side. Torsten handed her a torch. She lit it over at the campfire and walked back with it. She set the flame to the pyre and stepped back once it caught.

"In ashes you pass," Claris said, and doused the torch in the snow.

"We pass in ashes," the garde returned.

Worried about grief overwhelming her and crying in front of the garde, Claris moved away to the smaller campfire where Halvar already sat. They exchanged a brief glance, but neither spoke a word. When Dalfin returned, food was cooked, and Claris was grateful for the change from elk meat. Flore kept watch over the pyre as the others gathered around the campfire.

With food in hand Claris stood and went to her tent, where Pepin already curled himself up. She sat beside him.

"Did you find yourself food?"

He purred in response and took to grooming himself.

Torsten stopped at the tent's opening. "May I?"

Claris nodded and watched as he came in and seated himself beside her, so close the sides of their bodies pressed against each other. The extra warmth was welcome.

"You didn't kill today," Torsten said.

She stared at her food. "Perhaps my aim was bad."

His hand was ungloved, and she shivered as he touched her chin, coaxing her head to face him. "Your aim is perfect."

"They may die from injury yet." Her gaze went to his lips. She swallowed. "And why does it concern you?"

"Because you can't die." His hand loosened from her chin, but Claris pressed her own hand against his, trapping his hand against her neck.

"Because I can kill the demi-lich?" Her voice soft, almost breathless. His words, his actions twisted her insides. Part of her wanted to believe him sincere, and the other still whispered he was only manipulating her for whatever gain he'd receive from the vicomte.

"Because I couldn't live with that."

She sucked in a breath. Her heart kicked in a few extra beats. Weight on her lap drew her attention. Pepin climbed atop her, his tail swishing slowly. Her hand fell away from

Torsten to pet the lynx. Torsten's fingers lifted from her flesh, and she already missed the warmth of his touch.

"Why did we choose to doom ourselves?" Claris asked, her fingers absently skimming through Pepin's fur.

"That is what we are asked for," he replied. "And that is what duty expects. You threw yourself on this path for a reason only you know."

She looked over at him. "What if I now question those reasons?" She set out with the original task of ending the demi-lich, but it'd gotten twisted up with treacherous plots, and ulterior motives. It wasn't so simple anymore. Perhaps even beyond what she could manage.

"I'm not sure I'm wise enough for such answers." He returned her gaze, his mouth pulled to one side in a small smile.

Pepin mewed and laid his head down, closing his eyes.

"We have still six, maybe seven, days of travel left," Claris said, breaking eye contact from Torsten. Even her feelings were twisted within. A part of her pulled towards him, but that persistent reminder of his loyalty to the vicomte kept rearing its head.

"Our supplies will last until then."

She lifted her hand from Pepin, shuttering her expression. "It is probably wise for you to leave now."

Torsten waited a beat, but Claris refused to look his way or say anything. He stood and paused at the tent's entrance. "Perhaps you'd like a lesson in that hatchet one day."

"Are you hoping for now?" She glanced at the hatchet. She really should know how to wield it well.

He lifted one shoulder in a small shrug. "Unless you want rest?"

She shifted the lynx from her lap and stood. "We can try." None would raise a question at having her practice with Torsten. She'd done that countless times before with Ziri without issue. This would be safe to do.

Torsten smiled and led her not far from the rest of the camp, but enough distance to practice safely.

Claris held the hatchet in her right hand and all that came to mind was to throw it, but likely that wouldn't end well.

"So, feet shoulder-width apart, with one foot in front of the other. Then cut the area in front of you. Try some over-head and side-cut movements."

Claris tried to ignore the fact it was Torsten watching her like a hawk, not Ziri. This was for learning only. Nothing more. With each cut the more foolish she felt.

Torsten moved in behind her, leaning over and gently gripping his hand over hers. "Now, stop at the end of each swing. You want to keep that blade straight as you cut."

She inhaled; a shiver slithered down her spine. She let him guide her through the movement.

His grip loosened and he straightened. "You're a quick learner."

Claris twisted to look back at him, her eyes locking with his. "Perhaps it is the teacher."

His gaze drifted to her lips, then her neck. "I can teach many other things too." She snapped her gaze forward, hoping to hide her blush. His breath tickled the back of her ear. She bit her lower lip. "Especially to one eager to shuck the mantle of demoiselle."

A small, illicit thrill tingled through her. She knew she'd spoken of having to adopt a blade-maiden persona, but the idea of throwing it all away held a small temptation for her. She wouldn't have the weight of so many dead on her shoulders, treason to the king, none of it.

Though deep down Claris knew she never would really do that. Not to her father.

"Not the mantle," she whispered. "Merely the expectation I cannot be more than that."

"So, what is stopping you?" His lips grazed at her ears. She trembled.

Clearing her throat, she held up the hatchet. "Is that all to know?"

His warmth retreated, coming back to stand before her. "You can use it to hook an opponent's weapon down and out of the way and then strike with another weapon."

"Like a throwing knife?"

Torsten shook his head. "Like a sword, another axe, perhaps even a dagger." He looked towards the camp. "There is always Roul's sword."

"I am sure it is far heavier than what I can handle," Claris replied. She knew blade-maidens fought with such weapons, much like the garde, but her father didn't want any close combat for his daughter. The throwing knives were a consolation. That, and woman in Onvillia weren't known to ever raise a weapon of any sort.

"Only one way to know." He jogged off and returned soon with the sword. "Put the hatchet in your left."

Claris switched hands and took the sword. As expected, it wasn't light. "I am bound to hurt myself more than another." She struggled to lift and hold it without a waver.

"I'd never let you hurt yourself."

Another voice sliced through the air. "That sword won't work, Torsten." It was Flore. "She should try Sigibert's dagger instead."

Claris turned and they held out their hand to take the sword and in exchange gave her the dagger.

"Thank you," she said. Flore nodded and promptly left.

"They had a point," Torsten said with a smile. "Let us not tarry and give this a try before sleep beckons." He unsheathed his sword. "We will go slow."

They shouldn't have been training with sharpened blades, but Claris raised her weapons regardless. It was now or never. She couldn't predict when the next threat would appear, and she needed to do all she could to prevent another of her garde dying.

"As I bring the sword down at you, attempt to hook with the axe," he said.

She tensed, holding in her breath, waiting. As the sword cut down, she brought the axe down too, hooking the sword and pushing it aside, while bringing her other arm with the dagger up towards his chest. Its sharpened point stopped a finger away. The movements were slow, controlled, and allowed for Claris get a feel for the motion. They repeated the same steps at least ten more times, each time the tempo increasing. Her muscles burned, and all traces of cold chill vanished from her limbs.

Torsten sheathed his sword. "That's enough."

Claris took a ragged breath. "I am bound to feel that in the morning." She held the dagger back out to him.

"Keep it." He leaned forward, reaching towards her face. She became motionless. His fingers brushed aside a stray strand of hair plastered to her cheek.

Her hands ached from the cold. Her back throbbed. Her hair a tangle of wind, sweat, and days-old braids. Yet he still looked at her like that.

He slid behind her, his fingers in her hair, gentle and slow. He combed through it with his hands, separating each knot with care.

"You don't have to," she said quietly.

"I know," he said. "But I want to."

She swallowed, her throat tightening.

The wind carried a wail through the trees, but she stayed still.

When he finished, he pressed a hand to her shoulder. "Sleep well, Demoiselle."

He left her to walk back to the tent alone, Pepin still curled asleep inside. She lay back with a sigh and her mind drifted to his earlier words, and how she was tempted to invite him into the tent, just so she wouldn't have to sleep alone.

A Stolen Moment

DAY 9

A grey mist settled over the camp, casting an eerie pallor on the surroundings, while ash swept over the snow, carried by the biting wind. A sad smile passed over her; Sigibert's remains were free, just like his soul.

Brahim engaged in a deep conversation with Odo and Flore, their voices barely audible over the howling gusts. Dalfin came towards the tent, his limp still pronounced.

"These are for you," he said and held them out to Claris.

It was a new thigh strap for her knives, and a wrist sheath to hold two blades.

"From Brahim?" she asked.

Dalfin looked towards him. "He had me fashion them. Do you need a hand with them?"

Claris shook her head. "I will manage."

She looked again at his braces on his wrists and ankles. "Did you make them too?"

Dalfin turned one of his wrists around. "I did. My joints are a little more mobile than most, and this helps give them that stability."

"You are very skilled," Claris said with a smile. "And your leg? How does it fare?"

His face shuttered. "Do not worry about me, Demoiselle. I will not hold us back." With a polite nod he left her alone.

With determined focus, Claris first secured the thigh strap, the familiarity of the task easing her into it. But when it came to the wrist sheath, she encountered some difficulties. It took a few attempts to position and tighten it properly, her fingers struggling to find the right grip. Eventually, she managed to transplant her knives from the arm strap into their new sheath.

As if sensing her accomplishment, Brahim approached her, his presence grounding her amidst the swirling chaos of the camp. "They fit then?" he asked, a hint of satisfaction in his voice.

"Thank you," Claris replied, flexing her wrist to test its newfound weight. The pressure felt unusual against her skin, but she'd already adapted to a lot in the past week.

Brahim gestured towards her wrist. "Get used to it and practice retrieving the knife from there. We'll have time for that at our next camp."

"Where will we locate this aurichalcum?" Pepin reappeared and twined himself through her legs. She'd never heard of the metal before and knew it must be rare.

"The mage will let us know." Brahim looked down at the lynx before moving to take the lead.

As they continued their journey through the snow-covered landscape, Dalfin's limp became more pronounced, causing him to stumble several times. Odo acted as a sturdy support, offering himself as a leaning post whenever Dalfin required balance. Brahim's words of leaving him behind echoed through her each time he staggered, though. When he fell for a fifth time, Claris knew they couldn't continue their current course. The wind had intensified, whipping up snow around their feet, and decreasing their visibility.

They adjusted eastward, angling towards the forest. As the sky darkened, revealing the looming presence of the forest, alder trees stood abundant within its depths. Frost clung to their branches, transforming them into delicate webs of ice. Within the sheltered confines of the tree line, they found a small clearing where a fire could be built.

Claris was tired and cold, but she knew it was time to practice throwing from her new sheaths.

Excusing himself from Flore's presence, Brahim approached her. "You ready?" he asked.

Flexing her wrist, Claris admitted, "It feels unnatural."

"Give it a few days," he advised, his voice reassuring. He guided her away from the others and into the sheltering embrace of the forest. "You'll barely notice it then."

Unsettled by her conflicting emotions, Claris couldn't help but voice her concerns. "I am likely to cut my wrist before anything else."

A hint of amusement danced in Brahim's eyes as he smirked. "The sheath protects you from that," he reassured her. His gaze shifted momentarily, scanning their surroundings. "Where is your cat?" he inquired, his voice tinged with curiosity.

"Hunting for food. He will be fine."

Brahim pointed towards a sturdy tree nearby. "Then let's begin, shall we? Wrist or thigh only."

Taking her position, Claris prepared herself for the task at hand. But Brahim shook his head, denying her proximity. "At a distance," he said. "I've seen it before."

Respecting his guidance, Claris took a few paces back, creating the necessary space between them. With focused determination, she threw her first knife from her thigh, feeling a surge of satisfaction as it hit its target. After three throws, she found her rhythm, growing more comfortable with each motion. Finally, she reached for her wrist sheath, her fingers instinctively finding the loop of the knife. However, in her eagerness, she fumbled, and the blade slipped from her grasp, falling into the pristine snow below. Frustration threatened to consume her, but she managed to retain hold of the second blade, albeit with an awkward grip. Taking a moment to gather herself, Claris painstakingly adjusted her grip until it felt natural once again.

Brahim held up his hand but said nothing. Claris tried to keep still, tried not to stare towards him. She started to understand that Brahim sought to help, to improve her skill. He wanted to enhance what she had.

In swift, precise movements, he showcased his own mastery, throwing three knives effortlessly from his own wrist sheath. "You need to think less," he said, his words echoing in the stillness of the forest. With purposeful steps, he headed towards the trees to retrieve the blades.

Claris followed in his wake, her mind still grappling with the conflicting thoughts and emotions swirling within her. "Is the weight of the blade a factor?" she asked.

Pulling free one of the knives from its resting place, Brahim turned to face her. "Once again, you're thinking too much," he said. Sheathing the knife, he continued, "Let your instincts guide you. Trust in your training."

Sighing softly, Claris realized the truth in his words. Following directives that went against her nature was a challenge, but if it meant honing her skills as a blade-maiden, she was willing to try.

"Still thinking." Brahim smirked and held out her knives for her.

With a renewed determination, she accepted the knives he offered, their weight familiar and comforting in her hands.

He reached up, letting a braid run through his hand. "If you must, think on this. You don't dress like a demoiselle, your hair is certainly not appropriate, and your figure belies your status." He raised an eyebrow and shrugged. "You want more. If you want more, you must take it." Claris frowned a little. Without waiting on her response, Brahim stepped around her to leave.

The scent of cooked meat and onion wafted her way. She slid her knives back into their sheaths. The campfire wasn't far. She smiled when she spotted Pepin stalking through the trees, but Brahim's words needled at her. Bold words none in the court would dare speak towards her. He wasn't wrong, yet Claris didn't not want to be part of the nobility. She simply wanted more as well. Pepin and the impalement arts were the beginning.

She slipped deeper into the forest, seeking solace in the embrace of the towering trees. Resting her hand against the rough bark of a sturdy trunk, she bowed her head, allowing herself a moment of vulnerability.

"Mother," she started, "I think I have lost myself. I am not sure how to correct my course. My resolve to serve our kingdom has strengthened, for treason is afoot and Father needs my help more than ever. Yet being free from such courtly confines has opened me up in ways I did not think possible." She leaned her head against the bark. "I hope you are keeping an eye on Father."

Pepin rubbed against her legs, purring. Claris stood back from the tree.

She turned to leave, intending to rejoin the camp, but stopped abruptly when she found Torsten standing before her. A flicker of panic shot through her, wondering if he had overheard any of her private musings.

"We should stop meeting like this," Claris said, attempting to lighten the mood. She clucked her tongue three times at Pepin, who looked up curiously before bounding away into the undergrowth.

Torsten kept a respectable distance. "And yet," he replied, his voice low, the sound scraping against her very soul. "You don't seem to mind."

A blush crept up Claris's cheeks as she realized the truth in his words. "And why are you out here?" She gestured to the surrounding trees.

His eyes went to her weapons, then back to her face. "You shouldn't be out here alone. Not after what happened with Sigibert."

An involuntary shudder passed over her. "Then I shall return to camp with haste."

"Let me escort you," he said.

Neither of them made to move first.

Everything inside Claris twisted up and tangled. Logic warred with her heart, with her temptation. His proximity making the scales tip unfavourably for her station.

She sucked in a deep breath. Claris knew she shouldn't risk looking up at him, yet she couldn't dislodge her eyes from his. His gaze trapped her. There was an undeniable pull between them.

"We should go," she whispered, her voice barely audible amidst the hushed silence of the forest. "It is not proper." Her heart ached at the thought of denying her desires, but she knew the consequences of crossing that line.

Torsten's gaze held hers, eyes hooded. "And yet," he murmured, his breath warm against her skin, "that thought is anguish." His eyes dropped to her lips, and Claris felt her resolve weaken, vicomte or not. Two garde had died, and she was alive, but she had no idea for how much longer.

She stepped closer. Torsten tilted his head down towards hers. Anticipation coiled within her, and she stretched up on her tiptoes, her hands finding their way behind his head.

Their lips met in a gentle, intoxicating union. Warmth spread through Claris's veins as she parted her lips slightly, welcoming Torsten's tongue. His hands found their place at her hips, holding her securely. In that moment, everything else faded away, and all that remained was the sensation of his touch, the taste of his kiss.

But just as quickly as it had begun, the kiss ended. Torsten pulled back, leaving Claris breathless and yearning for more. She reached up with a trembling finger to touch her lips, savouring the lingering warmth.

The silence between them grew heavy with unspoken desires.

"Claris..." Torsten started. "What truth does your heart say?"

Her gaze lowered. "My heart has no place here." Claris took a step back, creating distance between them.

The coldness of reality settled over her once again, reminding her of why she had ventured out into the snow in the first place. She looked around, hoping none had witnessed their forbidden moment. The risk was too great to take.

"I..." Claris struggled to find the right words; her voice choked. An ache bloomed within her, tearing at her very core. "No words are necessary," she finally said, her voice barely above a whisper. "You know where this ends."

Torsten offered her a small, understanding smile before turning and walking away, his footsteps fading into the distance. Claris stood rooted to the spot, the urge to scream building inside her. Instead, she released a knife from her grip, watching as it soared through the air, landing perfectly on target. Again and again, she threw the blades, feeling the tension ease from her body with every precise movement.

Retrieving each blade with deliberate slowness, Claris then made her way back to her tent, where Pepin waited. The lynx curled up at her feet, a comforting presence amidst the turmoil within her. As she settled down for the night, exhaustion overtook her, and she drifted off into a restless sleep, though, again, no nightmares—nor dreams—plagued her.

A Quiet Reprieve

Day 10

In the cold, clear morning, they resumed their arduous journey, air thick with the sharp tang of frost. The biting wind persisted throughout the day, and all were grateful for the temporary respite provided by the shelter of the trees as they pressed on. Brahim, ever vigilant, ensured that they did not venture too deep into the forest.

As they walked, Claris seized the opportunity to practice pulling her knives free from the wrist sheath, determined to commit the motions to muscle memory. It didn't come as a surprise when Torsten, his presence seemingly ethereal, came up beside her. Claris fought the urge to be the first to speak, resisting the temptation.

"How was your practice last night?" he asked.

"You were watching me?" Claris kept her eyes fixed ahead, refusing to show any signs of surprise at his observation. She had thought he had left, but it seemed he had lingered nearby, ensuring her safety in silence.

"It is my duty," he said with a hint of pride. "Someone has to keep an eye on you."

She stole a quick glance at him, noticing the sly smile playing on his lips.

"Have we not been over this?" she asked, her tone laced with a hint of exasperation.

Torsten gracefully moved around her, positioning himself on the outer side, shielding her from any potential dangers that might lurk in their path. "Now you are shielded," he stated matter-of-factly.

Pepin, ever faithful and protective, padded up to Claris's other side. "He keeps an eye on me too," she said, her voice filled with playful defiance. Such lightness in her mood surprised even herself, after such loss, and pain.

Torsten glanced down at the lynx and chuckled. "He's not tall enough."

A sigh escaped from Claris's lips. "As your leader, I request you return to the rear guard."

Torsten's gait slowed, his steps becoming hesitant. "Of course... Claris," he replied, his voice carrying a hint of disappointment. He reluctantly obeyed her command, allowing a small distance to grow between them. She resisted the urge to look back at him, pushing aside the unsteady flutter in her chest. Pepin nudged against her leg, seeking comfort and reassurance, and she obliged, leaning down to give him a gentle scratch behind the ears.

She walked near the column of garde, her boots sinking into snow. She'd stopped feeling her toes two hours ago. Or maybe three. Time blurred when everything ached.

Boots crunched beside her. She didn't look up until they kept pace for more than ten steps.

Flore, she realised. They'd rarely spoken to her, though had jests plenty for the other garde.

"Alright, don't take this the wrong way," they said, "but you look like death."

She blinked. Flore's curls damp from snow, eyes too bright. They grinned like someone amused by their bleak surroundings.

She didn't answer. They kept walking, keeping pace beside her.

"I have a snack," they said, holding something out. "Could be venison. Could be horse."

She took it. "Thanks?"

They mock-bowed mid-step. "Your gratitude humbles me."

A long silence followed. After losing two garde, Claris wasn't sure she had it in her to smile anymore.

"You're doing fine, by the way," they said.

She stared at them. "We have lost two."

"Mm. Yes. Observant. And you think what, that makes you a fraud?"

Her jaw tightened.

"Don't give me that look. I've seen it before. You know what that tells me?"

She didn't answer. She might've now understood why she'd rarely seen others laugh when Flore prodded at them.

They leaned in, voice low. "That you give a damn. That's a good step."

Claris smiled, despite herself. Just a little.

"There she is," Flore said. "She still can smile."

She rolled her eyes. "You are ridiculous."

"Yet still alive." Their voice dropped slightly. "Their deaths aren't on you."

They walked for a while longer. Her grief had gone nowhere, but it had shifted.

"Thank you," she said finally.

They gasped. "She thanks me?"

"You are impossible."

They winked, then walked ahead alone. They hummed a cheery tune.

By nightfall, both the wind and snowfall had ceased, yet caution prevailed as they anchored their tents securely to the surrounding trees. While the aroma of cooking food wafted through the camp, Claris took a moment to observe those around her. Dalfin and Odo murmured quietly amongst themselves, their bond evident in their shared whispers. She was pleased that Dalfin's gait had improved, allowing them good coverage. Claris hoped it was a sign his leg was on the mend.

Seating herself near the flickering fire, she retrieved her knives and began the task of oiling and sharpening them.

Brahim dropped his own knives at her feet. "If you would be so kind."

Claris looked up at him, momentarily taken aback by his request. She glanced between him and the knives before pulling them towards her without uttering a word. After his gift of gloves and sheaths, she didn't begrudge the request. In fact, it took her aback. Having another care for your blade was seen as a sign of respect, of honour.

The familiar routine provided a welcome respite from the whirlwind of thoughts that filled her mind. As she diligently worked on Brahim's knives, Torsten approached, a bundle of swords cradled in his arms.

Her hands stilled. "What is this?"

His smile was warm. "We'd be honoured to have your skilled touch as well," he said, placing the swords before her.

She looked over at the garde and spied Brahim winking at her. Taking a deep breath, she returned her regard to Torsten. "They trust me?"

Torsten nodded. "You're their leader. You should see we fight with a fit blade. Mine is on top." She sucked in her lower lip, suppressing any retort that might escape. His playful nature was infectious. Seeing this, his smile widened, eyes gleaming with mirth. "I'll be sure to bring you food as payment."

Pepin had returned and gave the pile of swords a cursory look before slipping behind her into the tent.

Torsten lingered for a moment longer, his eyes locked with hers. Claris felt a flutter of anticipation in her chest, but quickly dismissed it, returning his gaze with a determined resolve. "You can go now," she whispered.

His smile widened further as he walked away.

Claris left Torsten's sword till last. Most of the blade and handle were unadorned and could easily be misplaced as a stock sword for the king's own garde. The only decoration was a single rune engraved up at the hilt. It entranced her, and she wondered if Halvar could use it in magecraft or not.

As if summoned by thought, Halvar loomed over her.

"Do mage-hammers need sharpening?" Claris asked. Pepin gave a small hiss from behind her.

Halvar chuckled. "No. They do not. Have you slept well?"

Claris keenly felt the loss of the brooch she had given him all over again. "I have. Thank you."

He gestured down at the sword. "Rune of luck."

Her finger traced the intricate lines of the rune, her mind filled with wonder. "Luck?" she repeated, her voice barely above a whisper.

Halvar nodded. "It has been done while the blade was cold. No magecraft."

"Maybe you will tell me where we will find this aurichalcum." Claris put the sword aside.

"Between wood and river, deep in lies," he replied. "Yes. A few days more." As if trapped in thought, Halvar ambled away.

Claris glanced behind at Pepin. "I may understand your dislike, boy."

The lynx mewed in response, satisfied with their shared understanding. With a smile lingering on her lips, Claris returned to the task at hand, focusing on Torsten's sword and pondering why he had chosen luck as its defining characteristic.

Once Claris had finished, and returned the blades to their owners, she nudged Torsten with her toe.

"I think I need more practice." She was aware of the other garde looking up at her, but she knew she spoke truth. One lesson alone wasn't enough for her to feel confident in using the hatchet, and now the dagger too.

Torsten came to his feet willingly, and the others cleared the way, leaving one side of the camp beside the fire free. Claris hoped to do it in a more discreet location, but that choice seemed to have been taken away. Yet, it was likely for the best. It was practice, as she'd stated, and nothing further could happen from it.

They started with the same, controlled movements he'd shown her previously. Not only for her to follow easily, but also not to harm one another. As her limbs loosened, and she forgot about being watched, her movements smoothed, becoming more automatic.

"You're dead," Torsten said, his sword pointed up at her throat.

"Again." Claris refused to give up. She had to be better. Dead couldn't be an outcome she accepted, not anymore.

Three more times Torsten showed how he would've killed her. Only once did Claris find her voice to make him stop and show her something in slower detail, going over it step by step until she understood the flow. Torsten was unexpectedly patient.

Brahim's voice then spoke up from the fireside. "Another night I can show you how to combine that with your throwing knives. Blend the two skills."

Claris tucked the hatchet and dagger away. "That would be most welcome."

Flore glanced up. "I can show you a few tricks as well."

"If you don't tell my father, I will be most grateful," Claris said and smiled, for surely, he'd see this type of combat skill a step too far. But something else niggled within. A spark of hope that perhaps the remaining garde respected her, for surely, they'd not offer if they didn't.

Perhaps she was now a step closer to embracing what it meant to lead.

What it meant to be a blade-maiden.

A Life Taken

Day 11

As dawn broke, fiery orange hues danced in the deep blue sky. Claris stood before her tent, a sense of awe washing over her as she admired the breathtaking view. Pepin weaved between her legs.

Meanwhile, Odo diligently worked on dismantling the tent, his hands skilled and precise. Catching Claris's attention, he spoke up, his voice tinged with excitement. "Demoiselle," he began, "I must confess, I'm not sure I've ever had my sword so sharp before."

"Then, you are welcome." She pulled the hood up over her head. "How is Dalfin's leg?"

Odo's face softened with concern. "The wound appears to be healing well, but he still struggles with putting too much weight on it."

Claris nodded. "Thank you for tending to him," she said before stepping away from the tent. With Claris out of his way, Odo moved swiftly, his actions reflecting a newfound agility.

Later, as they walked, Brahim fell back from the front to walk beside Claris. His brows furrowed with worry. "We may have a problem," he said.

Claris surveyed their surroundings, searching for any signs of danger. "What is it?" she asked, unable to detect anything alarming. Pepin loped at her side, also unperturbed.

Brahim's forehead creased further. "I've sensed something on the ley traces, and it isn't our demi-lich."

"Can you tell what it is?"

Brahim's voice dropped to a hushed tone. "It could be a faierie or even a goblin."

"You've likely sensed the Goeblin," Halvar said from behind. "The underground we must seek. Goblins love aurichalcum. The Goeblin is their home."

She sighed. "That does not sound promising." The idea of an underground destination didn't sit well with her, especially if it involved goblins; creatures that mostly kept to themselves and caused little grief, but woe to those that stumbled into their area. She would've preferred the faierie.

"Should be easy," Halvar said.

Claris looked to Brahim, but he shook his head. "We will have to assess once we're closer."

As the day progressed, clouds crowded the sky, attempting to obscure whatever light was on offer. Torsten approached from behind, his voice laced with concern. "I think we might have a problem," he said.

Claris's step faltered, a sense of trepidation settling in. "That is the second time today I have heard those words."

"There may be a tail," he replied.

"Are you certain?" Claris asked, her eyes scanning the surroundings. Pepin had darted towards the trees not long ago, perhaps sensing something amiss.

Torsten's tone was resolute. "Yes, there is definitely someone following us."

She gazed at him a moment before she nodded. "They may simply be foraging. Do you think it more than one?"

"I'm no tracker," he said, "but it appears to be one man."

She glanced again towards the trees. "Then one man is no threat."

Torsten's hand strayed to his sword. "Unless his own party are camped deeper in."

A chill ran down Claris's spine as she pondered the implications of his words. "Let us hope that is not the case."

Torsten nodded in agreement and moved towards the other garde, readying themselves for whatever may lie ahead.

Worry nipped at Claris. She knew Torsten spoke of a true possibility, but she needed the garde strong and rested if they had to enter goblin territory. They were three days out from Ladonnes, so the likelihood of a foraging party (especially in this weather) was slim. The prospect of more marauders caused a shudder through her. They were still in her father's county. Had it always been this bad and she was too blind to see it? Or had her father simply not shared such information with her because it wasn't seen as a womanly concern? An almost sliver of begrudging gratitude rose up in her for the demi-lich's presence. Without it, she'd still be sheltered.

Just as anxiety threatened to overwhelm her, Pepin emerged from the trees, bounding towards them. Instinctively, her hand reached for a knife, her grip tightening in anticipation. However, Pepin's actions quickly reassured her, as he circled once around her before pressing against her leg with a purr. A wave of relief washed over Claris as she realized there was no immediate danger.

Halvar and Brahim had stepped aside for a private conversation while the rest of the garde continued forward. A soft blue glow emitted from Halvar's arm, catching Claris's attention. Pepin mewled up at her, sensing her restlessness.

"Stay with the garde, boy," she instructed him softly before making her way over to join Halvar and Brahim. They had crouched down in the snow, their expressions grave.

"Is there something I should know?" she asked.

Brahim glanced up at her. "We're two days from the Goeblin."

"And is the ley telling you that?"

Halvar stood and Claris resisted the impulse to step back. "The tunnels are deep underneath us. We hoped to be closer."

Claris looked between them. "We should keep moving. We may be followed."

"By the marauders?" Brahim stood.

"No," she said. "Could be hunters. May simply be one man."

Halvar lifted his hammer from the ground. "Then we stay alert."

With their conversation concluded, the three of them rejoined the rest of the group, Pepin once again by Claris's side. As they continued their journey, Claris couldn't shake off the feeling of impending danger. Every rustle in the underbrush and every gust of wind sent a shiver down her spine. She remained on guard, waiting for an ambush that never seemed to materialise.

Only when they finally set up camp did some of the tension dissipate. Odo and Dalfin took charge of cooking food, while Flore and Torsten approached Claris.

"We think two garde should take watch rotations," Torsten said.

Her eyes widened a little in surprise. "Because of our tail?"

"Yes, though I have not spotted them for some time."

"We don't want to be caught unawares," Flore added.

"They would be longer watches," Claris said. "Tiredness can also be a liability."

"It will not impact the distance we cover tomorrow," Torsten replied.

Claris sighed. It wasn't their travel abilities that worried her. But she didn't want to concern them with the looming prospect of goblins. Not until they were closer.

"Demoiselle?" Flore prompted.

"Yes. Do as you suggest."

Flore nodded and headed back to the campfire, but Torsten lingered.

"Was there something else?" she asked and pulled back her hood. She sorely wished to sit.

"Pepin sleeps with you all night?" he asked.

Her eyes narrowed. "Yes. It would not be wise to sneak into my tent."

A faint smile tugged at the corners of Torsten's lips. "I have no intention of attempting to infiltrate your tent, Demoiselle Claris." He chuckled softly. "I am merely ensuring that Pepin remains by your side, in case our tail proves to be less than friendly."

A mixture of relief and amusement washed over Claris as she glanced towards the forest. "Let us hope our worries prove to be unfounded," she murmured, her voice laced with a hint of optimism.

"If that is all?" Torsten looked between her and the tent.

She swallowed. "Yes. You may leave."

"As you wish." He returned to the others.

Seeking solace and comfort, Claris retreated into her tent, grateful for the opportunity to finally rest. Pepin uncurled himself and settled onto her lap, providing a sense of warmth and companionship. She stroked his fur gently, whispering words of reassurance.

"Promise not to stray far tonight, boy," she said, scratching at his head. He purred. "Good boy."

The scent of cooking meat made Pepin restless, and he walked from the tent in hunt of his own food. Claris stretched out her legs and flexed her wrist. Though she was hungry, she was in no rush to eat. With Pepin gone, and with everyone distracted by the food, she could take a chance to practice some more. Claris told herself she wouldn't go too far.

Slipping out of the tent, Claris walked towards some trees nearby that offered good targets. She could still see the camp, but knew she wasn't too close. It was the solitude she needed.

Just then, cold metal pressed against her neck and a hand clamped tightly over her hip. Warm breath ghosted over her.

"Be silent." The voice was masculine and raspy.

Claris flexed her wrist and tried to grab a knife but failed.

His fingers dug in sharply. "No struggling."

His body odour was mixed with wood smoke. He must have a camp nearby to smell like that.

Was she still in sight of her own? The thought had her head turning, but the blade pressed in further.

"Take her weapons," her captor said.

Another man walked from behind her and unbuckled her thigh straps, though didn't see her wrist sheath.

"You sure she's noble?"

A thumb stroked over her chin. "Those men are garde. They don't go nowhere without a fat purse."

They wanted her for a ransom. She figured gaining attention would be worth the risk. Claris clicked her tongue.

Her head snapped to one side, pain searing through her cheek. Blood trickled into her mouth, the metallic taste a bitter reminder of her vulnerability. She hoped the commotion would alert her companions, providing them with an opportunity to come to her aid. Though she loathed the idea of being saved.

"We gotta go," her captor said and pulled her backwards. The other was still before her, the knife away from her throat.

She squirmed in his grasp while reaching to her wrist. Swords drawing clattered over at the campfire.

A low growl came from her left. Pepin had returned.

"What the—" The man before her fell sideways with Pepin's jaws around his neck.

Claris pulled a knife free and thrust it back into her captor's side.

His grip loosened and she pushed forward. He fell back into the snow, her knife still lodged in his side. She didn't dare to get near, instead pulling free her other knife and aiming for the jugular. His body jerked, he gurgled blood, then stilled.

Tears stung her eyes as Brahim, Odo, and Torsten all closed in around her. Pepin pushed through their legs and pressed up against her. Blood dotted her fingertips and her entire body shook.

Brahim wrapped an arm around her shoulders. "Get rid of the bodies," he said to the garde.

Claris leaned into Brahim. She wanted to collapse down, wanted to hold Pepin and weep freely. She didn't even notice the warmth of the fire as Brahim coaxed her down to sit. Flore hovered nearby.

"Take Halvar and check to see if there may be others," Brahim said.

Despite the flames, Pepin remained close by Claris's side, licking away the blood from her fingers, offering a small measure of comfort in this dark moment. Brahim's hand moved soothingly up and down her arm as she silently wept, her body trembling with the remnants of adrenaline. She noted the wrinkles on the back of his hand, reminding her how long Brahim had survived doing such a deadly profession.

"I... I killed him," Claris whispered through choked sobs, her voice barely audible even to herself. She looked down at her bloodstained hands, her heart heavy with guilt and remorse.

"You did what you had to," Brahim said. "The moment he laid hands on you, his fate was sealed."

His jaw was set tight, though lines pinched at his eyes with evident worry. Pepin chirped and pushed his head at her hands.

She thought she was fine, but a fresh wave of tears fell.

Brahim kicked the fire out. She wondered if it was to give her privacy in her weeping, or to hide their location.

"I was sixteen when I first took a man's life," Brahim started. "Bandits came to our village." Claris sniffed and pressed in close to his side, her body seeking a new source of warmth. He took her hands into his, giving them heat. "There weren't many, but none would go quietly. I'd gotten myself separated, and then there was one. Just me and him."

She squeezed his hand. "Put my sword right through him. He didn't die straight away, but I was so stunned that it didn't occur to me he wouldn't." He freed his hands and lifted a hand to her chin, lifting her head. "How you feel is normal."

Claris wiped away her tears, her breathing steadying as she absorbed Brahim's words. "But I threw a knife... into his neck," she whispered, her voice filled with a mix of disbelief and self-doubt. "Without hesitation."

He held her gaze. "You didn't let him die suffering."

Claris swallowed hard, grappling with the weight of her actions. "I am not sure if mercy makes it any easier," she admitted, her voice trembling.

Brahim's smile was filled with compassion and reassurance. "Perhaps not, but it speaks volumes about the strength of your character." He paused for a moment before adding, "You did what you had to in order to protect yourself and those you care for."

She sat up from Brahim and reached out to Pepin. "How many have you killed?"

He sighed. "It is a count I don't indulge. I do try and keep the killing to malevolence only." He stood. "But sometimes killing is the only action one can take to survive themselves."

Her hands stilled in Pepin's fur. "I do not want to sleep now."

"You'll surprise yourself," he replied.

Claris nodded and took a deep breath, wiped away all her tears and stood. She'd keep a brave face on for the garde. She didn't think they'd respect her for breaking down like that.

Flore found their way towards her, guided by the low blue light of Halvar's hammer. "It appears to have only been the two."

"Did we burn their bodies?"

"No," they replied, "we want to minimise any attention we could draw."

She swallowed, a heavy lump settling inside of her. "But... their souls." Taking a life was one matter, but not releasing their souls seemed almost inhuman.

"An unfortunate reality for many who die in combat," Flore said.

"As we near the Goeblin, undue attention is unwise," Halvar added.

"We should all get sleep," Claris said, and headed towards her tent. Pepin padded at her side, his head swivelling to both sides. She needed to be alone more than ever.

A Language Revealed
Days 11 & 12

Claris gave up sleep and slipped out of the tent. Pepin was content to stay near the blanket. Under the moonlight she noticed with a furrowed brow that there was no one on watch. Unless they had scouted further than she could see. She settled herself near the now dead fire, her delicate fingers instinctively caressing the familiar weight of her knives on her thigh.

His face wouldn't leave her. The way he staggered. The way his hands had twitched before going still. The way her knife had sunk in.

She hadn't wanted to watch him die. But she had. And now she couldn't blink without seeing it.

"You know," came Flore's voice behind her, "if you're going to sit out here brooding in the dark, you could at least make it dramatic."

Claris looked up to see Flore standing behind her, their presence almost ethereal in the darkness. Their large eyes caught the dim moonlight, giving them an owlish appearance. She sighed softly, feeling comforted by their company.

"You also shouldn't be out here alone."

"That is what they tell me," she replied, a hint of weariness in her voice.

"You've been doing well, given everything," they said.

Claris patted the ground beside her. "Please. Sit with me."

They glanced around and sat. "Odo is out there somewhere."

"Are you also on watch?" Claris asked, trying to peer out into the darkness, hoping nothing foul had befallen Odo.

Flore ran a hand through their hair. "I'm afraid I'm little help in this gloom. My night vision is poor."

Claris glanced at their profile and sighed. "I should know all of you better. Should have known Sigibert and Roul better." She pulled her knees closer to her chest, seeking solace.

"What matters is the skills we offer," they said, and grinned. "Dalfin, for example, is an excellent shot with his bow. Well, I fancy myself to be quick." They cleared their throat. "Some households are so large that many garde go unnoticed, unknown. You're doing fine."

She hugged her knees closer. Silence enveloped them for a moment. Claris stared into the darkness, trying to clear her mind from the weight of their journey and the uncertain future that lay ahead.

"You want to talk about it?" they asked. They held out a flask. She took it. Didn't drink.

"No."

"Want to pretend it didn't happen and talk about something else?"

"Yes."

"Romance, then. Easy."

She blinked. "Romance?"

"Obviously." They leaned back. "Tell me, what's your type? Other than below your station and soon-to-be-dead?"

She didn't answer.

"Perhaps, a certain garde by the name of Torsten?"

Heat flushed her cheeks. "You are mistaken."

"Perhaps," they said. "But not blind. Now, me? I like them sharp. Quick with a blade. Bonus points if they might poison me at dinner. Keep things spicy."

She finally took a sip from the flask. Bitter. Strong.

"Do you always do this?" she asked. "Jest until people forget what hurts?"

Their smile didn't reach their eyes. "It's either that or cry before the others. Can't ruin my image."

"We cannot have that."

"Exactly."

They shifted closer, their presence offering a comforting warmth in the cold night.

"You're still breathing," Flore said. "That's what matters."

"It should not feel like this," she whispered.

"It shouldn't. But it does. First kill always does."

She looked at them then. "Does it ever go away?"

"No," they said. "But you learn to carry it."

They sat in silence a little longer, the flask passing between them. And when Flore finally stood, they left without another word.

She sat a while longer.

Pepin purred lightly as Claris lay back down beside him.

Cold air rushed in as someone jostled her blanket.

"We need to move soon," Brahim said.

Pepin stretched out, yawned, and padded past Brahim to go outside.

Claris's eyes were sore, and she felt the bruises down at her side and hips. The areas were tender to touch.

"I will not take long," she said.

Brahim lingered. "Did you sleep well?"

She pulled her cloak back on. "I will be fine to travel."

The first person her eyes landed on after leaving the tent was Torsten. Her cheeks flushed as she recalled Flore's words, a mixture of curiosity and uncertainty swirling within her. She quickly looked away, busying herself with securing her belongings onto her back. Her reputation was already on unsteady ground, with whatever the vicomte now believed about her absence at court, so she surely shouldn't continue such a reckless path to ruin. She had to think of her father.

"We will be in goblin territory tonight?" she asked Brahim, as he packed down the tent for her, his movements swift and efficient. She was eager for distraction to such thoughts of Torsten. Her passion wasn't important to the journey. That wouldn't defeat the demi-lich.

"Yes," Brahim replied and moved over to Halvar.

She swallowed. At least goblins weren't humans. Likely she'd be fine.

As the garde moved out, Claris walked to her usual position between Halvar and Brahim, and the garde, while Pepin returned to her side.

As did Torsten.

"Flore said you didn't sleep."

"I had some," she replied evasively, not wanting to delve into the details of her restless night. She hoped Flore had kept their conversation private.

"You should have woken me," he said, eyes filled with concern.

She glanced at him, a mixture of gratitude and hesitation in her gaze. "So more of us could be tired?" she said, trying to hide the flicker of emotion that threatened to surface.

He smiled, a warm and genuine smile that tugged at her heart. His lone dimple drew her eyes. "It would have been worth it," he said, his voice filled with sincerity.

Claris shook her head, a mix of frustration and admiration coursing through her veins. "I am sure I have told you before, you must also look out for yourself."

His smile widened, and she couldn't help but feel a flutter of something deeper within her. "Perhaps I am."

Pepin mewed from his place beside Torsten, as if he understood the unspoken exchange between them.

"He seems to disagree," Claris quipped.

Torsten chuckled softly now, his laughter like music to her ears. "Let the cat think what he wants," he said. "But I am staying by your side this walk."

"Do not think me a great conversationalist." Claris already felt the brush of unease. If Flore had picked up something between her and Torsten, had the others? She wasn't sure she'd last an entire day with him at her side.

His smile vanished. "That is fine. Armour has no voice."

Claris held back a sigh. She turned her attention to adjusting the wrist strap, determined to improve her skills. Every so often, she felt Torsten's gaze upon her, a silent reminder of his presence. If he had no words for her, then she too would stay silent, lost in her own thoughts.

On their occasional momentary halts, she watched Brahim kneel and press a hand into the snow. She figured he was ley tracing, correcting their path towards the Goeblin.

"What would you prefer?" Torsten asked.

Claris pushed the knife back into the sheath.

"The forest or the river?" he continued.

"River," she said, thoughts straying to the estate in Grecy, and the short walk it was to that nearby river. Many called it the capital river.

"Because a river will always be there?"

Claris's forehead creased. "Never given it much thought."

"I'd prefer the forest," Torsten said and waved towards the one they walked beside.

She already warned herself to not grow close, to not become too familiar. But the conversation seemed innocent. "And why?"

"The mystery to it. Go deep within and you'll never be quite sure what you'll find."

Claris glanced up at him, studied the wistful expression on his face. Torsten fell silent when she said no more, but he continued to stay at her side.

With night's arrival, Claris was keenly aware of Torsten's absence as he assisted with the camp's set-up.

Dalfin sat with his bad leg stretched before him as he lit and encouraged the campfire.

Claris stood nearby, her awkwardness colouring the rest of her face. She cleared her throat. "Is there anything I can do?"

Dalfin looked up, bewilderment in his eyes. "Are you sure, Demoiselle?" Everyone else was preoccupied. She nodded and Dalfin pointed at the pot. "You could set that to melt snow. Overnight it will cool, and we'll have more water."

"Of course," Claris said and crouched by the pot. She scooped in the snow until Dalfin indicated it was enough. Once she set the pot over the flame, Claris left Dalfin in peace. The tents were erected and Halvar drew runes in the snow around the perimeter. His skin flared blue on the completion of each one.

Claris wandered over. "What runes are these?"

"Wards," Halvar said. "Won't work on humans. Suitable for goblins."

She looked down at the design. "Thank you."

He grunted and moved to draw another.

"You should not go off on your own," Brahim said from behind her.

"Pepin was with me before," she replied and turned around. She hadn't even left the perimeter.

"Even runes are fallible." He gestured at her wrist. "How does it go?"

Claris slipped free a knife and held it out to Brahim.

"Good," he said. "But can you follow it with a throw?"

She looked around before pulling free the second knife and threw it towards the closet tree. Brahim walked over to the tree, and Claris was quick to follow. He pulled the knife free and held it out towards her.

"You're a quick study."

She took the knife. "It did seem prudent."

Pepin's yowl cut the air and Claris spun in his direction. He raced from the trees with his tail tucked low. Claris crouched and let him barrel into her arms. His body trembled under her hands. A complete check over his limbs showed no visible injuries.

"What spooked you, boy?" She pressed her face close to his.

Odo and Torsten moved over in their direction with hands ready to draw their swords.

Pepin purred as he rubbed his cheek against Claris's.

Nothing came out of the forest in chase of the lynx.

Claris only stood once Pepin had calmed.

"We should move back inside the runes," Brahim said.

She clucked her tongue at Pepin, signalling "come, boy."

Brahim's head tilted to one side. "Ziri taught you that tongue, didn't he?"

Claris stilled. Since he'd yet to comment, she'd hoped he hadn't noticed her using one of the Djeya dialects in her communications with Pepin. Ziri had taught her some of the click languages in Djeya used by the central nomads.

"Only a few commands," she finally said, looking down at her lynx.

"Not many foreigners can master those pronunciations."

It was true, Claris had initially struggled with creating the necessary pocket of air between her tongue and roof of her mouth, but she'd eventually mastered what she needed.

"I would be unable to have a conversation in it," she admitted. "But he thought it a smart choice to use a different language in my communication with Pepin, in case a need ever arose where I was in danger. I could mask my intentions."

"Nevertheless, it is impressive." Brahim gave her a rare small smile and went over the fireside.

Snowfall came down in light flakes and Claris sought shelter in the tent, with Pepin still close at her side. She checked Pepin over once more for peace of mind but still found nothing.

"I am glad you are okay."

He curled up on her lap, letting Claris scratch the top of his head.

Brahim poked his head into the tent. "Join us at the fire. We must talk of our plan for tomorrow."

She shifted Pepin from her lap and stood. "Stay in here, boy."

"I do advise that Dalfin shouldn't join us in the Goeblin," Brahim said, his gaze settling on Dalfin as they walked towards the fire.

"He moves slow." Claris glanced towards Dalfin. "If you think it safer."

Food and wine were passed around the fire and she sat beside Brahim. Halvar remained standing. Whatever conversation the others had died away at her presence.

"Our goal is to retrieve aurichalcum tomorrow," she said to the garde. "As we do need speed, I must ask you, Dalfin, to remain at camp here."

"You'll have no complaint from me, Demoiselle," Dalfin replied and took another swig of wine.

She swallowed. There was a faint churn to her insides. "Therefore, I must ask another to stay with him." She sensed Brahim's gaze on her, but she refused to look his way. She wouldn't be the one to say.

Eventually Flore spoke, "I'll do so, Demoiselle."

"Thank you," Claris replied.

Brahim leaned towards her and whispered, "The cat should stay too."

Claris shook her head. "He goes where I go."

Brahim stood. "We should avoid the goblins where possible, or risk being overrun."

Halvar spoke. "Their home, the Goeblin, its walls are lined with that we need and we should not have to travel far within."

"And they die as easily as men?" Odo asked.

"Yes," Brahim said, "but their short stature gives them easy evasiveness." He waited but no one else spoke. "Be ready at first light."

A Dark Journey

DAY 13

The forest was oddly absent of sound. No animal noises; not even the sound of wind. Their trek through the snow and ground cover was silent, as if they were mere ghosts. Pepin's ears twitched but Claris couldn't be certain if he heard anything either. There was no tell-tale blue glow from Halvar. Only the constant visual checks assured Claris that everyone else was still nearby.

They exited the trees, and the river sat far in the horizon. Then they returned into the forest.

Claris went up to Halvar. "Why have we returned to the forest?" She paused. "You said between wood and river."

"It also lies," he said. "It is not much further."

Claris shook her head, not understanding his sentiment about lies, but at least comforted they were close.

Halvar hadn't lied and halted the group before a crude hole in the ground. The path down had a gradual incline.

"Weapons ready," Brahim whispered. "And keep the noise minimal."

"And no light," Halvar added.

Brahim handed Claris a small bag. "Put the aurichalcum in there and be careful not to get it on your skin. It's golden, hard to miss."

"You aren't to leave my sight," Torsten said, coming up beside her.

Claris looked over at him. "Even seen a goblin before?"

He shook his head.

"I have in drawings," she said. "Some say they were once faierie babes, but they were unwanted. Abandoned. Grew up wrong."

His lips twitched. "Not sure I'd believe that."

She smiled. "I do not either."

"Claris…"

She looked sharply up at him.

He shook his head. "Nevermind."

An ache inside told her she should ask what he was going to say, but she remained silent.

With everyone alert, Brahim took point. True to his word, Torsten stuck close to Claris, with Odo taking up rear guard. Claris slipped one of her knives free. They all had to stoop, especially Halvar, as goblins had no need for tall passages.

Though Halvar said they wouldn't have to go far, the entry fast faded from sight and darkness pressed around them. Goblins clearly had no need for light either, for not even in the distance could Claris see signs of torches or lamps. Pepin brushed against her frequently, which assured her of his presence.

She reached out, and Torsten squeezed her hand in return. Claris told herself it was only to reassure herself the others were nearby. But with the darkness pressing in, she couldn't shake the familiar feeling of being stuck within a nightmare, and his returned comfort helped ground her. Her eyes had adjusted to the dark, but she couldn't discern much of anything.

A metal object clattered against the rocky ground.

The group stilled, but no other sounds proceeded. Halvar pressed them on. Eventually they made a left turn.

A golden glint fell from the walls ahead. A shimmer one only saw at a particular angle. They all gathered around the space.

"Fill the bag," Halvar whispered.

Claris pulled out the bag and one of her knives. Heavy gouges into the rock proved something had previously worked at the wall for the aurichalcum. The garde stood guard around her.

The rock was soft and easy to scrape away, but she winced at the noise the metal made. She also soon held her breath against the powdery residue that puffed up with every motion of her blade, fearing what it might do to her if she inhaled.

The bag seemed to fill far too slow. If she took too long, she risked them all. She swallowed, willing herself to go faster.

A rumbling noise from further up interrupted her work. Claris quickly hid the bag.

"Get us out of here, Halvar," she said. Whatever amount she'd collected would have to do. She'd not risk them being caught.

They did not get far before a reverberation shuddered wall and floor alike.

Claris glanced towards Halvar, but he gave nothing away, leading them through the tunnels in quiet.

The place shuddered again, and this time she almost lost her footing. Pepin chirped softly at her side.

Halvar paused at a junction, glancing back and forth one too many times before choosing a path.

"Halvar?" Claris asked, but her voice was lost as another reverberation echoed around them.

"Is he lost?" Torsten whispered beside her.

Claris nodded. It had to be the only explanation. She'd never seen him falter before.

A laugh suddenly echoed around them. Claris's hand went to her knives. Her movements, though, were sluggish. She shook a hand out, unsure what was going on.

"That's no goblin," Brahim said. His voice was strained, as if he felt more than the others. Halvar had one hand clutched at his head, his brows drawn together.

She hoped they were moving back in the direction of the exit, but Claris swore the air around them was getting warmer.

"It's hot in here." That was Odo's voice, somewhere close. Elsewhere, Pepin yowled, displeased with the surroundings.

Her eyelids grew heavy now. Becoming harder to open each time she blinked. She only managed a few more steps before her legs gave way, and she barely registered the flare of pain from her knees crashing down as her eyes closed to darkness.

Other footsteps swallowed up the silence around them.

Claris could still feel rocky ground under her hands when she roused. Light filtered around the space, which was wide and open. Pepin curled close beside her. She pushed herself up; everyone else stirred awake as well. She realised she still had her weapons.

Seated on a throne built of stone and vine was a man. Or what appeared to be a man. She rubbed at her eyes, then took back her initial thoughts. It appeared to be a man, but it wasn't human. Facial features like a human, but sharper, more angular. The eyes absent of colour, and skin translucent that seemed to pick up all the colours around.

Examining her surroundings, she then spotted the goblins. Squat creatures, with elongated ears and tiny goat-like horns protruding from their temples. They were hiding in crevices and alcoves, watching and waiting.

Brahim rubbed at his head as he sat upright. He stilled at the sight of the throne.

Claris learned towards him and whispered, "What is it?"

The creature stood from the throne. "I'm the goblin sovereign."

Halvar rose to his feet.

"A faierie," Brahim whispered back.

Claris roused Pepin awake and stood beside Halvar. The walls around them had a gold sheen in many spots, more aurichalcum.

"Why have you trespassed into the Goeblin?" the sovereign asked. It was unnerving to look upon it for long. Multiple necklaces of bone and animal parts hung from its neck, with no visible collarbones.

"We seek aurichalcum only," Claris said, though her voice wavered unwillingly. She patted her cloak but couldn't find the bag.

The sovereign took steps forward. "So, you came to steal?" The faierie lifted the bag up, as if plucking it from the air.

"We—"

Brahim was beside her and placed a hand on her shoulder. "You will have no price from us."

Claris looked sharply at him.

"Let us have the bag and we'll leave," he continued.

"Leave?" The sovereign smiled, and it was decidedly unfriendly.

Her eyes grew heavy again and her legs threatened to give way.

Halvar touched a rune and blue flared up around the group. Claris shook the feeling off, which left her wondering why Halvar had not done so before. Or had the reverberations affected his magic? And if Brahim had sensed faierie on the ley, wouldn't Halvar have taken precautions?

The sovereign's smile widened. "Mages. Such fascinating creatures." A few goblins had crept from the shadows, and she tried not to look towards them. Pepin trained his attention onto the faierie; his tail swished slowly back and forth.

"The aurichalcum," Brahim said.

The sovereign looked between the bag and them. "You're very persistent. But I preferred when the girl spoke." It turned in her direction. "Speak."

Claris swallowed, racing to recall what she'd read from the faierie tales. She knew they took glee in pain, suffering, and death. "If you would be obliged, the aurichalcum would do us no favours. Only bring doom closer." A lie bundled with a trace of truth, certain that Claris did indeed court death by hunting the lich.

"There. That is better," the sovereign said. Claris was certain it hadn't blinked once, and it did nothing for her nerves.

"Will you let us keep it then?" she asked.

"Are you sure it is death you court?"

"Yes. Our blood will spill and feed the earth." She wanted to look away from the faierie but that felt wrong.

It came close as possible, the thin blue light a barrier between them. "I'm sure it'd taste sweet." Its head tilted at an odd angle. "But what death is that to be?"

Claris found she didn't even want to blink before the faierie. "We hunt a demi-lich."

Its face broke into a wide smile, sharpened teeth prominent in its jaw. "Indeed, death is what lies that way." It gestured to the space beside it. "Come, step free from that. Show death is not your master and you can claim the aurichalcum."

Claris turned the words over in her head, trying to find the trap. "Claim the bag of aurichalcum and all of us walk free from the Goeblin." She tried to ignore the pounding of her heart, how her throat constricted. She had to get herself under control, not show weakness to the faierie, or in front of her garde. Though she knew little, the rules that governed faierie meant they usually spoke plain. This would save them.

The faierie's smile returned. "No goblin will harm you in these walls."

She knew if she looked at anyone, she'd doubt herself. She clicked her tongue for Pepin to stay put and stepped out beside the goblin sovereign. There was an absence of warmth in the space it occupied.

The faierie leaned down, bringing its face close to hers. It reached out and touched a single finger to the mark on her cheek. "Death already tried once." Its touch was icy.

Claris held her breath and remained still.

It straightened and held the bag out to her. "Claim it."

She looked the faierie over, checking to see if it was a trick, but it couldn't be lying. She recalled that riddles were their friends, but lies a poison to them. She reached out, took hold of the bag, and the faierie remained impassive. Claris tucked the bag back into her cloak.

Brahim didn't let her linger and reached out to pull her way from the sovereign. The faierie stayed where it was.

The group took a few steps away from the throne but there was no exit. All that surrounded them was rocky wall and goblins, who all had now crept out of the shadows.

Claris spun back to face the sovereign.

A smile crept over its face. It lifted a hand and pointed towards its throne. Off to one side was a darkened space, a tunnel.

"Halvar, go first," Brahim said.

Claris looked back at the faierie, a chill settling over her skin at its silken smile. A blue glow still wrapped around Halvar, and no goblins stood near the tunnel, but Claris didn't want to go back into darkness. Pepin's ears twitched, as if picking up sound far from her hearing.

"No," she said, "let Pepin lead us." Pepin mewed, clearly not fond of the idea. She clicked her tongue twice and the cat bounded towards the tunnel.

Once they were all in the tunnel, and away from the throne, Brahim spoke again. "Let's move quickly. The faierie may change its mind."

They all fell silent and followed the pace Pepin set as he led them through the tunnels. Halvar's blue glow had dissipated and the air pressed chill through them. She still expected the sovereign or the goblins to appear at any moment.

They soon reached the exit, their pace now cut, but Brahim didn't let them stop until they were deep into the forest of trees.

"Check the bag," Brahim said.

Claris pulled it free from her cloak and drew it open. The aurichalcum gave off its gold sheen. "It is fine, yes?" She held it out towards him.

Brahim took the bag, looked, and handed it to Halvar. The mage stuck his hand into the bag. "It is all there." Halvar handed it back to Claris.

"Were you worried it tricked us?" she asked.

"Deals with the malevolent can always end poorly," Brahim replied. "But you seemed to know what to say to persuade him. For that, you have my thanks."

"The faierie is kin to many men in power," Claris said. "Underestimating women, thinking we will cave, falter, give in easier. They seem to forget that all our strength is hidden, or at least, not permitted to shine."

"May we not do that again," Brahim said, though Claris swore he still wore a smirk.

Torsten came over. "Night is almost upon us. We should head for camp."

"Yes. Let us not worry Flore and Dalfin any longer," she replied. It was her that had saved them from the faierie and goblins. Her leadership finally did some real good. Tension ebbed from her limbs, making her knees shaky. She did allow herself a satisfied smile. Not only had she secured the metal, but had the thanks of Brahim.

The man himself nodded and pointed in a direction. Claris was surprised how long they must've been down in the Goeblin though. She shivered at the thought she had been unconscious for some of it.

As Brahim led, Torsten returned to her side. "I didn't stay at your side like I said."

"Yet no harm befell me." She allowed herself another smile. "I got us out of there, harm free. And I was glad to do it. That is what one does, when one wants to lead. Take care of those in their charge."

"You did let a faierie touch you."

Her hand reached up to her face. "They claimed death tried once before." She'd had the mark for as long as she remembered, being told that it was a mark from her birth. But the faierie's words had her wondering if it was some-thing more. Something else to tuck within, to ask her father, should she get the opportunity.

"I wouldn't dwell on words from such a creature," Torsten said.

"Of course," she said. "I did expect goblins to come after us, but that now seems unlikely."

She saw his smile from the corner of her eye.

"Yes, I understand that. You do not trust easily," he said.

"Keep a closer watch again tonight?" She peered up at his eyes, remembering how her hand felt tucked into his back at the Goeblin. Flore's words circling back to her.

He nodded. "As you request."

It was dark when they returned to the camp. Flore sprung up the moment they saw them. Pepin puffed proudly as he laid a rabbit before Flore's feet then sprung away from the campfire.

"All went well, Demoiselle?" Flore asked.

"Yes," Claris said. "All was quiet?"

"Not a peep," they replied, bending to retrieve the dead rabbit. "I'll prep this."

Claris turned back to Torsten. "Remember the watch."

He held a hand over his heart with a small smile, before walking away.

She barely restrained her smile as she approached Brahim. "We reach Ladonnes tomorrow."

"And then we'll travel to Gien," he said. He was hunched over his blades, inspecting them.

"Where the rest of what we need will be?"

"Yes," he said. "The hardest part is done." He glanced at her, acknowledging her presence as he hadn't done before. "Ziri would be proud of how far you've come."

Her eyes stung with the threat of tears. "Tell me what you knew of Ziri," she said. It had been nestled in the back of her mind, and she finally needed to know what Brahim knew of him.

He looked sharply at her. "Are you certain?"

"What you say will change nothing," she replied. Pepin came over to her side, rubbing up against her leg.

"He was complicated. Kept much guarded."

"But you said you were kin?" Claris sat down beside him.

"Yes," Brahim said, setting aside his blades. "In the way all Djeyun are kin. All of us linked in spirit."

Claris leaned over to scratch Pepin's head as she took in Brahim's words. For all her studies, she realised how little she knew of other countries, other cultures. She promised herself to remedy that. "Then how did you meet?"

"The impalement arts, of course." Brahim picked out one of his knives. "A competition I suppose. It was there I saw how far a distance his blade flew."

"Which is why you wanted him. Your distance couldn't match his," Claris said.

"It was at that competition where your father employed Ziri." Brahim sighed. "As you can tell. It was a fleeting encounter, but as kin, we did stay in touch. Although my profession made that hard."

Pepin gave up his quest for affection and slinked towards their tent.

"You've ley traced a long time?"

"Yes," Brahim said, but his tone made Claris think there was more to that story. "Will you keep the aurichalcum on your person?"

Claris touched the spot on her cloak. "Yes. We will need a blade smith, won't we?"

Brahim nodded. "Let us hope we find one in Gien."

A Person Behind

Day 14

Claris was startled to see Flore directly outside her tent as she emerged. Pepin mewed up at her for suddenly stopping.

"Sorry, Demoiselle," Flore started, "didn't mean to scare. Is it okay to pack down the tent?"

Claris reached back in for the bedroll and blanket. "Thank you." She went to wait by Brahim and Halvar, who were already packed and waiting. She checked again that the aurichalcum pouch was still on her person.

"How long you think?" Brahim asked.

Claris looked up, expecting herself to answer, but Brahim was talking to Halvar.

"Should be there at the sun's peak," the mage replied.

"Good," Claris said, "that will give us light to acquire further supplies."

Torsten came over. "We're ready to move."

She cleared her throat. "We will pass into another comte's territory. Comte de Gien." She looked over the garde. "We cannot show ourselves to be from my father's county. Do not refer to me as Demoiselle. I am merely another member. Doing so could jeopardise our mission. We would have to submit to their hospitality, their questions. We do not wish to raise any panic."

Brahim raised an eyebrow. "And what should we say we are travelling for, if so asked?"

"We could say we hunt the Cheval Mallet," Claris said, thinking of the first thing that might be plausible. Stories had originated in the Comte de Gien's county of the evil horse said to appear at night as a beautiful black horse, saddled and bridled, all to tempt travellers. It was said any who rode the horse never returned. "A demi-lich poses too much risk to announce. Have the people believe we are simply ley tracers trying our luck."

Halvar shrugged. "It works."

Brahim nodded and everyone fell into their standard positions. He took them a little wider around the forest, none eager to tempt the goblins that may be lurking.

Claris glanced back, debating when she'd speak to Dalfin. He was only leaning occasionally on Odo for support, but she couldn't let him continue... it wouldn't be right. The deepening clouds overhead threatened more snow in the future. Claris settled on telling him once they were in Ladonnes. She couldn't back out then.

A sense of relief washed over her as they came upon the well-weathered thoroughfare. It would take them towards Ladonnes, and many travellers used it to continue onwards to the capital. She ached knowing that if they took the path past Ladonnes, they'd eventually reach Briarcilly. Claris longed to have word from her father, to know that he was recovered, or at least improved. That he wasn't worrying over her absence.

Ladonnes sat a little away from the path and a low goblin wall rimmed the city. Goblin walls were only high enough to ensure no goblins could scale them without aid, tiny spikes protruding at an angle from the base. The gates were wide open, and a sole city guard stood watch to one side. Claris felt his gaze on Pepin as they passed through.

"Stay close to me, boy," she said to the lynx.

City dwellers and travellers alike gave the group a wide berth, but it wasn't because of the lynx; it was because of Halvar with his large mage-hammer. Any who spied him either suddenly stopped or backed away to give him space.

"Let us secure lodgings at the inn, The Black Horse," Claris said as the group clustered off to one side, out of the main thoroughfare.

As they moved through the people, Claris searched for signs of a local physician. She'd have to ensure everything was arranged for Dalfin before they left the next morning.

The inn had a sign out front claiming that rooms were still available. Claris went in first with Brahim close behind, Pepin still tailing Claris.

"Greetings travellers..." The innkeeper trailed off at the sight of the lynx. He cleared his throat. "How can I help?"

"How many rooms do you have available?" Claris asked and brought Pepin to a sit.

The innkeeper's eyes stayed on the cat. "I've five."

"We will take four, with three needing to accommodate two occupants," she said. "The cat stays with me."

"For the night?"

"Just the one," Claris replied.

The innkeeper rang a little bell, and a boy appeared out of the back room. "Prepare rooms three to six, with four to six requiring an extra cot." The boy nodded and shuffled up the stairs. "They'll be ready within the hour."

"Thank you," Claris said and turned to leave. They had a lot to cover before the daylight was lost.

Outside the inn, she addressed Dalfin and Odo. "Please remain here, in case the innkeeper feels like changing his mind." She placed a few coins in Odo's hands, then turned to Flore and gave them a couple more. "And Flore, please take Halvar and purchase us necessary supplies."

"Find me once errands are done," Brahim said, and Claris reined in her disappointment. She had hoped not to be left with Torsten alone, and it was too late to change other assignments without it being obvious to all.

Everyone dispersed on their tasks and Pepin took to grooming himself as they stood around.

"And what will we be doing?" Torsten asked.

"Finding a physician," Claris said and peered up and down the path.

Torsten cleared his throat. "For..."

"Dalfin," Claris finished. "I want to ensure he'll be in good hands."

Torsten moved in one direction. "This way then."

Claris looked down at Pepin. "Come, boy." She made a mental note to also see a butcher; Pepin wouldn't be able to hunt inside the city.

The trio earned their share of stares, most directed towards the lynx. A gaggle of children took to following, daring each other to see who could get closest. Claris clucked her tongue at Pepin, warning him not to engage.

Torsten soon turned off the thoroughfare and knocked on a door, a neat sign declaring a physician.

A young girl opened the door, coming face to face with Pepin. "It's a cat, Father," the girl announced.

Claris couldn't help her smile.

An incredulous sound preceded footsteps. He was a tall man with muscled arms and a neatly trimmed beard. His eyes went straight to Claris.

"What can I do for you, ma'am?" he asked. The young girl moved behind his legs. Pepin sat, his tail swishing slowly.

"A companion of mine suffered a leg injury on our travels," she said. "We are lodging at The Black Horse, and I'd appreciate you being able to call upon him."

He looked between Claris and Torsten. "Has he got use of the leg?"

"In a limited capacity," she replied. "Would you have the time?"

"I will call upon you in the evening," he said. "I'm Lothar."

Claris inclined her head. "Claris, though your patient will be Dalfin."

Lothar nodded. "We will discuss a fee then."

"Thank you," Claris said.

The door closed and she looked to Pepin. "Did you happen to note a butcher?"

"They tend to be away a bit," Torsten replied, "the smell and that."

"Then let us seek one out."

Claris deferred to Torsten's sense of direction, hedging he had been to Ladonnes at least once before. The path they ended up on had few people, but the coppery tang of blood was undeniable.

Claris went to stop at the first butcher, but Torsten pressed on. Pepin mewed his displeasure. It wasn't until the third butcher when he called for a stop.

"Why this one?" she asked.

"Cleaner, and you hear live animals," he said. "Fresh is better."

Pepin's tail was straight in the air.

A man in a black apron walked out from the shop front. "Is there cause to your loitering?" His gaze drifted over to the lynx.

"We need food for our cat companion," Claris said.

The butcher narrowed his eyes at her, before settling on Torsten. "Need your wife to talk for you?"

"I am—"

Torsten's hand clamped onto hers and he squeezed. Claris blinked but stopped talking. She'd never been deferred over before. But she knew she no longer had the appearance of nobility.

"Would you be willing to part with a live fowl for my wife's pet?" Torsten asked. Claris held her tongue, she had no wish for attention or to cause a commotion. Though it didn't stop her mind wondering: What if Torsten really was her husband? She closed her eyes. What a nonsense notion.

"You can take a look at them, if you'd like," the butcher said. "The cat has to stay out here though."

Torsten released Claris's hand. "I will select one."

The butcher gestured for Torsten to follow, and Claris stroked her hand through Pepin's fur. A few townsfolk had paused in their own tasks to gawk at Pepin and Claris both. She hoped they weren't thinking she was selling him for meat. The sun had begun its earnest descent, and Claris was keen to be at the inn before darkness encroached. Towns had bad reputations for ill nightly activities.

Both the butcher and Torsten soon returned; Torsten held a wooden cage with a single fowl inside. She hoped he hadn't paid too much for it, as it was a little on the skinny side. Pepin's attention went straight to the fowl, his tail swishing slowly.

"There's no good open spaces inside the walls," the butcher said. "Here is as good as any."

Claris knelt at Pepin's side. "You will have to be quick, boy." She nodded at Torsten. He set the cage down and Pepin lowered his belly to the ground. Torsten unlatched the cage door, swung it open, and gave the cage a nudge to startle the fowl. It gave an indignant squawk and scattered out into the open.

Pepin watched it a moment, and Claris clicked her tongue three times. He leaped at the fowl, one paw trapping its neck while his jaws clamped its body. Blood spattered the ground, and all around had their attention trained on Pepin while he ate.

The butcher turned back to Torsten. "She trained the cat?"

Torsten smiled. "She raised him." Claris resisted the urge to smirk at the butcher.

A few bystanders stood further back, not eager to be the lynx's next meal. It didn't take long for Pepin to pull the fowl apart and get his fill of meat, and once finished, he took to licking his paws. Claris walked over and gave Pepin a pat, he chirped in return. She looked down at the remnants of the fowl; she'd have to deal with it.

A woman hurried up to her, three children close behind. She gestured at the remains. "We'd have that."

The butcher made a noise of disgust and returned to his shop.

"There is little meat left," Claris said. The children had already crouched near the carcass, and Claris shooed Pepin back to not scare them. She'd heard from the court gossip that many struggled in the colder months to feed their families, but to see it firsthand gave her a lump in her throat.

"Bone broth, and feathers can be used," the woman replied. Claris offered her a small smile.

Claris caught Torsten's subtle shake of his head. "You may take it." She stepped around the children and came to his side.

"Good. I thought you might give them coin," he said.

She peered up at him, unsure if he thought her charitable or if he disapproved of her kindness. "A fellow lowborn would not offer another a coin."

"But they'd let another take the scraps?"

Claris sighed. "We clearly have at least some coin."

Torsten took the lead back to bring them back out onto the main thoroughfare. "Where do we go tomorrow?"

"Gien has something we need," she replied and headed towards the inn.

"Aren't you worried we'll lose the lich trail, or someone else will get to it first?"

"No," she said. "We will find it once more, and when we do, we will be ready."

Halvar stood outside the inn, hammer resting at his side.

Claris paused before him. "Is all well?"

"Flore has the supplies inside," the mage replied, and continued to stare out into the town.

Pepin and Torsten followed her in. The innkeeper looked up on their entrance. "Your rooms are ready, but the others are seated in the parlour awaiting food, if you'd like to join them." He gestured to a door behind him on the left. Claris nodded her thanks, and they went in, but Brahim was not there.

Torsten sat beside Flore, who looked at Claris. "I put the supplies in a room. Odo and I can sort them tonight."

She nodded. "Brahim has not returned?"

The man had told her to find him after finishing her errands, but she thought he meant back at the inn. Had he meant to literally find him out in the town somewhere?

Odo and Dalfin exchanged a look.

"He did, briefly, and then mentioned he was headed to a den of ill repute," Odo said, his eyes unable to meet her own.

She looked over her four remaining garde. "None of you are to leave here." She gestured for Pepin to follow, and she returned outside, beside Halvar. "You know where Brahim went?"

Halvar looked down at her. "Place known as The Jewel." He glanced back out over the town. "A place you should not be in once darkness falls." She waited another moment and then he pointed in a direction. Claris wondered why Brahim would want her to meet him in such a place. Was he gambling with knives again?

The townsfolk in the streets had thinned but Claris wasn't too concerned with Pepin beside her. None had shown a true inclination to get near the lynx. Her gaze did roam the surroundings though; a few guardsmen with bows perched on rooftops at junction points. They probably did that every night.

The Jewel's outward appearance had no indication of ill dealings, and inside was tame. A few games of chance were happening in corners while men drank and smoked. A couple of women wended their way through the groups. But all the men were white that she could see, and none even gave her and Pepin a second glance.

She went up to the bar. "I am looking for someone. He is Djeyun."

The barkeep stilled his movements, and a few of the men at the bar had hands drift to their sides. Claris pulled out a coin and slid it towards the man she was talking to. "I am not here for trouble."

"He's in a back room," the barkeep said. "But I can't let you in. You'll have to wait out here."

Claris glanced around. "I must decline. I would appreciate if you would retrieve my friend without delay." Her neck prickled with the added attention from more patrons.

"And you must be patient," the barkeep replied. "I would hate to get the proprietor."

Claris tapped the counter; Pepin stood on his hind legs to put his front paws up. The barkeep took a step back. "And I would hate to see you eaten." She smiled.

The barkeep glanced around, eyes wide.

"Perhaps it best if you retrieve your friend," he said.

Claris gestured down, and Pepin returned to sit. The barkeep gestured over at a door under the stairs. She looked at the other patrons before heading to the door, leaving the coin on the counter.

The door didn't lead down as she expected, but to a hallway with a few doors lined along both walls.

Claris crouched at Pepin's side. "Where is Brahim?" The lynx mewed and padded in front of her; she stood to follow.

It didn't take long for Pepin to stop before a door. Outside, Claris couldn't discern any troubling noises. With one hand at the ready, she opened the door. Around a corner warm light spilled and voiced drifted her way.

Brahim sat at a card table with four other men. All five looked up at her entry.

One man, whose beard threatened to overgrow his face, began to leave his chair. "You can't—"

Pepin growled and Brahim put a hand on the bearded man's shoulder.

"She's with me," he said. "And appears my game is done."

Claris watched him gather his money while also keeping an eye on all the other men and their hands. Brahim tipped his head to the others before coming to her side. They left the room and out through the front. She felt all the eyes in the bar upon them as they exited the establishment. Pepin visibly relaxed once they were back in the open.

"You've good timing," Brahim said.

"I hope your plan didn't hinge on my timely arrival." She looked over at him.

"I knew you'd bring Pepin," he said. "There was no other way they'd let me leave with any money elsewise."

The sun had dipped almost from view, and the rooftop archers had multiplied.

"You made me walk this way, into a seedy establishment, risking my life, to save you from a card game?" Her eyebrows rose. "And the coin you won?" Claris's frown deepened.

"The mission. What we need in Gien will not be cheap."

Halvar no longer stood outside the inn, and as Brahim opened the door a voice called out to them. "Ma'am."

Claris turned around to find the physician, Lothar, and his daughter standing there. The man had a large leather bag with him.

"Good evening," she said and waved them inside the inn. "Let us find your patient."

The girl couldn't keep her eyes off Pepin.

"Brahim, this is Lothar, a physician," Claris said.

Lothar held out his hand. Brahim reached out to take it. "Pleased to have your service."

Torsten wandered into the entryway and Claris motioned to him.

"Torsten," Claris said, "please show the physician to Dalfin." She turned her attention back to Lothar. "Please see me once you have completed your assessment."

"Ma'am," Lothar said and followed Torsten up the stairs, his daughter dutifully following behind.

Claris sighed. She'd have to face the difficult conversation soon. Out in the parlour, only Flore and Halvar remained.

Flore looked up on their entry. "I will let them know you are here. I got them to put food aside."

Claris took a chair at the table. "That will be most welcome."

Brahim sat across from her while Flore left.

Halvar let out a low rumble of a laugh as he stood. "I would've thought you'd come back looking worse." He clapped a hand on Brahim's shoulder. "I guess the girl does have many surprises."

In Flore's place, the young boy came into the room bearing a serving tray with a selection of meats, fruits, and cheeses.

He gave Pepin a wide berth. Once he set the tray down, he stood to one side.

"That will be all, thank you," Claris said.

The boy hurried from the room.

"I have not known Ladonnes to be attacked by goblins in any recent time, yet they seem ready for such," Claris said.

"You noticed the archers too," Brahim replied. "Perhaps it is more a criminal deterrent." She chewed at her food longer while she thought, and he added, "But you think it something else?"

"The goblins may be wanting to expand," she said. "But we encountered not one, but two roaming marauder bands." Swallowing the food became harder as her throat constricted. The pattern of wrongness wasn't just in her father's county. The Comte de Gien was a close ally to her father, and to the king. She had to figure it all out, especially if she wanted to ensure her father's position continued at court.

"You're thinking of the faierie too."

Claris pushed the food aside and stood. "We may not be gifted a peaceful rest."

Brahim pushed the tray back towards her. "Which means you should eat. Don't seek out what doesn't seek you."

Her eyes went between the doorway and the food. She knew it unlikely to magically discover anything at night, but the niggling need to do something lingered. It was as if she was transported back to the estate, with her father cautioning her in her activities once her mother passed. A pang lanced through her. She longed to stand before the mourning stone and air her worries, to seek guidance. She didn't know why she expected herself to be able to do this.

"Please Claris, sit." Brahim spoke with a quiet voice.

She flicked her gaze back to him, then sat and plucked some fruit from the tray. Claris knew lingering on thoughts of the faierie would lead nowhere, but no place her mind wandered seemed good refuge.

Torsten came back into the room, the physician and his daughter close behind. Torsten went to stand in a corner. Pepin's head turned towards the girl.

"What news?" Claris asked.

"High chance of a stress fracture," Lothar replied. "I wouldn't recommend he keep putting weight on it."

Her heart sunk a little. "But will it heal?"

He nodded. "Given rest and proper recovery, it will be good again."

She refused to look at anyone but the physician. "How much coin to see him for the next five days?"

"With my fee tonight—"

"Fifty-five gold," the girl replied.

Claris couldn't help her smile.

Lothar's eyes widened. "I'm—"

"Do not apologise," she said. "Fifty-five is a fair price."

The girl beamed up at her father.

Claris stood and pulled out the coins, her purse now incredibly light. Perhaps Brahim had the right idea in procuring more coin. She handed the money over. "If you ever tire of working in Ladonnes, please seek out my father, Comte de Grecy."

His skin flushed at his neck. "That is most kind."

The girl took a keener interest in Claris. "You're a real demoiselle?"

Claris's smile widened. "True, though my clothes would not give it away so easy."

"Is there anything else I may do for you?" Lothar asked.

"Only your discretion, for I am not truly here," she said. "Would you like an escort back home?" She gestured at Torsten.

The physician shook his head. "That is most kind, but we will be fine. Safe travels, Demoiselle." The girl hurried a curtsy before following her father.

"I must see Dalfin," Claris said and went to head upstairs.

Torsten followed behind. "Should we recruit more men?"

"No..." New men wouldn't be loyal to her house, only to coin that was becoming scarce. And they would come with looser tongues. "We have no need of mercenaries," she replied. "What we have will be enough."

Torsten stopped at another room, leaving her to continue to knock at Dalfin's door.

"Dem... Claris," Odo said, opening it. He stepped aside to let her in.

Dalfin was in a cot, his leg elevated.

"How are you?" she asked, and seeing no chairs, she kept standing as casually as her uneasiness would allow. She didn't want her guilt on display.

He looked at his leg. "It will get better. I can still serve." His fingers played with the straps at his right wrist brace.

"Of that I have no doubt," she said, shifting her weight to the other leg. Nothing seemed comfortable. "But we cannot delay, and that you know too."

Odo quietly exited the room.

Dalfin let out a heavy sigh. "If my joints were just like everyone else's, this wouldn't be an issue."

Claris's stomach churned; she didn't want him to feel that way. "No one recovers quickly from that wound." She swallowed, staring directly at him. "No one."

"But if I wasn't—"

"No, Dalfin," Claris interrupted. "This does not make you weak. It is a strength to admit when one must rest. That physician will see you until you are healed."

"I will travel straight to the comte, then," Dalfin said, nodding, eyes a little brighter. "Report on our progress."

"Do not paint a dire picture," Claris said, smiling softly. "We need not fret him." She pulled out more coin and laid them on the table beside Dalfin. "This should cover what you need."

He looked at the coins. "Most kind, Demoiselle."

Claris wasn't sure what else to say, and the air hung expectant.

"Is there anything else?"

"No, I will let you rest." Claris gave him a brief smile and exited the room. "Be ready to leave at light," she said to Odo as he went to head back in.

She sighed and headed for her own room, Pepin already comfortable upon the bed.

She splayed out beside him, reaching out to scratch behind his ears. "Now we are six."

He chortled.

"Seven." She smiled, but it seemed hollow. They'd lost three men, though at least Dalfin lived. Brahim insisted he needed the garde to defeat the demi-lich, and their numbers dwindled. The odds did indeed look dire.

A Helping Hand

Day 15

Everyone said their farewells to Dalfin, and Claris ensured the innkeeper was paid for the garde's continued stay. Outside in the streets, she noted that archers were still like gargoyles perched atop roofs, while beyond them the sun buried itself behind darkening clouds. She knew it would take only three days to travel to Gien, but a storm could delay progress.

Claris glanced back at her three remaining garde. Would anyone have been able to do better in her stead? How would the other garde see her upon their return, knowing she'd lost a few of their own? She shook her head. She knew the thought of return folly. Pepin rubbed past her legs, drawing her attention.

The Ladonnes gates were still closed when they got there. A guard walked out on their approach, holding up her hand.

"We don't open the gates for another hour," the woman said.

The near emptiness of her purse told Claris a bribe would be a poor solution.

"You are far from home," Torsten said as he approached the guard.

She removed her helm, showing one side of her head shaven like Suevik warriors. "So are you." Her gaze went to Halvar before snapping away.

Claris swallowed her small thrill; the guard was a blade-maiden, or at least used to be one. She had no idea that blade-maidens would forgo their home country for another, but Torsten too was far from his home.

"Would you let us through the guard door at least, if not the gates?" Torsten asked.

The guard looked at the wall and back at them. She gave a single sharp nod. "If you wish to tempt fate of the goblins, I will not stop you."

"Thank you," Claris started.

"May Svafa guide you," Halvar said. Claris figured it was a Suevik thing and let her remaining words die.

The guard took them inside the narrow passage between wall and the doors. She undid five bolts, turned a key, and pushed the heavy oak door open.

Everyone filed out and Torsten whispered something to her as they passed. Brahim and Halvar continued to walk in the direction of Gien.

Odo came up to Claris's left. "Demoiselle, permit me to stay by your side." He glanced towards the nearby river. "The closer one draws to Briar Bay, the closer one gets to opportunistic thieves."

"Would you have counselled us hire services of a river raft?" she asked. Surely it would've been the faster route. The nag of doubt scratched at her mind.

Odo looked aghast. "I'd never be that foolish. The Briar Channel that feeds to Grecy may be well manned, but smaller riverways are prime targets if one does not have sufficient protection."

Her eyebrows pinched together. "Would our numbers and weapons not be deterrent enough?"

"Marauders beset us when our number were more."

A sting pricked at her eyes, recalling Sigibert's fall. "Yes, true. It is good we then go on foot." She wished she'd never said otherwise.

Odo nodded agreement. "So, you'll allow my presence?"

She offered him a smile. "It would be most welcome. But remember, I am merely Claris while we are in these lands."

With her protected, Pepin quickly loped off to find his morning meal.

The lapse into silence between Odo and herself was easy, as he took his role of garde with a rigidity that Torsten and Flore did not. He also seemed the most reserved.

That was until they'd travelled a little further and Pepin returned, tracking bloody footprints behind him. Odo called a sudden halt, his voice loud across the countryside.

Brahim eyed the bloodied tracks in the white snow. "Is that from a kill?"

With rising horror, Claris looked Pepin over, noting with relief he was unhurt, but he wore no bloodied muzzle. "No," she said. "This is something else. We should follow quick before the snow removes the tracks." There could be someone out there in trouble. It may not be her father's county, but that didn't mean they shouldn't help someone in need.

She clicked her tongue a few times and had Pepin walk beside her.

Brahim led them, retracing the path the lynx had left. It didn't take long for them to come across a small stone hut.

The door hinged open, right where Pepin's footprints began. As the lynx had been unharmed, Claris didn't sense a need for caution. Regardless, the three garde drew their weapons at the ready.

She stayed just outside the doorway, staring around in horror. Blood spattered over the walls and floors, with three bodies strewn across a rug. It appeared to be a family; a man, a woman, and a child no more than twelve years of age.

Halvar knelt by the bodies. "Barely a day since passing."

Claris pressed her lips together in a thin line and took a tentative step inside. Each of their throats had been slashed.

Torsten placed a hand on her upper arm. "You don't need to be here."

"Is it safe to say this was no lich attack?" Claris did her best not to look again upon their bodies. The smell of blood churned her stomach, but she refused to be sick, not in front of them all.

Brahim crouched down by the bodies. "No malevolent traces. Likely bandits." She closed her eyes with the pain of it all. So many bandits. It couldn't be a normal state. She rubbed at her temples.

The simple furniture and very limited extras strewn about the hut made Claris shake her head. "This winter must make many desperate." Desperate enough to kill those with barely enough themselves to survive. "Can we track where they went?"

"We could," Brahim said. "But we should not let this waylay our true purpose."

She closed her eyes, calming her thoughts, her breaths. "Very well. We push on. But we should be on alert. Bandits already took one of us. I do not want that to happen again."

Her eyes flicked down to the bodies. "We burn the bodies first." It was the least she could do, especially if she was unable to track down those responsible.

The garde gathered as much as possible, even using the furniture, and set the entire hut alight.

It wasn't long after leaving the hut that snow fell in earnest. The group clustered closer as they continued to press on, each cold flake doing its best to find their exposed faces. Claris was glad the winds were subdued, even if the snow refused to relent. Even when dragging their feet up and out of the deepening snow they didn't pause. There were few trees in their path, and thus little shelter to use anyway.

With cloud cover in all directions, the snow blocking the horizon, Claris found it hard to judge what the time of day would be. Pepin positioned himself between her and Odo, the trek seemingly no bother to him.

Brahim drifted back from Halvar's side to take position beside Claris. She looked towards him expectant.

"We'll find no shelter out here," he said.

She didn't like where his words may go. "I will not send us back down to caverns." She may not have lost any garde last time, but it wasn't a chance she'd take twice. Not when there were fewer of them.

"No," he replied, "but Halvar has an idea. I think it is our only option. Go, talk to him."

Claris stared a moment at Brahim, wondering why he didn't force it if he thought it the only way. She braced herself for something she'd surely not like. Pepin stayed behind while she approached the mage.

"He did not tell you," Halvar rumbled.

"Is it reasonable?" she asked.

"It will be taxing, but we'll not survive the night without it."

Claris thought the statement a bit alarming, yet she waited for him to continue.

"We use my magic for shelter. The space would be tight."

"And you will not get rest. But that is not the taxing part, is it?" The sinking of her insides grew.

"Sustaining magic for extended periods will render me unable to use it again for at least two days." He reached back to tap his mage-hammer. "Although I will still have this."

Claris looked back at the others; they were all capable in a fight, and surely their luck was not that ill they'd run into trouble soon. Though that niggle in the back of her mind cautioned her otherwise. They hadn't come across those, or what, was responsible for the massacre at the hut. At last, she agreed. "We'll push for as long as we can." She went back to Odo's side, while Brahim moved back to Halvar's.

"Is all well?" Odo asked.

"Yes," she lied, her eyes drifting to Torsten's position.

"You'd not fare well if you played cards," Odo said.

Claris smiled, though internally it didn't seem right to smile. "Good thing I have never tried."

"Is there anything I can do to ease the worry your face wears?"

She glanced over at him. "Is your father also in our service?"

"No," Odo replied. "I'm the first in our family to swear for you."

"Then I am grateful you sought your own path."

The wind whipped up more snow, stealing away any further chance of conversation. Everyone pressed in closer, eager for whatever reprieve could be found. The smells of sweat and wool surrounded them. Torsten was right behind her, her neck prickling in recognition of his proximity. Every step became slower and harder. Eventually all they could do was stop. Brahim looked to Claris, as if expecting her to speak up. Her eyebrows shot up in surprise.

"We cannot use our tents," she said. "But Halvar has offered to keep us sheltered and warm while we rest. I still want a watch rotation, but we will all rest side by side."

Pepin purred and rubbed at her leg. She knelt to give him a pat. "Yes, you too. Find yourself food."

Flore opened their pack. "We have food here that will not require fire."

"Good. Let us hope this storm passes soon," Claris said.

Halvar's runes lit up and a slight shimmer in the air around them was the only sign of his magic. The snow and wind stopped outside the pocket of space he created.

The garde set to scraping away as much snow as possible to clear a space where they could lay down some blankets. Warmth pricked the air, and at least seven runes remained aglow on Halvar's skin.

Claris looked about, suddenly realising what the plan meant. She'd have to sleep next to others, something she hadn't done in years. She swallowed and added her own blanket to what was already laid out. Blade-maidens would do this all the time, she reasoned.

They all waited until Claris had sat before the rest followed suit. Flore passed around salted meat and hard cheese for everyone to eat.

Halvar sat with his eyes closed and the mage-hammer rested across his lap, and a couple of different runes now pulsed as if they breathed along with the seven sustained.

As Torsten worked out the watch rotation, Claris nibbled at the food and kept her eyes out for Pepin's return. She was not long in waiting. Pepin soon reappeared and stopped at the fringes of the barrier, his mews insistent as snow whipped around his face. Claris glanced towards Halvar and thought against disturbing him in case it broke the magic. Instead, she reached through the slight shimmer, her fingertips instantly feeling the cold, a tingling prickling all over her limbs sending her hair on ends. She scooped Pepin up into her arms and pulled him close to her chest. He mewed in displeasure before giving her a lick on the face. "You will be fine for one night, boy." The lynx eyed the magical barrier warily.

Torsten had settled on a blanket to one side of her. Flore eyed the cat as they took the other space beside her. "Does he scratch at night?"

"You have nothing to worry about," Claris said, giving Pepin a rub behind the ears.

Exposed in the open, Claris kept expecting to feel a chill on her skin, but the warmth Halvar's magic generated was surprising. She lay down on the blanket, letting Pepin stay pressed in close against her back.

Torsten lay down too, his face towards hers.

In such close quarters, she didn't trust herself to say anything. Yet no one else spoke; the only sounds were ones of general movement; everyone attempting to get comfortable. And she couldn't take her eyes away from his face.

In the end, she relented. "You should rest while you can," she said.

She appreciated the distance he'd granted her that day, and she'd by lying if she said she didn't miss his presence. But she knew she wouldn't voice that aloud.

His lips twitched into a small smile. "Of course."

She took her own advice and forced her eyes shut.

A Bad Throw

Day 16

Hard warmth rested underneath her fingers. She splayed them out, feeling her head raised higher than the rest of her body as if upon a pillow. Claris's eyes shot open, awakening fully. She'd fallen asleep with her head upon Torsten's chest, and her hand resting upon his abdomen, and even her leg thrown over the top of his own.

"It's natural to seek warmth." Torsten's quiet voice jarred her further.

She snatched her hand back to her own chest. "I am sorry," she whispered. "That must have been uncomfortable for you." Who knows how long she'd trapped him under her limbs. A flush raced up to her cheeks.

He smiled easily. "Your presence made sleep easier."

Claris restrained her own returning smile, ignoring the sudden quickened pulse skittering through her. She cleared her throat, focusing her gaze anywhere but on Torsten. A tingling sensation spread from her fingertips to her toes, leaving her feeling both exhilarated and apprehensive. A part of her reasoned that she had indeed sought out Torsten for warmth, but her body had clearly gravitated towards him, and not Flore, who had also slept beside her. Her subconscious betrayed her rational side.

Sweat sheened all over Halvar's skin, but he only let go of the magic once everyone awoke. Snow mounded around where the barrier was, but the snowstorm had passed. Only a few white clouds spotted the sky.

Claris watched on as Halvar consumed some of the dust Brahim had handed over all those days ago. The mage's runes blinked once.

"Will you be okay for the walk ahead?" Claris asked him. She'd heard stories what drugs did to men, and knowing Halvar was using one, a magical one, disquieted her. Though it seemed beneficial, she had no idea if it had any ill side-effects.

The mage nodded and fitted his mage-hammer onto his back. "Of course. Sleep will come tonight."

Everyone had gathered to continue the journey, and Claris watched as Brahim walked out to search for the ley trail. His usual routine.

He bent low, shoving his hand through to the earth, shook his head, and stood. Claris's brows furrowed as he went to another spot and repeated the same process, before standing with a grim look. Then he walked back, fitting his gloves back on.

"I've lost the ley."

Halvar knelt to press his palm through snow to reach the ground underneath. He stood and shook his head. "Something has leeched the land dry of ley. Or someone has masked it."

"Both being bad," Brahim said. "A ley masker is usually one of malevolence."

"Can a lich do that?" Claris asked.

Brahim shook his head. "No, but the one who warded it could."

She took a deep breath. It was her responsibility to ensure this group succeeded. "We keep moving towards Gien. If they have manipulated the ley here, does that mean they may be near?"

"The demi-lich was not moving this way." Brahim frowned. "It may not be related. I'll keep checking for it as we go."

Though once they were back walking, Claris couldn't help her mind straying to horrible possibilities. That the mastermind behind the demi-lich may also be riling up the goblins, leeching ley to throw ley tracers off their trail.

Unfortunately, she couldn't see why. She was clearly missing something important.

Part of her itched with the want to throw knives. She hadn't the chance the last couple of days and it felt wrong. Nor had she found a moment to speak to her mother. Perhaps she was more unmoored than she truly knew? Such fantastical thoughts flittering through her head must simply be because she hadn't centred herself recently.

"You look worried," Odo said, having once more taken position by her side. Torsten kept his distance. "I can always listen if you want to air your thoughts. I'm not one to judge them."

Claris knew if she returned home, she'd speak highly of Odo to her father.

"That is a kind offer, but I would not burden you so," she replied.

He did not press the idea, and they continued in silence.

With no snowfall to slow progress, the group made good ground, and despite Brahim and Halvar's concerns, nothing made itself known. Not even the thieves that Odo cautioned her on. There were trees in the distance, but night's descent meant they wouldn't reach them before dark.

Once the camp had been set up, Brahim lined up the three garde, each holding a small shield before them. Torsten held his in front of his neck, his eyes visible over the top.

"Are you using my garde as targets?" Claris came over.

Brahim's eyes lit in amusement. "No, you are."

"But—"

"You need to continue practice," Brahim replied. "And your restlessness is plain to see."

Claris immediately wondered if Odo had reported anything to Brahim, but she had not seen the two speak. "And if I miss?"

He grinned. "Is that your plan?"

She slipped free one of her knives. "No."

"Good. Hit the three in quick succession."

Claris flexed her wrist. If he wanted quick, it meant using the wrist sheath. Flore held his shield before his knees, while Odo's was before his chest. Flore was her greatest risk. She'd never aimed that low before.

She mapped it in her mind first: low, high, mid.

"I'm still waiting," Brahim said.

She resisted throwing him a dirty look. Claris took a breath. She threw her held knife, and readied for another, barely registering if the first struck the target or not. Brahim was timing her for sure. Once the third knife left her fingers, Claris finally surveyed her attempt. Her throws all landed at least. Not perfect targets, but at least no blood was drawn.

"Switch!" Brahim's voice startled Claris. "Throw. No hesitation."

Her eyes widened. All three garde had changed the positions of their shields. With the wrist sheath depleted, Claris would have to pull from the thigh. She'd already taken the hesitation that Brahim didn't want. She grabbed one knife, breathed, and then took both her first and second throw.

Her third throw aimed towards Torsten, his shield positioned low over his hips, leaving his chest exposed.

The knife rotated, its constant spin creating a sick feeling inside her.

She'd thrown it too high.

Her voice caught in her throat.

Reflexively, her eyes shuttered for a moment.

The knife thudded precariously at the shield's edge, right before his heart.

Their eyes met and her hand trembled. Her heart hammered.

Brahim made a noise of disgust. "Almost lost another." He moved away. Clearly, he was done with Claris for the night.

Odo and Flore gave her a wide berth as they too went back to the camp. She'd have to retrieve her knives later.

Torsten walked towards her, the knife in one hand. He held it out to her.

Claris waited for him to say something, but he remained stoic. The silence stretched. She swallowed.

"I am sorry," she finally said, almost choking on the words. Her throat thickened. "I would never mean you harm."

She reached out to take her knife. His fingers lingered over hers.

Claris looked up at his eyes, concerned by his silence. "Torsten?"

His eyes met hers. "Even if it did not strike, you'll still hurt my heart."

She swallowed. "How?"

His hand went to reach for her face, before falling back to his side. "You're afraid of what someone as boring as Alain may think." Claris's eyes widened; she'd barely given a thought to her impending betrothal to the vicomte's son in the past days.

Then he lingered no more. They stung her deep, those words. She couldn't make her legs move from their spot. Pepin eventually came to her, nudging her legs with his face.

She forced a smile down at him. "You are right, boy, I should move."

The tents were butted up against each other and she followed Pepin into hers; her knives lay in a pile at the entry. She would oil and sharpen them before rest. The garde wouldn't likely welcome her company tonight.

A Room Shared

Day 17

When Brahim approached her in the morning, Claris expected a reprimand. Her fingers dug into the palms of her hands.

"We'll reach Gien by nightfall," he said.

"How long will we need there?" she asked, still waiting for another remark.

"Two days at most."

"And you are sure we will be able to trace the demi-lich once more?" She couldn't, wouldn't, go back to her father without the task completed. She'd not be seen as a failure.

He waved down at the ground. "Provided the ley returns."

"Best not waste the light then." Everyone was ready to move out.

Brahim raised a hand to Halvar, who set out, the garde following behind. Not even Torsten had spared a glance in her direction. She had grown used to his gaze, and its absence sat wrong against her. Pepin purred as he rubbed up against her legs. He too was keen to get moving.

"There'll be trees near Gien to try again." With those words, Brahim set out after the others.

As Claris took up the rear position of the group, eventually Odo fell back to take his place beside her.

"You should not walk behind us," he said.

She held in the sudden flare of irritation. Claris wanted to be seen as their equal, their leader, not a noblewoman needing protection.

"Have you been to Gien before?" she asked after a few beats.

"No, Demoi... Claris," he said. "I've been to Cervoy, but didn't have the pleasure at stopping in Gien."

"Are the beaches as pleasant as they are in Briarcilly?" she asked. She liked them in winter, none ventured there.

"If by pleasant you mean quiet, then yes. Though one such as I had little time to relax while there."

"And where do you call home Odo?" she said.

"I was raised in Meauchy."

She smiled, but it faded fast. The last time she had spent time in Meauchy was when her mother was alive; it was her mother's birthplace. Though not far from Grecy, the closest neighbour by river, it harboured too many memories for her to want to go back there. Now all she knew was Grecy and Briarcilly. At least now she was getting to see more of her homeland.

"I'm sorry if I've said something wrong."

She cleared her throat. "No, you have said nothing to offend."

Odo nodded and remained quiet.

Claris turned her attention outwards. Flore and Torsten stood quite close together, and she found herself wishing Torsten was the one by her side. A foolish thought, but one that had taken root. It wouldn't be easily dislodged.

The journey had clearly scrambled some of her sense, she couldn't seriously be contemplating any kind of relationship with Torsten, no matter how much her pulse raced in his presence.

She glanced sideways at Odo. "What is Torsten to you?"

He blinked in surprise, clearing his throat. "A fleeting moment. A stolen passion. It only happened that once."

Claris hummed lowly. "Had you met before this journey?"

"The once, when I accompanied your father to Chavers," Odo said.

They fell to silence once more.

She was grateful the weather remained complacent for the day. The snow depth was enough for a tough traversal. The trees were now on the outskirts of their path, but they didn't press closer towards them.

Brahim was right; they reached Gien as the sun descended out of sight.

If the river and proximity to the capital encouraged thieves, Claris was surprised no wall surrounded the town. Yet there were at least two watchtowers she spotted.

Everyone fell in closer to Claris and Brahim, but there were few signs of life as most townspeople were likely already indoors. The inn they found had a dishevelled air, and only low light spread out of the windows. Claris couldn't see anything else nearby, not even a tavern. The sign outside the inn depicted a white rabbit. With no other nearby prospects, and the late hour, Claris motioned for them to stop here.

Her hand rested against the door, then she stopped. She loathed the churning inside her. Claris cleared her throat. "I cannot be the one to request rooms, this close to the capital. Brahim, please."

Claris followed behind Brahim to a room filled with tables and benches. A hearth burned brightly against one wall, and a few patrons sat at tables with both food and drink. Heads turned in their direction, and Claris followed Brahim over to the counter.

"Yes?" the man said on their approach.

"We need rooms," Brahim said. "There are six of us, and we travel with a lynx."

The man peered over the counter and down at Pepin; he arched an eyebrow. "So you do."

"Only three rooms. You'll have to share," he said and fixed Claris with a stare. "And there ain't no others in town."

Claris couldn't be sure it wasn't a lie. Brahim didn't take his eyes from the man. "How much for the night?"

"Fifty silver, but ten silver extra for the cat."

Brahim slid the coins before the man. He took the coins but didn't bother looking up. "Rooms three to five."

Claris took the keys from him. She went up the stairs first, Pepin bounded up before her. At the door to three, she turned to face the group.

"One..." She cleared her throat. "One of you needs to share with me."

"Halvar and I shall share," Brahim said, clearly opting from the dilemma Claris faced. She handed a key to Brahim, allowing him to leave to his room with Halvar.

"Then we garde will draw for it," Odo said, fishing out a pouch of stones from a pocket. He looked sheepishly down at them. "I like to collect them from riverbeds."

Claris peered over the stones and pointed to one that appeared smooth with a blue hue. "That one."

Odo nodded, put them back into the pouch and shook it up. Flore went first and retrieved a small black stone.

Torsten stuck his hand in, and out came the exact stone Claris had chosen.

Claris wondered if Halvar would say that the Will made it so, or if indeed some portent from the gods. Her nerves tingled.

"Here," she finally said, holding a key out to Odo. "Looks like you and Flore."

"Meet back downstairs for a meal?" Flore asked.

Claris nodded and turned with key in hand to her and Torsten's door. Her breath quickened at that thought.

Pepin scratched at the door, eager to be let in.

It was perhaps the smallest room Claris had encountered, with a bed tucked into one corner and a wash basin in another. She was glad to unburden her back as she removed her pack, but there was only one bed. A bed large enough to share, but she didn't think that was what the innkeeper meant when he said she'd have to share.

Based on her attire, and that she travelled freely among men, the innkeeper likely thought nothing of it.

She turned, and found Torsten filled what little space there was. Pepin leaped up onto the bed, turned in a few circles, and laid down. Torsten then went to open his mouth, but Claris fled the room before he spoke. She'd face the inevitable later.

A cooked meal eaten inside was a luxury she missed, even if they had this not long ago in Ladonnes. The others were already at one of the tables, and Claris took a spot beside Brahim. Of course, that meant Torsten sat across from her.

Bowls of soup were brought out with a chunk of bread each. Thankfully for Claris they all ate in silence, though Torsten did his best to catch her gaze.

Brahim turned to Claris once they were done. "A word, if you will."

The garde took their cue and left the table.

"Tomorrow I will seek my contact for the glass," Brahim said.

"And then you need a weaponsmith?" Claris asked.

"Though that may be harder."

"The blade will need two days," Halvar said.

"So, we must hope whoever we find can do it immediately," Brahim finished.

"And that is where your coin comes in," Claris said. "I cannot use my status."

Brahim tapped once on the table, and Halvar stood and left.

"Do you know why I gave you that challenge last night?" Brahim asked.

She knew this would come and was grateful he had chosen not to talk about it in front of the others. "Because everyone needs to practice."

"That is only half of it," he replied. "What is important is to be prepared for the unexpected. We may only have one shot with the demi-lich and it cannot be a miss."

Claris looked down at her hands. "I thought you were beginning to trust my abilities."

"Yet neither of us want to fail." She looked up and couldn't decipher his expression, but it didn't seem one of contempt. "You may leave," he said.

"I would go with you tomorrow," she said as she stood.

He looked up at her and nodded.

Not wanting to push further, Claris led Pepin back up the stairs and to the room. Torsten wasn't there and she figured he had gone somewhere with Flore and Odo. Her insides knotted at the mere thought of him returning and what could be said between them. She had been hot and cold with him, and she wondered if she'd done irreparable damage to their relationship. He hadn't spoken a word to her since last night. Since he had confessed she'd hurt his heart. She pressed a fist into her chest, willing the ache to subside.

Pepin mewed up at her and made himself comfortable on the bed. She had too many thoughts skipping through her mind. She knelt before the bed and took a deep breath.

"You were meant to help guide me," she started, "with the matters of the heart I will never be able to talk to Father on. It is consuming me and leaving me missing you more than normal." She smiled. "Though I am sure you would disapprove of my choice."

Footsteps outside her door made her stop and stand. Torsten stood at the threshold for a moment before entering and closing the door behind him; his eyes strayed first to Pepin.

There was little space in which to go, so Claris sat beside the cat, while Torsten stood in the small space. She gave over her position to allow his height to tower over her. She clasped and unclasped her hands, uncertain on to how to fill the silence.

To her surprise, Torsten knelt before her, head bowed. "I'd give it all up for you. Reach in my chest, offer my heart."

Her forehead creased, her lips parting. Her pulse pounded.

"When I saw you in that courtyard," he started, "I thought I found a piece of home. But you are noble, not Suevik. Not one with the freedom those of Suevia are afforded."

Claris felt her eyes moisten, but she willed herself to not cry.

"But I know that is not your wish. Allow me to serve by your side, and I can be content."

Her frown deepened. She needed to see his eyes. She reached out and gave his chin an encouraging lift upward. Her mouth dried at his stare. Claris longed to be seen as an equal, and he offered such a prospect.

"Demoiselle?"

Claris swallowed. "I..." She couldn't find the right words. "It is not easy for me, to have the weight of my status, my expectations on me. It feels like I am unable to do what my own heart desires. That I must live by my mind alone." She took a shaky breath. "And please, you know my stance on that title."

His lips twitched. "Of course... Claris."

"Now, please, stop kneeling."

As he stood, Claris turned her head aside, heat flushing up the back of her neck. He shifted to collect his bedroll to lay down on the floor. She was about to question why he wouldn't join her on the bed, for there was room, but shut the thought down. Perhaps she and Torsten could have a comfortable truth between them. Even if that meant she lived with a permanent pain in her chest.

Claris manoeuvred around Pepin and got as comfortable as possible on the bed.

"I do apologise in advance if Pepin jumps on you," she said as Torsten doused the lamp.

"Sleep well, Claris."

"And you... Torsten."

Claris found she couldn't close her eyes, letting them adjust to the new gloom and watching him. His own eyes were closed. She tried to still and quieten her breaths as much as possible. Her mind recalled Flore's words, and they were right. They could die.

"Is there something you need?" His voice startled her, Pepin mewling at the disruption from the movement of her legs. Torsten's eyes opened and he gazed up at her.

"Sleep alludes me," she whispered.

He propped himself up on one elbow. "And how may I help?"

She bit her lower lip, thoughts straying to the last private moment they stole together. It was more than a week ago. She swallowed.

"Claris?" His voice but a whisper, a caress against her. She closed her eyes briefly. Her heart fluttered traitorously.

She clacked her tongue in command at Pepin, who slunk off the bed, albeit reluctantly. She reached out a hand, placing her palm against Torsten's cheek. He stilled under her touch. Claris smelt the musk of his body, the chilled sweat and dust in his clothes, longing skittering down her spine.

Her fingers drifted down to his shoulder. He shifted and came up on his knees, bringing himself closer.

Torsten leaned in. Claris closed her eyes. Whisper-soft kisses fell over her eyelids, down her neck, and to her shoulder. She shivered at the contact, at the gentleness. His fingers drifted along her arms, and she leaned towards him.

His lips traced the curve of her neck back up to the shell of her ear. "I'd like to kiss you."

Claris realised she'd like his presence, his close presence, to help chase the coldness still clinging to her. She wet her lips.

"Please." It barely came out as a whisper, but Torsten shared her need.

He pressed his lips gently against hers. Claris dug her fingers into the back of his shoulders, pulling him closer. He deepened the kiss, sending shivers all over her skin, and a hot demanding heat pulling at her insides. She didn't want this to end, tightening her fingers up behind his neck, one hand tangling up with his braid. Torsten was both tender and passionate.

Their breaths blended, and the press of their bodies communicated the urgency of all they dared not speak aloud. His fingers smoothed down her side, brushing against her breast, and slid to her hips. A small gasp left her lips, which Torsten eagerly smothered with his soft lips and lash of tongue, his insistent mouth intensifying the curling heat down past her navel.

Torsten moved from her lips, kissing the curve of her jaw, her neck. She swallowed heavily, feeling each kiss, each touch as if time stopped with each flash of desire jolting through her.

Her fingers dug in deeper in his back and scalp, pressing herself as close as she could to his body.

Pepin mewed.

Claris and Torsten stilled, with Claris's breaths coming out a little heavier.

A small knock sounded at the door. Pepin had stood and had his head bowed towards the door.

Torsten planted a kiss on her forehead and went to the door. He missed her entire body blushing with that one action.

He wedged it open, but Claris couldn't see past his frame to see who it was that had interrupted them.

Soft light swept into the room from the hall, and Torsten twisted to see her. "It is Odo. I will be back."

A frown pulled her eyebrows together, but he gave no more before stepping out and closing the door behind him.

Pepin immediately leapt up onto the bed, nuzzling his head under Claris's hand. She let out a heavy sigh and gave Pepin the attention he demanded. At least he distracted her from her swollen lips. Though she longed to finish what she'd started with Torsten.

A Soul Required

Day 18

Brahim and Halvar were already breaking their fast when Claris joined them downstairs. She'd fallen asleep before Torsten had returned last night, and she'd tasked him with watching over Pepin while he hunted for his meal.

"Halvar will seek us a blacksmith while we go to our contact," Brahim said and slid over some of the cheese and fruit.

"And what of my garde?" she asked.

Brahim looked away and shrugged. "A day of rest wouldn't go amiss."

"Will your contact be hard to locate?"

"No, they aren't one who hides."

One of the serving girls from last night came out and set a plate of cooked sausages between them.

Halvar pushed the plate towards Claris. "You first."

She had missed hot meals in the morning and gladly helped herself to one of the sausages. All three lapsed into silence while they ate.

Halvar was the first to finish. "I will see you back here at sun's peak."

As Brahim and Claris were leaving, Torsten returned with Pepin, who immediately wanted a scratch from Claris. She blushed at Torsten's gaze and tried to rein in her emotions.

"You and the others may fill the day as you please," Claris said to Torsten. "Just be sure to cause no unwanted attention."

Torsten nodded and entered the inn, while Pepin remained at her side.

Claris glanced back. "He will likely follow us."

Brahim sighed. "Of course, but it will not matter."

He led Claris to a tiny shop, unassuming with a tidy appearance, and even a planter box with well-tended flowers. Pepin went to investigate the smell of the blooms while Brahim knocked on the front door.

Claris didn't expect the contact to be a woman. Her skin was lighter than Brahim's and her brown eyes almost golden, but clearly of Djeyun descent. Claris's insides twisted at the thought of how free she must be, to live alone, unbeholden to the whims of a husband.

"Brahim," the woman said, "it's been a long time." Her eyes cut to Claris, some of her smile fading. "And who is this?"

"Aida," Brahim replied, "this is Claris, and she can be trusted." Aida's eyes flicked over the knives strapped to Claris.

"In you come then," Aida said, stepping to one side to let them inside.

The interior was as well-maintained as the exterior, with a variety of plants and paintings of flora tastefully placed in corners and on walls. Claris saw no sign of any other living being in the home.

Aida took them into a small, but cozy, sitting room. "Tea?"

Claris nodded. "That would be most appreciated."

"Thank you," Brahim said and settled onto one of the couches. Claris sat at the other end of it. She wanted to know how they knew each other, and how long it had been. Despite what Aida had said, neither behaved like it had been a long stretch of time.

Aida returned with a pot of tea and three cups. She poured out each cup before taking a seat on the opposite couch.

Claris took a small sip and tasted a hint of a spice, but one she couldn't place. Pepin stirred beside the couch.

"He is yours?" Aida asked.

Claris set the teacup down. "Had him since a kitten."

Aida turned her attention back to Brahim. "I doubt you visited for tea alone."

"We need some volcanic glass," Brahim said.

She didn't even blink. "How much, and how soon?"

"At least two bags, and now." Brahim sat forward. "We've got everything else we need, and time is of the essence."

When Aida stood, Pepin also got up from the floor. Claris reached over to give him a comforting pat as Aida left the room. "It's okay, boy."

She was about to ask Brahim a question but then noticed the faraway look to his eyes. So she let the silence continue, until Aida returned with two small leather pouches and set them down on the table in front of Brahim. He picked up one and checked the contents inside.

"And in return?" he asked.

Aida pointed to Pepin. "I'd have some lynx fur."

Pepin growled in her direction. Claris stilled.

"You would call that a fair trade?" Brahim said.

"I only want a little," Aida replied.

Claris unsheathed one of her knives. "You are not to come near him." She bent closer towards Pepin. "You will not even notice," she whispered to him. Claris took hold off some of his chest fur and slid the knife through it. Pepin licked her hand afterwards. Claris held the fur out in her palm.

Aida leaned over to collect it. "Much obliged."

"Do we get to know what you want that for?" Brahim asked.

She smiled and shook her head. "That's between me and my clients." Aida stood. "If there is nothing else?"

Brahim grinned. "You've never been this eager to get rid of me before."

Aide winked. "I've got a scheduled client coming soon."

Pepin mewed and Claris schooled her face to show nothing.

"We should return to Halvar," she said.

Brahim nodded, and they both followed Aida back to the front door and left without any more exchange of words. Claris checked the sun's position and was glad to see they still had time.

"You trust her?" Claris asked.

Brahim looked towards the house. "She poses no threat."

Claris frowned. It wasn't an answer to her question, not exactly.

"Do you see him?" Brahim said as he headed back towards the inn.

Claris nodded, even as her heart skipped a beat. "Three buildings back to our right." Had Brahim picked up on what was between her and Torsten?

"At least he is trying to improve."

Halvar leaned against the wall of the inn, and pushed away upon sight of Brahim, Claris, and Pepin.

"Did you find one?" Brahim asked.

"There is one near stables," Halvar replied. "He understands what we need but will not do the final blow."

Pepin pressed behind Claris's legs, and her skin prickled at the back of her neck. "That does not sound good."

Brahim looked around. "Not out here."

A sick clawing sensation began in the pit of her stomach. If a blacksmith, whose job it was to forge weapons, would not do the final step, it made her ill to think of what this knife would really cost them.

"We should get the blacksmith started," Halvar replied. "Time is precious."

Claris held her tongue and followed behind while Halvar led the way, but Claris was certain Torsten still followed. It made her think that Brahim had not wanted what Halvar spoke of known to the garde.

The stables were quieter, and smelt cleaner, than she would have expected. Pepin moved from her side, but a clack of her tongue had him remain. She didn't need him spooking any of the horses within.

The blacksmith was tucked behind the stables, and it appeared quite deserted. No fires burned.

Halvar knocked on the door, while Brahim peeked at the blacksmith's equipment and forge. Claris stayed near Halvar, at least maintaining the light sense of propriety her father would've expected.

The door swung inwards and revealed a man younger than one Claris imagined, especially for a master of his trade. She had expected someone quite advanced in years, though his brown hair did sport many grey hairs at the side.

"Best come in," the blacksmith said. The interior had a fine coat of dust over all the furniture and fixtures, with only a few smudges providing evidence of use.

The man directed them to a wooden table with mismatched wooden chairs. Claris took a seat. The blacksmith watched as Pepin settled beside her.

"You have everything?" he asked.

Together they turned over the special ingredients required to forge a lich-killing dagger.

"And you have one for the final blow?" he said.

Claris cleared her throat, but Brahim spoke first. "We have a group; one will do the honours."

The blacksmith's eyes narrowed. "You've more than one willing to give up their life for this?"

Claris's eyes widened, her mouth falling open, but no sound coming. They couldn't be serious. This blacksmith expected someone to die. Her vision blurred as her heart thudded.

Pepin's head nudged into her hands. Her eyes narrowed towards Brahim. Both him and Halvar had known this and hadn't disclosed it. She would have words with him once they had left. How dare they not mention a sacrifice was required. A sacrifice of someone she'd grown close to, someone who trusted her.

"They are loyal," Brahim replied, as if he wasn't discussing the demise of one of her garde.

Claris grew hot as her hands clenched into tight fists. She had three garde left. All good warriors. None deserved such a fate. It sunk deep into her insides.

She let out a forceful breath. "When will you need them for sacrifice?" She choked on the final word, and Pepin chortled towards the blacksmith.

"Tomorrow afternoon," the blacksmith said. "Is there a throwing dagger I can use as a template?"

Brahim nodded and slipped one free from his sheaths. Claris would need to practice more with the one she had of Brahim's style.

"Bring your man and the remaining payment tomorrow as the sun falls, and you'll have your weapon."

"I will stay with you," Halvar said. "You will need me here."

The blacksmith looked between the three of them before nodding. "Very well."

Claris and Brahim left the blacksmith, before Claris grabbed tight to Brahim's forearm. "With me."

He put up no resistance as Claris pulled him towards the stable.

"If I had told you earlier, you wouldn't have agreed," Brahim said, his face almost void of any emotion.

Pepin growled as Claris tried not to lose her calm.

"The garde are mine, my father's soldiers, and I am responsible for their wellbeing," she started, doing her best to keep her voice low. Her pulse quickened. "You are a bastard." She shook. "An utter bastard."

Brahim raised an eyebrow but stayed silent.

She took a deep calming breath. "We have three left. Three. And we still need to face the demi-lich. You know you deceived me. Deceived them."

Pepin rubbed against and between her legs. She reached down to give him a pat, feeling tears at the corners of her eyes.

"Leading is making the hard calls," Brahim finally said. "The calls no one else wants to make. The ones that could break your soul, if you let them. I protected you from that for as long as I could."

She clenched her hand momentarily. Closed her eyes. Let out a shaky laugh.

"Protected me?" She rubbed at her forehead. "That was not protecting me. That was cowardice."

Brahim stepped closer.

Her eyes opened. "Go back to the inn. I want to be left alone."

He glanced at Pepin before nodding and taking his leave.

Claris crouched and wrapped her arms around Pepin. She laid her head down on his back.

Horses shuffled restlessly in their stalls. One gave a low whinny. A shadow fell over her.

"Is everything okay?" Torsten asked.

She lifted her head to look up at him. "Not entirely."

"Halvar stays with a blacksmith, Brahim walks from here alone, and you're on the ground." Torsten held out a hand. "Let me help."

Tears pricked at her eyes. She swallowed. She must not cry before him.

"Claris?"

Pepin shifted away from her. She put her hand in Torsten's.

"I must talk to the others," she said.

They walked in silence back towards the inn. She tried to collect all her thoughts, and exactly what she could to say to Odo, Flore, and Torsten. But the words forming in her head all seemed insufficient. She wondered if her father had ever had to ask a garde to give their life outside a battle before.

Would he think her a monster? Would he recognise his own daughter upon her return? Her step faltered. She could offer herself in place of the garde. That would be a noble action. Claris sucked in a breath. Brahim would talk her out of it, so would the others. She wished there was another way. She cursed whoever warded the demi-lich, her resolve to hunt them down intensifying.

She stood at the entrance of the inn but couldn't make her legs take her any further.

Torsten remained at her side. "Shall I gather Odo and Flore?"

Claris nodded. "Yes. I will meet them where we sup."

He entered the inn, and Pepin pushed his head against her leg.

"I know, boy." She couldn't delay any longer. Whoever it was deserved some time before facing their end. She pulled her shoulders back and went inside. There was no way they could see her own reluctance. She had to be brave for them.

The three garde were already seated at a table. It took all her strength not to turn heel and walk back out.

They went to stand at her approach, but she shook her head. "No need for that. Please."

She took a seat opposite them.

"First, let me thank each of you for staying by my side, for proving yourself over and over again," she said. "Our journey has not been easy. We have lost men. But we still have far to go."

Claris reached down for Pepin, who licked her fingers.

"And what I must now ask is not easy, and it is not done lightly." She looked at each of them. "But the weapon we must forge demands a high price. It requires a soul."

None of the garde spoke. She swallowed and set her hands into her lap.

"I thought of offering my life in your place, but I know your honour would never allow that." She clasped her hands together, for fear their shaking would become visible.

The garde all tried to speak at once, each volunteering. Numbness spread through her insides. Her vision unfocused. They couldn't expect her to choose.

Odo cleared his throat. "Perhaps we draw for this, as well."

"Are you sure?" Her voice caught, and she swallowed.

"We would all volunteer," Flore said. "This way, the choice is out of all our hands."

Odo frowned at Torsten. "Though, my lady, it should be one of your own garde. Flore or I."

"He too has volunteered. I wish to lose none of you." Claris gave a small nod, refusing to make any eye contact.

Odo retrieved his pouch of stones. Claris chose a stone with a greenish hue this time. Odo handed the pouch to her. Her hands trembled as she shook up the stones and then opened the pouch, holding it out towards them. Pepin rubbed against her legs.

The garde all looked between themselves before Odo reached in first. Claris held her breath. He held a smooth white stone in his fingers. He set it aside, and Flore reached into the pouch. Claris still hadn't taken a breath. Flore pulled out the blue stone she'd previously chosen. She closed her eyes as Torsten took his turn. The pressure in her chest built.

"Me," Torsten said. The air rushed out of Claris. Between his fingers he held the green stone.

"Then..." She took a deep breath. "Then we thank you for your sacrifice." Her eyes stung with the threat of tears.

"It is an honour," Torsten said, his tone light despite the dire gravity of it all. "I'm okay with this. When will it happen?"

Her heart ached. "At dusk tomorrow." Pepin purred up at her, nuzzling his head into her lap. She thought of all the times Torsten told her he was her shield; he'd die for her. Every part of her ached and tingled, for he truly meant every word. He'd never been false with her. Her throat tightened.

Claris forced herself to look at both Odo and Flore. Their faces crestfallen, Odo's mouth partially open.

"We'd like the time to honour Torsten tonight," Flore said. "His sacrifice saves our own lives. We must thank him."

"Of course," she said and stood. "Rest assured this sacrifice will not go unacknowledged." With a nod, she dismissed them, watching Torsten leave behind the others.

Pepin mewed at her.

"If only I could throw some knives," she murmured towards him. Brahim must have taken refuge in his room, for she had not yet spied his presence.

"We can at least maintain our knives," Claris said and headed to the room, Pepin close on her heels.

Up in the room, her eyes strayed to Torsten's small set of belongings. She sniffed and returned her focus back to her blades. She shouldn't dwell on events she couldn't control. Besides, that was tomorrow, and the future would have to wait.

She choked back a sob. She flung the blade she held at the door, its point sticking in the wood with a wobble from the force. Claris couldn't change the draw, couldn't alter Torsten's fate.

A quick rap against the door stirred her from her task.

She opened it to find Brahim standing there. Her eyes narrowed, and she debated slamming the door back in his face.

"Would you like company for supper?" he asked.

"That is what you have to say?" She bit the words out; Pepin now stood beside her, his ears flattened.

Brahim looked to the lynx. "Please. Join me."

"Fine." She blew out a breath and encouraged Pepin to stay in the room. She didn't need her temper rubbing off onto him.

Even when food was served, Claris wasn't inclined for any conversation.

"It'll be a shame to lose Torsten's skills," Brahim finally said.

She stopped swirling her spoon through the stew. "They are all skilled." Claris minutely shook her head, lowly chuckling to herself. "But honestly. Their welfare must mean nothing to you. First, the secret about the warding." Her hands clenched. "Now, this. Both times costing a life."

"I'm—"

Claris cut him off. "No. I do not want your words." An ache throbbed behind her eyes. "I want none of your lies."

Brahim pushed aside his bowl. "I've done what is best for the goal. I will continue to do that." His tone measured.

She crossed her arms. "What is best is not losing good people."

"This is necessary," he said with a bit more force. "Relinquish your garde to me and you can run home."

"The garde are mine." Claris stood and walked from the room. She shook her head as she recollected his words. The nerve he had. The folly she had in believing he'd started to trust her.

She turned the corner and collided with Torsten.

They both took a hasty step back.

"I thought you were with the others," Claris said, her face flushing.

He looked down. "But that wasn't where I wanted to be."

Claris wished they were anywhere but there. Brahim could see them if he came this way.

Torsten looked at her. "Would you welcome my company?"

Her heartbeat fluttered, even as regret weighed at it.

"If that is your wish," she whispered, holding still in anticipation. Claris wanted to shed the notion that she'd failed him. She wanted their last moments together to be memorable.

"No," he said, voice lowering. "As you wish." The look he gave her was unhindered, the rawest she'd ever seen.

A Shared Moment

Day 18

"Where shall we go?" Her voice trembled.

Torsten drew his hand gently over the slope of her shoulder, her skin prickling at the touch of his warm fingers.

He leaned down towards her, his breath warm against her neck. "We can seek solitude elsewhere."

Claris sucked in a breath. "Where?"

Torsten held out his hand. "Your choice."

She wiped her sweaty palms against her clothes, before laying a hand in his.

He smiled and led them out of the inn. They walked side by side in silence as he guided her through the town. The sun had made its descent, and a low light pooled over them. Flickers of moonlight glinted from windows.

Torsten stopped before an unassuming building, but Claris was not entirely naïve. It was a pleasure house, a place where people could rent a room for a night. Some houses had dedicated staff, while others acted as a room rental service only.

She looked at him sideways, her fingers clenching over his own. "We already had a room."

"This would stay between us... but we don't have to," he said.

"Torsten..." But Claris didn't know the right words. Her eyes glistened with unshed tears. She very much wanted to, told herself the other night this was something she willed, even before his imminent demise.

His warmth radiated over her.

Claris turned her head towards him.

He put one hand gently at her back and leaned towards her. Her pulse picked up. His lips pressed against hers. She reached a hand to his face. They leaned into the kiss. A kiss filled with longing, regret, and unspoken desire. The taste of him was wood smoke and ale.

"Shall we go in?" he whispered, sending chills skittering down her spine. Nerves fired through her. She nodded, choking down a sob. She wouldn't cry. Claris didn't want this to be a sad moment.

Taking her hand once more, Torsten led her into the building. It was dimly lit with the sweet scent of incense burning. Stopping briefly near the front, Claris hanging back, he took possession of a key. He took her up a spiral staircase made of mahogany, the balustrade inlaid with gold. The door he paused before had a golden leaf motif inlaid above the handle. Torsten turned the key and led her in.

The room was larger than the one at the inn. A canopied, curtained bed sat proudly in the centre.

Her fingers fell from his as she approached the bed, sitting uncertainly on its edge. Torsten shuffled closer, their hips against one another.

His hand cupped her face. "We should make a memory you cannot forget."

Her hand closed over his, her head leaning into his touch. "I am sorry."

"Don't be." He leaned forward, pressing his lips gently against her forehead. "I'm where I chose to be."

Claris heart pounded. She ached for this, and a thousand consequences swarmed at the forefront of her mind, screaming at her how reckless she'd become. She was about to give her virtue to a man fated to die, a man without noble status. She closed her eyes, willing such thoughts away. This is what she'd chosen. She had just as much right to do as Torsten did. It'd be a moment between the two of them alone. No one else would ever know.

She shivered involuntarily as he ran his tongue over her lips, waiting for her permission to deepen the kiss. She parted them, and he bit her lower lip gently, drawing a moan from her. Claris's hands roamed over Torsten's broad back, feeling the warmth of his skin beneath her palms. His heart raced, beating in sync with hers, as if they shared a single pulse.

He rumbled with approval, snaking his arms around her back and lifting her towards his chest. Claris was atop his thighs, legs pressed on either side. His body was so hard against her own.

His hand strayed up to her hair, his lips shifting away. She immediately felt the loss. "You okay?" he asked.

Claris looked into his eyes. "Do not stop."

His mouth pressed back to hers. Her hands ran down over his chest, back over his arms, taking in all his hard muscle. Then his arms encased her, bodies pressing closer. His chest crushed to her own, his kisses deep and demanding. Claris submitted herself to the sensations, letting all her worries fall away. No longer a noble, no longer on a mission, no longer facing an imminent end. She freed herself, giving herself over to the pure sensation of pleasure.

Torsten unfastened both their cloaks, running his hand down her side, catching the fabric as it slid. His lips dropped to her neck; Claris tilted her head to the side, allowing him better access. Her inner core clenched, her fingers digging into his back.

His fingers crept up under her surcoat, featherlight against her flesh.

She knew what he wanted, the same thing as her. Claris released her grip on him, and tugged the surcoat up over her head, tossing it aside. His hand went to the tie of her breastband and let it loose, the fabric falling to her lap. Torsten covered one breast with a hand, while he dropped his mouth to her other. She whimpered at the contact, her flesh tightening.

It felt right. Her body against his. Their breaths both hot. Her body arced into his, his tongue flicking over her nipple. Claris dug her hands into his head, tugging his closer. His teeth scraped over flesh, sucking her nipple and breast into his mouth. Her breaths turned ragged, wetness pooling between her thighs.

She pulled his face back to hers, eager to taste his mouth once more. His thumb stroked over a nipple, letting her gasp, his tongue flicking inside her mouth.

He wrapped his arms around her back, and in one fluid motion had Claris on her back atop his cloak, his arms and chest caging her. She smiled shyly up at him.

He smiled back. "Perfect," he whispered, kissing the shell of her ear, nipping the lobe with his teeth.

His mouth fell back to her breasts, and her hands dug into his back. Tightness coiled low inside, the bundle of nerves aching for touch. She gripped his own shirt and tugged it towards his head. He helped her remove it and she splayed her palms over his naked chest, the warmth of his skin and the roughness of his hair, a contrast that sent shivers down her spine. He rumbled his pleasure at her touch.

Claris knew what she wanted, and was no longer happy to wait. She pushed down her trousers, knowing he watched the movement with hooded eyes. She flicked them off her feet, and though totally exposed, only heat caressed her body. His mouth fell back to hers, while he drifted a hand to rest over so close to the ache between her thighs. His fingers made lazy circles, quickening in a startling, but pleasurable, way. Claris bit his lower lip in response. He growled. She grabbed the band of his breeches and attempted to push it over his hips. She huffed out in frustration. His laugh rumbled through his chest.

The sound stunned her, stilling her fingers. His laugh flooded warmth through her, and tears threatened at the very thought of never hearing that sound again.

He finished the job for her, and Claris bit her lower lip, a little shocked, a little self-conscious of having Torsten fully naked atop her own naked body.

"Please tell me to continue," he breathed.

Her eyes went back to his. His eyes spoke volumes, that this moment was right. She saw nothing but her own longing reflected in them. A moment she'd not forget. "Continue," she whispered.

She swallowed heavily, feeling him pressed up against her. She wasn't uneducated in such matters and did her best to relax as much as possible. He held one hand against her hip, and shifted his weight, pressing into her, stretching her slowly. She gasped at the initial flare of pain, digging her fingers up around his waist and back. He moved in little by little, and peppered her neck, lips, and shoulders with tiny kisses as he fully eased and seated himself inside her. Claris's breath hitched, torn in separate spasms of an ache twisted up in both a tender pain and pleasure. She angled her hips and wrapped her legs up and over his waist, letting him fill her further. He lavished her with his mouth, tongues and teeth clashing together.

Torsten eased himself out and thrust back down inside her. She clenched at the movement, then gave herself over to the jolts of pleasure racing through her as Torsten repeated the motion, gathering a rhythm and tempo. Claris rocked her hips up, her body aching for more fiction.

His hand left her hip and slipped between them, thumb providing the much-needed friction. "Does this feel good?" he breathed heavily.

Claris opened her eyes. "Yes."

He kissed her on the forehead as her breathing increased. They moved together, Claris finding her own rhythm against Torsten, sighing from the almost painful coiling deep within her, pressure bubbling up, aching for release. Her fingers buried into his back, whole body tensing. Claris moaned as her body found release.

Torsten stopped. "You okay?"

Claris nodded, placed her hands on his face, and pressed her lips to his. His forehead dropped to hers, resuming his movements, hand retightening over her hip, his movements faster.

His breathing intensified, and Claris felt him throbbing inside her. She held him tighter, fervently kissing his neck and shoulder.

His muscles tensed underneath her. He groaned, pulling out from her suddenly. Torsten held himself as he grunted, spilling his seed over the sheets instead of inside her.

Claris's breathing evened, as she lay back on the bed, exhaustion creeping through her. Even on the verge of his own demise, he'd cut short his own pleasure to ensure Claris wouldn't have to worry about falling pregnant. A sharp pang lanced through her internally. So foolish, she thought, wishing she'd trusted him sooner.

Torsten lay down beside her, hand resting on her stomach, giving her his warmth.

She turned her head to face him, taking in his heavy breaths, his chest rising and falling.

As their breathing slowed, he rolled onto his side, pulling Claris close. He kissed her forehead, his fingers tracing patterns on her bare back.

Claris snuggled closer, her tears finally falling as she faced the harsh reality of their situation. "I needed this," she said. "I needed you."

He kissed away her tears. Her feelings defied all sense and sanity.

"I should get you back," he said, gently extracting himself from her, getting to his feet, and gathering up their clothes, holding them out to her. "Thank you for trusting me."

She smiled, torn between sadness and contentment. "I should thank you." Though she wouldn't say it aloud, she'd given a piece of herself over to Torsten, and hoped his soul would carry it with him once he'd passed.

Once they both were dressed, he rested a hand at her back as they left. Back at the inn, Claris was very thankful she encountered none other from their party on the way back to the room.

A sniff and meow behind the door cleared Claris's head.

She opened the door. Pepin raised up from the floor, turning his head between Claris and Torsten. Claris bent down to run her hands through his fur, and he gave her fingers a lick.

"You will have to sleep on the floor," she told Pepin. "Someone else is sharing the bed."

Torsten raised his eyebrows, and her cheeks flushed.

He draped an arm over her as they settled down on the bed, pulling her closer into the curve of his body. Cocooned within his warmth, she found her mind already drifting asleep.

"I'm here for you... Claris."

She swallowed. He wasn't going to be there after dusk tomorrow.

A Sacrifice Made

Day 19

She woke in the same position as she fell asleep. Torsten still pressed up against her back and his hand curled over her waist.

"Morning," he said. The thin curtains let the early dawn light into the room. No one else was likely awake yet.

Claris smiled. "You are awake."

"But at peace."

She took a deep breath and sat up. She wasn't sure her resolve would last long.

"We should not waste this day."

The bed shifted underneath her as Torsten sat too, his presence once again welcome at her side. "We can stay here?"

His fingers brushed lightly against her cheek, the calloused pads contrasting with her smooth skin. He leaned closer, pressing a tender kiss to her forehead. His lips trailed down, leaving a warm path against her brow, then her closed eyelids, before finally finding the curve of her mouth. The kisses were soft, deliberate; he treated each connection as if it were a quiet secret, savouring the intimacy that the morning allowed.

Claris's breath hitched, a swirl of conflicting emotions unfurling within her.

Torsten pulled back just enough to meet her eye. "Well?"

Her face flushed. He chuckled softly, the sound deep and resonant, as he brushed a stray strand of her flaxen hair behind her ear, fingers lingering by the port-wine stain near her left ear. A mark she had always been conscious of, but that he seemed to regard as a point of beauty.

"I'm at your command," he whispered into her ear, sending shivers down her back, even as her heart clenched.

A knock came at the door. Pepin stirred and stood, alert. It didn't sound like Brahim's hand. Claris slid free a knife and went over to it. Torsten shadowed close behind.

She opened it a sliver and widened it.

"Odo is missing," Flore said, lines etched on their forehead.

"When did you last see him?" Claris asked.

"He was with me as we returned for rest, but now there is no sign."

Claris turned to her belongings, fitting on her knife straps, cloak, and boots.

"And have you checked with Brahim and the proprietor?" Claris said.

Flore nodded. "Neither have seen him."

A sinking feeling weighed her insides. "Get Brahim. Meet us outside."

At the bottom of the stairs, the scent of cooked sausage stirred her stomach, but she pressed forward.

"What are you thinking?" Torsten asked, strapping his sword at his waist.

She looked up into his eyes. "He has done the one thing I dread."

Torsten's eyes widened. "He wouldn't. We drew for it."

Claris shook her head. "I fear he has."

"But you said dusk."

Brahim and Flore exited the inn.

Pepin, sensing Claris's volatile mix of anxiety and anger, growled towards Brahim.

He raised his hands. "I have no part in this."

"How would he know where to go?" Claris said, stepping towards him, unsheathing a knife. "I have put up with a lot, but my patience wanes."

"You think I would encourage it? I care not for which garde of yours dies for it, but we need that weapon." His brow was furrowed.

Claris looked into his eyes. "Best hope I am wrong on both counts."

She turned, clicked her tongue, and led them through the streets towards the blacksmith. The forge was still. Her brows furrowed. Knocking at the door had no response.

"Torsten, if you will." She stepped aside.

He broke the door down. Pepin darted in first. But the place was empty. No sign of even Halvar was to be found. There was no sign of struggle either.

She spun on Brahim. "Where did they go?"

He shook his head. "I know not."

Claris took a deep breath. "I am tired of games. Prove your worth. Halvar is magic. Surely your skills can track him and not just a lich."

Brahim looked at her. His eyes twitched. "Of course. Let us go outside."

She let him go first, and whispered to Flore as they passed, "Kill him if he tries to run." Flore gave a small nod and continued close behind Brahim.

They couldn't lose the weapon, nor the mage.

Brahim crouched down in the dirt, his fingers dug in through the fine layer of snow. Pepin paced around Claris's legs, feeding on her anxiety.

Torsten took a step towards her, but she shook her head. She needed no comfort. What she needed was to stay stoic, to focus on finding Odo. To prevent a foolish action.

Worry gnawed at her, unsettling her insides. Lines creased her forehead as she watched Brahim. She had no idea if he was doing something or not, adding to her disquiet. Her hands tapped against her knives.

Brahim stood. "They're towards the sea, but close to the river."

"Flore, walk with Brahim," Claris said. "I'll follow."

Pepin took the space between Brahim and Claris.

Torsten fell into step beside her. "What do you wish of me?"

Claris glanced towards him. "Look for signs he may be misleading us."

"After all this time?" Torsten had a hand rested near his weapon.

"We have come too far to lose now," she said.

They left the bounds of the town and headed towards the river, moving east. The snow was a minor nuisance, but only a light layer coated the earth. Claris watched the sun in the sky, keenly aware of time's passage.

The longer they took, the less likely they'd find Odo still alive. Two emotions warred within Claris: relief and anguish.

Torsten may be spared by Odo's action, but it gnawed at her that Odo would do this, especially without so much as a goodbye to his fellow garde. To her. Pepin purred at her side, giving what comfort he could. Her fingers twitched beside her knives.

She should've done better. Counselled her garde. Ensured they knew everything. That all were on the same page. Surely then Odo wouldn't have felt his action necessary.

Water trickling over rocks grew louder as they closed in on the river. Brahim paused at its bank, staring across its watery passage before moving on. Claris looked, but could not see what he was looking at, or for. Pepin took the chance to lap at the water before quickly returning to her side.

The sun had climbed higher towards its peak, and there was still no sign of Odo, Halvar, or the blacksmith.

"Are we close?" Claris called.

Brahim gave no response, except for a subtle shake of his head. Flore glanced back towards her, and Claris also shook her head. They may have made no progress, but Brahim gave no outward signs of betrayal. She couldn't let Flore execute him without good cause.

The river flowed south, and Claris wondered if they'd be able to return to the settlement before darkness draped the sky.

Brahim held up his hand and the whole party went still; even Pepin crouched low to the snow. Claris closed her eyes, willing her ears to hear more than the flow of the river, the breeze in the branches, or the breaths of those around her. A hand rested at the ready at her knives.

A long moment stretched in the air.

Her eyes snapped open as Brahim stepped towards the river. He took one more. She edged out a knife.

Then he turned to face them, his lips set flat in a grim line. He held one finger to his lips and gestured across the water. Rocks and shrubs sat upon that riverside bank, with the land receding behind them.

Claris assented and followed Brahim towards the river's edge. Its span was not too great, but enough she'd feel its icy bite long after they left its depths. He picked a spot to cross—the water came up over his knees—and the rest followed his exact path. One wrong step could see them plunge deeper down into the river.

She gritted her teeth as she took that first step, then another, the water eagerly enveloping her legs in cold. Pepin splashed in beside her, not concerned by its chill. Claris kept her arms up high, doing her best to keep balance and less of herself wet.

Torsten stood at the other side, arm reached out to help Claris from the river. Brahim and Flore were crouched at some rocks. Claris tried to ignore the chilly bite and knelt near Brahim.

"Well?" she asked.

"They should be down this decline and to our east," Brahim said. "The magic has intensified."

Her insides clenched. "That does not bode well."

"For your man, no."

She went to stand and Brahim's hand shot out to grip her upper arm. Pepin growled lowly.

"We must not interrupt Halvar if he is mid-rite," Brahim said.

Claris twisted her arm free. "Why?"

"They'd have to start anew, blade and all." Brahim's eyes drifted to where Torsten crouched. He didn't need to add what the true cost would be. Another of her garde's life.

Torsten shuffled closer. "What do we wait for?"

Brahim cleared his throat. "Let me go."

Her eyes narrowed, and her gut clenched. She couldn't let Odo die without him knowing she came for him, that she did care about all their lives.

Claris stood. "We will all go." She turned to Torsten. "Prepare for the worst, but we cannot interfere."

They moved tentatively down the slope, knowing rocks could be hidden beneath the snow cover.

Brahim had not lied. Odo was on his knees, with Halvar poised over him. Torsten took a step in front of Claris, but she reached out and grabbed his arm gently. He put up no resistance.

Halvar and Odo noticed their presence. The blacksmith paid them no mind. He held a dagger in one outstretched hand towards Odo.

Though she knew it impossible. She couldn't sense magic like Brahim. Though Claris swore she felt an unknown energy, almost another presence in the air around them.

Halvar gripped Odo's shoulder.

Odo looked up towards Claris and Torsten.

"Death with no regrets," Odo said, a small smile on his lips.

Halvar sliced the dagger across Odo's throat.

The light left his eyes. His body slumped forward. All around them went quiet. Pepin put a paw on Claris's foot. No one moved, and no one spoke. Claris wondered if Odo's last words were for her, or for the other garde. The sting of tears blurred her vision. She couldn't bring herself to action.

Halvar broke the silence. He took the knife from the blacksmith, and walked over to Brahim, presenting it to him hilt first. Claris couldn't take her attention away from Odo's lifeless form. From the blood staining the snow crimson.

Flore went before her. "Demoiselle?"

She watched as Brahim took the knife. Fury burning through her veins, giving her extra warmth amongst the snow, she went to stand before Halvar.

"What right of yours possessed you to such action?" she asked. Though Pepin disliked the mage's proximity, he stuck by Claris's side and bared his teeth.

Halvar looked over the party. "Odo came to me. Urged it was the only way."

"The knife was to be forged as sun falls," Claris said, sure the time of day had held importance.

"Time has no sway to magic," Halvar said. "He even came with the remaining payment."

Claris looked away. She couldn't believe Odo would betray her trust, go through her belongings in such a way. Her gaze fell to Brahim.

Before he could speak, Halvar held up his hand. "He had no knowledge. If you must place blame, then it lies at my feet."

She took a deep breath. They still had the demi-lich to hunt and kill; they now had the means to do so. Flore still awaited her orders. Torsten's focus was all on Odo's body. Falling apart couldn't happen.

She couldn't shake the unanswered question of why Odo would do such a thing, why those were his final words. She rubbed at her temples. He was the youngest of her remaining garde. He had so much future ahead of him and yet chose this. She shook her head. It didn't make sense. She sorely wanted it to.

"We will send Odo on, and daybreak tomorrow we resume our hunt," Claris finally said, snapping out of her thoughts.

The blacksmith still stood nearby.

"Do you have your payment?" Claris asked, and the man nodded. "And do we have your silence?"

He looked between them all. "Of course. My reputation is important, but a good word from you would be most welcome."

Claris knew he only did the task that was asked of him. "If your blade succeeds in its task, you will have it."

The blacksmith gave a small bow. "Thank you. If I may?"

Claris nodded and he made his departure.

"Should we move Odo's body?" Flore asked.

"No," she said. "We do not want the town's attention. We will do so out here." She turned back to Brahim. "You need to find where we next head."

"I will prepare the wood," Flore said and headed for the nearby trees.

Torsten broke from his solitude. His shoulders still curled over his chest, his whole form crumpled in; a posture she'd never once seen from him. "I will help."

Claris remained silent, letting her two remaining garde carry out the necessary task. Brahim had moved a distance away, crouching down to tune in with the ley lines. At least the ley had returned. Pepin curled within the snow, close to Odo's body.

Halvar stepped towards her. "Can I offer any assistance?"

She couldn't bring herself to look at him. "Are you sure the blade will work?"

He tapped at some runes adorning his flesh. "Magic doesn't lie."

There was no one to truly direct her anger at. The deed was done. Nothing could undo it. "Return to the inn. We need the rooms another night."

Halvar moved away.

Claris let her hands run down over her knives. She itched to throw them. It would take time to build the pyre to burn Odo's body. She moved towards trees, away from where Flore and Torsten chopped at others. Pepin raised his head, watching her leave, but he stayed put. Though she ensured she'd stay in sight of the others.

She freed her first knife from its sheath, took aim, and released. The motion was freeing, breaking her free from thoughts. Claris swallowed back a lump that rose suddenly in her throat. It was harder to forget. Throwing knives wasn't going to be the answer this time. She went to the tree, pulled the lone blade free, then knelt in the snow.

"I hope you have seen the ways this journey has changed me," Claris said, head bowed. "Travelled further than you could have imagined seeing your daughter go, especially without Father. All the choices I have made, the deaths I carry on my shoulders, are ones I know you would not have wanted for me, but I do hope you are proud of me."

Snow crunched behind her.

She closed her eyes momentarily, then stood. Brahim had approached but kept a respectful distance.

"What have you found?" she asked.

"It is somewhere to our north-west," he replied.

"Then we should head to Montes." She closed the gap between them. They'd cross over another boundary, into another territory, a march. She knew little of the marquis, but knew he'd lost two wives to illnesses. Her father had received a missive from the marquis enquiring about Claris, as if feeling the comte out to see if he'd be open to offering her hand as his third wife.

He frowned. "We should not waste time. We should cut a direct route."

"Through the woods and wilds?" Claris questioned.

"Would there be farmlands?"

She shook her head. "Not that far north. Mining and fishing are their province."

"I would find some maps to chart a route," he said.

Claris remained silent. He phrased it in such a way as if he asked her for permission. Brahim waited for her response. She watched Flore and Torsten pile up chopped wood.

"My garde will keep me safe," she said. "Return to our lodgings. Find our best path."

The sun started its descent, and she knew they wouldn't be done until darkness was well established.

Brahim placed a hand on her upper arm. "You did all you could. Do not carry Odo's death upon yourself." Claris didn't trust herself to speak, so she nodded. He took his leave, and Claris returned to Pepin and Odo's body. There she sat until the pyre was complete. They had finished the grim work under night's glow.

"Shall we light it?" Torsten asked, once he and Flore had shifted Odo's body.

Claris stood, brushing away snow. "Yes."

Together the three of them stood before the burning pyre, their heads bowed. The wind blew the smoke away from where they stood. Insects flew near, attracted by the light from the fire, but repelled by the heat.

Tears pricked at her eyes. She kept circling back to the unanswered question as to why he did this. The only hint he might've been displeased about Torsten was he was not one of her own garde, not truly responsible for her safety. She pressed her fist into her chest, willing the hurt away. No one should ever have to be put in that position.

Torsten turned to her at first sign the fire was dying. "You should head back."

"Flore, please start ahead." They looked between Claris and Torsten before giving a short nod and went on their way.

"Torsten." Claris swallowed, finding it hard to form the words. "Are you okay?"

His eyes went to the fire. He shook his head. "I've lost friends before, but this is different. Odo didn't just die. He sacrificed himself when he didn't have to." His throat bobbed. "He had such ambitions. Now..."

Claris reached out, fitting her hand into his.

But Torsten let his hand fall away from her. "I think I might stay a little longer."

She sucked in a breath. The colour appeared to be leeched from his eyes. She understood his desire to be alone, and hoped he'd be okay.

A Heavy Burden

Day 20

By the time she reached her room back at the inn, dawn was not far away. Claris collapsed onto the bed.

The silence of the dimly lit room at the inn felt oppressive. Her breath trembled, shallow and frantic. Pepin perched close by, his amber eyes glistening with a sense of understanding and concern as he leaned against her thigh.

The weight of Odo's sacrifice pressed upon her chest like a boulder. The flicker of the lone candle cast wavering shadows that seemed to dance and mock her. Taunting her for not restraining herself better.

She buried her face in her hands, stifling a choked sob that threatened to escape. Tears cascaded down her cheeks. The fire that had consumed Odo's body—the crackling of the flames and the smoke that had risen—was seared into her memory. She watched as the remnants of his brave soul were reduced to ash, his noble sacrifice a bitter irony against the passion she shared with Torsten.

Her heart ached, a jagged wound that felt insurmountable.

"Why, Odo?" she whispered, as the truth lingered in her throat. She'd gained one life while losing another. A cruel twist of fate.

As Pepin moved closer, nudging her leg with his furry head, she felt the warmth of his presence grounding her. She stroked his fur, seeking comfort.

Claris exhaled a shuddering breath, releasing the pent-up agony in a visceral wave. The tears flowed freely now, un-abated, a cathartic release of all that had fractured within her.

At some point Claris must've succumbed to sleep from her grief, the streaks of dry tears on her face a reminder of all that had transpired. Pepin raised his head as she stirred. They'd need to leave soon.

Sitting up, she realised Torsten hadn't returned to the room, though his belongings were absent.

She frowned. He had come back, only to leave without her knowledge.

Claris found Brahim and Flore downstairs, packed and ready.

"How long?" Claris asked Brahim.

"If we make good ground, five days," he replied. Claris looked but saw no sign of Halvar or Torsten. "They wait outside." Her mouth dried at the thought that perhaps Torsten avoided her.

"You have the blade?" Her eyes went to his knives.

He tapped his thigh. "It will work."

Claris couldn't let doubt trap her; she simply nodded and headed outside. The sooner they completed the task, the better.

They had decided against using horses for this journey; the path Brahim had charted was treacherous enough without the added burden. The snow-covered terrain would make progress slow, perhaps even slower than if they had chosen to ride. They would follow the course of the river for as long as possible, navigating its twists and turns.

As they made their way outside Gien, Claris went to approach Torsten, desperate for him to at least look at her, when Flore came to her side.

"Odo made his choice."

Claris clacked her tongue, waving Pepin onwards before her. "You were there when Torsten drew the stone."

"I did say we were not blind," Flore replied. "Our service is yours, Demoiselle, and he sacrificed himself more than for this quest. He did it for your happiness."

She stumbled, Flore grabbing her arm to steady her. With a small intake of breath Claris gaped at her garde. She couldn't believe such words, that they all knew, and didn't care? Didn't think less of her for it? She had to have misheard.

"You okay?" Flore asked, letting her go.

Claris shook her head. "That cannot be true. Garde must do what is best for the mission."

Flore gave her an almost sad smile. "A broken heart would have no hope to pierce another."

Claris opened her mouth, then closed it. She knew they needed a response, reassurance she was okay. "Thank you, Flore."

They gave a small nod before allowing her to fall back into her thoughts.

Though Flore's words were intended to bring her solace, they pricked at Claris like thorns. She glanced at Torsten, who walked alongside Halvar. She had allowed her own emotions to cloud their mission. Her father's voice echoed in her mind, admonishing her for such recklessness. She hoped that by Odo taking Torsten's place, even after drawing lots, it would draw no ire from any gods or higher power.

"Much weighs on you."

Claris hadn't noticed Halvar come up beside her, and her hands instantly went to her knives. She shouldn't let herself get lost in thoughts. Not while travelling. They'd encountered plenty to keep her wary. Even Pepin putting distance between her and Halvar should've registered.

"Am I that obvious?"

"There is much I've witnessed," he said, "and I know a heavy soul when I see one."

She knew she shouldn't blame Halvar for what happened to Odo, but it was hard to take. It couldn't have happened without his involvement.

She breathed deep. "I have led Roul, Sigibert, and now Odo to their end. Left Dalfin behind." Claris shook her head. "I know this is what the code of a garde means... but it does not make the burden easier."

"Voicing this is good." Halvar nodded to the white wild landscape before them. "The wind will carry it away, lighten your soul. Know attachments amplify burdens and grief, and what comes from such emotions."

Claris stopped in her tracks and looked to the open land-scape. She didn't feel any lighter; the ache in her chest threatened to widen to a chasm. She yearned to prove herself, be a leader, but with how hard her heart was hurting, she doubted she was strong enough to follow it all through.

Gien now stood in the distance behind them as they stuck close to the river. They sky was dim from cloud cover, but there were no outward signs that spelled trouble.

She gazed towards Brahim; he had brought them on this quest for the demi-lich, the very reason they were trudging through the snow, the tops of their noses pink from cold. A month hadn't even passed, yet so much had changed. He wasn't outwardly trying to antagonise her anymore, but his lies had fractured whatever accord they had.

As the sun reached its peak, they stopped for a quick respite.

Pepin took the opportunity to hunt food for himself, while Claris opted for practice. Brahim couldn't keep away.

"Have you practiced with my blade?"

Claris kept her eyes on the target. "I have the one." She knew it wasn't a good response, and she couldn't help the instant need to defend her actions, to explain herself.

"Then you throw it, then retrieve it. Repeat."

She threw another of her blades. "I will keep that in mind."

Brahim's eyes sparked in what she took for amusement. He said no more and went back to the others. She should ask him to test the ley lines again to ensure they stayed on course.

The blade to kill the lich was forged to match Brahim's blades. Claris knew she'd have to master a throw with them, in case it all fell to her. A scenario that seemed likely with their numbers already so low. She took a deep breath and did exactly as Brahim said. She threw his knife, retrieved it, and thew again.

Flore and Torsten packed up the few belongings, ready to continue their way. Claris sighed; she should have been the one to tell them to move on. She went to the tree and removed her knives, safely tucking them back into her sheaths. Claris made a mental note to be the one to stop them at day's end. She needed to do better; be the leader she convinced her father she could be. She couldn't let grief win a battle she'd fought long for.

The running river was a constant noise, almost soothing to Claris. It made the landscape less lonely. She'd surely miss its presence once they cleared its path. She let out a heavy sigh, her mind straying to Ziri. For Ziri, every day had to end with something new learnt. Claris wasn't sure what she learnt on this journey, but hoped she'd become better.

"Demoiselle?" The concern in Flore's voice must've meant they'd been trying for her attention.

She looked down, but Pepin's familiar presence wasn't there.

"Are you okay?" Flore asked.

Her brows furrowed, her first thought thinking it would've been Torsten checking in on her.

Claris let out a deep breath. "Of course. I did not mean to cause worry."

Flore gave her a small nod and moved back to their position. Her eyes sought out Torsten, but his shoulders were hunched as he marched forward through the snow. Not even a glance back at her.

With his presence absent, she was keenly aware of Pepin's whereabouts. He was not in sight. He must've been hungry, or bored as she daydreamed.

Based on the sun's position, they'd still be near the river when they broke for camp. Both the weather and landscape put any thoughts of pushing far into the night from her mind. Time was against them, but they had to survive the trek to defeat the lich.

She went up to Brahim. "Would others now be tracking the demi-lich? It's path surely has not gone unnoticed."

"It is likely," he said with shrug, "but unlikely they have the right weapon."

"Because self-sacrifice is rare, or mages are rare?" Claris asked, a bite to her reply.

"Because demi-lichs in this state are rarer."

It did little to bolster her confidence. A small part of her hoped they'd meet others of the mind to improve their odds. More bodies would surely be a boon. A few small farms made their homes close to the river, yet they seemed almost abandoned and desolate in winter.

As the sky darkened, they still had the river by their side. They wouldn't depart from its path until likely midday tomorrow, where they would head more north-west, towards forest and Montes.

Brahim pushed them as far as the dying light permitted.

Pepin curled up tight, but not too close, to where the fire danced. She watched for a moment longer, for when Torsten would make his way to her side. But he had his back towards her, busying himself over the campfire.

Halvar once again came to her side. He held a small piece of parchment in one hand.

"Some say writing a burden down to burn will help one release it from their shoulders," he said, offering the parchment to her.

"Has it helped you?" she asked as she took it.

"My burdens are many, the weight of my hammer reminds me of this."

Yet he offered her a path that might help ease all on her mind. She doubted it would work, but it wouldn't hurt to try.

She searched the supplies but turned up no quill and ink. Claris tucked the parchment into her clothing, promising herself to write something when she could.

A STORM DESCENDS

DAY 21

As the sun arced towards its zenith, the group departed from the riverside. All morning, Claris waited for Torsten's approach, but it never came. Even as she had stood in the chilly air, he hadn't come to her to offer her warmth.

Her heavy breath was a visible plume before her face. The snowfall thickened and the wind gathered its strength. Flurries grew heavy, each flake adding to the blinding white threatening to erase their path ahead.

Claris drew her cloak tighter around her shoulders, the weight of her knife sheaths reassuring against her limbs. She kept her eyes wide and alert. Pepin pressed in close to her legs.

They all grouped closer together, and though Torsten moved to her side, he remained silent, not even sparing her a glance. Her heart clenched.

Brahim marched ahead of them, cutting through the growing tempest with resolve. Halvar's skin emitted a soft blue as he activated runes, but Claris couldn't discern any visible change in their surroundings.

Each step took them further from the river's comforting murmur.

She squinted against the vengeful sky, her vision snatched away by a maelstrom of white. The world had become an ever-shifting veil of snowflakes. They swirled with malicious grace around her, stinging her cheeks, blinding her to all but the vague shapes of Brahim's cloak and Torsten's hunched shoulders.

She trudged forward, focusing on the rhythm of her breath; a metronome of survival. Each inhalation pierced like a frost-laden dagger, while each exhalation released a ghostly plume into the tempest. The relentless wind howled around her, challenging her resolve and threatening to erode her will.

Beneath her booted feet, the terrain conspired against her every movement. Snowdrifts appeared deceptively soft, yet treacherous as she plunged through their crust. The powdery depths grasped at her legs, seeking to pull her down. Hidden beneath lay unseen dangers, crevices that yawned like open jaws of the earth, ready to swallow the unwary.

She trusted in Pepin, who leaned against her legs, giving her nudges as needed when she strayed to a path he didn't approve of.

With each faltering step, her senses heightened, attuned to the shifts in the density of the snow, the slight depressions that hinted at voids beneath. She refused to succumb to the land's insidious traps. Ice crystals adorned her lashes, and she knew they'd need warmth soon, or they'd perish in the cold.

"We should stop." Wind snatched away her voice. None gave any indication that they'd heard her. She knew it was foolish for them to continue, but not even Brahim seemed eager to halt his pace.

Visibility had all but vanished.

She'd lost sight of Brahim and Torsten, and soon the warm press of Pepin against her side vanished.

She called out once, twice, thrice. "Pepin!" But her cries were unheard.

Claris closed her eyes momentarily and strained to hear any sound that didn't belong to the storm. The subtle crunch of snow beneath boots, the muted jingle of equipment, all absent. She sniffed at the biting wind, hoping to catch a familiar scent. But nothing.

She halted, her heart a drumbeat of alarm. Isolation crept upon her.

Claris trusted the others to seek shelter and weather the storm until it passed. But she had to find Pepin.

"Pepin!"

Her voice, thinned by desperation, barely cut through the howling gale.

Memories of her and Pepin, side by side, flashed before her like spectres; hunting in the woods, sharing quiet moments beneath starlit skies, the lynx's chirp a soothing constant in the backdrop of her life.

She called again, her voice hoarser, her throat raw from the effort. "Pepin!"

Claris pressed forward. The wind lashed at her with icy tendrils, stinging her eyes.

Her throat, raw and aching, bore the burden of her desperation as much as her legs bore the weight of her body through the deepening drifts.

How had she not yet come across any of the others? Were they not looking for her? Surely Torsten would be searching for her as much as she searched for Pepin.

A dim outline emerged, a mere whisper against the stark whiteness that surrounded her. Claris's breath hitched, a shard of hope piercing the numbness that had settled in her bones. Her eyes, red-rimmed and squinting against the fury of the storm, focused on the small figure huddled at the base of an ancient tree, its limbs gnarled and bowed by the weight of winter.

As she drew closer, the figure took on the familiar contours of her faithful lynx. "Pepin," she whispered, her lungs seared by the frigid wind. "The gods must not be vengeful."

She dropped to her knees, oblivious to the ice that bit into her flesh, her focus solely on the small, shivering form before her. Claris reached out to him, pulling him close to the warmth of her chest.

She buried her face in his neck, her breath hot and ragged against his skin. He purred quietly.

"Forgive me," she murmured into his ear. She never should have lost sight of him.

Pepin nuzzled into her, his breaths syncing with her own.

With him safely in her arms, she almost forgot the chaos of the storm they found themselves in. She swallowed hard. The others couldn't be far.

As if summoned by thought, a blue glow loomed through the veil of white. Halvar stood tall, Brahim, Flore, and Torsten close behind his massive frame.

Claris blinked up, noting the wind easing a little within Halvar's presence, his whole body and hammer alight with lit runes.

Brahim knelt at her side, while Flore fussed over on her other side, checking both her and Pepin for obvious injuries.

"Steady now," Brahim said, offering a hand to help her rise.

A gentle warmth fell over her limbs, the chill thawing a little from her bones. A few of Halvar's runes pulsed with the new use of magic.

"Is there shelter nearby?" she asked, her throat thick and parched.

"We passed a cave mouth not too far back," Flore said.

Even in the storm's fury, the dimming of light told Claris twilight bled into night. They couldn't stay out in the open.

"Better there than here," she said with a nod.

Huddled close, the thick layer of snow muffled their footfalls. The cave's entrance yawned wide, inviting them into darkness.

Inside, the air was heavy with the scent of damp stone and ancient earth. Halvar increased his blue glow to illuminate their surroundings, casting long shadows that danced across the rough-hewn walls. Torsten set about gathering fallen branches and dry moss to create a small fire in the centre of the cave. Claris let Pepin out of her arms.

Outside, the storm raged on, giving no signs of abating.

The flickering fire cast a warm glow over their faces as they huddled together, eager to share warmth. Pepin lay curled next to Claris, his presence a comforting weight against her side. Torsten had placed himself away from her.

"We should have stopped," Claris said, breaking the silence, her gaze focused on Brahim. "I told you to."

Brahim's gaze met hers. "If you did, I heard not."

"But it would have been prudent to, even without my words," she insisted, her eyes narrowing.

"It came on quick," he replied. "Then I lost sight of you all. We're lucky none of us were lost."

"Even I said to stop," Flore added.

Brahim swallowed, she'd never seen him unsettled. "I was adamant we could press before the storm worsened."

Claris turned her eyes to Halvar. "And your magic, why not use it sooner?" Flore busied themselves with sourcing food from their supplies.

He rapped his knuckles against his hammer. "I did. That is why we are all here now."

"Let us hope we reach this demi-lich soon," Claris said, sighing. The cold would only harshen as they travelled further north. "We cannot afford to lose another to foolishness."

The crackle of the fire filled the quiet.

"The cold is unnatural." Halvar broke through the silence. "We must be close to the demi-lich."

Brahim shifted in his spot. "There... there is something I should share."

Claris braced herself, hoping he'd not hidden something else vital about their journey.

A shudder passed through him. "It was a night much like this. A storm that snatches all sight and sound." His eyes lifted from the fire to snag Claris's own. She frowned, an unease settling over her from his words.

"In that storm, a demi-lich arrived in our village. My wife held our babe close to her chest." His eyes closed. Pepin raised his head, also focused on Brahim's words.

"I'd yet to face such a creature. I stood defiant, confident I'd save them." The firelight carved deep lines of anguish into his visage. "It battered me aside from my futile attempt. Then it wrenched their spirits away from them. My beloved, my child, lost to an eternity of silence."

He looked away, outside the cave, as if expecting the demi-lich to materialise.

"It is..." His voice fractured. "The demi-lich we hunt is the one that stole them from me. It's why I am so determined not to fail. Not again."

Claris sat motionless; the gravity of his loss pulled at her.

Flore reached across and rested their hand atop Brahim's own. "We will kill the demi-lich."

"Not just for your family," Claris said, "but for all those lives lost in Arson."

"For Roul, Sigibert, for Odo," Torsten added. Her eyes flicked over to him, but his gaze was trained on the fire.

Halvar stamped his hammer into the ground. "For all of us."

As they shared the meal over the fire, Claris looked towards Brahim, now understanding him a little better, his dogged determination. She didn't think he harboured any more secrets, for that one seemed like the biggest. The most personal. Surely she could trust his word, his actions, once more?

"We should take rest," Brahim said, "we will have much ground to make up for."

Pepin nuzzled into her as Claris lay down close to the fire. She watched as Torsten made himself comfortable, again not near her. The gulf between them yawned wider. She didn't understand it. The pain in her chest refused to abate at the thought of him and his distance.

A Repeated Practice
Day 22

The dawn unfurled its pale light over a world washed clean by the tempest's fury. The storm's rage subdued into a whispering breeze that caressed Claris's cheeks with an apologetic touch.

As they set out from the cave, she made her way to Torsten's side. If he wouldn't seek her out, she'd have to do so. Pepin padded silently beside her.

She steadied her heart, taking a measured breath. "Torsten." It came out in a whisper.

He turned slightly, only to offer a nod, the movement curt and guarded.

"Demoiselle," he replied.

Claris hoped he'd at least use her name. "You are avoiding me." She stepped closer, careful to keep her voice low. She didn't need the others to hear their conversation.

"I'm not," he countered.

"You cannot expect me to believe that." Frustration edged her voice. "You shun my company and maintain a distance like I am a plague you wish to avoid. I need to understand why."

He halted, turning to fully face her. "It is for your own good," he murmured. Claris caught sight of the others continuing to walk on.

"My own good?" She fought to keep her voice steady. But she sensed her own words being thrown back in her face. She almost laughed at the irony.

Torsten's jaw tightened. "I am afraid, Claris. Afraid of what this—what we, together—entails. Odo's sacrifice weighs heavily on me."

Her chest twisted at the mention of Odo. "I need you. You cannot push me away, not after what we shared."

She laid a hand against his chest. His heartbeat thundered beneath her palm.

He looked down at her, eyes conflicted. He took a step back. "I... can't." Torsten turned on his heel, increasing his pace to catch up with the others.

"You shouldn't lag behind." Halvar's sudden voice caused her to startle, her heart leaping into her throat. Pepin mewed and bounded away.

Hand pressed to her racing heart, Claris let out a heavy breath. "How much did you hear?"

Halvar's gaze went to Torsten's retreating figure. "Love is complicated."

Claris blinked, then staggered to follow as the mage walked faster. He surely couldn't mean that Torsten loved her? That wouldn't make sense. Surely if you loved someone, you wouldn't push them away.

As the hours slipped by, marked only by the steady cadence of boots crunching atop the snow, she couldn't shake the sting of Torsten's words. She also couldn't keep her eyes off him. Yet eventually her attention waned and her gait slowed, her boots sinking slightly into the soft earth beneath the blanket of snow. Once more she dropped back from the rest of the group. Hopefully they'd reach a sparse forest the next day, giving them some reprieve from the open white expanse. Once they were through those trees, they'd be in the march, the marquis's land.

The distant call of a raven punctured the air, its dark wings etched against the pale sky. Pepin watched it as he trailed behind her.

After the camp was set for the night, Brahim led her to a lone tree, its skeletal arms winter-stripped of leaves.

"Here," he said, passing her another of his own knives. "You need the practice."

She took the blade. "I would like to practice alone." Pepin settled nearby in the snow.

He glanced between her and the tree before nodding and returning to the campfire.

Claris took aim. Threw. Missed.

Again.

And again.

By the fourth throw, only one blade had struck true. The rest skittered off bark or thudded into the snow. She needed to clear her mind. Steady her heart.

"Tragic," said a voice behind her. "If that tree had a mother, she'd be weeping."

She turned. Flore stood there, arms crossed, wearing a lopsided grin.

"It is an off day." She walked to retrieve her blades.

"Good. I came to offer assistance."

She bent, snatched the knives, and turned back to face the tree. "I do not need help."

"Sure you do. You're thinking too much." They stepped into the clearing beside her.

Their words echoing ones Brahim once said.

She threw again. Better this time, but still not dead centre. Flore gave a low whistle.

"Now we're talking. Alright, hatchet time."

Her gaze flicked briefly to Torsten. He sat near the fire, sharpening his blade. He didn't look her way.

She hesitated. "You will mock my stance, will you not?"

"Undoubtedly."

She knew they were right. She'd been remiss in her practice.

"Very well. Show me what you can." Claris unhooked her hatchet, unsheathed Sigibert's old dagger, and took her stance before Flore.

Flore nodded and stepped into stance. They sparred. The rhythm of training, the repetition of movement, the sweat and breath and ache, all of it became her refuge.

They corrected her grip once with a touch that was quick and impersonal.

The cold bit at her skin, and her muscles screamed, but her mind was finally quiet. The noise of doubt, of longing, of Torsten's voice, was gone. She only heard the clash of blade against blade, the heavy inhale and exhale of exertion.

"Again," Claris said. She'd lost track of how long she'd been practicing with Flore. She welcomed the absence of worry in her mind.

Flore leaned over their sword, taking deep breaths. They flopped down with a grunt.

Claris wiped her brow and sat beside them. The campfire burned lowly. Only Halvar stood watch at a distance.

"You noticed it too, then?" Flore asked.

Her shoulders tensed. "What?"

"Torsten."

She didn't look at them. "What about him?"

"He's barely made eye contact with you since Odo died."

Her fingers stilled over her blades. "I had not noticed."

Flore gave a soft scoff. "Liar."

Claris's jaw tightened. She stared into the fire. "Being close to me is a liability."

"He's not wrong," they said.

She turned sharply.

"I meant no ill," they added quickly. "It's a truth. You are nobility. You get to decide what happens to us."

Her throat went dry. She hadn't felt that at all. Every death seemed out of her hands.

"And some," Flore went on, "don't want to look fondly on those who might send them to die. Especially if those eyes ever truly looked back at them."

She didn't say anything. Not at first.

"It was not like that with Torsten."

"No?" Flore gave her a sidelong glance. "Because he looked at you like it was."

She opened her mouth. Closed it.

'I'm not judging," they said. "I'm saying... some choose to stay at sword's length so they won't shatter if you fall."

"And you?" she asked, voice low. "What do you do?"

They smiled, wide and bright. "I jest until no one notices I'm still bleeding."

They were quiet for a long while. The fire crackled.

Flore touched her shoulder. "Let him find his way back or not. But do not lose your focus."

She stared into the fire. "Sleep well, Flore."

She moved back to the tree. One by one, she threw knives into the dark, over and over, until every blade was spent.

Only then did she retreat to her tent. Only then did the weight return.

A Raven Warning

Day 23

Claris stood at the edge of their camp, her breath forming ghostly tendrils in the frigid air. Pepin prowled nearby, as the first light of dawn painted over the snow.

She watched as Torsten and Flore packed up. She hadn't had much to eat, and the weight in her chest refused to leave.

Odo had sacrificed himself in the belief it'd likely grant her happiness with Torsten. Instead, it'd been a catalyst for sadness. Claris didn't know if she'd be able to repair things now between her and Torsten.

They'd not ventured far when Brahim signalled for a halt. He hadn't stopped to test the ley. Claris tried to listen for any sounds that didn't belong, but nothing seemed unordinary to her. Pepin hadn't gone on alert either.

"Something is amiss," he said. "In the air. Halvar?"

A chilling wind howled through them, ruffling the fur of Pepin as he paced restlessly beside her. She shivered, pulling her fur-lined cloak tighter around her shoulders. The frigid air seemed to seep into her very bones.

Halvar touched one of his runes, it faintly lighting up for a moment. Pepin chirped and flattened himself against the snow.

An eerie stillness fell, as if the wind never existed.

"Look," Brahim said, gesturing towards a cluster of snow-dusted trees.

A raven perched on one of the gnarled branches, its beady eyes glowing with an unnatural malevolence. With a guttural caw, it launched itself at them, talons extended and beak snapping. Claris instinctively drew her knife, but Halvar slammed down his mage-hammer, sending a burst of energy that knocked the raven from the sky. She hadn't seen Halvar ingest any of that powder recently, and hoped his magic was holding up, that he wasn't expending himself too hard.

As the raven's body hit the snow, it vanished in a puff of black smoke. Claris frowned. Had it been but an illusion?

"Is this from the demi-lich?" she asked.

"They can do such magic," Brahim said. "It could also be traps laid by the one in charge."

"It means loss and ill omens," Halvar added. "A warning to all venturing this way."

Flore shuffled restlessly nearby, their fingers toying with the hilt of their sword.

"Then we travel the right path," Claris said, a surge of renewed energy sparking through her. Finally, some good news.

Brahim nodded. "We should be careful as we go now."

The tree line stood within eyesight now. Claris wondered if they'd encounter more illusionary ravens within.

Brahim knelt in the snow, removed his glove, and plunged his hand within the snow.

A few beats passed before he stood. "The demi-lich is underground."

Claris swallowed, knowing of only one place nearby that dwelt under. "The Mines of Montes."

"Those mines?" Flore gasped, their face blanching.

Brahim looked between her and Flore. "Something to know?"

She sighed. "They have long been abandoned. It is said a darkness killed all the miners, and after days of protests, the marquis was forced to shut them."

Flore shook their head. "It's a labyrinthine maze, filled with chasms and subterranean rivers. One wrong step and we're doomed."

"They mined gold there," Claris said. "They say many have tried to go in, claim some gold for themselves, but no one ever sees them again."

"A curse," Halvar added. "The very air in the mines can be our enemy too."

Her eyebrows arched up, surprised Halvar had travelled so far north before, or at least knew about the mines.

Torsten shifted closer, and Claris resisted the urge to look towards him.

"If we want to reach those mines today, we must move," Torsten said, pointing up at the sun's position.

Having the best knowledge of the location of the mines, Flore took the lead. Claris figured with their pace they could be there before losing the sun entirely. Pepin loped beside her, never straying too far.

As the sun dipped below the horizon and an icy darkness enveloped them, Flore spoke up suddenly.

"There," they said.

Hidden behind trees loomed the entrance to the Mines of Montes, a gaping maw of darkness that seemed to swallow all light. Claris had expected it to be boarded up to dissuade foolhardy adventurers. Yet she was able to stare into the abyss, conflicted if they should enter or not.

"Are there any other exits?" Brahim asked, coming to stand beside her and Flore.

Flore shook their head. "None that I know of."

Brahim looked up at the trees surrounding them, and then back into the mines.

A chill wind whispered through the air, carrying with it the scent of decay and a palpable sense of foreboding.

"Then our quarry is in there," Brahim said.

"Perhaps we camp outside tonight." Claris didn't like the idea of being trapped within the mine's walls while they slept if the demi-lich had made the place its home.

"But what is it doing in there?" Flore asked.

"The end for it and us," Halvar said.

Claris shuddered. "We should rest while we can."

Brahim agreed. "Once inside, we will not rest until our task is complete."

Claris reached down to pet Pepin, who stood sentry near the mine entrance. "You too, boy." Pepin purred at her, before focusing back on the mines.

Torsten went to light a fire, but Brahim stopped him. "Let's not attract attention."

It'd be cold without any fire, and Claris had no intention of asking Halvar to use magic if they were so near to the demi-lich. If it was just Pepin and her in the tent, she may not wake in the morning. So she took a tentative step in Torsten's direction. He noted her approach but made no attempts to move away, instead his eyes tracked her movement towards him.

"With no fire…" Claris trailed off, finding herself at a loss for words as she looked up at him, recalling his last words to her.

Torsten looked to the two tents being pitched. "Finally asking me to share my warmth?" His face showed no spark of joy or playfulness. The words almost lifeless.

"It needs to be nothing more than keeping one another alive," Claris said, her heart hammering. She wanted his eyes to hold warmth.

"What would the others think?"

Claris recalled Flore's words and knew that it didn't matter. It probably never had. "That you do your duty as a garde," she finally said. "Nothing more."

His shoulders dropped. "As you wish."

With no fire, they ate dry rations, and all turned in for early rest.

Claris settled into her tent, tucking Pepin in close to her body as she lay on her side. She told herself not to stay awake, that Torsten would arrive when he willed it. He wouldn't break his word.

She focused on the steady rhythm of her heartbeat, trying to ignore all else, willing herself to sleep.

Her eyes flew open as she sensed Torsten's presence, but she resisted moving to give away her wakeful state.

"You should be sleeping," he said.

"I'm cold." Claris wished things were different. That she'd met Torsten under different circumstances.

He settled down beside her, her breath catching as his body pressed against her own. Warmth radiated from him.

"Better?" he murmured, her nape of neck tingling from his breath.

"Only if this was forever." The words spilled out. Claris felt Torsten stiffen behind her, but he didn't move away. Her heart skipped a beat, and she closed her eyes. She had to control herself. Even if she meant such a sentiment, that traitorous reasoning within her knew it was futile, because he wasn't a noble. It couldn't be forever.

Silence stretched out, but she allowed the tension to ebb from her body as his warmth made her comfortable, sleepy. Safe.

A Magic Trap

Day 24

"We stay close," Brahim said, "and we need to find the best place to engage the demi-lich. We want to set the trap, not let it trap us."

They'd all been woken before the sun rose, Brahim eager to have them on the move. Claris noted that Torsten had reverted to silence towards her.

A lone torch was all they had in their supplies, but they all agreed it'd be better than Halvar using his magic.

"Worst case scenario?' Claris asked, her fingers resting along her knives.

"All of you distract it," Brahim said, "allowing me to take the shot."

"Ready?" Torsten asked, drawing his sword, poised at the very entrance. He'd volunteered to go first.

Claris clacked her tongue at Pepin. "Be careful."

The air inside was heavy and stale, thick with the scent of damp earth and decay. They were forced to move in single file, the cramped passages winding like gnarled roots. The dim torchlight barely penetrated the gloom. Shadows danced upon the rough-hewn walls.

Having never been in a mine before, Claris wondered if such narrow passages were normal. She dared not voice such a thought, worried how easily it might carry.

In the distance, the faint trickling of water could be heard.

Flore stood before her, holding the torch, while Brahim and Halvar stood behind her. Pepin tucked in close to her heels.

They'd yet to reach any form of junction, but the sloping path gave away they were descending deeper into the earth.

Further on, the passageway widened and soon opened into a chamber where glimmering specks of gold dust littered the ground. Remnants of long-abandoned mining equipment lay rusting to one side.

Brahim took a cautious step further into the chamber. "This could work."

Claris blinked. "To lure the demi-lich into?"

Halvar set aside his hammer. "It is quite large."

Flore stepped in another direction, before unleashing a strangled cry of pain. Claris hurried to their side, horrified to see the sharp metal spikes of a bear trap closed around their leg.

It didn't make sense. Claris knew if it had been on the floor, Flore would've seen it. Pepin mewled, pressing his body against the ground, his ears flattening back.

Brahim knelt beside her. "Appears an illusion hid it."

She cursed under her breath. "Hold on, Flore."

Flore gritted their clenched teeth as they attempted to pry open the vicious jaws of the trap with trembling hands. Torsten came around the other side to help.

"Save your strength," Claris urged Flore. "We will do it."

Halvar and Torsten pried the trap apart, releasing Flore's mangled limb. The sight of their torn flesh and splintered bone sent a shudder down Claris's spine, but she knew she could not allow herself to succumb to revulsion.

"Can they... Can you save them?" she asked Halvar, her voice barely a whisper. Somewhat luckily, Flore had passed out from the pain.

"We must staunch the bleeding and set the bone before it is too late," Halvar said. Claris's mouth set into a grim line, knowing it likely meant the chances were slim.

"Tell me how to help," she said. She'd not lose another garde.

"Help hold them down, in case they wake," Halvar replied, his hands already working at the leg.

Claris pushed down with all her weight on Flore's foot, while Torsten steadied their torso.

"Stay with us," she murmured.

With sudden force, Halvar pushed the bone together. Flore's eyes snapped open; their shout muffled by Brahim's quick thinking, as he clapped his hands over their mouth.

Halvar wrapped clean cloth over the wound and stood.

"A word," he said to Claris.

She looked down at Flore, whose breathing had steadied. Claris followed Halvar out of earshot of the others, though she eyed the floor warily.

"That was no ordinary trap." Halvar traced his fingers over runes on the mage-hammer. "Watch." As blue flared over the weapon, Halvar swung and slammed it into the earth.

Her jaw slackened as probably twenty more of the same traps materialised. She swallowed when she realised one was not two steps from where they stood.

"Because they were hidden by magic?" She pressed a hand to her stomach.

Halvar shook his head. "They are magic. Wounds inflicted by them are magic."

Her eyes darted to Flore. "Tell me straight. What does that mean?"

"They will not survive it." The light from the hammer winked out. "We don't have what we need as a cure."

Claris's eyes shuttered, swaying slightly on her feet. A strangled sob escaped.

"You should say your goodbyes," Halvar said. "I'll clear these traps."

She drew in a shaky breath. It couldn't be real. Claris took careful steps and knelt back by Flore's side, their chest rising and falling in ragged gasps.

Torsten hadn't moved away. His eyes met hers briefly.

"Halvar says magic will kill them," Claris finally spoke. "That they don't have long."

She reached out and took one of Flore's hands into her own. Sweat dotted their brow.

Halvar soon returned to them, with Brahim close by his side.

"We shall scout on ahead," Brahim said, "clear any other unseen traps. See what else there is to find."

Claris cleared her throat. "Do not go too far."

Brahim nodded. "Ease their passing. We'll be back soon."

Flore slipped in and out of consciousness, whatever magic within their blood burning through them quickly.

Claris choked back another sob. "I am sorry we cannot save you, Flore."

Torsten slipped out a dagger. "They don't deserve to suffer."

Tears stung her eyes. She wanted to scream, but bit it back.

She held her hand out, her hand shaking. "It should be me."

Torsten looked at. "Are you sure?"

"I have to be."

He rested the dagger in her palm. She laid her hand on Flore's chest. "Be at peace." Before losing all nerve, she plunged the dagger straight into Flore's heart.

Their body jerked once before falling still.

Tears streamed freely down Claris's face. Her fingers slackened around the hilt. She couldn't bring herself to remove it.

She had none of her own garde left, just Torsten, garde of the vicomte. She choked on another sob, biting down on her fist to prevent screaming out. Her chest ached more than when her mother passed. Pepin nuzzled at her, purring quietly. Her fingers absently found his fur, seeking his comfort.

"Claris." Torsten's voice cut through her haze.

She looked up. "Torsten, I—" Her words faltered.

"I'm sorry," he said, bowing his head.

Footsteps drew her attention; Brahim and Halvar had returned.

She stood and wiped her bloodied hands on her pants. "Well?" She took another deep breath. Claris knew she couldn't break down. They had a demi-lich to kill, even though they were another down.

"We found another chamber," Brahim said. "It appears the one responsible was here."

Claris wiped away her tears, her mind racing. The truth could be so close.

"Any signs they might still be?" she asked, recalling Brahim said if the one responsible for warding the demi-lich died, so did the ward. It could make their task a lot easier.

"Perhaps deeper within," Brahim said with a shrug. "But we cannot say with certainty."

"Show me." Pepin stirred at her feet, sensing the urgency in her voice.

"We all go," Halvar said.

Claris sucked in a breath, her gaze falling to Flore's lifeless form. "We cannot leave them like this."

"Time is not our friend," Brahim said. "You can respect them properly once the demi-lich dies."

Torsten gave her a small nod. "We can't risk a fire in here."

Claris hesitated, hating it all the same. "Very well."

As they ventured deeper into the mine, the darkness pressed in on all sides. The torchlight revealed strange markings etched deep into the rock. Claris stared at them, a chill skittering down her back.

"Lich runes." Halvar tapped one of the markings. "Twisted variations of true runes."

The chamber Brahim led them to was smaller than the last, but with high ceilings intersected by heavy beams of aged wood, remnants of a time when the mine thrived. Cobwebs draped across the beams, but Claris spied no signs of spiders. The lich runes were etched into every space of wall, pulsing with a dim luminescence, a tinge of purple instead of Halvar's blue.

An otherworldly energy filled the air around them. Pepin mewed, refusing to step into the chamber itself.

Claris knelt before him, scratching behind his ears. "I will be but a moment."

Torsten cleared his throat. "I'll stay at his side."

She offered him a small smile, before moving deeper into the chamber. Cracked vials filled with iridescent liquids rested on crude stone benches, while a large, circular altar took centre stage. Claris stepped closer, noting a dark ichor staining the altar's surface. She swallowed, taking a step backwards.

What she needed was tangible evidence. Something to help her find and punish the one responsible.

"Can we learn anything from this?" she asked, eyes seeking out Halvar.

"They've done more than control a lich," Halvar said. "That ichor belongs to faierie. Whoever it is, they are mixed in with a lot of malevolence."

Her insides hollowed, her hands clenching. "Then they cannot go free."

Brahim rifled through old parchments gathered in a corner. "This may help."

A jolt spiked through her as she moved over to him. Brahim held a couple of pieces and let her take them. She held her breath as she skimmed over the writing, noting it was all the same hand. But it was the tiny mark in the right corner of each that caused the sick spooling in her stomach. She knew that mark. Seen it on letters to her father.

"This is the marquis's mark," Claris said, the words tasting unfamiliar on her tongue. "Either he is our culprit or being framed to be." She folded them up and tucked them into her clothes.

"We should lay our trap," Halvar said. "The demi-lich might have sensed us by now."

Her throat dried.

"We'll go back to the other chamber," Brahim said. "It is the best we've found."

Claris fell in behind them, her stomach churning. Pepin rubbed against her legs.

Back in the vast chamber, Brahim turned to face her. "Let me check your sheaths."

She shifted on her feet, suddenly feeling thirsty. But she did as Brahim asked, and held out her wrist so he could inspect it as well.

Her chest tightened, her breaths a little quicker, barely registering Brahim's hands checking each knife was in place and her sheaths secured.

Torsten rested a hand on her shoulder. "Deep, slow breaths."

Claris's gaze darted up to his. He took a deep breath in, and then out. Claris soon followed his motions, the tightness in her chest abating. Pepin was pressed close against the back of her legs.

"There." He smiled. "It's normal to feel that way on the eve of battle."

She let out a shaky laugh. "Thank you."

In the quiet, Claris leaned into Torsten, feeling the warmth radiating from his body and the steady rhythm of his breaths.

"Torsten," she whispered.

He didn't get to answer.

"It is ready," Brahim called, from where he stood in the chamber's centre.

The trap was set, and now they had to wait.

A Lich Encountered

Days 24 & 25

Claris avoided glancing in the corner where they'd put Flore's body, covering them with a tent canvas.

She found she couldn't sit or stay still, so she remained standing, her eyes peering towards the deeper depths of the mines. Brahim assured her the demi-lich still was somewhere in its bowels. It would come to them.

The torchlight had died out, and now they had a single source of light, a rock Halvar had enchanted with a blue glow.

Claris shifted her stance ever so slightly, her muscles tense. Pepin prowled around the cavern, also growing restless in the wait.

Torsten still stood nearby, his hand resting at the ready on his sword hilt.

"Torsten," she murmured, "promise me something."

He stepped closer. "Yes?"

"Promise me that whatever happens, you will face it with me. I cannot face the darkness alone."

"Claris," he said, as his fingers grazed her chin, tilting it up slightly, so he locked eyes with her. "I swear it on my life."

His hand fell away as Brahim approached them both.

"Remember the plan?"

Claris nodded. "Lure it to Halvar's trap, and then you will take the shot."

It seemed so simple when she spoke it aloud, but she knew it would be nothing but. The demi-lich wouldn't simply follow like a loyal pet.

Brahim's gaze went to Torsten. "Don't let her fall."

The air around them suddenly came alive. It crackled with an unseen energy that set their teeth on edge and sent shivers coursing down their spines. Pepin chortled, bounding over to Claris's side. The temperature warmed, as if they stood right near a fire.

"Be ready," warned Halvar, his mage-hammer held in front of him. Torsten unsheathed his sword. Claris readied a knife and stepped to one side of the entrance, Brahim taking the other. Torsten stood centre.

Darkness thickened around them, the air crackling with ever greater intensity. The demi-lich was nearby.

Claris's heart pounded while she bounced on her toes.

A chilling gust of wind snaked through the chamber, the air shimmering with a spectral light. The demi-lich emerged from the shadows, its skeletal form illuminated by an ethereal glow that cast eerie patterns across the walls.

Brahim launched an initial flurry of knives, blades glinting in the dim light before clattering harmlessly to the ground. Claris winced as the sound echoed.

Pepin, coiled like a spring, darted forward underfoot.

The demi-lich howled in discontent and threw out a pulse of dark energy. Claris barely ducked in time, feeling the icy tendrils whip past her.

She lunged, letting her knife fly, the blade singing as it sliced through the air. As her knife bounced against its wards, it moved towards her. Shadows thickened, creeping along the floor. She took quick steps back, angling towards Halvar's trap.

Torsten stepped in now, arcing down his sword in between her attacks. Each turn they took, each strike, acted as a distraction. A momentary respite for one another.

A cackle from the demi-lich froze Claris in her steps. It swivelled on the spot, hurling Torsten halfway across the chamber. Pepin skirted around the lich, hunkering down in front of Torsten's prone form, teeth bared.

Adrenaline shot through her.

Brahim, saving his knives, closed the gap and swung with his own sword from behind. Shadowy tendrils lashed out from the demi-lich's body, arcing in a spiral outward.

"Brahim!" Claris shouted.

He flattened his body to the ground as she skittered closer to Halvar, unleashing another two blades.

"You shall die, mortals," the demi-lich growled.

Her mouth dried upon hearing its voice. It grated at her nerves, sent chills all through her. A sound that shouldn't exist.

The monster surged towards her. Dread clawed at her mind.

"Now!" Brahim bellowed.

Claris darted closer to Halvar.

He swung his hammer, the weapon gleaming with blue light, at the ground.

Her heart raced as the trap was set, triggered runes emitting a soft blue glow. She couldn't move yet.

The demi-lich closed the distance, its chilling laughter echoing through the chamber.

Pepin raced towards her. Torsten struggled to his feet. He was meant to be in this position, not her.

"Move!" Torsten shouted.

But Brahim said, "Stay!"

He flung another blade towards the lich, but it wasn't deterred.

Claris dashed backwards, keeping the trap in its path. Her pulse raced.

The demi-lich raised its arms. Pepin was almost upon her.

The ground shook underfoot.

"Get it in now!" Brahim dashed on the outskirts, circling to Claris's position.

She let it all out. Her anger, her loss, her fear in a primal scream. Her throat raw, her ears deaf to the noise. Her eyes shut.

The ground stilled. Warmth caressed her face.

Claris opened her eyes. The demi-lich was almost upon the trap. But then it stopped, a smile creeping across its skeletal visage. She shuddered.

"Force it in," Halvar said, his hammer poised, ready to finish the trap.

Pepin leaped, crashing into Claris's side. She fell heavily to the ground. The knife in her hand skittering away across the ground.

With a thunderous roar, the demi-lich unleashed a new wave of lashing tendrils towards them all. She rolled, tucking Pepin into her body. An icy lash across her back forced out a cry. Hot pain followed.

She clacked her tongue at Pepin and rose to her feet. Torsten clutched at his sword arm, while a blue glow engulfed Halvar as he fended off a fresh onslaught of shadows.

Claris's eyes found Brahim's in the chaos.

He gave her a nod and threw a blade directly at her.

Her eyes widened, and she stepped to the right as the blade struck the ground at her feet. The lich-killing blade.

Brahim took her distraction and charged at the demi-lich, sword raised.

He swung. The demi-lich grabbed the blade in one hand. But Brahim made no move to wrench it free. The demi-lich thrust its other straight into Brahim's chest.

"Now!" he shouted at Halvar.

"NO!" Claris screamed, her voice cracking.

Halvar's hammer crashed down, the runes flaring brighter than the sun. The creature screamed, a sound that clawed at Claris's ears.

Brahim's body crumpled to the ground.

An eerie blue glow bathed the chamber as tendrils of thorns and vines burst through the cold, unforgiving ground. They twisted and writhed, ensnaring the demi-lich within a cage. The creature's howls echoed off the walls, its skeletal form struggling against its newfound prison. Shadows lashed against the thorns, but none escaped.

"It won't hold long," Halvar called, leaning against his hammer for support.

Her gaze locked onto the creature's exposed ribcage, where the faintest glimmer of ethereal light pulsed, betraying a sliver of vulnerability. But the demi-lich thrashed, refusing to stay still.

Pepin paced in front of the demi-lich's cage, teeth bared.

With a deep breath, Claris tightened her grip on the knife. She had one chance. This blade wasn't a copy of Brahim's, but a copy of her own.

She closed her eyes, steadying her breaths.

The snap of wood had Pepin growling.

With the exhale of her breath, she released the blade.

A Soul Saved

Day 25

All sound ceased. The demi-lich crumbled to dust. Sudden icy chill permeated the air.

Claris's knees buckled and she fell to the ground, letting out a cry.

She'd done it.

Pepin leaped into her arms, licking at her face.

Halvar's magical cage vanished, his blue light extinguishing, plunging the chamber into darkness.

Tears welled in her eyes. She was alive. Pepin's insistence to be close had her arms wrapping around him to keep him still.

A lingering buzz tingled through her nerves, as her heart finally slowed to a steady rhythm. Fatigue seeped into every joint, making everything feel heavier than it should.

"One moment." Halvar's voice cut through the gloom.

Fire flared from where the mage stood, he'd made a campfire. A shaky laugh fell from her lips.

Torsten came and knelt before her. Her eyes glanced to the gash on his upper arm. Concern etched on his brow as he looked at her.

"I... I did it." Her voice came out thick. More tears spilled over her lashes. Pepin squirmed free from her hold.

"Let me check you for injuries," he said.

His words hitched her breath. "My back." She leaned against him, allowing herself this moment of vulnerability.

She felt his fingers go to her back and flinched as they touched a tender spot. His fingers withdrew with blood.

"We should get it cleaned." His warm breath tickled her cheek.

She hummed in agreement but made no effort to move. Torsten wrapped an arm around her, pulling her in closer to his chest.

Claris raised her head a little, her gaze resting on where Brahim's body had fallen. But a faint glimmer nearby caught her eye.

"Is that..." she said and sat up straighter. "The soul gem!"

She moved suddenly, startling Torsten as she scrambled from the ground, all tiredness momentarily forgotten.

Where the demi-lich had crumbled away, right near Brahim's outstretched hand, was its soul gem. Her heart lurched.

Halvar reached down and picked it up, examining it closely.

"It's intact," he said.

Claris peered down at the amber-hued jewel. "Does that... does that mean Brahim's soul is inside?"

Halvar nodded, holding the gem a little higher. "Along with those of his family."

A bitter taste rose in her throat. "Do they suffer?" Pepin purred softly.

"Soul gems are complex magic," Halvar said. "The souls within live as if a second life. Dead souls cannot power it."

Claris's mouth opened and then closed again. She struggled for the words.

"Meaning, we destroy the gem, the souls pass on," Torsten said, filling her silence.

Her chest tightened. "Is it a kindness to keep them alive then?"

"This is what he wanted."

Claris startled. Brahim had wanted to die? Charted the path to ensure his death? She swallowed. She should have seen it sooner.

"The magic will wane over decades, without new souls to recharge it," Halvar said.

"Then we protect the gem until that time arrives," Claris said. "Give time for Brahim with his family, no matter how short. Then, the souls will be released, free?"

Halvar nodded. "I can place an enchantment to ensure it will not break."

A fresh wave of tears pricked at her eyes. Everything, internal and external, ached though her. She hoped Brahim had found his peace. That he knew his sacrifice was worth it. "Thank you. It is the least we can do for Brahim."

Halvar stepped away, runes igniting along his skin and hammer. Air shifted and twisted around them.

"It is done." The mage came back and held the gem to her.

Claris took the gem and tucked it safely away, her eyes once more falling to the bodies of Brahim and Flore.

"Let us gather what we can to burn their bodies," she said.

They ended up using some of the old furniture from the foreman's chamber. Halvar and Torsten moved the bodies of the fallen onto the makeshift pyre.

Torsten held the lit torch to her.

Claris had hoped not to have to do this task again, and this time she was to burn two bodies. She went forward, setting the torch to the pyre.

"In ashes you pass," she whispered.

Ignited, the chamber echoed with the symphony of crackling fire.

Her hands clenched as her mind fell back to the Marquis of Montes. She had to know the truth.

Smoke filled the chamber; Claris pressed a hand to her mouth.

"We should leave," Torsten said, coming to her side. "We've done all we can."

She nodded, knowing he was right. Pepin bounded towards the exit before them.

As they made their way through the winding passages of the mine, Claris's limbs weighed down heavily. She needed rest but wouldn't stop until they were at Montes. It was close to the mines.

Soon enough they emerged into the cold, fresh air. The sun had already dipped below the horizon, casting long shadows through the sparse trees.

"We must reach Montes," Claris said, shrugging the supplies from her back. "We'll move light." Pepin sniffed down at the supplies, nudging them with his nose.

"Claris," Halvar's voice rumbled from behind her. "I must take my leave."

She blinked. "You will not join?"

He shook his head. "The matters of court are not for me. Duties call me elsewhere."

Claris looked to Torsten. She'd sorely miss Halvar's magic. "We survived thanks to you."

"Safe travels, friend," Torsten added, extending his hand to the mage.

Halvar gripped Torsten's hand in a brisk shake. "May Will be it so." He smiled, before moving southward.

Torsten looked to the moon. "Are you sure we should travel at night?"

Her eyes were heavy with fatigue, her limbs ached, but she still nodded. "I must reach Montes." She clicked her tongue at Pepin and set off north-west.

Torsten took his position beside her. "And what is your plan?"

"If the marquis is there, ask him the truth. But he may be in Briarcilly, as all nobility should be."

"So?"

She felt his gaze upon her. "We question the seneschal. But I will not leave without answers."

"You also should have this." Torsten stopped and held out the knife that'd killed the demi-lich.

The knife appeared unblemished, as if never used. "Would it still work?" she asked.

"Even if it doesn't," Torsten said, "you should keep it."

Claris removed one of her knives and replaced it with that one. It held a piece of Odo after all.

"Torsten," she started.

He shook his head. "Let's reach Montes first."

The city of Montes sat nestled within the craggy terrain, its stone and timber buildings rising steeply against the landscape. Its wall, constructed from thick stones, had served as a bulwark against gold thieves back when the mine was operational. The watchtowers remained manned though. At such a late hour, Claris expected to find the main gate to be closed, but it stood open. The guards within the towers didn't halt their entry in.

Claris knew she'd have to make herself presentable to gain an audience, but that would be the problem for the morning.

They walked through the winding streets that snaked through Montes until they came upon an inn, the sign marking it as the Golden Fox. A lone candle lit the innkeeper's desk, barely a whisper of sound to be heard.

A man walked from one of the closed doors, a lamp held in his hand. He beheld their ragged states and eyed Pepin warily, taking a sudden step back.

Claris cleared her throat. "Sorry to alarm you at the late hour," she said. "But would you have a room?"

The innkeeper's brows rose. "You can pay?"

She pulled out coins. "Just for the night."

He leaned over, taking the offered coins. "Follow me."

They followed him up the narrow stairs, a few creaking under their weight, and opened a door for them.

As Claris turned around to thank him, he'd already shut the door and left.

She eyed the lone bed, but her bones were too weary for much thought. Claris collapsed onto the mattress, letting Pepin leap up to nestle at her side.

"We still need to tend to that wound." Torsten spoke softly.

Claris murmured, already her eyes weighed down.

"Claris," Torsten said, his hand upon her shoulder. "Please, you can't risk an infection."

She pushed herself upright, Pepin mewling at the disturbance. Torsten peeled away her tattered tunic and her breath caught in a painful groan. His fingers were featherlight, her back arching as he touched close to the wound.

"I am sure it is nothing," she murmured, her voice hoarse. "You have your own hurt."

"Hush," Torsten said. He cleansed the wound with water. "My arm is nothing compared to this."

Her eyelids fluttered, her body trembling with weariness.

"Almost done." She was only dimly aware of a bandage tightening around her mid-section, as he bound the wound. Until finally he said, "There." His voice offered a comfortable warmth that cut through the unrelenting ache within her.

With a sigh, Claris closed her eyes and leaned on him, feeling his broad chest solid against her. Torsten's arm circled around her waist. Then as he shifted them to lie on the bed, her body finally succumbed to rest.

A Traitor Unmasked

Day 26

Gentle pressure on her shoulder roused her from sleep.

"We should wake," Torsten said.

Her eyes were gritty and heavy, struggling against the lingering pull of sleep. No part of her didn't ache, and a throbbing persisted at her temples, along with a stinging on her back.

"Give me a moment," she finally said, wanting to curl up into herself, cracking her eyes open only a sliver.

"There's a bathhouse not too far."

Claris sat up, wincing at the sudden flare of pain. "You've already been up?"

Torsten grinned. He was dressed in fresh clothes and appeared well-groomed.

She rubbed at her eyes. "How long have you let me sleep?" Pepin sat upon the lone chair in the room, his tail swaying softly as he looked in her direction.

"It approaches late morning." Torsten cleared his throat. "And I hope you don't mind, but I got you a gown." He gestured to where Pepin sat.

Blinking, Claris made out a deep green fabric behind her lynx's body.

"That..." She felt her cheeks warm. "Thank you."

"But first, let me look at your back."

She stood, turning to let Torsten have a clear look. His fingers sent shivers up her body as he unwrapped the bandage, and Claris wished things were different. That he didn't work for the vicomte, that he wasn't lowborn.

The warmth of his presence left from behind her. She glanced over her shoulder. "Well?"

"Much better," he said. "I can take you to the bathhouse."

She let her eyes meet his gaze, hoping she'd be able to repair all between them. "Do you remember your promise?"

"I will face whatever you wish." His eyes darted to her exposed neck.

She smiled slowly. "Good," she whispered. "I need that bath, then we get the truth." She clicked her tongue at Pepin and then addressed Torsten. "While I bathe, take Pepin outside the walls."

Pepin mewed at that, eager to hunt.

At its entrance, Claris carefully extracted the soul gem and placed it into Torsten's hands. "Keep this safe for me." He gave her a solemn nod.

Once inside the bathhouse, Claris presented herself to the matron. Soothing aromas of lavender and sandalwood infused the warm, moist air. It was no longer time to hide. If she wanted the truth, she needed to be in a position of power, even one as limited as it was for a woman.

"Morning," she said. "I'm Demoiselle Claris, daughter of Comte de Grecy."

The matron's eyes widened, as she took in Claris's dishevelled appearance, letting out a small gasp. "Are you okay, Demoiselle?"

Claris smiled. "Quite fine, thank you. But my trip was hard. Are you able to lend someone to help me bathe and dress for an audience?"

"Of course," the matron said. "Please wait here and it'll be but a moment."

Claris eyed the plush seating draped in rich fabric, but knew if she sat, she wouldn't want to stand again soon.

Two attendants, dressed in garments of silken fabric, came through the doorway. "This way, Demoiselle," one said.

Claris followed them into a private bathing chamber, adorned with delicate mosaics and potted plants. The attendants deftly prepared her bath, pouring fragrant oils and herbs into the water, before helping her disrobe. One let out an almost inaudible gasp when they spied the wound on her back but said no more.

In her tired and sore state, Claris didn't mind them fussing over her, settling into the steaming water, relishing the soothing sensation over her tense muscles. They cleansed both her skin and hair, and Claris couldn't believe it had almost been a month since she last had a proper bath.

Once dried, Claris had them braid her wet locks and pull the gown on. She gathered up her sheath of knives and affixed them back to her body, outwardly displaying the wrist sheath.

One attendant bundled up her soiled clothes. "These, Demoiselle?"

Claris shook her head. "Dispose of them."

Outside, Torsten and Pepin waited. Torsten raised his eyebrows at her appearance.

"What?" she asked, glancing down at herself.

"The gown is different," he said. "I'm used to you in pants."

She chuckled. "Me too."

At the heart of Montes stood the marquis's estate, its stone façade adorned with intricate tapestries flailing in the breeze. Tapestries meant to depict their storied lineage. Claris thought little of such grandstanding.

Gardens, meticulously maintained, ringed the stone building. Two of the estate's garde stood at the entryway.

Claris forced a smile at them. "Demoiselle Claris, daughter of Comte de Grecy, here to see the marquis."

The garde exchanged looks, and then glanced at Torsten, who once again looked every bit a garde again. One kept their attention on Pepin, who sat attentively at Claris's heels.

"Or is he not in residence?" she asked, noting their silence.

One shook their head. "He is here. Is he expecting you?"

"No, but I am here on urgent courtly business." Claris maintained her smile, hands clasped together at her front. She knew they'd spied her wrist sheath. "May I enter?"

She knew she had less standing than the marquis, and he'd be well within his right to refuse a meeting with her. But suspicion already rose within her. He shouldn't be here. He should be at Briarcilly.

Finally, one of the garde pushed open the door. "Please wait in the receiving chamber."

Claris nodded her thanks and entered the estate, Torsten and Pepin close behind. It wasn't lost on her that the marquis had golden statues, and gold inlaid wood within the chamber. They'd profited well when the mines were still operational.

Butterflies fluttered in her stomach, and she took to pacing before the fireplace while they waited. Torsten stood stoically to one side, while Pepin curled up on a chaise.

The marquis entered the chamber, stilling her pacing. He stood tall and imposing, with silver-streaked hair cascading in waves around his strong jaw and high cheekbones. His brow was furrowed as he took her in. A dagger rested at his hip.

"Demoiselle Claris, I presume," he said and stepped further into the room.

She curtsied. "Marquis."

He waved a hand, walking over to the serving trolley. "Evander is fine." He raised a decanter of wine. "Drink?"

Claris shook her head. A sour taste settled in her mouth. She looked to Torsten, who gave a nod.

"Mar... Evander," she said, "I have come across correspondence bearing your mark."

Evander poured himself a drink and sat in a nearby chair, his gaze settling on Pepin. "Oh?"

Her hands trembled a little as she withdrew a single piece of parchment, leaving the rest concealed, and handed it over to him. "That is your mark, yes?"

His eyes roved over the writing, then snapped up to her. "Where did you find these?"

"The Mines of Montes," she said, pulling her shoulders back.

Evander smirked. "You went into the mines, an area forbidden entry by the king." He tsked at her. "One might think that treason."

Pepin mewled, leaping from the chaise, his eyes trained on the marquis.

"Even if the king's garde were to go in there," Claris said, ignoring the roiling in her stomach, "and find what I did?"

The marquis sat his drink down, slowly stood, and smoothed down his clothes. "It will be my word against yours."

A low, menacing growl peeled from Pepin's jaw. Torsten's hand fell to his sword.

Claris blanched. It was him. The one responsible for the demi-lich. Her eyes widened. Surely, that couldn't be right.

"But why do it?" she asked, her voice low. "It took so many souls."

Evander's face split into an unsettling smile. "To show the people the king is weak. Your father is weak. All the king's allies are. Closing mines in fear, cowing to Suevia and Hodoyin."

She swallowed. "And Lannes?"

He sniffed. "Misdirection. If blame lies at Suevia's feet, then our people will beg for retaliation."

Pepin growled again.

"Garde!" The marquis grinned. "Either relent to my garde, or you shall die."

She readied a blade. "I survived a demi-lich."

Five garde barrelled into the room. Torsten moved to stand beside Claris, sword drawn. Pepin flattened to the ground, growling.

For an instant the tableau held, all unsure what action would unfold.

"Dispatch them," the marquis ordered, exiting the room.

Claris's eyes narrowed and she flicked out her wrist. The blade whistled through the air, striking the marquis in his right shoulder. He cursed.

With a yell, the garde flooded towards them. One charged, sword low. Torsten met him, his sword swinging in an arc. His blade crashed into the charger's arm, blood spraying.

Pepin leaped towards another, claws digging into the chest while his jaws went for the throat.

One came for Claris, a dagger point raked along her ribs. She gasped and flung out another knife towards their neck. She side-stepped another flash of the dagger and flicked another knife from her sheath, this time taking her attacker in the eye.

Torsten bled from a wound on his arm, as he parried another garde's blade. Pepin leaped aside another garde's sword.

In the small room, Claris wished she had her hatchet on her. She readied another blade, glad for the respite, pivoted on her heel, and threw towards the garde harried by Pepin.

He fell to the floor, hands clutching at his throat, and the blade embedded in it.

"Go after the marquis," Torsten grunted, taking the impact of another blow.

Claris clacked her tongue at Pepin, who bounded towards her. She gave one last look towards Torsten before racing out of the room. A trail of blood splattered the polished marble floors.

"Find him," Claris told Pepin, and followed as the lynx dashed before her.

They found the marquis in his study, slumped within his chair behind a grand walnut desk. Her throwing knife still jutted out of his shoulder.

His eyes widened at the sight of her.

"Now the choice is yours," Claris said. "Admit to treason, this plot, before the king, or die."

The marquis chuckled. "You will not kill me, girl."

"I do not desire that," she said, and glanced down at Pepin, "so I hope you do not force it."

He stood. "You know, I heard whispers about the Comte de Grecy's daughter, how she was wild, perhaps even a little feral." He grinned. "I did ask for your hand, but your father declined. I'm sure it would've been a pleasure to have you submit."

Her gaze narrowed as she watched him step around the desk. Pepin kept by her heels, another growl rumbling through him.

She readied a blade. "Well?"

The marquis grinned mirthlessly. Shedding all noble actions, he lunged towards her, dagger gripped tight in his hand.

Pepin let out a deep, guttural sound, akin to a roar. She ducked and spun, launching her blade at the marquis's back.

Before he turned, Claris let another knife fly at the back of his knees. Him being alive would make her cause easier.

He staggered but turned and righted himself. "Whore," he spat, lurching once more for her.

Pepin lunged, jaws clamping over the marquis's wrist. He howled.

"Yield," Claris demanded.

The marquis's glared at her, before smiling. Her insides hollowed. She saw the shiny glint of the blade he'd had hidden in his boot.

Her heart leapt into her throat. She would not see Pepin die before her!

In quick succession, she released two blades towards the marquis. One struck his forehead, the other his throat.

His body fell backwards, and Pepin leaped away, unharmed.

Claris's heart hammered as she knelt to pull Pepin into her arms.

The marquis gurgled blood before falling silent.

"Zut," she muttered.

"Claris!" Torsten's voice echoed down the hall.

"Here," she called, sitting back onto her heels. She now had the death of a marquis on her hands.

Torsten had his blade at the ready but lowered it upon taking in the body before her.

His hand rested on her shoulder. "Are you okay, Claris?"

She looked up at him. "I am fine."

"More garde will be on us soon."

Claris let out a heavy sigh and retrieved her blades from the marquis's body, wiping the blood along the skirts of her gown. Pepin mewed.

A feminine gasp rang out behind Claris.

In the doorway stood the marquise, and four garde, weapons drawn at her back. The marquise could only be a few years her senior.

Claris curtsied before her. "Marquise de Montes, I am Demoiselle Claris, daughter of Comte de Grecy." Torsten sheathed his sword.

"I..." the marquise stammered. "Explain yourself."

Claris cleared her throat, tucking her hands behind her back. "The marquis attacked me and my garde after I levelled an accusation of treason upon him."

The marquise's hand fluttered to her mouth. Her legs wobbled and one of her garde caught her arm before she collapsed.

"He... he left me no choice but to defend myself," Claris added, looking down at the floor.

"Well." The marquise walked into the room. "You won't mind my garde escorting yours elsewhere so we may talk."

Claris looked between Torsten and the marquise's garde. The marquise was unexpected; Claris had no idea the marquis had found his third wife. If that wasn't enough, the marquise's hand fell to her belly and Claris only now noticed the roundness, almost hidden beneath her skirts. She was with child.

"Go," Claris told Torsten.

Once he and the other garde had exited the room, the marquise slumped down into a nearby armchair. Her eyes looked towards the body of her husband. "I'm Enna."

Claris quietly clicked her tongue at Pepin, who padded over to her side and sat on his haunches.

"He said it was a mere hobby," the marquise said. "That I was being silly." She let out a mirthless chuckle as she looked up at Claris. "But, perhaps not silly after all?"

Claris licked her lips, taking a tentative step forward. "What hobby?"

Enna waved a hand towards the bookcases along one wall. "Middle one. Hidden room."

Claris's eyes widened. She had set out from Grecy to hunt a demi-lich, and now she was in a noble estate with hidden rooms. When Enna made no further movement, Claris went over to the bookshelf and gave a strong push. It swung easily inwards.

The room within was eerily reminiscent of what she found at the mines. She didn't even want to step within, fearing invisible traps like the one that got Flore. She swallowed and turned back to face the marquise.

"I need to tell the king," she said. "Can you post a trusted garde here, and at the entrance to the Mines of Montes? Ensure none go in, until the king can send men." She took a deep breath. "My word alone will likely be insufficient."

"That I can do." Enna rubbed at her temples. "My garde can help you gather what you need to return to our king." She rested both hands over her belly. "I will not be making the trip. It's... why Evander had stayed here with me." She looked forlornly around the space. "Not sure what will happen now."

"Thank you, Enna. I am sure the king will ensure you are cared for." Claris curtsied once more. "We will let you mourn."

After they got the letter signed and sealed from the marquise, Claris charged Torsten to work with the marquise garde for their horses and supplies.

She took time charting their route to the capital in the fastest manner. She figured it would probably take a good twelve days of horseback travel to get to Briarcilly. She frowned down at the map, her finger tracing lines over and over.

"Why not a ship from Atigy?" Torsten said from behind.

Claris's frown deepened. "Merchants will not take a woman on board, much less a cat."

She thought for a few moments more, realising only one path lay before them. "Very well," Claris said, folding the map away. "I'll send a messenger ahead and hope we aren't way-laid." With no longer having the need to track the demi-lich or stay hidden, they'd take the most direct route.

A Hasty Travel

Days 26-31

Claris and Torsten pushed their horses fast as they left
Montes. They cut a direct line over land, snow biting into the horses' hooves as they forced their way south
towards Gien. Once there, they'd take the trade routes to
Cervoy, Belleres, Treille, and finally Briarcilly.

Pepin rode astride Claris's horse, unable to keep up with
the pace for long periods.

By the time they reached a thin crescent of trees, gnarled
and wind-blown, Claris conceded to the night and cold.
They'd make camp.

She stripped the sweat-soaked tack from the horses
and rubbed them down with gloved hands, whispering her
thanks into each trembling flank. Torsten set out the bedrolls
in silence, his movements efficient, practiced.

Claris kept her gaze trained on the fire, the flames catching
in the hollow of her throat like something half swallowed.

They hadn't spoken, not really, since Montes.

She'd thought the ache in her chest would've abated after
the demi-lich was gone, but it persisted. Deep down she
knew it would constantly be there. The ache, a hole, that
Torsten would leave once they arrived at Briarcilly. Once he

went back to the vicomte, and she went back to her proper place as a demoiselle.

Pepin roamed off to hunt for a rabbit. She settled down on her bedroll near the fire, pulling a blanket up over her shoulders, shielding herself from the cold.

"Torsten," she said, her voice lower than she expected. "Please, sit."

He obeyed without a word, lowering himself beside her. His body heat rolled off him in waves, and she leaned in before she could decide not to. Her temple brushed his shoulder, and she let it rest there.

"I miss your warmth," she whispered, her voice barely audible above the crackle of flame.

His arm curved slowly around her back, hand resting against her hip like he was afraid to press too hard.

"I'll gladly give it."

Her heart hammered as she stole another glance at him. A small smile graced his lips.

"Halvar said something to me," she said, eyes still fixed on the fire. "Four or five days ago. Though it feels like months."

"Mm?"

"He said that love was complicated."

His shoulders tensed, barely. "Did he?"

Claris shifted, the wool of her blanket sliding off her shoulder, baring her to the cold and to him. "Yes."

She reached for him, fingertips brushing along his jaw.

Torsten's breath caught. "You're not making this easy."

"I don't want easy," she said, her voice low and certain. "I want you."

Her lips met his. Urgent, hungry, no room for preamble. He answered with equal fire, his fingers threading into her hair, anchoring her to him. There was desperation in the way their mouths met.

She broke away, breathless, trailing kisses down his throat. His hands gripped her hips, grounding her. The earthy scent of eucalyptus and thyme, mingled with his sweat, enveloped her.

She pressed her body closer to his. "I am waiting," she whispered into his ear, hands splaying over his chest. He shivered underneath her.

"Claris..."

"Fight for us."

A deep breath escaped him. "You're...everything."

With a quickened heartbeat, she leaned back in, brushing her lips against his. Torsten's thumb brushed against her cheekbone.

"Kiss me," she said. He captured her lips in a deepening kiss, and for a moment everything else faded away, as heat radiated between them.

Breaking away, their breaths mingled together, Claris traced her fingertips along Torsten's jawline.

"Stay with me until we reach court," she said. Her eyes looked up at him, his gaze bore into hers.

"And then?" His voice was low.

She resisted the impulse to pull away. "Then we are inevitably separated."

Torsten pulled Claris closer, their bodies fitting together, as if a perfect match. "Then I'll remain waiting."

Their lips met again, this time with a newfound intensity. Each kiss became more passionate than the last. The touch of their skin, the taste of each other's breath, and the rhythm of their beating hearts, all creating a perfect harmony.

Sweat slicked over their skin, the salty taste clinging to Claris's tongue. Torsten peppered light kisses over her cheeks and temple.

"We should rest," he said. "Or we'll never reach the king."

Claris kissed his cheek before disentangling herself. "I should be the voice of reason."

He smiled in response, tucking her body close to his as they lay down.

Torsten fell asleep quickly.

Claris lay still, her cheek pressed against the back of his shoulder, the curve of his spine a steady rise and fall. The fire had died down to embers.

Her body was warm, sated, but her thoughts wandered.

She should have been happy. Instead, that ache pressed against her chest again.

She thought of Flore.

Of their voice, of their jests. They had known. Of Torsten and her. And they had never said a word. Not openly, not to others.

She blinked against the sudden heat behind her eyes.

Flore had made things easier. And now they were gone. Her own hand ending their pain.

Claris turned her face into Torsten's back, breathing him in. The scent of someone still here.

She swallowed.

Torsten stirred sightly in his sleep. She didn't wake him.

Flore would have liked this. Would've told her not to mess it up.

Claris smiled against her grief. Then closed her eyes.

They arrived in Gien at night, hushed beneath a skin of frost. The river moved like a dark ribbon at the city's edge, quiet and slow. A thin fog clung to the alleys.

Pepin dashed to her side, pressing closer as they walked near the stables. A stableboy watered and fed their horses, letting them rest before they continued the last days of their travel.

The air bit at her cheeks. Torsten came to stand beside her, his cloak drawn tight.

"I have a room at the inn for us," he said, voice low.

Claris smiled faintly. "The one?"

"Unless you prefer the other place?"

She didn't answer. Though Gien held a perfect memory, it also carried a great burden. Odo gave his soul, his life, not too far from where they stood.

The inn behind them glowed faintly with light in the windows, but out there, Claris felt the ghost of all that had happened. They hadn't spoken of it much, but Gien had marked them.

"I keep thinking about the morning after," she said, "when I woke thinking I would lose you when the sun left."

Claris turned to look at him. "I was already worrying about the end of us. But we fast approach a different end."

He studied her for a long moment. "Perhaps."

She leaned her shoulder into his. "I wish we had more time."

"We'll make time," he said.

Her fingers found his under his cloak, twining tight. Pepin mewed up at them.

Claris sighed and drew away. "Come. Let us rest."

From Gien to Briarcilly, the travel was easier, quicker. They'd made good time. Claris couldn't believe their good fortune.

A King Approached

Days 32 & 33

The sun hovered low behind them, painting the fields in tired gold. Claris slowed her horse atop the last rise before the city, her breath clouding in the still, frigid air. Pepin ran a few circles around the horses' hooves. From this vantage, Briarcilly sprawled wide below them.

Even in winter, the southern road teemed with motion. Cloaked riders with crest-stamped satchels galloped past, their horses' hooves throwing up ice-muddied slush. A string of carts carried caged fowl and bolts of fabric, guarded by armed garde more concerned with the wind than bandits.

Claris leaned forward in her saddle, eyes narrowing.

"Trade has not died for the cold," she murmured. She'd never seen this before. She'd normally be holed up behind the walls before the snow would even fall.

They urged their horses down the slope and joined the churn of traffic. Claris tugged her hood lower over her brow, brushing snow from the shoulders of her worn cloak. The weight of her knives felt heavier now. Not dangerous, but questioned. Judged.

Briarcilly's walls rose like teeth from the valley floor, bastioned with age and flecked with snow in every crack. Above the gates, royal pennants flapped in the wind, their silks limp with damp. Beyond them, the scent of brine drifted inland from the bay.

As they approached, a shout rose from the cluster of soldiers stationed inside the stone archway.

"Demoiselle Claris."

She blinked into the wintry glare.

There he stood, Dalfin, his hair shorter than when they'd parted.

"I told you I'd be fine," he called, grinning through the cold.

Claris was off her horse before Torsten could dismount beside her. She crossed the space between them in four strides and threw her arms around Dalfin's shoulders.

"I am so glad to see you." It lightened her soul a little, seeing his face. A pleasant reminder that not all her garde had perished.

He grunted at the unexpected embrace. "Demoiselle," he said. "We got the message. I've waited here every day since."

Torsten approached them, offering Dalfin a solid clasp on the shoulder. "Didn't expect to see you on your feet this soon."

Dalfin shrugged. "That doctor you sent worked a miracle."

Pepin chirped, forcing Dalfin's attention to him.

She swallowed. "And my father?"

"He is better," Dalfin said. "That message gave him great relief. But seeing you will be better."

The sting of tears pricked at her eyes. "I must meet with the king first."

He gave Claris a sharp look. "They won't let you in like that."

Claris glanced down at herself. To face the king, the court, dressed as such, would surely cause a scandal. This would appall her father. She lifted her chin. "They'll have to."

Dalfin's grin faded. "You've been summoned to the palace. But you'll have to wait for the official audience."

Her stomach sank. "They mean to stall me."

Dalfin didn't confirm it, but his silence said enough. He motioned for them to follow, stable hands coming out to take the horses.

As they neared the palace, three garde stepped from another pathway, their surcoats adorned with the Vicomte de Chavers crest.

"Torsten," one said, stepping forward. "The vicomte requests your report."

Pepin growled; Claris clucked her tongue at him to stop. Though her own heart pounded, hoping Torsten would deny the request.

"Send my regrets to the Monsieur," Torsten said. "The king's summons must come first."

Claris sucked in her lips to hide her smile.

The garde who spoke looked to her. "Demoiselle." With a curt bow, he turned on his heel and led the others away.

To her surprise Pepin then rubbed himself against Torsten's legs, freeing her smile.

The palace's towering spires were seen before the rest of the stone structure. Large, arched windows with leaded glass broke up the stone, and broad stone steps—lined with statues of previous kings—led up to its grand entrance. Claris steadied her breaths in front of the colossal entrance doors, crafted from dark wood.

The royal garde opened the doors for them, their movements stiff and practiced.

Claris stepped into the vestibule, boots thudding against
the polished stone. Pepin padded beside her. The servants
on either side of the hall flinched at the sight of him, but said
nothing.

From the shadows of an archway, a woman emerged.

She was tall and fine-boned, with a hawk's profile and
greying gold hair pulled into a braided coronet. She walked
with measured steps and spoke before Claris could offer
greeting.

"Demoiselle Claris. I am Madame Vautier, Mistress of the
Queen's Inner House." Her tone was cool. "His Majesty has
received your petition for an audience. Until he can review
your account in full, you are to be quartered in the southern
wing."

Claris's jaw tensed. "I would speak to my father, the Comte
de Grecy."

"The council is aware," Madame Vautier said smoothly.
"He will arrive when they deem it necessary."

Claris turned to Torsten and Dalfin. "And my garde?"

A pair of palace garde had moved between them.

"They will be housed in the king's west barracks," Madame
Vautier said. "Demoiselle Claris, your rooms await. You will
find a bath waiting. Your... pet may accompany you."

Pepin gave a warning chuff.

Torsten's voice was low. "I'll find you once they let me."

Her fingers twitched, wishing she could touch his hand.
Instead, she gave a nod.

She turned away before she could change her mind.

Madame Vautier led her down a corridor of gilt-framed mirrors and high arched windows. Everything gleamed, too polished, too distant from the snow-covered world outside. Servants in palace livery bustled through side doors. At last, they stopped before a carved walnut door flanked by wall sconces shaped like antlers.

"This is your chamber," said Madame Vautier. "The bath has been drawn. You will be seen shortly by a lady-in-waiting. Please refrain from wandering."

With that, she turned and disappeared into the long hall.

Claris stood still for a moment. Then she opened the door.

Inside, steam rose from a copper tub nestled before a low-burning fire. A tray of honeyed tea and sugared figs sat untouched by the window.

She unbuckled her knives slowly, each one placed on the table beside her. Pepin curled silently onto the rug, eyes narrowed at the chamber door.

Claris sat on the bed's edge, boots still on, damp cloak wrapped around her like armour.

A soft knock echoed against the chamber door.

Claris didn't answer right away. Pepin raised his head with a low growl but didn't rise.

The knock came again.

She stood and cracked the door open.

The girl who waited there couldn't have been over sixteen, with ink-dark curls and a wary look in her eyes.

"Demoiselle Claris?" she said. "I'm to help you bathe."

Claris stepped back, allowing the girl inside. "And your name?"

"Isabeau, my lady."

Claris nodded once. "Very well. Let us get on with it."

The girl took one look at Claris's state and did not so much as blink. Instead, she moved with careful, practiced efficiency. She didn't even seem perturbed by Pepin's presence.

Steam clung to Claris's skin the moment she undressed and sank into the hot water. Her muscles cried out.

By the time she emerged and let Isabeau brush the knots from her hair, she felt less like herself than ever.

Isabeau worked silently, hands nimble, though her eyes darted to the knives once or twice. Claris caught the look in the mirror.

"Who is your father?" she asked.

The girl stilled. "Baron Alric de Leau."

"I have not seen you at court before," she said.

Isabeau resumed twisting Claris's hair into braids for the night.

"I've been here two years," Isabeau said. "Often passed between noble guests and court officials."

Claris met her gaze in the glass. Isabeau flushed and looked away.

"Rest well, my lady," she said once she was done. "You'll need it tomorrow."

"Thank you," Claris replied. Perhaps she might want another lady to help her, and perhaps Isabeau could be that person. She didn't seem to flinch away from the knives, or Pepin.

When she'd gone, Claris went over to Pepin to sit beside him, letting her fingers drag through his fur.

The marble beneath Claris's boots was polished to a near-glass sheen, the gold-veined stone cold through the soles of her shoes. She walked alone down the vaulted corridor. Isabeau had come back to help dress her in the morning.

Gone were the breeches and leather, gone was the dust of the road and the bite of wind at her cheeks. She wore the palace's version of her. Cleaned, perfumed, her hair braided with silver ribbon. She had reduced her arsenal to two knives, hidden deep in her sleeves within the wrist sheath.

At the far end of the corridor, two figures stood beside the heavy wooden doors of the audience chamber.

Torsten and Dalfin.

Torsten's presence stole her breath. Straight-backed, sword at his hip, his gaze locked onto her the moment she came into view. His expression unreadable, his jaw clenched tight.

They waited in silence until she was only paces away.

Royal garde stood nearby, guarding the chamber's entrance.

Dalfin was the first to speak. "Your father is sorry he couldn't see you last night."

Claris gave him a tight smile. "It is okay."

She turned to Torsten, who didn't speak, only looked at her in that way he did. Not as a noblewoman. Just her.

"You clean up nice," he said.

"And you look like you might stab someone," she replied, voice low.

"I might."

They were so close. She longed to reach out, to take his hand just for a moment, but the garde flanking the door shifted, impatient.

Dalfin nodded towards the chamber. "They'll be expecting decorum."

Claris lifted her chin. "They'll get the truth."

With that, the doors creaked open.

At the far end of the chamber sat the king and his advisors. The king's throne was constructed of dark oak and inlaid with gold, raised on dais, surrounded by plush carpets woven with the royal colours of deep blue and crimson. Flanking the throne, the advisors sat on two simpler, but still ornate chairs.

Off to the left, in front of the large stained-glass windows, stood the rest of the king's governors of his provinces, marches, and counties.

Her eyes settled on her father. He stood with his shoulders set proudly. How she wanted to sprint over to him, but she kept her proper noble composure and showed nothing.

A few murmurs followed Claris's path towards the throne.

At a respectable distance, she went into a deep curtsey, while Dalfin and Torsten bowed beside her. Pepin flattened himself to the ground.

She stared at the marble floor, waiting for the king to speak.

"Rise," he finally said, his voice deep and steady.

Claris looked up, meeting his grey eyes, and straightened. She spied more grey strands within his brown hair, neatly groomed and tied back.

"Demoiselle Claris," the king said. "I'm most pleased to see you well, and uninjured. The message bore tidings of dire news." He leaned forward. Claris knew her message had been sparse, for fear it might fall into the wrong hands. "But, let us hear it true."

She launched into her account, from her discovery in Lannes, the deaths of her men, the demi-lich and mines, and finally her encounter with the marquis.

"I have a letter from the marquise here," she said, pulling out the folded and sealed letter.

The king leaned back into his throne, glancing over to his advisors. "The Marquis of Montes is dead? By your hand?"

She swallowed, her pulse fluttering. "A task I took no joy in. He left me no choice." She pulled out the other parchments. "But this will corroborate the truth of his treachery."

Claris knew not to approach the king directly and waited for one of the royal garde to step forward and take the documents from her.

The king waved towards one of his advisors, who took the documents.

Claris clasped her hands together while she waited for the advisor to read. She resisted the urge to look over at her father again. Though she noted the king's eyes fell to her wrists, and the sheath of knives strapped to one. Her sleeve had fallen back.

She couldn't hide her hands now, it'd be too obvious. She took a soft, shaky breath.

The advisor finally nodded, passing them to the king.

"Your father did pass on your message about the bourgmestre in Lannes," the king said. "And you say marauders and bandits are more populous?"

She nodded. "Especially for the weather."

"And these men who stand at your side helped in this endeavour?"

"Yes." She licked her lips. "Torsten and Dalfin," she said, gesturing to each in turn. "And my lynx, Pepin." He purred in response.

The king quirked an eyebrow. A few murmurs from the nobles drifted towards her.

"Then it seems you have done this kingdom a great service," the king said. "You not only have my gratitude, but you may request a boon."

Her fingers pressed harder together. Again, she resisted looking towards her father. She had so much she could ask for, recognition to be her father's rightful heir, her father to be elevated from comte, but her heart clenched. She glanced towards Torsten beside her.

Her throat thickened, her pulse quickening.

"I would ask for you to grant a lordship to Torsten," she said, keeping her gaze forward and on the king. She wouldn't waver under his gaze. "Without his aid, I would not be standing here to tell you all of the marquis's treason."

Her heart pounded. If granted, she'd be able to betroth Torsten, if he so desired. Torsten stayed deathly quiet as her side.

"And your other man?" the king's look was pointed.

"A chevalier," she said. "He would be a good addition to your ranks, if he too wishes for that."

Dalfin's eyes widened in surprise, but he dipped his head slightly. "Such a boon would be immense."

The king pursed his lips and looked to his advisors.

Finally, the king gave a sharp nod. "Consider it so. Sieur Torsten and Chevalier Dalfin, I welcome you to the gentry."

Her whole body tingled. The other nobility politely clapped at the king's pronouncement, and generosity with his boon.

Claris curtsied. "Thank you, King Eldric. May your reign last long."

The king gave a soft smile and dismissed them with a wave. Claris took a deep breath as she turned to make her exit with Torsten, Dalfin, and Pepin at her heels.

Outside the audience chamber, free from scrutiny, Claris leaned against a nearby wall.

Dalfin beamed at her. "There aren't words enough to thank you, Demoiselle."

"I spoke true," she said, "you will make a fine chevalier."

The audience chamber doors opened and closed again. Claris stood from the wall hurriedly.

Her father took long strides before pulling her into an embrace. She squeezed her arms around him.

"Father," she breathed. "You look so well."

He stepped back, hands resting on her shoulders. "So do you, Claris."

Then he turned to Torsten, holding out his hand. "Sieur Torsten." Torsten gripped his hand. "You have my gratitude. For keeping her safe. For bringing her home to me."

Pepin chortled up at her father. The comte looked down with a small laugh. "I had no doubts about you, Pepin."

Claris's heart felt full.

"Come," her father said, "let us retire back to our manor."

Claris's heart leaped, for she truly had missed his smile.

She held her hand out to Torsten, biting her lip.

Torsten looked between her and her father before taking her hand in his.

PRONUNCIATION GUIDE

Characters

- Claris: Kla-REE

- Pepin: PEH-pin

- Torsten: TOR-sten

- Brahim: BRA-him

- Halvar: HAL-var

- Flore: FLOR

- Odo: o-DO

- Dalfin: dal-FAN

- Sigibert: si-ji-BERT

- Roul: RUL

- Aalis: ah-LEES

- Yvain: ee-VAN

- Henri: an-REE

- Jehan: zhe-HAN

- Arnoul: ar-NOOL

- Levlan: lev-LAN

- Ziri: ZI-ri

- Argine: ar-JEEN

Places

- Grecy: gre-SEE

- Lannes: LAN

- Arson: ar-SON

- Ladonnes: la-don-NES

- Gien: zhee-AN

- Montes: mon-TES

- Dosse: DOS

- Meauchy: mo-SHI

- Chavers: sha-VER

- Briarcilly: bri-ar-SEE-yee

- Argentum: ar-zha-TUM

- Onvillia: on-vi-LEE-a

- Suevia: SUE-vi-a

- Hodoyin: HO-do-yin

Acknowledgements

This book would not exist without the people who helped me through its creation.

First, to my husband, Matthew. Thank you for your unwavering patience, and your endless support. You held our world together when I disappeared for this endeavour.

To my mother and my sister, who have always believed in my writing.

To the editors who helped polish and elevate each page: Olivia, Dan & Angela. A huge thanks to JV Arts, who created the exceptional cover.

And finally, to you, the readers. Thank you for giving your time, attention, and imagination to these pages. Your willingness to take this journey is beyond amazing to me.

Thank you for being part of this first step. Here's to the stories still to come.

*Photo by Alise Black
Studios*

MIA K ROSE lives in the Gold Coast, Australia (Yugambeh Country) with her husband, two children, and two Cavalier King Charles Spaniels.
Instagram: @miakrose